KEEPING LARYN

RESCUE ANGELS
BOOK 1

SUSAN STOKER

This book is a work of fiction. Names, characters, places, and incidents are products of the author's imagination or used fictitiously. Any resemblance to actual events or locales or persons living or dead is entirely coincidental.

Copyright © 2025 by Susan Stoker

No part of this work may be used, stored, reproduced or transmitted without written permission from the publisher except for brief quotations for review purposes as permitted by law.

This book is licensed for your personal enjoyment only. This book may not be re-sold or given away to other people. If you would like to share this book with another person, please purchase an additional copy for each recipient. If you're reading this book and did not purchase it, or it was not purchased for your use only, please purchase your own copy.

Thank you for respecting the hard work of this author.

Edited by Kelli Collins

Cover Design by AURA Design Group

Manufactured in the United States

AUTHOR NOTE

This is a work of fiction. I have taken great liberties with many things having to do with the US Army, and the Night Stalkers specifically. Ranks, missions, deployments, the people who work with the esteemed pilots, location of where they're stationed...all of it. I have the utmost respect for all things military, but I realize that many things in this book and series are improbable or even impossible for an Army unit like the six men I've depicted as Night Stalkers. Enjoy the stories for what they are... triumphs of good over evil, love and respect, and some strong women kicking butt.

CHAPTER ONE

Laryn Hardy swore as the wrench she was using slipped and she scraped the hell out of her knuckles.

"You good?" asked one of her favorite Army personnel she worked with, Sergeant Wells—or Chuck, as she called him.

"Yeah!" Laryn told him brightly. But honestly? She wasn't good. She was frustrated, hungry, and frankly, exhausted. She might be one of the best MH-60 mechanics in the world, but she was also human. And right now, all she wanted was to walk out of the hangar and say to hell with her job, working with the Army, and tiptoeing around all the BS she had to deal with on a daily basis.

Her worst nightmare had come true last month when one of "her" choppers went down in Iraq and was lost. The Army freaked out. The Navy freaked out. Everyone wanting to know if the pilots had been able to destroy the helicopter so the highly classified information onboard, and the machine itself, wouldn't fall into enemy hands.

But Laryn remembered the first thought *she'd* had after hearing about the crash. It wasn't about the thousands of hours she'd spent making the chopper as safe as possible. It wasn't the additional hours and hours of time she'd have to spend in the future to redo all the work that was destroyed by one enemy RPG.

It was the absolute panic she'd felt at not knowing if the people onboard had survived the crash.

Especially helicopter pilot Tate "Casper" Davis.

Sighing, Laryn slumped against the side of the chopper and closed her eyes as the fear and worry she'd felt the moment she'd heard about the crash swept over her once more.

She'd been in love with the Night Stalker pilot from almost the first moment she'd met him, but it was more than obvious he didn't feel the same. Which wasn't exactly a surprise. She wasn't the kind of woman men fell head over heels for. She was on the short side, at five foot five. Her long dark hair was nothing special, particularly when it was usually just pulled back in a bun at her nape to keep it out of the way of the engines and mechanical parts she worked on every day. She never wore makeup; there was no point, because she would've sweated it away before ten in the morning. Her daily clothing consisted of oversized coveralls, usually stained with grease and who knew what else.

Her nails were short and often broken. Her hands were covered in old scars, and scabs from more recent injuries—like the one she'd just added to her collection of scrapes. And being the only child of a single father, whose idea of a good time had been taking her to the dirt races around rural Tennessee where she'd grown up to teach her everything there was to know about working under the hoods of cars...Well, she was more comfortable around older, somewhat crass rednecks than smooth, confident, best-of-the-best helicopter pilots.

And yet, the first time she saw Tate, she fell hard and fast.

Which should've been ridiculous. He was...well, he was *Casper*. The hotshot Night Stalker. Probably conceited, and rightly so. Yet, when she'd been introduced to him, he'd looked her in the eye, made her feel as if he was one hundred percent focused on her and what she was saying...and he *didn't* make her feel as if she was beneath him, as many other pilots had done simply because she was a mechanic.

For twenty minutes, they'd had an in-depth, intense conversation about the upgrades she was making to his chopper. He'd had good insights and suggestions, and when she contradicted something he said, he didn't get weird or egotistical about it. By the time he walked away, showing off his perfect ass in his flight suit, he'd killed any chance she might've had at a relationship with anyone else.

It was stupid. Absurd. Juvenile. And yet, in the three years since she'd met him, Laryn hadn't dated anyone. She'd held on to the tiniest hope that maybe someday, if she was extremely lucky, he might see her as more than just the head mechanic assigned to work on his precious helicopter.

Since then, she and Tate had fallen into a weird kind of dance in regard to their relationship...if what they had could be *called* a relationship. She'd berate him for treating her "baby," his helicopter, too harshly, and he'd pick on her for being too much of a perfectionist. They'd gripe at each other good-naturedly back and forth. Things were light and superficial between them, and Laryn had no idea how to change that. She liked that he was at ease with her—at least, she thought he was—but hated that they didn't talk about anything personal.

And anyway, why would they? She was just a mechanic. He was a Night Stalker. One of the most highly decorated pilots in the Army. He and his team of five other pilots had even been awarded a coveted special contract out of Norfolk, Virginia, which was *extremely* unusual. They were deployed on special missions with Navy SEALs and were even utilized for dangerous rescue missions in the civilian world. They were regularly deployed at a moment's notice, and could literally be on the other side of the world, flying between mountaintops, over oceans, or across valleys full of soldiers eager to shoot them down one day, and then lounging at their favorite hangout, Anchor Point, the next.

And because she was the best of the best, she'd been hired as the head mechanic to look after the helicopters the Night Stalkers flew—so she went wherever *they* went. She'd spent more time on huge Navy ships in the last year than she had in her own small apartment near the base.

Her thoughts circled back around to the moment when she'd heard that Casper and his copilot, Pyro, had crashed, and she shuddered. She'd been terrified that the man she was head over heels for had died. The relief she'd felt when she'd heard that he was all right, that everyone on the chopper was alive and well, was followed by a determination to stop being such a coward. To let the man know she was interested in him…personally.

But from the moment they'd returned to Virginia, she'd been neck deep in chopper parts. In making sure the next helicopter Tate flew would be just as safe as the one that had been lost. They'd fallen back into their usual banter…Tate joking with her as if she were a male buddy, and her sniping at him for being careless and not taking his safety more seriously. In other words, she fell back into the role she'd assumed early on—that of a nitpicking harpy.

"Are you sleeping on the job?"

Laryn's eyes popped open and she looked over at Chuck. He was standing next to the door of the chopper, staring in at her.

"No," she said a tad bit defensively. "Resting my eyes."

"Why don't you go home?" he asked. "You've been here for…" He looked down at the watch on his wrist. "Way too long."

"I need to finish retrofitting the rigging system for the fast ropes," Laryn protested. "Need to make sure everything is perfect for the flight trial in a couple days."

"No, you don't. Everything is fine. You've already made sure of that. You need to get more than three hours of sleep at a time. Go home," he insisted.

He couldn't actually order her to do anything. Chuck was in the Army. Laryn wasn't. She was an independent contractor. Yes, she had to adhere to some of the Army's rules, but she was the senior mechanic. The person in charge. The head honcho. In the hangar, she was *his* boss, actually. But the truth was...she was ready for a break.

"Okay," she said a little belatedly.

"Okay?" he said skeptically.

Laryn chuckled. "Is that so surprising?"

"Well, yeah. You never do what anyone tells you to do. I think if someone told you to run out of a burning house, you'd run *into* it instead, just to be contrary."

"I'm not that bad," Laryn protested.

In response, he simply lifted an eyebrow.

Chuck was pretty young at twenty-four, but he was an excellent mechanic, and Laryn enjoyed working with him. Though, right now, his reaction made her press her lips together.

She couldn't help the way she was. Her dad had taught her to be strong, tough, independent. He never took any excuses from her. Even when she was in elementary school, he'd had her at the track and under the hoods of cars. Homework was put on the back burner. Boys were *definitely* off the table when she got older. But she'd gladly spent every minute she could with her dad. When he'd unexpectedly died when she was nineteen and at her first duty station in the Army, she'd been devastated.

So yeah...she was her father's daughter, and she didn't like anyone telling her what to do. And if someone dared tell her she *couldn't* do something? Wasn't strong enough, smart enough, tall enough...she did whatever it took to prove them wrong.

And now she was the most sought-after helicopter mechanic in the country. Even internationally. She'd even gotten several very lucrative offers in the last couple of years to work overseas for other countries' governments, but she'd turned them all down.

Because of a stupid crush.

Tate would be fine without her. Probably wouldn't even realize she'd left. And yet, she couldn't make herself go. That weakness was ridiculous.

Shaking off the thoughts that threatened to send her into a self-deprecating downward spiral, Laryn fisted the wrench she'd been using when she'd scraped another layer of skin off her knuckles and shoved it into one of the deep pockets along her thigh before standing. The interior of the chopper was tall enough that she could walk to the opening without having to stoop. Chuck stood back, knowing better than to offer his hand to help her out, and she nimbly hopped to the ground.

"Are you really going home?" he asked.

"Yes. I'll be back tomorrow afternoon," Laryn told him, making a split-second decision.

His eyes widened. "You're taking the rest of today *and* most of tomorrow off?"

"Yup. I've been working my ass off. I need a break. And you're right, I also need sleep. Lots of it." Since Laryn was a contractor, her hours weren't as rigid as those of the military guys she worked with. And since she was the boss, she had more leeway to come and go as she pleased. But it wasn't as if she took unfair advantage of that. She was usually the first to arrive and the last to leave. Many nights she'd still been working at one or two in the morning. She hated leaving things unfinished, and when she thought about what could happen if she got lazy on the job—namely, pilots getting hurt because of something she'd done or not done—it made her physically nauseous.

But Chuck was right, she'd worked her ass off to get this chopper up to speed, and it was as ready as it was going to be. She had no doubt that Tate and Pyro wouldn't find anything wrong when they took it up to test it out.

"Wow, okay. Enjoy your time off," Chuck told her, sounding sincere.

"Don't fuck with my machine," Laryn warned, narrowing her eyes. "I mean it. Keep everyone away from her."

"I will," he reassured her. "We all know how you are with your choppers. We wouldn't dare touch so much as a bolt without your say-so."

Laryn internally winced. There she went, being overcontrolling again. It was a good thing she worked with all men; women wouldn't be able to take her brash and demanding attitude. She had to admit that she'd gotten worse over the years while trying to fit in, be one of the guys.

Now, for the first time in a long time, she didn't *want* to be a guy. She wished she had some girlfriends she could call up for a girls' night. Wine. Relaxing. Watching ridiculous reality TV and eating junk food. Instead, all she had was her empty apartment, coworkers who were half-scared of her and way too young for her to hang out with, and a man she pined for who didn't know she existed, except when he had a question about his precious chopper.

Not for the first time, she had the thought that she needed to get out of the rut she was in. Maybe she *should* consider taking one of the offers she'd received and move away from Norfolk. Go to Turkey to work for the Gendarmerie Special Operations Unit. They had a couple of MH-6os and had been desperately trying to recruit Laryn to come work for them. Tate Davis and his fellow Night Stalkers wouldn't even know she was gone. She was just another mechanic. Someone else could maintain their helicopters.

Of course, it wasn't that easy, considering what she did now was top secret and the US government wouldn't just shrug and let her go work for another country. There would be nondisclosure agreements to sign and tons of other legal hoops to jump through.

But she was being ridiculous. She wasn't leaving. No matter how much money was dangled over her head to try to woo her away from her current position. Not as long as Tate Davis was flying her choppers. The thought of leaving his safety to someone else was...unfathomable.

Laryn nodded at Chuck and headed for the hangar door, bracing herself for the heat. It was the end of August and the weather was still hot and muggy here on the Virginia coast. Soon the cooler air would move in, and Laryn couldn't wait.

She was so out of it with hunger and exhaustion, and with all the thoughts swirling in her head about her future and her pathetic social life, that she almost ran smack dab into someone entering the hangar.

"Whoa!" the deep voice said. His hands landed on her shoulders, keeping her from falling back on her ass.

Looking up, she saw it was the one man in the world she both desperately wanted to see, and the last man she wanted to be face-to-face with at that moment.

Tate.

"Where ya going? I thought you lived here at the hangar," he joked.

But Laryn wasn't in the mood. Even if he wasn't exactly wrong. "Home. I've been here all day and I'm fried. I'm assuming you're here to check my work. If you find anything off, let Chuck know. He'll pass along your complaints when I get back tomorrow afternoon."

"I'm not here to check up on you. I was just curious as to what you'd gotten done," Tate protested. His copilot, Pyro, was behind him. He clapped him on the shoulder and continued toward the chopper Laryn had just left behind.

"I've gotten *everything* done," she told him with a sigh, and without her usual sassiness. "It's more than ready for you to test her out in a couple days. And I've told the colonel that I won't sign off on the chopper being ready until I'm one hundred percent sure it *is* ready *and* that you, the pilot, thinks it's ready."

"I know, that's what makes you an amazing mechanic," Tate told her.

She stared at him, and a pang hit her as it always did when she looked into his blue eyes. He had a twin brother, Nate, but she thought Tate was the better looking of the two. Which was kind of silly, considering they were identical. But to her, there were subtle differences. Tate was more confident, outgoing, and even though he was only thirty-four, he had a bit of silver in his hair that his twin didn't, giving him a more distinguished air. His hair was also a little longer than military regulations stipulated, but she supposed as a hotshot Night Stalker, he had a bit of leeway where that was concerned.

And she couldn't deny the freckles on his face were adorable. She wondered if they covered him…everywhere.

Aware that her thoughts went where they always did when she was around this man, Laryn was more abrupt than usual. "We done here?"

Tate blinked. "Yeah."

Laryn gave him a nod and stepped to the side and continued on her way. Her skin tingled, as if she could feel his gaze on her as she walked, but she refused to look back at him.

She was going home to heat up a frozen meal, shower, then crash for hopefully a good eight hours.

But her intentions of not looking back at Tate faltered, and before she walked out of sight of the hangar, she couldn't help glancing over her shoulder.

Her heartrate increased when she saw Tate standing where she'd left him. And he was indeed staring right at her. He gave her one of those chin lifts she saw him and his fellow pilots using all the time. He wasn't smirking at her, as usual. He looked serious and…concerned?

No, she had to be imagining that, because Tate Davis didn't look at her with concern. Ever. She was simply the mechanic he relied on to keep his chopper running at top form.

But something about the way he was looking at her, and hadn't moved from where they'd had their short conversation, struck her as...atypical. In fact, ever since he'd crashed in Iran, he'd been acting a bit differently toward her. She wasn't sure why, or even exactly *how* different it was until right this moment. Now she realized the old Tate would've shrugged off her words and continued into the hangar to check out how the work was progressing on his chopper.

Also in the last month, she'd found his gaze on her more than once. Caught him staring at her, almost as if he was trying to figure her out.

Under no circumstances could he ever learn that she'd had a massive crush on him for years.

Was that even the right word? Crush? She didn't think so. She wasn't thirteen. She was a grown-ass woman. She admired Tate. Respected him. Loved him.

Sighing, she continued on toward her car. It was her dad's old 1990 Honda Civic Hatchback. It looked ancient, but Laryn kept her running as smoothly as a brand-new car. Sure, she'd had to replace the engine and most of the parts, but every time she saw it, she smiled, because it made her think about her dad and all the time they'd spent in it together going to and from races. It was the first car she'd changed the oil in all by herself...under her dad's watchful eye, of course.

She was barely awake by the time she arrived home. She stumbled up the stairs to her second-floor apartment and decided food and a shower could wait. She collapsed onto the couch after taking off her steel-toed boots and reached for the fluffy blanket carelessly draped over the back, where she'd left it. She was asleep in seconds, not even the mystery of why Tate was acting so differently around her enough to keep her awake.

CHAPTER TWO

Casper stared after Laryn...and couldn't help but let his gaze drop to her ass. She was a powerful dynamo in a small package, and he couldn't get her out of his head. It had started on the deck of the naval ship after he'd returned from that goat-screw of a rescue. Thankfully, his brother Nate, the woman who'd been a captive of the Iranian government with him, Nate's team leader, and Pyro were all fine after their chopper had been shot down and they'd had to land in the mountains of Iraq.

He'd been kind of dreading facing Laryn when she found out her precious chopper had been destroyed. And she'd said everything he'd expected, giving him a rash of shit. But it was the look in her eyes that had stopped him in his tracks. The look of fear.

Fear for *him*.

He'd known Laryn for three years, and in all that time, he'd only seen exactly what she'd presented to others: an incredible mechanic. The person who made it easy to be a pilot without having to worry about the inner workings of the chopper he was flying. But seeing the distress in her eyes that day, and knowing she'd actually been worried about *him*, not the machine she lovingly cared for, had shaken him.

It made him realize just how much he didn't know about the amazing woman who literally held his life in her hands when he flew. One bolt left untightened, one overlooked routine maintenance item, could mean the difference between life or death for him and his copilot.

Casper had dated his fair share of women. But the ones who seemed to want him most were specifically looking to date a pilot. Wanted to be on his arm not because of who he was, but because of what he did, and the status they thought he could give them.

When he'd first become a Night Stalker, he'd soaked up the attention. Reveled in it. Now? Those women annoyed him. When he went to Anchor Point with his fellow Night Stalkers, he wanted to relax. Have a beer or two. Chill. Not fend off women who made his eyes water with the amount of perfume they'd bathed in, or wore clothes that were two sizes too small in their bid for attention.

Those women were a stark contrast to Laryn. He couldn't remember a time when he'd seen the diminutive mechanic wearing anything but gray coveralls. They swam on her frame, which meant he hadn't really gotten a chance to see much of her body. Except her ass. She was well-rounded there, which made him suspect the rest of her was much the same way. The thought of digging his fingers into her soft flesh as he held her against him made his cock immediately stiffen.

Which was another change...not the erection, per se, but getting one every time his thoughts strayed even one inch over the line when thinking about Laryn. He'd become extremely curious about the woman who'd been in his life for the last few years, yet who he knew so little about.

He walked toward the chopper she and her team were working on, the one that he and Pyro would be testing soon. His copilot was talking to Sergeant Wells, a younger mechanic who Casper had seen working with Laryn quite a bit.

"How's she doing?" Casper asked.

For the next five minutes, he and Pyro were treated to a monologue from the eager younger mechanic, who told them everything that was being done to the helicopter and how, in his opinion, it was going to run even better than the one that had been destroyed.

Casper listened with interest, and when the young man took a breath, he grabbed the opportunity to interrupt and clarify what he'd *really* been asking with his earlier question. "How's *Laryn* doing? She looked exhausted when she left."

"Oh, she is," Chuck said with a small shrug. "She's like a dog with a bone. She refuses to take a break when something isn't working right. She constantly reminds all of us that if something breaks or isn't installed perfectly, or if a part isn't kept perfectly lubricated, that it could be a matter of life or death for the pilots."

"She seems like a ball buster of a boss," Pyro chimed in.

"Yes and no," he said. The admiration and loyalty he had for Laryn was easy to hear in his voice. "She's a perfectionist for sure, and expects the same in anyone who works under her. But she's also the first person to tell us to go home when she thinks we're overworked. She's kind of like a mother hen that way. Always wanting to make sure we've eaten, and that we aren't doing anything stupid, like drinking and driving on the weekends."

For some reason, that surprised Casper. Which made him feel like shit. He just hadn't imagined Laryn being the kind of woman who'd be so protective with the younger men who worked under her. Which wasn't fair. She bitched about how hard he flew his chopper and the work it created for her and her team, but she also always asked how his missions had gone before she asked how the machine flew during his operations. Wanted to make sure he and the rest of his Night Stalker teammates were all right. And when he spoke, she listened intently to what he was saying...if the steering seemed off, if the rotors made unusual noises, if the engines seemed to be working harder than they should.

She made him feel as if they were the only two people in the world when they were talking.

It wasn't until right that second that he realized how rare that was. Most people were constantly on their phones, looking at them in the middle of conversations. Or they were distracted by people and things around them, their eyes roaming. Especially the women he met...always casing a room as if looking for someone who might have a higher rank or more money.

Even his teammates weren't entirely focused on him, or each other, when they hung out, their attention half on their conversation, half on their immediate surroundings. Casper was guilty of that too. Because of their training, the missions they'd lived through, and the general lives they led, they were constantly on alert. Aware of who walked in the door, of who was milling around them, what kinds of bags they carried...who might look innocent but could actually be a suicide bomber.

It was an intense way to live, but life experiences and training had made them who they were.

Laryn wasn't that way. All her attention was on whoever she was talking to or whatever she was doing. Casper frowned, now that he thought about it. That wasn't safe. To be so absorbed in the moment.

"She went home?" he suddenly blurted, wanting confirmation of what she'd told him. And probably sounding like a lunatic, butting into the casual conversation Pyro and Chuck were having about the upcoming flying tests that were scheduled for the chopper two days from now.

"Laryn? Yeah. She said she was," Chuck told him.

Casper could feel Pyro staring at him intently, and he had a feeling he was going to be in for an interrogation as soon as they were alone.

"I need to talk to her about a hydraulic issue we had in the last test flight," Casper said, lying through his teeth. The last test had gone perfectly. The chopper flew like a dream. The controls were extremely responsive, and he and Pyro hadn't found anything that wasn't working properly.

"Oh, something that wasn't already reported? Laryn isn't going to like that. You know how she is," Chuck said with a worried frown.

Casper *did* know. If he'd actually forgotten to tell her about something that wasn't right on a test flight, she would tear him a new asshole. But since he was fishing for information and had no intention of actually telling his mechanic that anything was wrong with her work, he wasn't too concerned.

Ignoring the way his brain had claimed Laryn as *his* mechanic, Casper did his best to sound completely nonchalant as he asked his next question. "The thing is, I'm not sure where she lives. Can you give me her address so I can go talk to her?"

Chuck's frown deepened. "I don't think—"

"I could call her, but we both know how she is. And you said it yourself. She's already been here too long today and works too hard. I can just stop by on my way home and tell her what I need to tell her, while making sure she doesn't get into her car and drive her butt back down here to immediately check things out. Do you know where she lives?" Casper asked, both praying the young mechanic had the info he wanted and trying to tamp down the desire to beat the man to a bloody pulp for possibly knowing where Laryn lived when he didn't. It was irrational, and Casper wasn't exactly happy with these new feelings coursing through him.

But ever since his twin had found a woman he wanted to spend the rest of his life with, Casper felt as if time was running out for him. He wanted what Nate had. His brother had been through hell, losing his Navy SEAL teammates on an op, then getting taken captive during another mission. But things were looking up for him now...he was engaged, had a new team he clicked with, and he'd seemed to break through the mental shit he'd been dealing with since his former teammates had been injured and killed.

Casper was thrilled for his twin, but he felt as if he was missing out after seeing how content and happy Nate was with Josie, his fiancée.

"I'm still not sure," Chuck hedged.

The more the specialist hesitated, the more determined Casper was to get Laryn's address. "Look, I trust her more than I trust my own instincts," he cajoled. "She literally holds my life in her hands. It's her work that keeps my ass in the air." That was a small stretch, because as incredible as Laryn was, it was *his* skills in the cockpit that had gotten him through some extremely harrowing missions. But he'd say whatever it took to get Chuck to spill the beans on Laryn's address. "I'm not going to hurt her or anything, that would just be stupid. Besides, you know I'm going over there, so if anything *did* happen to her, you'd just go to the MPs and tell them I was the last one to see her."

"True."

"And Laryn can take care of herself. I bet she has one of those giant wrenches she uses on a daily basis right next to her door, ready to bash in someone's head if they so much as look at her sideways."

To his relief, Chuck laughed. "Right? I can totally see her brandishing a wrench in someone's face instead of a pistol. She's not too far from here. Said she wanted a place close by in case she needed to get here in a hurry. She's at 147 Little Creek Road. It's a small apartment complex. She's in 2B."

Casper desperately wanted to ask how the hell Chuck knew so much about his boss, but he kept his mouth shut. He knew where all his fellow Night Stalkers lived, so it wasn't much of a stretch that Chuck would know the same kind of info about *his* coworker. This new jealousy making itself known was annoying and surprising at the same time.

"Thanks," he said as casually as he could.

"If she's mad about you showing up, you aren't going to tell her that I spilled the beans about where she lives, right?" Chuck asked, sounding worried.

"Nope. She'll be too irritated that I forgot to give her necessary intel to worry about that, anyway."

"Okay. She said she wasn't going to come back in until tomorrow afternoon, hopefully you can hold her to that," Chuck said.

"I will," he vowed.

Someone called Chuck's name from across the hangar.

"I gotta go," the mechanic said.

Casper nodded and braced as the young man walked away. Sure enough, Pyro immediately laid into him.

"What the hell, man? Something was wrong and you didn't say anything to me or Laryn?"

He turned to his copilot. His friend. One of his very *best* friends, who he trusted one hundred percent to always have his back. They'd been in more than one fucked-up situation and every time, Pyro had come through. "Nothing's wrong with the chopper," he said.

Pyro frowned. "Then what was that all about?"

"I don't know," Casper said honestly.

"Dude," Pyro drawled.

"I just...something's up with Laryn and I want to check on her. That's all."

Pyro stared at him for a solid twenty seconds without saying a word. Long enough for Casper to want to squirm. He didn't, he'd been trained better than to let what he was thinking or feeling show. But it was extremely difficult to hide what was going on in his head from one of his best friends.

"You've never felt the need to check on her before," Pyro

finally said. "You aren't going to fuck over the best mechanic the Army has ever hired, are you? Because we need her."

Irritation swept through Casper, but weirdly, he was glad Pyro was looking after Laryn. "No."

"What's changed?" Pyro asked with a tilt of his head. "Because for the last three years, you've never felt the need to check up on anyone other than Obi-Wan, Chaos, Edge, Buck, or me. And your brother, of course. Not that I think you're unfeeling, you're just...focused. Your only old lady has been the choppers we fly. Does this have anything to do with your brother getting engaged?"

"No. Maybe. Look, I'll admit that the mission to pick up Nate shook me. And seeing him with Josie made me think about what I could be missing out on. But that's not why I want to check on Laryn. Not entirely. She's been with us for three years now, and we know nothing about her. That's not right. I know *everything* about you and the guys. She's literally worked her ass off to make sure our choppers are top of the line, and we never have to worry about anything mechanical when we fly. I feel as if I've been a dick for not knowing her better than I do now. That's all."

Pyro gave him another long look. Finally, he said, "You're right."

Casper's tense muscles relaxed. Then tightened again with his friend's next words.

"I'll go with you."

"No!"

The denial came out a lot harsher than Casper intended.

"I mean...thanks, but that's okay. I'm just going to stop by real fast and make sure she's good, then I'll go home and rest up. The next couple of days will be intense with the flight trial coming up. And you know if everything goes all right, we're being deployed to the Middle East again."

A grin formed on Pyro's face—and Casper realized he'd had

no intention of going with him in the first place. And he'd walked right into his copilot's little trap.

Then the grin faded, and Pyro got serious. "If you're just looking for a quick lay, there are lots of women at Anchor Point who would gladly hop into your bed. Hell, if you wanted some excitement, you could bring one of them back to the hangar and do her in the chopper. Don't fuck with our mechanic," he warned. "We need her."

"I'm not looking for a fast fuck," he told Pyro in irritation. "I'm just going to check on her."

"All right. Call if you need a wing man," Pyro said with a wink.

Casper rolled his eyes and did his best to relax his shoulders, which had hunched up defensively at his copilot's warning. "If I did, I'd call Edge."

Pyro fake gasped and laid a hand on his chest. "I'm offended," he said.

"Whatever."

"Seriously, bro. You need anything, you call me. I've got your back," Pyro told him.

"I know, and I appreciate it. Go get some rest. We'll have our hands full with the trials the day after tomorrow."

"I'm just gonna check things over here then head home. Go, Casper. Assuage your curiosity about Laryn. Don't think I haven't noticed something about you has changed when it comes to her. Go see if you can figure it out. Because the last thing we need is your head somewhere other than behind the stick in two days."

"I'm always focused when I need to be, and you know it," Casper complained.

"Except when we were flying and you heard about your brother's team being taken out," Pyro reminded him.

He nodded in recognition. He wasn't wrong. He'd felt Nate's despair that day.

"Or when he was being tortured in Iran."

"Right, point made," Casper said irritably.

"Throw a woman into the mix? Someone who means something to you? You'll be a hot fucking mess in the pilot seat if shit goes south with her. And hey, I'm not warning you off or nothing. I'm thinking you could use someone to iron out your rough edges. We all could. Go. And don't be a dick like you usually are to her. Be nice...You *can* be nice, right?"

"Fuck off."

"Right, maybe you *can't* be nice," Pyro teased.

Casper turned and walked away from his copilot and the chopper, throwing up his hand with his middle finger extended as he did.

He could hear Pyro chuckling as he neared the large hangar doors. But he couldn't deny his friend had a good point. He and Laryn had fallen into a kind of routine. They sniped at each other, but Casper had never really meant anything by it. It was just how they were. But when he thought about Laryn being exhausted from working double shifts just to make sure the chopper he'd be flying was in as good a shape as it could be, it made his belly clench.

He didn't want to simply be the asshole pilot who flew her choppers anymore. What *did* he want to be to her? He wasn't sure. But he needed to find out. And this evening was the perfect chance to make the first move toward changing their relationship.

He wanted to be her friend...for now.

For three years, wherever the Night Stalkers went, Laryn went. Why he and the others had never invited her to have a drink with them, to eat with them, he wasn't sure. He and his fellow pilots bunked together, ate, shit, showered together. They were connected at the hip. He hadn't thought twice about where Laryn was sleeping, when she was eating, or what she did during her down time.

When they debriefed after a mission, she was usually there in the background, listening as the performance of the choppers was discussed and learning what kind of enemy fire they'd faced, if any. Then she'd leave as the debrief continued, off to do whatever she needed to do in order to make sure their choppers were ready to perform perfectly once more. Casper often wouldn't see her again until he was headed out on another mission.

He felt like shit now for not really thinking about where she was, what she was doing during the days, weeks, or even months they spent on naval aircraft carriers during missions. She was simply always there, in the background, reliable as the men he flew with.

A relationship with Laryn wasn't off the table. She wasn't in the Army any longer, she was a contractor. There were no actual barriers to them being friends...or more.

It was that thought that had Casper picking up his pace as he headed toward his Ford Taurus.

His buddies gave him crap about his nondescript car, but he liked his helicopters flashy, not his vehicles. He wanted to blend in on the road. A thought occurred to him—maybe he could use his car as the excuse he needed to be knocking on Laryn's door. It was making a funky noise, and he could ask if she'd take a look at it. It would still be weird, him showing up out of the blue and asking her to look at his car, but it was better than lying about the performance of his helicopter or admitting that, after three years of knowing her, he was suddenly concerned for her welfare. If she was getting enough sleep. If she was eating.

Feeling better now that he had a plan, even if it was lame, Casper unlocked the door to his car and slid into the driver's seat. He put Little Creek Road into the map on his phone and started the engine. It wasn't until he was halfway there that he realized his heart was beating fast and he felt the same way he usually did while on a mission. Adrenaline was coursing through his veins and he was looking forward to what was about to happen.

Casper smiled. He hadn't felt this way about seeing a woman in a very long time. He hoped that boded well for what was to come. If not, he was about to crash and burn *hard*...and he could ruin the relationship he and his fellow Night Stalkers enjoyed with the best mechanic they'd ever had. His friends would never forgive him.

But then again, maybe things would work out. Time would tell.

Casper pushed his foot down a little harder on the accelerator, eager to see how this evening would play out.

CHAPTER THREE

Laryn was dreaming that she was somewhere in Africa after being kidnapped, standing in front of a pile of miscellaneous car and airplane parts. She was ordered to put them together to make a helicopter. All the while, the elders of the tribe were beating drums behind her while they prepared a huge bonfire to use to cook her if she didn't succeed in two hours.

Gasping, she sat upright and blinked. Her apartment wasn't too dark, so it hadn't been very long since she'd collapsed onto her couch and obviously fallen asleep immediately. But that dream was fucked up.

It wasn't until she'd blinked a few times that she realized how hot she was. The blanket that had felt so good earlier now felt as if it was suffocating her. And the drums she'd heard in her dream were actually the beats of someone knocking persistently at her door.

Annoyed, and still feeling off-kilter from just waking up and from the crazy-ass dream, she abruptly stood and stalked over to the door. She had no idea what time it was, but it had to be too damn late for someone to be knocking so obnoxiously. She didn't have visitors. Ever. So it had to be someone trying to sell something. She didn't know her neighbors, so she didn't think it could be them. And if there was an emergency at the base with her choppers, someone would've called. Not come over in person.

That's why she didn't bother to look through the peephole in the door. With the way she was feeling—irritated and needing another fourteen hours of sleep—she wasn't thinking about someone being there to do her harm. She unlocked the bolt and slid the chain off before wrenching open the door and blurting, "What?"

It took her brain a moment to catch up to her eyes.

What in the world was Tate doing on her doorstep? Panic immediately swamped her.

"Tate! Are you all right? The others? Are we being deployed? You haven't had a chance to test the chopper yet! It's not ready—!"

"Breathe, Laryn. I'm fine. Everyone is fine. We aren't being deployed, not yet, that will wait until after the trials. And I have no doubt whatsoever that the chopper is absolutely perfect. How could it be anything else when she had *you* working on her?"

Laryn blinked in confusion. "Then...what are you doing here?"

To her surprise, Tate looked a little nervous. Had she ever seen him anything other than confident? She didn't think so.

"Why do you call me Tate when everyone else calls me Casper?"

"What?" She was having a hard time understanding exactly what was happening.

"Sometimes—usually when we're around my friends—you call me Casper, but most of the time it's Tate. Not that I mind. I kind of like it, actually. Hardly anyone around here uses my real name. I was just wondering."

If she hadn't just had a nightmare, if she wasn't still half asleep and exhausted, Laryn probably would've shut the door in his face and gone back to bed. But since she was still off-kilter, she shrugged and gave him an honest answer. "You don't seem like a Casper to me. You're tan, and Casper the cartoon ghost is white. And so friendly. And smiley. And you aren't like that."

Tate chuckled. "I should probably be offended, but I'm not. You're right. I'm not like that at all. But you know I got the call sign because I'm like a ghost in the sky. Showing up as if out of thin air to cause havoc on the bad guys."

Laryn rolled her eyes. "Duh. Of course I knew that."

"Can I come in?"

Her brain was having a hard time following his fast change in topics. "Why?" she asked.

"Because."

Too damn tired to exchange quips, Laryn took a step backward.

Tate took that for the consent he was looking for and stepped over the threshold into her apartment. As soon as she shut the door behind him, Laryn knew she'd made a mistake. Having the man she had a huge crush on inside her apartment would forever change the space. She'd constantly envision him there from now on.

Walking through the tiny foyer into the living area, turning to lean against the counter that separated it from the galley kitchen, Tate stared at her for a long moment without saying a word.

"What?" she asked a little defensively. Looking down at herself, Laryn saw she was still wearing the coveralls she always had on while at work. Hell, the wrench she'd stuck in the pocket along the thigh was still in there too. Her hair was probably no longer in the neat and tidy bun she always wore to keep it out of the way while she worked. She felt grubby next to him, and that irritated her.

"You fell asleep as soon as you got home, huh?"

"Yeah. And I'd still be asleep if you hadn't rudely woken me up," she said a little peevishly. That was a lie. That dream had definitely woken her up even before he'd started knocking on her door.

"Right. Sorry about that."

Laryn stared at Tate, waiting for him to explain why he was there. When he didn't, she tilted her head in confusion. "If we aren't about to be deployed and everyone is okay, why *are* you here, Tate?"

He ran a hand through his hair, and Laryn was surprised to see his cheeks heat.

Tate Davis was blushing. *Blushing*. It was confusing and... adorable.

When he met her gaze, his hair was mussed and his brows were furrowed. "I had this whole story about my car making a funny noise and wanting you to check on it, but the last thing I want is for you to tromp downstairs and work on something, only to find out that it's nothing important. And you should know that I told Chuck I needed your address so I could talk to you about something being wrong with the hydraulics on the last test flight, that I hadn't told you about."

"Wait—what?" Laryn asked incredulously. "Something was wrong with the hydraulics? On the fast-rope rig? I didn't notice anything when I was working on that today. Why didn't you tell me before? Shit. Now I need to go back to the hangar and see if I can figure out what's up before the next test flight. If you lose hydraulics in the middle of an op, that could have serious ramifications for everyone. I should—"

She didn't finish her thought, because as she rushed to walk by Tate to grab the boots she'd left against the wall, he took her upper arm in his hand and stopped her. "I said that's what I told *Chuck*. But it was a lie. The hydraulics are fine. As is everything else."

All Laryn could do was stare up at Tate as she struggled to process what he was saying.

He loosened his hold on her arm but didn't let go. Even through her coveralls, her skin seemed to tingle where he was touching her. This was bad. Very bad. She needed to put some space between them. But she was frozen. Wanting him to keep touching her and hoping he let go at the same time.

"Are you all right?" Tate asked. "You've been working extremely hard. And please know everything you've done for us, for me, has been noted and appreciated. But you shouldn't work yourself into the ground."

"Are you drunk? Or high?" Laryn whispered. His faculties being altered felt like the only explanation for this abrupt change in behavior. He'd never really asked if she was all right before. Not like this. Not by taking time out of his day, finding out where she lived, and just randomly stopping by. Something had to be wrong.

But he chuckled. "No. Nothing of the sort. I'm just worried about you."

He was *worried* about her? "Why? Did I do something wrong? Did I screw something up?"

"*No*," Tate said again, this time sounding more like himself. A little irritated. Abrupt. Although, also a bit out of sorts. "Can't I come by to check on a friend? Especially when she's been working fourteen- and sixteen-hour days to retrofit the helicopter I'll be flying on a mission in a week?"

Laryn had a feeling her mouth was hanging open, but she couldn't help it. Tate Davis had called her a friend. It was more than she'd ever expected, and so much less at the same time.

"We *are* friends...aren't we?" he asked.

Similar to his nervousness when he stood at her door, he now had a note of uncertainty in his tone. This was a man who was confident in everything he did. He had to be, in order to be a Night Stalker pilot.

"Yeah, of course." The words were affirmative, but she had a feeling her tone wasn't quite as believable.

He winced.

Yeah, she'd never been a good liar. Her dad had always seemed to know when she was stretching the truth.

"Have you eaten?" he asked.

Laryn shook her head. "No. When I got home, I was too tired."

"Why don't you go change. I'll see what I can find to make us."

Her mouth was open again. Laryn couldn't help it. "You're going to cook?"

"Well, that depends on what you have. But I was thinking more of putting something together, like sandwiches. But if you have something you want me to cook...casserole, steaks, grilled chicken and veggies...just let me know."

"I might have stuff for sandwiches," Laryn told him, quickly trying to do a mental inventory of what was in her fridge.

"Good. Go on. Take a shower. Change. Relax. I've got this."

But she still hesitated. This was such a bad idea. The worst. She still wasn't really sure why he was there, but she couldn't kick him out. She'd dreamed about this for years. Having Tate in her apartment, in her kitchen, making her dinner. Okay, maybe she hadn't dreamed *this*, but having him talk to her as if she was a normal woman, and not simply the mechanic responsible for the helicopters he flew? Yes.

"It's fine, Laryn. Good. Promise."

It was as if he could read her mind. He slowly released his hold on her upper arm, and for a second she wished her arms were bare so she could feel his calloused hand against her skin. What his touch would feel like on other, more intimate parts of her body.

But she immediately shut that thought down. As much as she was into him, she wasn't going to have a one-night stand.

Was *that* what this was? He thought she was desperate

enough to sleep with him? He needed to get his rocks off before the flight trials?

"I'm not sleeping with you," she blurted.

Tate didn't seem offended in the least by the question. "Okay."

"Okay?"

"Yeah. That's not why I'm here. Not that I'm opposed...but again, that's not why I came over."

She was still in the dark about why he *had* come over, but now she couldn't think about anything other than him saying that he wasn't opposed to sleeping with her. What would he do if she jumped him right now? Just threw herself at him and tore his flight suit off? The image made her lips twitch.

"Something funny?" he asked with a quirk of an eyebrow.

Laryn shook her head almost furiously. "Nope. Nothing. Not at all. I'm just going to..." She gestured down the hallway with her thumb. "You know."

He grinned. "All right."

"Yeah."

"Anything you don't like on your sandwiches?" he asked, as she began to back away from him.

"Pineapple."

He grimaced. "Gross. Is this a good time to discuss pineapple on pizza?"

Laryn shrugged. "Depends on which side of that argument you're on."

He grinned at her. "Go," he ordered with a chin lift toward the hallway.

Damn, that was sexy. Laryn turned to head to her room and realized she was smiling. That wasn't something that happened a lot after she spoke with Tate. He usually annoyed her or treated her as if she was his little sister or something. She wasn't getting little sister vibes from him right now though.

She decided that she didn't *care* why he was there, just that he was. It was possible she was still dreaming, and if that was the case, she never wanted to wake up. Because if she thought she'd liked the Tate Davis she knew from before, it was nothing compared to how much she liked *this* Tate Davis.

* * *

Casper watched Laryn walk away from him and, as usual, his gaze was drawn to her ass. How her coveralls could be baggy as hell everywhere but her ass, he had no idea. But he liked it a hell of a lot.

His heart was still beating hard from her casual comment about sex. He was appalled that she thought he'd shown up for a booty call, but he wasn't lying when he'd said he wasn't opposed to having sex with her.

Laryn Hardy was sexy as hell. He hadn't realized he was attracted to her until recently, and now he couldn't think of much else. She was rough around the edges, she didn't back down when she was challenged, she liked to be in charge, took no shit from anyone, wasn't afraid of hard work, and...Hell. She was a lot like *him*. And the opposite of most women who hit on him.

Turning, Casper headed for her small kitchen. It was nothing special, linoleum countertops, cheap appliances, no dishwasher... it felt like he was in his own kitchen. Except when he opened her fridge, she didn't have nearly the amount of food he did. She did have some sliced deli meat and cheese though. He pulled them out, along with some mayo and mustard, not sure which she'd prefer. There was also a package of bagels on the counter, which he used as bread.

It didn't take long to put together the sandwiches, and while he waited for Laryn, he used the time to look around her living room.

She had a couch that had seen better days but looked

comfortable. There was a blanket hanging off the cushions, as if she'd thrown it off when she'd gotten up to answer the door. The rest of the room consisted of an oversized, beat-up leather chair off to one side, wide enough to fit two people; a medium-size TV; and a bookcase filled to the brim with books —at a closer look, they were a mix of history, romance, dirt racing manuals, and of course, several how-to books on engines. Some were old, tattered and torn, and others looked pristine. Her bookshelf was a lot like the woman herself... eclectic.

There was a picture of who Casper figured had to be Laryn as a child, standing in front of an old Chevy Camaro on a dirt track with her arm around an older guy. They were both beaming, and Casper could see the resemblance between the girl and the man.

"That's me and my old man when I was around nine. That's the car we built from scratch, and my dad's old buddy drove it in the dirt track race in our town. I was so proud."

"As you should've been," Casper began as he turned around. Whatever else he was going to say got stuck in his throat as he stared at the woman before him. If he hadn't seen for himself that Laryn hadn't left the apartment, he wouldn't have recognized her.

The woman standing there looked *nothing* like the mechanic he'd gotten so used to seeing. For one, her hair was down. Casper couldn't remember a time he'd ever seen Laryn with her hair down. And it was beautiful. Dark brown with light brown highlights, long enough to touch her upper chest. It was still damp from her shower, and it took every ounce of control Casper had not to reach out and run his fingers through the silky-looking strands.

And she smelled...delicious. That was the only way to put it. Not that he'd ever really noticed how she'd smelled before. Probably because he was so used to the scents of the hangar and the choppers she worked on. Oil, grease, sweat. But now she literally smelled like cookies. Maybe cake. Vanilla. It made his mouth water.

And the body he'd wondered about was no longer hidden by the coveralls she always wore. She had on a pair of sweatpants and a T-shirt, both hugging her curves...and what curves they were.

He was right. Laryn was curvy as hell—and he'd never seen anything sexier.

"What? Do I have something on my face?" she asked self-consciously.

"No," Casper said. "I was just thinking that I haven't seen you in anything but your coveralls...like...ever."

"That's not true," she protested.

Casper shrugged. He was still trying to get his mind to work properly. This woman...she was like Clark Kent. Or Diana Prince. Hiding in plain sight. This was her superhero form.

"You grew up working on cars?" he blurted, desperately trying to keep himself from saying something stupid. His brain wasn't firing on all cylinders.

"Yeah," she said, sounding happy. "Loved it. My dad taught me everything he knew. Took me to the track every weekend. He said I took to it like a duck to water. He was so proud of me when I got a few certificates from the community college in their automotive technology program when I was still in high school."

"I bet he's *super* proud of you today," Casper said.

"He died when I was nineteen," Laryn said matter-of-factly.

"Oh, shit. I'm sorry."

"Don't be. I mean, it sucks, but he was *always* proud of me. I was Daddy's little girl and could do no wrong."

"I bet you were two peas in a pod," he guessed.

"We were." Laryn smiled at him, before her stomach suddenly let out a loud growl.

Her hand immediately went to her belly, and Casper couldn't

help but look down at where she was touching herself. He could see the small swell under her hand, and it took every ounce of control he had not to pull her hand away and replace it with his own.

It was almost alarming how much he wanted this woman. Why now? What had changed? He wasn't sure. Except for the look of concern she'd let slip on that naval ship, after returning with his brother and the others when his chopper had crashed. He'd seen her true emotions for the first time, and he'd been intrigued. And now, here he was, desperately wanting to know everything about Laryn.

"I wasn't sure if you wanted mustard or mayonnaise on your sandwich," he told her as he turned away, stepping toward the kitchen, more so that she didn't see the erection in his flight suit than truly wanting to end their conversation.

"Both," she said, stepping past him.

Once again, her clean, sweet smell wafted up to his nose, making Casper want to lean in and sniff her neck. Truthfully, he wanted to do more than that, but the thoughts he was having about his mechanic were kind of freaking him out with their sudden urgency. So he kept his distance as she squirted a healthy amount of condiments on the top half of her bagel, then picked up the sandwich and took a huge bite right where they stood in the kitchen.

It was something else they had in common. Casper didn't sit to eat much. He was too used to eating on the go. And when he was by himself in his small apartment, he didn't bother setting a table. Sometimes he ate on his couch while he watched football, but usually he saved time by eating his meals standing in the kitchen as well.

He also wasn't surprised by the speed with which Laryn ate. Like him, she had a profession where enjoying a leisurely meal was a luxury. They were both done with their sandwiches in minutes.

"That was delicious," she told him. Then they stood there a little awkwardly before she asked, "You want to sit down?"

Casper nodded, and they headed over to her couch. She sat on one end and he settled into the other.

"So...you came by to check on me. I'm good. How are *you*? How's your brother and Josie doing? Have you talked to them much?"

Casper shouldn't have been surprised she remembered his brother's fiancée's name, and yet he still kind of was. He didn't even think the two were introduced to each other when they'd been on the naval ship, but she'd obviously found out Josie's name somehow.

"They're good. They got engaged."

"Really? That's awesome," Laryn said, pleasure lighting up her features.

She seemed genuinely excited for them both. Casper felt guilty for all the times he'd thought this woman was a robot, going about her business all emotionless and stoic. It was obvious she had plenty of deep feelings—she'd just kept them locked down around *him*. Which was a blow for some reason.

Another awkward silence filled the air, and Casper wasn't sure what to say.

"Sooo..." she said, drawing the word out. "If you aren't here for your car, and you aren't here to tell me something's wrong with the chopper...why are you *really* here?"

"We've worked together for three years or so now, right?" Casper asked.

"Yeah. Why?"

"In all those years, we haven't ever sat down and had lunch together. Or hung out. Or talked about anything other than work. Why is that?"

Laryn looked at him as if he had two heads. "Because. I'm the mechanic and you're the pilot. You're, like, a god or something. I'm nothing."

"Bullshit!" Casper exclaimed, wincing when Laryn flinched. "Sorry, didn't mean to be so loud. But that's bullshit," he repeated. "Everyone knows a pilot is only as good as the mechanic who works on his machines."

"Now *you're* spouting bullshit," Laryn said with a small laugh. "*No one* notices us. No one cares about the grease monkeys behind the scenes. It's been that way everywhere I've ever worked. With no exceptions. The drivers get all the accolades. All the press attention. All the women...or men. And that's fine," she rushed to add. "I'm fully content to stay in the background with my head under the hood, so to speak, keeping the engines purring."

Casper was getting exasperated with his body. His damn cock wouldn't stay down. Just hearing her say "engines purring" had him thinking about very different things other than helicopters and cars. "How many job offers have you received since you started working on the MH-60s?" he asked.

"What does that have to do with anything?"

"How many?" he insisted.

"A few."

Casper arched a brow.

"Fine. I get about five or six a year."

"Laryn, you're underestimating your worth. I can think of half a dozen companies—hell, *countries*—off the top of my head that would kill to lure you away and have you work for them. You want to know how many companies are trying to get *me* to work for them?"

"It's not the same. You're in the Army. You can't just up and leave," Laryn protested.

"It's a little different, sure, but my point stands. I'm a good pilot. But good pilots are a dime a dozen. Good mechanics? Who know their preferred chopper like the back of their hand? Not so easy to find."

"Good pilot?" Laryn leaned toward him a little. "Tate, you're a Night Stalker. The best of the best. I've seen videos of some of the things you can do with a chopper. It's scary as hell and just as impressive. Good pilot, my ass." She huffed that last part and sat back.

Casper couldn't help but grin at her reaction. The truth was, he was a hell of a pilot, but he stood by the point he was making. "You ever think about it?"

"About what?"

"About taking one of those job offers."

Her gaze dropped, and she looked everywhere except at him.

Casper's heart fell. "Holy shit, Laryn. You have."

She shrugged and straightened. "I'd be an idiot not to at least consider what's being offered."

"What *is* being offered?" Casper asked, shifting to face her.

"A lot more money than I'm making now, I can tell you that," Laryn said, with a bit of nervous laughter.

"And?"

"That isn't enough?" she asked a little defensively.

"Are you truly not happy here?" he asked her quietly. He felt defeated. Sad.

"It's not that," she hedged.

"If I've said or done anything to make you feel unappreciated or not wanted, I'm sorry," he told her.

"No!" she said immediately, which made him feel a little better. "Working with you and the other Night Stalkers has made me a better mechanic," she went on. "It's brought home in the most visceral way possible that everything I do makes a difference. If I'm tired and don't put all my attention on my work, it could literally have life or death consequences. If I don't tighten a bolt correctly, or if I cut corners, you could *die*. Or your friends and the Navy SEALs you transport. And if you can't complete a mission, a bad guy might get away, and he or she might plot against the US and execute another 9/11. That's an extreme example, but that's what I think about every time I get a job offer from another country."

"What other countries have you heard from?" he found himself asking.

"Oh...here and there," she said offhandedly.

"Where?" Casper pressed.

"Bahrain, Greece, Saudi Arabia, Turkey, Egypt...even Australia. I'd love to go to Australia. Have you heard about these adorable animals called quokkas? They're known as the selfie kings and queens, because they look like they're smiling in pictures."

"Laryn!" Casper burst out. "You can't go work for Egypt! Or Turkey! Or Saudi fucking Arabia!"

"Why not?" she asked, sounding genuinely puzzled.

"Because!"

"That's not an answer. And I know there have been some issues between them and the US, but that's in the past."

She was so naïve, it was infuriating and adorable at the same time. Casper forced himself to take a deep breath.

"Besides, I'm not *really* considering it. But some of the people offering me jobs have been pretty unrelenting. They think I'm playing hard to get and angling for better offers." She laughed. "I've even been offered my own harem of men, ready and willing to do whatever I want. It's crazy, actually."

The thought of Laryn with another man made Casper's skin crawl. It was a surprising reaction, considering their past...or lack thereof.

His body moved before his brain could catch up, scooting over on the couch until he was sitting right next to her. His thigh touched hers, and this close, her vanilla scent drove him crazy. He couldn't resist, leaning in until his nose was almost touching her neck.

"What are you doing?" she asked, almost sounding panicked.

Casper had no idea *what* he was doing, except that it felt

right. This woman had been right under his nose for years, and he'd failed to see what a gem she was. The longer he was around her, the more he learned about her, the more intrigued he became. She didn't care about money, that was obvious; if she did, she would've been gone a long time ago, lured away by some other company's or country's monetary offer. She was loyal and patriotic. She was hard-working...and Casper liked that a hell of a lot.

He also hadn't missed the way she'd specifically mentioned cutting corners could hurt him. Yes, she'd included his fellow pilots and the SEALs they often carried, but they were almost an afterthought.

Now that he was paying close attention, it wasn't hard to see that she was interested in him. Casper wasn't being conceited, thinking all women wanted him, but he'd gotten very good at reading the signs over the years. And Laryn wasn't all that good at the game of being coy. All her emotions were there to read in her eyes. In her body language. Even now, though she'd sounded panicked, she wasn't pulling back, wasn't telling him to get the hell away from her. She sat stiffly, yes, but he could see her heart beating in the artery in her neck and the instant flush on her cheeks the moment he scooted closer. Could hear her breathing increase.

"You smell delicious. Is that soap? Lotion?"

"Both. Why?"

He should stay away from her. If he chased away the best mechanic the Army had ever had, he'd feel like shit. But he was drawn to her, was kicking himself for not paying better attention to the shy, liked-to-fade-into-the-background woman who'd been such a huge part of his life for years.

"Tate?" she asked uncertainly.

That was another thing. The way she called him Tate made him feel like a different man. Not the hotshot Night Stalker everyone wanted a piece of. The Army wanted to control him.

Women wanted him in their bed. Men felt that if they could get close, some of his supposed badass-ness would rub off on them.

All Casper wanted was to be himself. To find someone like his twin had, who would let him be who he was...the guy who liked to read instead of watch TV at night, who loved to cook, who could sit for hours in a quiet garden, soaking in the outdoors.

Was Laryn that person? He had no idea, but when he was around her, he felt more like the person he'd been when he'd joined the Army—naïve and fresh-faced, excited about the future—than the cynical, jaded man he'd started to become over the years.

His nose brushed against the skin under Laryn's ear, and he felt her shiver at the slight touch—before she abruptly leaped from the couch and turned to face him with a frown.

"What the hell was that?"

"What?" Casper asked with a slight grin. He'd definitely felt her reaction to him. It was heady. He liked being the pursuer for once. It had been years since he'd found a woman he was interested in who made him work to woo her. And it was quite clear that Laryn Hardy wasn't going to jump into his arms at the smallest sign from him that he wanted her.

No, she wasn't like the women at Anchor Point, who went there trolling for sailors and pilots and didn't care which one they ended up with.

"You think you can come here and knock on my door, make me dinner, then sweet talk me to get me into bed? Not happening, hotshot. I wouldn't sleep with you if you were the last man on the planet! And I don't appreciate you trying to seduce me to keep me from entertaining any other job offers."

"That's not what I was doing!" Casper protested, genuinely shocked that she'd think such a thing.

She snorted. "Yeah, right. You expect me to believe that after three years, you've suddenly discovered that you want me? Give me a break. I'm not that stupid. Get out."

"Laryn—" he started.

She shook her head. "*No*. I want you out, Tate. Now."

Casper slowly stood. This wasn't how he'd wanted things to go. He wasn't entirely sure *what* he'd wanted to happen, but it wasn't for her to get pissed off and kick him out. But if she thought things between them were going to go back to the way they were...she was very wrong.

"I'll go. I honestly didn't come here to get you into bed. I wouldn't disrespect you that way. Believe it or not, I came because...well...I was worried about you. You work really hard, and you've done an amazing job getting the new MH-60 ready for the flight trials. I have no doubt that everything is going to go perfectly, and we'll all be on our way to the Middle East next week.

"And yes, I've apparently had blinders on for the last three years, but they're gone now. I see you, Laryn Hardy—and I like what I see. I want a chance to get to know you better. To be friends. And maybe something more. Either way, things are going to be different from here on out. I'm going to be around a lot."

"And what if I don't want you around?" Laryn asked. "If I say no?"

Casper was frustrated, but it was a good question. "If you truly don't want to be my friend, I'll back off. I'm not the kind of man who can't take no for an answer. If you aren't interested, we can go back to being pilot and mechanic, only talking about the choppers and how they're operating. But I think if you give me a chance to show you that I'm serious about wanting to get to know you better, you'll find that I'm a pretty decent guy. My dad raised Nate and I to respect women. To treat them right."

Laryn didn't respond, simply stared at him.

Casper was taking that as a win...for now.

"I'm sorry I freaked you out, that wasn't my intention. But please...don't take any of those jobs you mentioned. Not yet. I'm happy to look into the offers for you. I know people who know people, and they can find out the working conditions and the reason why some of those countries might want you."

"They can't want me because I'm damn good at what I do?" she asked.

"Of course that's *one* of the reasons why they want you. But, Laryn, you also work on top-secret MH-60s that you've retrofitted for the United States. You think they don't want that intel?"

"I've told them that I've signed NDAs and can't talk about any of that or give them any secrets of the US military."

Casper blew out a harsh breath. "And the fact that you think they'll simply shrug and say okay is both naïve and exasperating at the same time. The men who run those programs can be ruthless. They'll do whatever it takes to get the information they want. Trust me, they aren't above torture."

Some of the color left Laryn's face, and Casper wanted to kick himself for scaring her.

But then again, maybe she needed to be scared a little.

"Some of them *have* been a little...insistent," she admitted softly.

Casper's protective instincts rose hard and fast within him. But he forced himself to stay calm. To not demand to know what was said and by whom. "Again, I have friends who can research the job offers you've received."

She nodded but didn't speak.

"I'm going now. You're still taking the morning off tomorrow, right?"

Laryn nodded again.

"Good. I'll see you in the afternoon then. I want to go over the final details for the test flight...not that I'm worried, I just want to check everything off. Okay?"

"Yeah."

"Sleep well, Laryn. Oh, and I'm hoping that after the trials, you'll come out with me and the guys. It's tradition for us to go out for pizza and beers after killing it in any kind of flight trial."

"I know."

Of course she did. And that made Casper feel even more guilty that she hadn't ever been invited, especially considering the huge role she'd always played in making sure the choppers they tested were in tip-top shape.

There was so much more Casper wanted to say. He regretted ruining the easy night they'd been having. But Laryn was tired, he'd interrupted her sleep. He felt better that he'd gotten some food into her, and she'd been able to shower. Which, again, was a change for him. He hadn't ever really wanted to take care of a woman; it was enough some days just to take care of himself. But it had felt good, knowing he might've made Laryn's night a little better...before he screwed things up.

He turned and headed for the door to her apartment, his steps heavy. He paused after he'd opened the dead bolt and cracked the door open. Turning back to look at her, Casper saw she'd followed him and was standing about five feet behind. Her hair was drying in waves around her shoulders, and her sweats and T-shirt clung to her healthy curves.

"Lock this behind me," he ordered.

Laryn rolled her eyes. "No, I'm going to leave it open for just anyone to walk in anytime they want."

Casper wrinkled his nose. "Sorry. Stupid comment on my part." He was stalling. He knew it, and he had a feeling she did too.

"I always bolt it and put the chain on. And I've got my dad's heavy-duty cast iron pipe wrench for self-defense," she told him.

Which made Casper smile, as he recalled his and Chuck's conversation about how she'd bash someone over the head with a wrench she kept by the door. Looks like they weren't too far off. "Good. See you tomorrow."

"Bye."

The door shut behind him, and Casper waited until he heard the bolt slide into place. Then he forced himself to walk away. There was so much he hadn't said, so much more he wanted to find out about the woman he hadn't been able to stop thinking about for the last few weeks. He was becoming obsessed, and the more he was around her, the more he realized the interest wasn't one way. Laryn was prickly and defensive, but he understood that. He'd need to go slow, gain her trust, show her that he wasn't going to screw her over. That he truly wanted to get to know her.

He was an idiot for not opening his eyes to what was right in front of his face before now. He had a feeling Laryn could be very important to him in the near future. He couldn't wait to see how things played out.

CHAPTER FOUR

The next afternoon, Laryn wasn't any closer to figuring out what she was going to do about Tate than she'd been last night, after he'd left. It had taken every ounce of willpower she had to get off that couch when he'd practically been nuzzling her neck, and she'd totally lied when she said she'd never sleep with him. Hell, it was everything she'd ever dreamed about...which made what he'd done even more confusing.

Why now? Why had he randomly taken an interest in her? Nothing had changed. She was still just the mechanic who worked on his choppers. And out of the blue, he'd suddenly had some epiphany that he wanted her? She didn't trust that, not for a second.

It was out of self-preservation that she'd kicked him out last night. It had been way too nice having him there. Talking with him. Having him make her dinner. She definitely couldn't get used to that. To him. Someone else would come along and he'd lose interest in her. Of that she was certain.

But she couldn't get the feel of him sitting so close out of her head.

She hadn't meant to tell him about the job offers she'd

received. Thankfully, she hadn't let slip just *how* insistent the Turkish representative had been about her joining their team.

Altan, the guy who'd contacted her about working for him, was upbeat and friendly at first. But after she'd put him off a few times, he'd gradually become more demanding. Emailing every day, even calling her, despite her never giving him her number.

Recently, his demeanor had changed from cajoling to downright threatening. Which was completely out of line. *He'd* contacted *her* in the first place, and she'd been willing to listen to his proposal. When she finally expressed her firm disinterest, as was her right, he became borderline abusive.

Thinking about what Tate had said the night before about torture, she shuddered. It was crazy that she was in the middle of this kind of situation. She was literally nobody. Laryn Hardy, daughter to the biggest redneck she knew. Her daddy wouldn't've stood for anyone harassing his little girl...but he wasn't around to protect her anymore. Besides, he'd taught her how to protect herself, how to stand up for herself, especially since she worked in such a male-dominated industry.

Which was why she hadn't hesitated to tell Tate to leave. She wasn't going to be taken advantage of, no matter *how* much she wanted the man. How much she wanted to lead him to her bedroom and have her wicked way with him. She couldn't handle the letdown if she slept with him and he returned to mostly ignoring her afterward.

The sleep she'd planned to catch up on last night hadn't happened, and she felt even more tired today than yesterday. But work wouldn't wait. She needed to get to the base and make sure everything was good to go with the chopper before the trials.

Tate had said he'd be there, which she wasn't looking forward to.

Sighing, she shook her head. She was lying to herself. Even though she had no idea how things would go between them now, of *course* she wanted to see him. It was a sickness. A flaw within herself.

"Laryn!"

She jerked at the sound of her name being called the second she entered the hangar. Surprised, she looked up to see Tate standing near the MH-60, along with all of his fellow Night Stalker pilots. She hesitated for a beat, before straightening her shoulders and walking toward them with all the confidence she could muster.

Just because things had taken a weird turn with Tate, that didn't mean she was suddenly a different person. She had shit to do. Most importantly, a machine she had to make sure was not only one hundred percent safe, but would pass all the tests it needed to pass in order to be used in a dangerous mission in a week or so.

She never knew the details of the Night Stalker missions, just enough to know it wasn't as if they would be taking a pleasure cruise up and down the coast of whatever country they were in. No, their job was to transport special forces into dangerous territories and perform maneuvers that would have most people, herself included, throwing up as they delivered and retrieved those troops.

"'Bout time you got here!" Buck called out as she neared.

Tate smacked his friend on the back of the head. "Shut up," he told him.

Buck simply grinned.

"You look like shit," Obi-Wan chimed in, frowning.

"Jeez, man, enough!" Tate scolded.

Laryn smirked. "Good to see you guys too," she told them dryly. "And I might look like shit, but you guys *smell* like it... which I think is worse."

"She's not lying," Chaos said, as everyone chuckled.

"The SEAL team we're being deployed with challenged us. Said we couldn't outrun, out-push-up, or out-burpee them.

Taunted us by saying we were nothing but a bunch of pansy-ass pilots. Of course, we had to show them how wrong they were," Obi-Wan explained.

Laryn grinned. The six pilots were covered in sand, as if they'd taken turns burying each other at the beach like kids did when they were little. Their hair was sticking up in spikes on their heads and it was obvious they'd been sweating like pigs in the not-so-distant past.

"Who won?" she asked.

"Are you kidding?" Edge asked, sounding affronted.

"We kicked their butts," Pyro said with pride.

Looking at the men she'd worked damn hard to keep safe for the last few years, Laryn couldn't help but feel pride well up inside her. They were conceited, but they deserved to be, since they were amazing pilots. The best. They were a little rough around the edges, but then again, so was she. They worked hard and played hard. But none of them were hard on the eyes. They were all incredibly good-looking. Stereotypical jock pilots. And she cared about each and every one of them.

True, she might not hang out with them when they were off duty, but she quietly celebrated their triumphs and was devastated when something went wrong on their missions. She knew them, maybe not like a true friend did, but they were a big part of why she hadn't seriously considered any of the job offers she'd received. Tate might be the biggest reason she hadn't left, but the other five men were a collective close second.

"That fast-rope rig you installed is sick!" Pyro told her, the excitement in his voice making Laryn's grin grow bigger.

"And I heard the new infrared camera can see a bug farting from three thousand meters. When are we getting that system?" Obi-Wan asked.

"Personally, I like the drink holder she added," Chaos said with a smirk.

"It's not a drink holder, jeez," Laryn teased with a roll of her eyes.

"What is it then?" he challenged.

Fine, he had her. It was totally a drink holder. She'd added it as a joke.

Thankfully, before she could respond, the colonel in charge of the Night Stalkers, Asher Burgess—and to whom she reported, as far as the military went—entered the hangar. The six men around her all turned and saluted him as he approached.

"At ease. Where do we stand on getting this bird in the air?" he asked impatiently.

Laryn stepped forward and began to debrief the officer in charge. It took almost ten minutes to satisfy him that the chopper was truly ready for the trials. He turned to the pilots.

"Debrief in thirty minutes. My office. We have a lot to go over before leaving next week for the Middle East."

"Sir."

"Yes, Sir."

All the pilots answered in tandem as they once again saluted their commanding officer.

It wasn't until the colonel left that Laryn let out a breath of relief. She'd been around plenty of officers before, but something about the colonel had always made her uneasy. He was a good guy, had his pilots' best interests at heart, but he had a forceful and no-nonsense presence that always kept her on edge.

"Darn it," Pyro grumbled. "I was hoping we'd be able to take her up this afternoon."

"No time," Tate told him. "Not with the colonel wanting to meet with us."

"I know."

"You want to go up with us tomorrow night?" Tate asked Laryn.

Her eyes widened. "Um...no."

"No? Don't you want to see how your baby handles firsthand?"

"Nope. No. Uh-uh. Forget about it."

Tate and the other men all grinned. "Why not? Don't you trust Pyro and me?"

"Yes. I know you're good at what you do. But I don't do helicopters. Or small planes. I actually don't like planes in general, but they're a necessary evil when we need to get to a ship in the middle of a far-off ocean."

"Are you scared of heights?" Buck asked incredulously.

"No. I'm scared of crashing," Laryn hedged.

Now all the men laughed.

"We don't crash," Obi-Wan informed her.

"We sometimes land hard, but that's not the same thing," Chaos said with a perfectly straight face.

Laryn rolled her eyes. "Still not happening."

"I would never let anything happen to you," Tate said, sounding completely serious. All signs of teasing were absent from his words. Which was unusual for him. "None of us would. We'd bend over backward to make sure you were safe."

"Because who else would keep your babies purring for you?" Laryn joked, feeling uneasy with the intensity behind his words. It was going to take a while for her to get used to this new Tate. The man who actually paid attention to her, who didn't just joke lightheartedly with her about "his" helicopters.

"I'm serious," he insisted.

"Yeah, you're one of us," Edge told her.

Looking at the oldest of the pilots—because it felt safer than looking into Tate's blue eyes—she swallowed hard. "Thanks."

"I can't believe you're afraid of heights," Buck said with a small shake of his head.

"I told you, I'm not afraid of heights. Only of falling to my death," she corrected.

"So I guess zip-lining is out."

"Or skydiving."

"Or tightrope walking."

Laryn found it impossible to hold back a giggle. "Zip-lining, I'd do. The other two, definitely not."

When she glanced at Tate, she saw a look on his face she couldn't interpret. Her belly swam. She'd learned to live with her crush on the man, had managed her feelings quite nicely for the last few years. But somehow in one evening, after he'd shown up unexpectedly, fed her, asked how she was doing, leaned in to *smell* her, all the shields she'd put up to protect herself had crumbled like dust.

He could hurt her. *Really* hurt her. And the weird thing was, even knowing the possibility of getting crushed existed, when he decided she wasn't...enough for him, and despite her protests last night, she'd still say yes if he ever made her feel as if he truly wanted to go out with her.

"We have about fifteen minutes, you want to show us anything in particular on the chopper before we have to go to our meeting with the colonel?" Pyro asked.

Forcing herself to concentrate, Laryn nodded. She'd just arrived, but she had the utmost confidence that the other mechanics wouldn't have messed with anything. They were a little scared of her, to be honest, which was perfectly all right with her.

Switching into work mode, she stepped to the open back door of the chopper and bent to reach for the small stool she kept nearby, to make it easier for her to get in and out of the helicopter.

Before she could grab it, she felt hands at her waist.

Then Tate's deep voice was next to her ear, saying, "Jump."

Instinctively, she did as he requested, and before she knew it, she was standing in the chopper. Tate and the other pilots leaped up without any issues, and even though the back compartment could hold at least a dozen fully equipped special forces soldiers,

Laryn felt crowded with the larger men all around her. At five-five, she wasn't exactly a shrimp, but she definitely felt at a disadvantage being around pilots who were all taller than her.

Tate and Pyro sat in the pilot seats, while the other men hovered behind Laryn as she began to point out the upgrades. "The terrain-following/terrain-avoidance radar has been improved. The controls are just a little more to the right than they used to be." She nodded as Tate's hands reached for them without any difficulty. "The AN/ZSQ-2 sensor turret has a more robust cover, making it almost impervious to icing over, or any stray bullet that might try to take it out."

The pilots nodded, and she could hear murmurs of appreciation from the four men behind her.

"The FLIR's been calibrated and the turret also has the standard laser range finder that all the choppers have, and can be armed with laser-guided missiles and rockets. Those, obviously, haven't been installed yet, but they'll be put in as soon as the trials are over and before it gets sent over to the Middle East."

"Assuming that's part of what the colonel will talk to us about. The timeline. Gotta get this baby where we need her before the upcoming mission," Pyro said.

"You've also got the usual jammers, warning sensors, and satellite communication antennas. As long as you don't decide to run into any RPGs again, you should be good to go," Laryn told Tate and Pyro.

Everyone chuckled.

The next ten minutes, Laryn listened to the pilots talk about the functionality of the chopper and what they might expect from the trials. They would take place tomorrow night, and would include simulated missiles being fired at them from ships offshore. Which wasn't anything new for the Night Stalkers, but horrible storms were also in the forecast. Laryn hated when any of her pilots had to fly in bad weather, but that was partly what the Night Stalkers were known for.

Flying in crappy weather, in difficult terrain, and getting in and out of locations without being detected thanks to their flying skills.

Tomorrow would be harrowing for her, and fun for Tate and Pyro, of that she had no doubt. But she'd do what she always did and pretend the risks they took didn't affect her in the least. It would take every ounce of acting ability she possessed, but she'd convince them. Just like she always did.

"We're all set. I'm ready to take this baby up," Pyro said, as he turned to climb out of the copilot seat. She took a step back, almost tripping over Edge, who was standing right behind her. He caught her arm, keeping her from the humiliating experience of landing on her ass in front of the guys.

"Sorry 'bout that," he said with a small grin.

Laryn nodded and returned his smile...but when she turned back around, she saw Tate staring at the hand still on her arm, his eyes narrowed.

As the other man moved back, she frowned at Tate. "What?" she said.

His gaze whipped up to hers, and she swore she saw his cheeks pinken.

"What, *what*?" he returned.

Shaking her head, Laryn let it drop. Tate was confusing the heck out of her. He'd always sniped and griped at her like a brother would to an annoying little sister. And she'd reciprocated because she had no idea how else to act. But this was all new. This...concern. Jealousy? No, that couldn't be it. Edge was one of his best friends. And he wasn't remotely interested in her. None of the pilots were.

Everyone hopped out of the back of the chopper, and when she started to sit down to make it easier to jump out, Tate said, "Hang on, Laryn."

She hesitated, watching him easily jump down, then he turned around and reached for her. "I've got you."

She stared at him in confusion. He had her? What did that mean?

"Laryn? Go ahead and sit, I'll help you down."

Oh! *That's* what he meant. She blushed at her lack of understanding. "I've got it."

"Of course you do. But I can help."

She would've continued to refuse his help, but she was just bringing more attention to them by drawing this out. So she quickly sat, and his hands closed around her waist once more as he basically lifted her out of the chopper and set her on her feet. For a split second, neither of them moved. Tate stared down at her, while she returned the look.

Then someone cleared their throat, and both of them took a step back.

"I'll call after our meeting and let you know what the mission timeline looks like, and if there are any updates to the trials for tomorrow night," he told her.

Which was a very considerate thing for him to do...and something else he'd never done in the past. When pilots met with the colonel for any reason—meetings that often went on for hours—she normally learned any pertinent info the day after, when she arrived at work in the morning.

"It's okay. I can find out tomorrow."

"I'll call. You need the info as much as we do. You're as much a part of this team as we are."

He wasn't wrong, at least about the first part, and pleasure bloomed in her chest even as another blush warmed her cheeks. Yes, it was three years late in coming, but she wouldn't turn down any intel if he insisted.

"Okay."

"Shit. You've had to wait until the next day every time for updates?" Obi-Wan asked.

Laryn shrugged. "It hasn't been a big deal."

"Of course it is. That's bullshit," Chaos swore. "Honestly, you should be in the meetings with us. You have top-secret clearance just like we do."

Laryn shook her head quickly. "No. I don't want to have to go to your meetings!"

Everyone laughed at that.

"Good point. Well, I know it probably doesn't mean much after all these years, but we'll make sure you're kept up-to-date with all the need-to-know info in the future," Buck told her.

That warm feeling returned. Again, she had no idea what had changed in the last month since Pyro and Tate's close call when the latter was rescuing his brother, but she liked it.

"Thanks."

"You guys go ahead, I'll be right there," Tate told his friends.

The other guys all gave her chin lifts, which made Laryn smile a little, then she braced herself as she turned to Tate. "Is everything okay, based on what you've seen of the chopper?"

"Of course. I wanted to apologize for being a dick."

She blinked in surprise. "What? When?"

"The last three years."

Laryn burst out laughing. "Um...okay."

"I mean it. You're an integral part of our team. We couldn't do any of the things we do without you. Don't think I've missed how often you've stayed up all night working on the choppers after we've returned from missions. You always make sure everything is perfect before we have to go out again. I haven't thanked you enough for any of that."

"It's my job," she told him honestly.

"I know, but you've gone above and beyond what most mechanics would do."

"I'm not most mechanics," she said firmly. "My dad taught me that a driver, or pilot, is only as good as the machine he's driving or flying. And if I wanted to work for the best, I needed to make sure he had the tools he needed to *be* the best. And you, Tate, are definitely one of the best. I'm not saying that to inflate your already huge ego, just stating facts. And if I ever do anything to make your job harder, that would be the ultimate fail on my part."

Had he stepped closer to her? He had. They weren't touching, but he was definitely standing closer to her than she could ever remember him being in the past, anytime they'd had a discussion.

"I was also a dick last night. I overstepped my bounds. It won't happen again."

Laryn wasn't sure how to feel about that.

"But I'm still going to do what I can to prove to you that I'm a better man than I've been in the last three years."

"Tate—" Laryn protested. But he talked over her.

"I mean it. I don't know why I've always been an annoying prick to you. But that ends now. I have to go. I'll talk to you later."

And with that, he turned and jogged after his friends, leaving Laryn standing in the hangar next to the chopper, still utterly baffled at his change in behavior. She had no idea what she'd done, or not done, to make him do a one-eighty in his attitude toward her. But she liked it. A lot.

Feeling lighter than she ever had before a flight trial, which was one of the most stressful things she had to endure as head mechanic, she turned toward the chopper to see what else could be perfected before tomorrow night.

CHAPTER FIVE

"What gives?" Edge asked Casper after their meeting with the colonel. It had gone way longer than any of them had expected, and it was now after ten p.m.

"About what?" Casper asked, even though he had a feeling he knew exactly what his friend was referring to.

"You and Laryn. I didn't miss that look you gave me when I kept her from falling on her ass. If looks could kill, I would've been dead meat."

"Nothing."

"Stop with the bullshit. You've been different around her ever since that incident after we picked you up in Iraq."

Casper ran a hand through his hair. He was tired. Stressed about the upcoming trials tomorrow night. They were fun, but also harrowing. Not life-or-death harrowing, but hoping the helicopter performed the way it was supposed to so they could get on with their next mission was always nerve-racking. A lot rode on his and Pyro's ability to put the chopper through its paces, to make sure that, in the heat of the moment, when every life in the helicopter was on the line, it did what was asked of it.

"You gonna try to hit that?" Edge asked crudely.

Casper acted without thinking. He shoved his friend aggressively, making Edge have to take several steps back to keep his balance. It was a good thing the parking lot was empty, because having someone observe them fighting wouldn't be good for either of them, or the Night Stalkers in general.

"Don't talk about her like that!" Casper growled as he stalked closer to his friend.

Edge might be eight years older than him and in his early forties, but the man was just as capable of defending himself as Casper. If push came to shove and they ended up actually fighting, it would be an even match, and neither would come out of it without some serious injuries.

But Edge didn't seem remotely willing to fight. He smirked and held up his hands. "Sorry, dude. Just had to make sure."

"Make sure of what?" he asked.

"That you weren't just fucking with her. I like Laryn. Always have. She's a hard worker and I respect the hell out of her. If you were just looking to get laid, I would've taken you out. Made sure you stayed away. But your reaction tells me everything I need to know about your intentions. My only question is—why. Why now? What changed?"

Casper did his best to rein in his anger at his friend. He actually appreciated that he was looking after Laryn. "Honestly?"

"Of course."

"It was after we lost the chopper in Iraq. She met me on the flight deck, giving me grief like she always does. We went to talk, she wanted to know how the chopper felt when it was hit, why we weren't able to avoid the RPG, everything about what happened. But unlike in the past, she seemed...upset. Her face went white when I described how we went down, and she literally started shaking. It was in that moment when I realized that the stoic, grumpy mechanic face she's always shown us, shown *me*, was a mask. She cares about the choppers—of course she does—but when she learned about what happened after Pyro and I went down, how serious the situation was, it hit her hard."

"And?" Edge asked. "That doesn't explain your interest in her now. Just because she was upset that you crashed—Er...landed hard, doesn't explain why you all of a sudden seem to want to tear me a new asshole for touching her."

"I've paid more attention to her over the last month, and she's...She's everything I've been looking for in a partner. In a woman. Hard-working, compassionate, funny, kind...and sexy."

"Sexy? Laryn?"

Casper frowned at his friend. "Yeah. Those coveralls are hiding one hell of a body."

"Huh. I hadn't noticed."

"Good. *Keep* not noticing," he growled.

Edge laughed. "All right. I'll buy all that."

"I've been taking it slow. Trying to come to terms with all these new feelings, while also figuring out how to approach her. She's a little prickly."

"A little?"

It was Casper's turn to chuckle. "Yeah. But I have a feeling she'll be worth the chase."

"As long as you aren't chasing her just for sex. You can get that anytime, anywhere."

"I know. And no, that's not why I want to get to know her better."

"Okay. Well...let me know if you need anything. I admire the woman. She's pretty amazing."

"She is. Now I need to call her and update her on what the colonel told us."

"All right. You'll be in tomorrow morning?"

"Of course. PT first, then we'll meet back at the hangar to go over last-minute shit for the trials."

Edge gave Casper a chin lift and headed for his car. Casper

leaned against the driver's side door of his Taurus and pulled out his phone. The parking lot was deserted and dark, but he wasn't worried about anyone jumping him. Not here on base at the hangar. For some reason, he didn't feel like going back to his lonely, small apartment yet. His heart was beating fast, and he was looking forward to hearing Laryn's voice more than he was ready to admit out loud.

Everything he'd told Edge was correct. What he *didn't* share was that when he and Laryn were in that meeting room on the ship, and he'd seen her shaking after hearing about his ordeal in Iraq, he also saw how relieved and emotional she was that he was all right.

Something had clicked in that moment. At least for him.

Close calls were a part of his life as a Night Stalker. He worked in a dangerous profession and dealt with life-or-death situations all the time. No one discussed it. No one in his circle really thought much about it. It was just part of the job they all loved. But seeing how relieved Laryn had been that he was alive and unhurt made him realize that the mechanic he'd worked with for years...*cared* if he lived or died.

It was an unforgettable feeling. One that sparked a sudden and almost jarring certainty that Laryn was meant to be his.

No one would believe him if he admitted it, but there it was. And he'd spent the last month trying to figure out what it was about her that drew him so much, especially considering she'd always been there, in the background...at least for the last three years.

He'd been an idiot. Hadn't opened his eyes to the possibility that the woman who completed him was right there all this time.

And he'd struggled with the revelation. So...he'd watched her closely, observing her at work, around her mechanics and his teammates. Seeing what made her tick. Now he could admit the feeling he'd had on that ship wasn't an anomaly. And his curiosity and the feeling of being drawn to her had just gotten stronger.

Last night, he'd moved faster than he'd intended. Had shown his hand too early. He hadn't meant to spook Laryn, and he needed to move slower, let her get to know him, to trust him before he tried to move things between them from the friend category to something more.

He clicked on Laryn's name in his cell—he'd gotten her number when they'd returned from the mission that had destroyed his chopper, using the excuse that he needed to be able to contact her with issues as she retrofitted his new MH-60.

It rang several times, and when her voice mail clicked on, Casper frowned. Instead of leaving a message, he called right back. This time, she answered. But it didn't sound like the Laryn he knew.

"Hello?"

"Laryn? It's me, Casper...er...Tate. What's wrong?"

"Nothing."

But he was already on the move. He'd opened his door and sat behind the wheel before thinking about what he was about to do.

"Don't lie to me. What's wrong?" He could tell by the shakiness of her voice that something was up. He just wasn't sure she'd tell him. He'd be the first to admit that they weren't exactly confidants. But he wanted to change that. Change a lot of things about their relationship.

"I just...Really, it's fine. I'm good."

She'd almost told him. As Casper pulled out of the parking lot, heading toward the base's exit, he pushed a little harder. "Talk to me, Laryn. I can hear in your voice that something's wrong. If you don't want to tell me, okay, but don't lie and say nothing's going on when I can hear that something's up."

"You don't know me well enough to be able to say something like that," she told him.

Casper wasn't thrilled she still wouldn't tell him what he wanted to know, but at least she was talking to him. If she was talking, she was breathing, which was good. "I know that you're particular about your tools. I know that you're a marshmallow when it comes to stray animals and trying to find them homes, even though you can't keep them yourself. I know you're a morning person and not a night person. I know that you prefer to eat a big breakfast and a light dinner, and you'd rather not socialize with the soldiers and sailors onboard the naval carriers —my team included."

He could hear her breathing, but she didn't respond right away. Relief hit Casper once he exited the base, because he could drive a little faster without worrying about being pulled over by the military police who strictly enforced speed limits on base.

"Laryn?"

"I'd love to have a dog. I want a beagle. I'd name him Waffles, and he'd be a pain in my ass, but so cute it wouldn't matter. I don't like the feeling of food sitting in my belly like a lump when I go to bed. And it's not that I don't want to socialize with people on the ships we end up on; it's that no one seems to want to socialize with *me*."

"What? Why?"

"I don't know."

She sounded so sad. So lost. It made Casper's heart hurt.

"Well, things are gonna change on that front. You'll eat with us, and I'll see if we can't get you a berth in a room near us."

"It's fine, Tate. I don't expect to be best friends with people on the ships. I'm a big girl. I am who I am, and if people don't like me, I don't care."

Casper had a feeling she *did* care. "*I* like you," he blurted. "Buck, Obi-Wan, Pyro, Chaos, and Edge all like you. Chuck likes you. Hell, most of the mechanics you work with like you."

She chuckled at that. It was a shaky sound, but it was definitely a laugh. "No, they don't."

It was Casper's turn to laugh. "Right. Because they're lazy assholes who don't like working?"

"Or taking orders from a woman. One who's not in the Army, at that."

"Tough shit for them," Casper told her. "You're the best at what you do, and they're idiots if they don't take the opportunity while working for you to soak up every ounce of knowledge you have. Now...what happened tonight to make you so upset?"

He heard her sigh, but she didn't respond.

"I'm on my way to you," he informed her. "I'll be there in a few minutes. Is a guy there you can't get to leave? If so, tell him to get the hell out or he'll be dealing with me."

Laryn snorted. "There's no guy here."

"Girl?"

"No girl either."

"Good. So if it's not someone physically there, what is it? Did you hear from the colonel? Is it the chopper or the trials?"

"No."

"Talk to me, Laryn," Casper pleaded. "I have to tell you, I'm low-key freaking out trying to figure out what happened that has you sounding as if you're two seconds away from either bursting into tears or running from your apartment, screaming at the top of your lungs."

"I'm not a crier," she informed him.

"Doesn't matter if you are or aren't," he said honestly.

As he turned on Little Creek Road, he heard Laryn let out another long sigh. "It was just a phone call."

"It wasn't 'just' anything if it rattled you this much," Casper said. "Who called?"

"Fine. Altan Osman."

"Who the hell is that?"

Another sigh, another pause. "You aren't really coming over here, are you?"

Casper couldn't tell if she was hoping he was or hoping he wasn't. "I am. I'll be at your door in about two minutes. Who is Altan Osman and what did he say to upset you?"

"You're kind of annoying, you know that?"

"Yes. Pyro tells me all the time. Who's Altan Osman?" he repeated.

"He's in charge of the MH-60 project in the Turkish Gendarmerie. They've recently acquired a couple, and he's been in contact with me about coming to work for them and helping them get the choppers combat-ready."

"Wait, Turkey uses the TAI T129 ATAK attack helicopter mostly, right?"

"Yes. Which is a very good choice. But they want to upgrade."

"And this Osman character wants you to retrofit them for their military?"

"Yes."

"How'd he get your name?"

"I don't know."

"How'd he get your number?"

"I don't *know*."

"And he called you tonight and freaked you out?"

A pause. Then Laryn said softly, "Yes."

"I'm pulling into your parking lot now. Meet me at your door," Casper ordered.

"Tate, I'm fine. There's no need for—"

"Thirty seconds, Laryn. Open the door for me when I get there."

She huffed out a breath. "You are *so* annoying."

"You already said that. I'm coming up."

Casper took the stairs two at a time as he ran toward the second floor. He didn't run down the hall toward her door, but he was definitely moving at a fast clip. He raised his hand to knock, but the door opened before his knuckles could make contact with the wood.

Laryn was wearing another pair of sweats, but tonight she had on a tank top, which made Casper's mouth water immediately upon seeing her. Her breasts...they were full and lush, and desire hit him so hard, thinking about what they'd feel like under his hands, in his mouth...what they'd look like as she sat astride him and rode him.

The thought was inappropriate as hell, and he was ashamed at the lust that coursed through his body, but he couldn't help it. Laryn standing up to him, going toe-to-toe, talking about the mechanical aspects of the MH-60, rolling her eyes at him, not taking his shit...all of that was hot. He'd recently come to his senses and realized he *liked* sparring with her. *Liked* their banter. That she was a much more complicated woman than he'd ever realized.

But *this* Laryn? Out of her coveralls with her hair around her shoulders, fire shooting out of her eyes at the audacity of him showing up at her door unannounced, *again*, shoulders bare, hands on her hips, irritation—and a hint of relief—in her eyes at him being there?

He couldn't resist her. Didn't want to resist her.

He'd been an idiot for not seeing what was under his nose for so long. But now that he had, he was going to do everything in his power to convince this woman that he had her best interests at heart and she was safe with him. That she could trust him... with her thoughts, her fears, her body.

"I'm fine," she told him firmly.

"I know," Casper said, taking a chance and pushing past her into her small apartment. Seeing it reminded him yet again of his own...kind of bare bones. But for some reason, just being here made him feel a hundred percent as if he were coming home.

He heard her shut the door, and bolt it and slide the security chain on, before she followed him. Turning, he leaned against the bar-height counter that separated the galley kitchen from the living area. "Tell me what Osman said to freak you out."

"I'm not freaked out," she denied.

"You are. So whatever he said had to have been intense,

because you aren't the kind of woman, person, to be freaked out by much. I've seen you barely blink when faced with a destroyed laser system on one of my choppers. Wires sticking out in every direction, sparks flying, and you simply shrug and say to give you two hours and it'll be as good as new." Casper gentled his voice. "Please, Laryn. What did he say?"

It seemed to be the "please" that finally got to her. She walked into the kitchen without a word and opened the fridge. She got out a gallon jug of sweetened iced tea and poured some into a large plastic cup sitting on the counter.

"That stuff'll rot your teeth," Casper teased gently, as he had many other times since learning she liked the sugary-sweet drink.

"Whatever," she mumbled as she put the jug back into the fridge.

She hadn't offered him anything to drink, but Casper wasn't there for a social visit.

Giving her a moment to collect her thoughts, praying she'd finally tell him what had upset her so much it had her voice shaking and sounding so off when he'd called earlier, he waited patiently.

She sat on the edge of the cushion on one side of her couch and stared into space.

Gingerly, Casper lowered himself onto the sofa next to her. Not touching, but not on the other side either.

Laryn took a long drink of her tea, then held the cup with both hands as she spoke without making eye contact with him. "I told you before that I was looking into other jobs. I knew a guy who'd worked in Bahrain, and I contacted him a while ago. Told him I might be looking for a position somewhere outside the US."

"Why?"

She turned to look at him. "Why what?"

"Why do you want to leave here?"

She shrugged. "Haven't we already had this conversation? It doesn't matter why. Anyway, I asked if he knew of any good contractor positions not just for mechanics, but for someone with my expertise."

It *did* matter why she wanted to leave, and he wasn't convinced what she'd told him yesterday was the real reason, but since she was talking, Casper didn't interrupt.

"He said he'd see what he could find out. Next thing I knew, I was fielding inquiries from all sorts of countries. People who knew who I was, what I do, the machines I work on...and it was overwhelming. Most understood when I politely turned them down. There were a couple I seriously considered, but none could really make such a big move worth my while."

Casper understood that. It was a huge deal to move out of the US, the compensation and incentive package would have to be big to be able to lure her away. He was relieved that, while she might have put out some feelers, she didn't seem all that eager to truly leave the country.

"Then Altan emailed me. We exchanged a few polite messages back and forth. He laid out what he was looking for, and explained how he'd recently acquired a couple MH-60 helicopters, but I guess they were only outfitted with very basic equipment. I'm not sure what that means, as he didn't go into detail, but he told me the Turkish government was looking to find an expert who could make the machines lethal fighting machines...his words, not mine. He named a very fair compensation package, but I told him I'd since changed my mind and wasn't interested in leaving my current position.

"He got persistent. Raised the salary he'd originally offered me by quite a bit. Threw in free housing, meals, and housekeeping. He even offered to find me a husband, which made me laugh."

The more she talked, the more tense Casper got. He could sense what was coming.

"When I still turned him down, I could tell by the tone of his emails he was getting pissed. He clearly thought all it would take was throwing more money at me and I'd jump at the chance to move to Turkey to work for him and his government. He started getting kind of belligerent in his messages. Telling me I was an idiot for turning him down. Saying that I could be married to one of their generals, that I'd have power and prestige."

"Power and prestige mean nothing to you," Casper said.

Laryn turned to face him. "How do you know?"

"I've been working with you for three years. I've seen you downplay your skills time and time again. You've helped others on the naval ships we've been on with no expectation of compensation. You go out of your way to teach the lowest privates who are just starting out everything you know, and you shrug off any praise or accolades that are aimed your way. You even let others who work for you take the credit. The *last* thing you'd do is take a job because of the power and prestige it could bring to you."

"Thank you," Laryn said softly. "I just love what I do. I don't want or need anything other than seeing a machine I've worked on operate to its full potential."

"So...Osman called you tonight?"

"Yeah. Again, I have no idea how he got my number, because I certainly didn't give it to him. He tried to convince me that working for him would be the best thing I could do for my career. He tried using the husband he'd find for me as incentive again. I finally had to get stern with him, and I told him that I wasn't interested in the job, though I appreciated the offer. Then I asked him to stop contacting me, and he got...upset."

Casper figured that was a tame word for what really happened.

"He started yelling at me in what I assume was Turkish. Then before he hung up, he said I was making a mistake. That his country needed me, and I was—and I quote—"a fucking

American cunt," and I'd regret turning down such an extremely generous offer that any other ugly, old, unmarried woman would jump at."

Casper was furious. He wanted to beat the shit out of this Altan Osman for daring to insult Laryn. And threaten her. But he wasn't here right now. Laryn was. And she needed to know she was safe, and that she'd made the right decision in being firm and turning the man down. She might be the best MH-60 mechanic in the US, and easily in the top five in the world, but that didn't mean she was at this asshole's beck and call. She wasn't required to share her skills with *anyone*. If she wanted to quit and move to a deserted island and live off the damn grid, that was her right and her choice.

Moving slowly, Casper scooted closer to her on the couch, until his thigh was touching hers. He didn't touch her in any other way, he'd learned his lesson the night before about moving too fast around this skittish woman. He simply let his body heat seep into her skin.

"I can understand how that call would have unnerved you," he said, keeping his tone as level as he could.

At the way she turned and raised a brow at his words, he figured he wasn't as calm sounding as he hoped.

"I mean, he wasn't completely wrong. I *am* single, and some would consider me old. Ugly? I suppose that's subjective."

"You aren't ugly!" Casper exclaimed.

"I know. I mean, I'm not ready for the runway or for the bright lights of Hollywood, but I'm okay, I guess. Plain is probably a better word."

"Laryn, you aren't ugly *or* plain. You're *real*. And that's way more attractive than anything I can think of." He held out his hand, palm up, and said, "Give me your hand."

She looked down at his hand in confusion, but let go of the cup she'd been holding on to as if her life depended on it and put her hand in his.

Casper ran his thumb over the back of her hand, over the small scars that were there, over the fresh scrapes, and the tiny smudge of grease she hadn't been able to scrub out of her skin. "This hand is magic. It can turn a hunk of metal into a sleek, purring powerhouse that can lift several tons into the air. This hand keeps me safe when I'm behind the controls in the cockpit. Knowing it was *you* who tuned the engine, turned the screws, checked over every inch of the bird I'm flying—in ways machines were never meant to fly—gives me the confidence to do what I do. To take the chances I do. Because *you* were the one who got her flight ready. That's fucking beautiful."

Laryn was looking at him with wide eyes so full of emotion, Casper felt as if he'd drown simply by staring into the gorgeous brown orbs.

"I'm so sorry you had to listen to that harassment. That's no way to try to recruit someone to work for them. Insults aren't exactly a good start to a healthy working relationship."

"I know."

"He threatened you," Casper said in a low voice.

"Yeah. And he scared me. I admit it," Laryn said. "But I'm better now. He's in Turkey and I'm here. He doesn't know where I live. It's fine."

"You didn't think he had your number either...and yet, he called." Casper hated to bring that up, but he needed her to be smart about this. "If he works for the Turkish Gendarmerie, the special forces, he's probably got connections."

Laryn stiffened and tried to pull her hand out of his grip, but Casper tightened his hold. "I'm not saying that to scare you."

"Well, *that* was a big fail," she griped.

In any other situation, Casper probably would've grinned at her tone. But this wasn't a laughing situation. Someone had fucking threatened her. Which was unacceptable. "Let me talk to some people. See what they can find out about this Osman guy. See if he's all talk or if he has the means and ability to actually follow through with a threat."

"I'm sure it's nothing. I don't want to be a bother."

"Trust me, you won't be a bother. Not to my guy. He loves this shit. Finding dirt on people, ferreting out info they think is buried deep enough to never be found."

"I don't want the colonel or my boss to find out I was even inquiring about another job."

That part was trickier. "I'm thinking neither man will assume anything if they hear through the grapevine about your troubles with Osman. You're the best in your field, Laryn. They'll probably just think Osman was fishing, hoping to lure you away by offering you tons of money and, of course, a husband. They'll be more concerned about someone trying to steal you away. Hell, you might get a raise out of this entire thing," Casper said, trying to lighten the mood.

But Laryn didn't laugh. "I don't want any more money. I make more than enough as it is."

And that was one more reason to like this woman. The more Casper was around her, the more he got to know her, the *real* Laryn, the more he wanted her.

"Let me talk to him. My acquaintance. He'll do some digging while we're deployed and by the time we get back, I'm sure he'll have all the intel we need to figure out if this is a real threat, or just a desperate man spewing vitriol. Please?"

She sighed. "Fine."

That was the second time using the word "please" had gotten him what he wanted. Casper filed that away and vowed not to abuse the power that word apparently had over her...at least coming from him. He'd heard some of the mechanics who worked for her pleading to leave early, or for a day off, and she'd stood firm and told them no.

"I have to get up early tomorrow for PT, and it's getting late, so I should probably get some sleep," Casper told her.

"Right," Laryn said, tugging at her hand once again.

This time Casper let it go, but not before memorizing the feel of her calloused palm brushing against his own.

"Thanks for coming over," she told him politely.

Casper nodded. "You're welcome. Do you have an extra pillow I can use?"

She frowned. "What?"

"A pillow. I can use the blanket you've got on the back of the couch, but a pillow would be nice."

"You aren't staying here," she said, almost sounding horrified.

"Yes, I am," Casper said firmly.

"No, you aren't," she told him, sounding just as stern.

"Laryn, you just got off the phone with a man who threatened you. Said you'd regret turning down his offer. A man who, at best, has access to a lot of money if he's responsible for hiring someone to outfit MH-60s, and at worst, connections at the highest levels of the Turkish government. There's no way I'm leaving you alone."

"I can take care of myself."

"I know you can. You're a grown adult. But you aren't a trained soldier."

"I actually *am* a trained soldier. I went through the same basic training you did," she countered. "Besides, you're a pilot. And I don't see any choppers hanging around my apartment."

Damn, he admired her spunk. But he wasn't going to be swayed.

"If I leave after hearing what you told me tonight, I'm not going to get any sleep. I'll be worrying about you all night. Wondering if Osman has any contacts here in the States. If someone has broken into your apartment overnight and stolen you away. Tomorrow morning, I could wake up and you could be halfway across the ocean, headed to Turkey to be detained and forced to work on their newest acquisitions. And while you'd resist, because that's who you are, they could torture you to make you spill the secrets about the latest technology the US is putting into their choppers."

"Oh my God, you're such a drama queen," Laryn protested.

Casper put on the most pathetic face he could muster and even pouted a little bit.

"I can't believe I'm agreeing to this. Fine. But only for tonight."

He wasn't going to agree to that, so he simply smiled.

Laryn shook her head as she stood and headed to the kitchen to pour out the tea that she didn't bother finishing. "I'm going to regret this," she mumbled.

Casper frowned at that. He silently followed her into the kitchen. When she turned around from the sink, gasping in surprise to find him so close, he put his hands on the counter on either side of her and leaned in. Her hands flew up and landed on his chest, but she didn't push him away. Simply rested them there.

"You aren't going to regret it. I'm just here to make sure all is well," he told her.

"Okay."

"I mean it. No regrets, Laryn."

"I...this...it's such a change from how things used to be."

"I know. I've been an idiot. I told you that. And I'm done. I'm standing up for a friend. For someone who's had my back and made sure I'm as safe as I can be while I'm in the air. I'm doing the same thing for you, even though it's a bit late."

His words seemed to have a profound effect on her. Her shoulders relaxed and her fingers curled into his chest.

"Thank you," she whispered.

"You're welcome. We'll work on your ability to ask for help."

At that, she rolled her eyes, and now she *did* push at him a little bit.

Casper grinned and stepped back, giving her some space.

"Don't blame me when you sleep like shit. That couch is uncomfortable as hell."

"Shit," he mumbled.

Laryn giggled, and it was the most carefree sound he'd heard from her tonight. He reveled in it. He had no problem getting a horrible night's sleep if it made this woman relax.

She walked out of the kitchen and Casper waited to see what she was doing. She returned in less than twenty seconds with a fluffy pillow in her hands. She put it on the couch and pointed down the hallway. "The bathroom's in the hall. We'll have to share, I only have one."

"No problem. I'll let you know when I'm leaving in the morning."

"What time is PT?" she asked.

"Five-thirty."

"I'll be awake. I usually get up at four-thirty to work out myself."

"You do?"

"Uh-huh."

An idea struck Casper. "Want to come work out with me and the guys?"

Laryn frowned. "Uh...hell no."

"Why not?"

"Because you guys probably run like forty miles, do a thousand burpees, and bench press those huge boulders lying around the base for security purposes."

Casper burst out laughing. "Not even close. I think we're gonna do a five-mile run tomorrow, then go to the park on base with the workout equipment—you know, the one with pull-up bars, bench jumps, triceps dips, monkey bars, and that small climbing wall. Come with us. It'll be fun."

"I don't know."

Casper couldn't help himself. "Please?"

She frowned. "Shit. There you go, being all nice again. *Fine.*"

Satisfaction coursed through him. "Great. We'll leave here around five-fifteen. Since you live so close to base, that'll give us plenty of time to meet up with the guys."

Laryn nodded and turned to head back down the hall toward her room. She turned at the last minute. "Tate?"

"Yeah?"

"The last person to do something so unselfish for me was my dad. I appreciate you being here."

His heart fell at her admission. This woman should've had all sorts of people bending over backward to help her out. To be nice to her. Including him. He'd fucked up hard. But he was going to do what he could to make amends. To make sure she knew from here on out that he was her friend. As were his fellow pilots. Laryn was a vital part of their team. They hadn't treated her as such, but that was going to change.

"Good night, Laryn."

"Good night."

He stood in the middle of the living room staring down the hallway for several minutes, listening to her puttering around in her bedroom. When he saw the light under her door go out, he finally moved, stretching out on the couch. She was right, it was lumpy as hell. But Casper didn't care. He didn't bother removing his boots. He wanted to be prepared for anything. Did he really think someone was going to smash through the door to get to Laryn? Not really. But until he spoke with Tex, the person he'd told Laryn about, he wasn't going to take any chances.

Tex would be able to research this Altan Osman guy and determine the true threat level he posed. Until then, Laryn would have to deal with having someone nearby at all times. If it couldn't be him, it would be Pyro. Or Edge. Or any of his fellow pilots. He was actually thankful they were going to be deployed soon. There was nowhere safer than on a naval ship in the middle of the ocean. While he and the other Night Stalkers did their thing, she'd be safely ensconced onboard. When they got back to Norfolk, they'd figure out how to mitigate any possible threats.

Casper was looking forward to this deployment. To showing Laryn what it meant to be part of a team. She'd probably resist, but she'd learn that he and his friends were stubborn. And when they set their mind to something—namely, bringing Laryn into their inner circle—nothing and no one would keep them from meeting their objective.

CHAPTER SIX

Laryn thought she was going to die. She worked out three mornings a week, but trying to keep up with Tate and his friends was making her feel as if she was going to hurl. She'd also slept like crap last night—which wasn't helping her performance this morning—because she couldn't stop thinking about Tate being just on the other side of her door. Using her pillow. On her couch.

If he wasn't staying there simply because he thought she was in danger, she might have gotten more enjoyment out of the situation. Though, she couldn't deny feeling warm and gooey inside that he even wanted to protect her.

She truly didn't believe that Altan would come after her, even though he'd sounded beyond pissed on the phone. So much so that it had shaken her usually unflappable confidence. Having Tate there last night was actually a huge relief. But she wouldn't get used to that. He couldn't just move in indefinitely.

And to her shock, he seemed fine this morning. As if her lumpy couch hadn't fazed him in the least. Then again, he'd probably slept in worst places. It was annoying how chipper he seemed though. He'd talked all the way to the base and seemed excited to meet up with his friends to inform them that she'd be joining them for PT.

The guys seemed genuinely happy to have her there, which was kind of a surprise, since they were so tight-knit. Everyone knew the team did PT on their own, didn't invite anyone to join them, and generally kept to themselves on base.

And now, after her first invite, she was doing her best not to puke up the water she'd gulped down before starting off on this jog.

By the time they got to the park to use the equipment there, she was done. Laryn flopped down into the grass and said, "You guys go ahead. I'll just do some sit-ups."

Everyone chuckled, but she could tell they weren't laughing *at* her.

After catching her breath and doing a few sets of sit-ups, Laryn rested her arms on her updrawn knees and watched the pilots do their thing.

And their *thing* was impressive. As were their physiques. They all wore Army-issued shorts and matching gray T-shirts with the word ARMY across the chest. Their arms bulged as they did pullups, their thigh muscles on full display as they did squats and burpees.

Even though these men were pilots, and their job required them to sit for long stretches at a time, Laryn had no doubt they were just as capable as the special forces men they carried to and from dangerous missions. Each of the six pilots had been through extensive training in hand-to-hand combat and being able to evade hostile forces if, God forbid, their choppers ever crashed behind enemy lines.

Seeing them work out, seeing their comradery, the way they joked and laughed and even how they encouraged each other, gave her a deeper understanding of their bond. They weren't simply coworkers, they were best friends.

To her surprise, after the guys were done working out, they

came and joined her in the grass. Buck and Obi-Wan sprawled on their backs and groaned. Pyro and Chaos laughed and told them to suck it up. Edge merely smirked, and when Laryn looked over at Tate, she saw he wasn't looking at his friends. Instead, his gaze was locked on her.

She immediately felt flustered and looked away.

"So...Laryn's being harassed by an asshole who wants her to work for him."

She gasped. His words all the more shocking because for a short while, she'd actually forgotten about the phone call from the night before.

"What? Who?"

"But she *has* a job."

"You aren't leaving us, are you, Laryn?!"

"Harassed how?"

The questions and exclamations came hard and fast.

"Long story short," Tate said, "we all know Laryn's the best MH-60 mechanic we've ever had. That the Army was smart enough to hire. Well, apparently word's gotten out and everyone wants her to come work for them. And by everyone, I mean other countries. Countries that would do whatever it takes to get someone who knows the technology we use like the back of her hand. A man from one such country has been recruiting her *hard*, and when she said she wasn't interested, instead of backing off, he's doubled down. Called her last night, even though she never gave him her number, and said some things that were worrying. I'll be contacting Tex as soon as I can to have him look into this asshole, to see if his threats were more than just frustration over not being able to hire her."

Laryn was embarrassed. She wasn't sure why, considering she was on the receiving end of the nasty threats. Maybe because she felt as if she'd opened herself up to Altan's behavior by letting him think there was a chance she might actually take him up on his offer, simply by listening to him in the first place.

"What do you need from us?" Edge asked. He said it nonchalantly, as if their support was a sure thing.

Laryn opened her mouth to respond, but Tate beat her to it.

"I stayed at her place last night, just in case, but I can't be around her all the time. Depending on what Tex says, we might need to take turns watching out for her."

"Done."

"Easy enough."

"Just let us know when you need us."

Their support was immediate and heartfelt.

Still, Laryn couldn't help but feel irritated at Tate's takeover of the situation. "I don't need a babysitter or a bodyguard," she told them as firmly as she could. "I admit that, last night, I was feeling a bit off-kilter. But now that I've had time to think about the situation, it's unlikely that Altan will actually do anything. It wouldn't be smart, because if anything happened to me, it would be obvious who did it."

"You think that's going to stop him?" Chaos asked with a small tilt of his head.

"Well...yes," Laryn said.

"Wrong," Buck said in a low tone. "You could be taken captive and forced to do the work he previously would've paid you to do. And you'd have to do what he asks, because the alternatives wouldn't be pleasant. Even if we knew who took you, we wouldn't know *where* you were taken."

"We've been on rescue missions for American prisoners of war, and trust me, the conditions those soldiers and sailors have been found in when we recovered them weren't pretty." Pyro sounded serious, and Laryn shivered as he continued. "The strongest special forces soldier is often no match for months of torture. You'd break, little Laryn. You'd go back on every oath you've made to our government to keep what you do to yourself, if only to make the pain stop."

"Enough!" Tate barked at his friends. "No one is going to take Laryn captive. And you're scaring her."

"You don't think she *needs* to be a little scared?" Chaos asked. "Maybe she doesn't understand how much the knowledge she has in her head is worth. How desperate enemy countries would be to acquire it...by any means necessary."

"I'm serious, no more," Tate growled in a voice that was so unlike anything she'd heard from him, Laryn almost felt afraid of *him*. "There's nothing wrong with Laryn knowing her worth and wanting to look for more compensation and better benefits because of her skills. Isn't that what we all did? We knew our worth, so we convinced the Army to give us a special contract so we could be stationed here, instead of with the rest of the 160th Special Ops Aviation Regiment at the bases in Kentucky, Washington, or Georgia. Doesn't matter how or why Laryn ended up on this asshole's radar, just that she has, and it's our job to protect one of our own. I don't want to hear one more fucking dire warning aimed at Laryn. *Period*. You guys in or out?"

"In," all five of the other pilots said at the same time.

"I'm sorry," Laryn couldn't help but say quietly. Tate standing up for her so vigorously and aggressively had taken her by surprise.

"You have nothing to be sorry for," he said without hesitation.

"I think I do. Chaos isn't exactly wrong. I did ask a friend if he knew about any contract jobs. How word spread so fast from there, I'm not really sure. But I *was* the first to reach out."

"Why?" Pyro asked. "Are you so unhappy here? With us?"

That was a tricky question to answer. And there was no way Laryn was going to admit that she'd asked her friend if he knew about any jobs because she was feeling down about being around Tate all the time, when he barely acknowledged her presence.

"No. I just...I think I was in a rut. I thought that going someplace new would make me feel..." Her voice trailed off. She realized almost too late that she probably shouldn't say what she was thinking. She didn't want to hurt anyone's feelings.

"Feel what?" Edge asked.

Laryn licked her lips, then sighed. "More like part of a team," she said quietly. "I mean, I know I'm not a pilot or anything, and I do like the other mechanics I work with, but they treat me strictly like a boss. For a long time now, I've been feeling as if I work in a bubble. Do my thing, go home, come back to work. I guess I kind of wanted to shake things up."

As soon as the words left her lips, Laryn felt bad, because all six men around her had stricken looks on their faces.

"You *are* a part of our team, Laryn," Pyro said. "You think we could do anything we do without you?"

"Without you, I'm not sure I'd be as confident as I am when I fly," Obi-Wan agreed. "I don't hesitate to do some crazy shit because I know the bird isn't going to fall apart under me... because you've gone over her with a fine-tooth comb to make sure everything's working properly."

"We've obviously failed in making sure you know how important you are to us," Edge agreed.

"From now on, we'll do better," Buck reassured her. Then he grinned. "You're going to be so sick of us. All up in your face, wanting you to hang out. Dragging your ass out of bed to come out to Anchor Point for a beer and to play some cornhole."

"I'm not playing cornhole with you guys," Laryn said. "I couldn't hit the broad side of a barn if my life depended on it. I'm sure you can all sink that stupid beanbag every throw."

Everyone chuckled.

"He's right. You're right," Obi-Wan said quietly. "We've let you down. Haven't made sure you realize what an integral part of our team you really are. Jesus, it's why the colonel insisted you be included in our contract in the first place, to be stationed here in Norfolk. Casper made sure you were assigned as our lead mechanic and would go wherever we went."

Laryn looked at Tate. Once more, his gaze was locked on hers. "You did?" she asked.

"Yes."

It was only one word, but the emotion and heartfelt honesty behind it made Laryn feel like an idiot for ever wanting to work elsewhere.

"I didn't know," she said lamely.

"Which was our mistake," Tate said. "We didn't make sure you knew, and we didn't make you feel as if you were one of us. Which ends now. Starting with making sure this Osman asshole knows you're off-limits. That you aren't going anywhere. No means no. And begging, threatening, or otherwise making you feel vulnerable isn't going to change your mind. Will you let us help you? Let us have your back, just as you've had ours for the last three years?"

How could she say no to that? Laryn nodded.

"Good. Now, I never did get around to telling you what the colonel told us in the meeting last night. Bottom line is that he has no doubt the MH-60 will pass the trials, so he's already arranged to get it to the Mediterranean Sea, to the destroyer ship positioned there. It's a change of plans from when we thought we'd be in the Arabian Sea. We'll follow and rendezvous with Navy SEALs preparing for missions in that area."

Laryn nodded.

"You want to talk about the trials?" he asked, still laser focused on her.

"Not really. The chopper is ready. You're ready. It's not a big deal."

Of course it was a big deal. They all knew that. If something went wrong, if one of the systems that had been installed failed to operate as expected, it could delay the upcoming mission, which would cause all sorts of upheaval in schedules.

"Right. So...I stink," Tate said. "I could use a shower. How about if we go to my place first, I'll shower, then back to your apartment so you can get ready? I'll make us some breakfast before we head over to the base."

Laryn's brows furrowed. "That's not necessary, Tate. Just drop me off at my place and I'll meet you at the hangar later."

"Not happening. Laryn, I was there last night. I saw how badly Osman scared you. We have no idea what kind of reach he has or what he might have planned. I'm not willing to leave you vulnerable until we have more intel from Tex."

"Who is this Tex guy, anyway?" Laryn asked irritably.

"His name is actually John Keegan. He's a former Navy SEAL who's a fucking computer genius," Buck told her, as he stood and brushed grass off his ass.

"He's had a hand in the rescues of more special forces personnel than we can count," Obi-Wan added.

"And many of their partners," Pyro agreed.

"The government trusts him, the SEALs trust him, the Deltas trust him...hell, all the men and women who've gotten out of the military trust him. He's able to dig up information on anyone and everyone. Nothing is buried too deep for him to find," Chaos told her.

"He'll let you—and us—know if this asshole who scared you last night is truly a concern, or if all he needs is some 'encouragement' from Tex in the way of a virus let loose on his country's computers to get him to back off," Edge said with a grin.

"Speaking of which, where is this Osman from? That's what you said his last name is, right?" Pyro asked.

"Turkey," Tate answered, before Laryn could.

The others all swore or muttered under their breath.

Everyone followed Buck's lead and stood. Tate held his hand down to Laryn to help her up. "Come on. Time's a ticking. And I know you don't want anyone else messing with your chopper before the trials. We need to get moving so we can shower and get a good breakfast in before we have to hit the ground running."

Laryn reached up for his hand without thought and the second his fingers closed around hers, goose bumps sprang up on her arms. She prayed Tate didn't see them, or any of his friends. As soon as she was on her feet, Tate turned and headed for the parking lot where they'd all left their cars...without letting go of her hand. She had no choice, if she didn't want to make a big deal out of him holding her hand, but to follow along with him.

The other guys chatted about their plans for the day without seeming to think she and Tate holding hands was anything out of the ordinary. And she couldn't help but feel all warm and fuzzy inside at how she was being included in their conversations. She'd been on the outskirts of their banter for so long. It was very different to now be part of the inner circle.

When they made a decision, they didn't fuck around. They were one hundred percent committed. Which wasn't a huge surprise. Night Stalker pilots were some of the most focused and determined people she'd ever met. Usually that was in regard to completing a mission, come hell or high water. But apparently it also included righting what they thought was a wrong, as well... namely, her not feeling as if she was a part of their team.

And honestly, she wasn't really...but it was sweet of them to *think* she was. Yes, she was responsible for their choppers being able to operate under the harshest conditions. For making sure the engines would do what was asked of them without hesitation. But did that make her one of them? In her eyes, no. But apparently these six men thought differently.

The feeling in her belly was one she'd been chasing for years. To belong. To be a part of something bigger than herself. To be an integral cog in the wheel. That's how she felt when she'd worked with her dad on the cars at the dirt track, how he'd made her feel. And that's how she felt right now.

She wasn't too keen on the idea of having a babysitter, but she couldn't deny that it made her feel a tiny bit better. Until she found out if Altan Osman was an actual threat, it wouldn't be a hardship to have Tate hanging around. She just had to keep her feelings under wraps. She never wanted him to find out how much of a crush she had on him. It would likely ruin the newfound camaraderie she had with him and his team. Laryn could deal with being his friend. Maybe.

CHAPTER SEVEN

Casper felt on top of the world. The flight trials had been flawless. The chopper responded beautifully to his commands and all the bells and whistles the Army had invested in, the radars, night-vision, missile launchers...everything worked perfectly. And he could tell Laryn had outdone herself on the engine, as it felt more responsive than the one in his last bird. Which was impressive, considering that had been the easiest helicopter he'd ever flown.

His mechanic hadn't been far from his mind all day. He couldn't stop thinking about how Laryn admitted that she hadn't felt as if she was a part of a team. He was ashamed and blamed himself for making her feel that way. He knew better than most how important it was to make everyone he worked with feel valued. As the highest-ranking pilot in his team of Night Stalkers, he felt it was his responsibility to take a leadership role. And he'd failed where Laryn was concerned. So badly that she'd been job hunting.

Of course, she was a grown-ass woman who could, and should, make her own decisions about her life, but he couldn't help but feel as if he'd let her down. That somehow, she was in the situation she was in partly because of his actions. If Casper had opened his damn eyes and realized how the lack of inclusion was making Laryn feel, maybe she wouldn't have asked her friend to be on the lookout for potential contractor positions. He wanted to fix this. One way or another.

And the first step toward that goal was to include their mechanic in their traditional celebration of a successful flight trial.

Still feeling the rush of adrenaline from putting the chopper through its paces with Pyro at his side, with the rest of his fellow Night Stalkers playing the roles of both ally and enemy birds, depending on what system was being evaluated—it was always a challenge to take on one of his friends because they were all unparalleled behind the controls of a helicopter—Casper walked toward where Laryn was standing with two of the younger mechanics who worked for her.

"I'll know more once I talk to Casper, but it seemed to me that she was pulling right. We need to double check everything to make sure the stick is properly aligned. Being off even half an inch could mean devastation for everyone on the chopper, especially when the pilots are maneuvering between mountain ranges."

She wasn't wrong. And once again, it reminded Casper of just how much this woman knew about their machines. He often took for granted how flawlessly they performed when he was flying, but Laryn was exactly right. If something was off even by the smallest margin, it could be a huge disaster.

"I didn't notice it pulling right, but if you say it was, it was," Casper said as he approached. He slung an arm over Laryn's shoulders and gave her a quick one-armed hug. "She performed beautifully. Thank you all for your hard work to get her up and ready to go."

The younger mechanics' faces lit up at the praise, and it hit Casper then that it wasn't only Laryn he should've paid more attention to. Building these men up would help not only him and his friends, but any future pilots these mechanics worked with.

As the two men—boys, really—babbled on about specific maneuvers he'd performed in the test flight, Casper was acutely aware of the woman at his side. He hadn't removed his arm from around her, and she hadn't shrugged him off. It might've been his imagination, but he could've sworn she leaned closer as he patiently listened to the effusive praise her coworkers were giving him on his flying prowess.

This would've been the perfect time to improve the relationship between him and the mechanics who worked on their choppers...but Casper was only interested in improving *one* relationship right this moment. The one with Laryn.

"Thanks, guys. But I truly believe a pilot is only as good as the machine he's flying. And thanks to Laryn and everyone who worked on my MH-60, today I got to be one of the best. Now, if you'll excuse me, I need to steal Laryn."

"Of course."

"Yeah, I'm sure you guys have an AAR to attend."

A pang of guilt hit Casper. He wasn't stealing her to go to a boring After Action Review. No, he wanted to convince her to go to Anchor Point with him and his fellow Night Stalkers to celebrate the successful trial.

He dropped his arm from around her shoulders and instead took her hand, turning her around and walking away from the mechanics who were still staring at them with interest. Reluctantly, he dropped her hand when they were out of hearing range of anyone around them. It was crazy how right her hand felt in his.

"What's up?" she asked with a slight tilt of her head.

"Come to Anchor Point with us," he said without preamble.

She blinked as if surprised. Then let out an adorable little huff of breath. "I thought you wanted to talk to me about the chopper leaning to the right."

"Nope. I want you to agree to come to the bar to celebrate with me and the guys. It's tradition."

"I don't know," Laryn hedged. "I have paperwork to do, and I want to take a look at the bird before she gets loaded up to head to the destroyer. Make sure nothing shook loose in the trials or needs to be replaced."

"The chopper is fine. Your guys can do that. Come on. Come out with us."

"You're just asking because you feel you have to babysit me after hearing about that call last night," she accused.

"I'm not," Casper said. "Remember, I told you last night that I wanted you to come with us when we celebrated the flight trial. And I'm asking because I honestly want you to come. I've been a shit team leader because I've excluded one of the most important people on my team for way too long. We all want to celebrate with you. Share in the triumph of being back in the air after losing that bird in Iraq. I've felt naked without a chopper, and now I can get back to doing what I'm good at."

He considered using the magic word that seemed to make this woman agree to whatever he wanted, but he didn't want to abuse the power that word seemed to have over her.

"I promise it'll be fun. The guys and I want to get to know you better. We never get hammered, and we won't stay out too late."

Laryn sighed, looking back at her employees, then over at the MH-60 sitting in the hangar, then finally back at him. "Fine. But not for long. It's already way late."

It was. It was twelve-thirty. "Awesome. And it won't be for long, as the bar closes at two." He wanted to grab her hand again but was cognizant of the many eyes on them, and the last thing he wanted to do was embarrass her or make her have to answer any uncomfortable questions from her staff. There were no rules against her dating a sailor or soldier, but instinctively, Casper knew she'd be uncomfortable with any attention being drawn to herself or her actions. She was much more comfortable flying under the radar.

The thought made him smile, as that's where he was comfortable too...literally. Flying his chopper under the radar, so he was invisible to enemy forces.

Instead, Casper put his hand on the small of her back as he urged her toward where his friends were waiting patiently. He hadn't had a chance to talk to most of them privately about what was up with him and Laryn, and honestly, he wasn't sure what he'd tell them. That he'd suddenly noticed she was a very attractive woman? That he was drawn to her? That he felt like an idiot for overlooking her for so long? All of that was true, but he was still formulating a way to inform the others what was going on.

But then again, he probably didn't really have to. He'd never brought a woman to PT before. And while Laryn technically *was* a part of their team, it was still unusual enough for him to have taken such an intense interest in what was going on with her. So much so that his friends—other than Edge and Pyro, who he'd already had conversations with about Laryn—probably had an inkling his interest wasn't entirely professional.

"High-five!" Buck exclaimed as they neared.

Laryn smiled and smacked his hand.

"She flew sweet and strong!" Pyro added, pulling Laryn into a bear hug.

She squeaked, but was still grinning as she returned his exuberant embrace.

"Did you see Casper turn her practically on her side as he circled around to get behind us?" Obi-Wan asked.

"Yeah," Laryn said with a nod, after Pyro let go of her.

"I almost shit myself when he cut the engines, dropped four hundred meters, then started her up again and came up behind us," Edge said with a shake of his head.

"Casper, you're a crazy son-of-a-bitch, and I'm glad you're on our side," Chaos agreed.

"You're coming with us, right?" Buck asked Laryn. "To Anchor Point?"

"For a while, yes."

The men all cheered.

"Let's get going then. Time's a tickin'," Pyro said as he looked at his watch.

"Climb on," Chaos ordered as he turned his back to Laryn and crouched down.

"Pardon?" she asked with a furrow of her brows.

"Climb on," he repeated. "I'll give you a ride to Casper's car."

She laughed. "I don't think so."

"Come on...it's a victory walk thing."

"Thank you, no."

"But—"

"She said no, Chaos," Casper said firmly, shoving his friend.

Chaos lost his balance and almost fell over, but he managed to keep his feet and snort-laughed. "Fine, but never say I'm not a gentleman and didn't offer."

"I've been walking on my own for as many years as I can remember. I think I'll make it," Laryn told him dryly.

They all headed out of the hangar toward the parking lot, and the mechanics still around called out farewells and more congratulations. Everyone seemed to be in a good mood, and Casper was still riding the high of the complicated maneuvers he'd executed earlier.

As soon as they exited the hangar, he put his hand back on the small of Laryn's back and led her toward his Taurus. When they got close, she smiled, reminding him how excited she was when she'd first seen his car.

"The two thousand five models have had issues with the engine misfiring at freeway speeds. You experience that?" she asked.

"No."

"What about the idle air bypass valve? That can sometimes cause engine performance issues."

"Not with this baby."

"The camshaft sensor magnet has been known to damage synchronizers." She was talking more to herself now, and her hand brushed the hood as she walked around the front of the vehicle. Casper had a feeling she was itching to raise the hood and check things out. "Have you ever blown a gasket? Or had white smoke coming from the exhaust? That could be why."

In response, he walked up to her and took the hand resting on the hood in his own. Without a word, he led her to the driver's side and opened the door. Gesturing to the seat, he said, "Why don't you drive and see for yourself how she goes?"

"Really?" Laryn asked, her eyes sparkling with eagerness.

"Wouldn't have offered if I wasn't serious," he told her.

She lifted an eyebrow, looking skeptical. "Most pilots I know are control freaks. They would never let anyone else drive their cars. Especially a woman."

"I'm not like most pilots. And it's obvious you know more about cars than I ever will. I trust you with my life when I climb into that MH-60. Why would I not trust you behind the wheel of my car?"

Still, she hesitated.

Casper took a chance. He stepped into her personal space, not touching but definitely crowding her. To her credit, she didn't cringe away or push him back. She simply lifted her chin to continue to be able to meet his eyes.

"I've seen your car, Laryn. Early nineties Honda Civic. Looks like a piece of shit, but purrs when you start her up. The state of someone's car tells me a lot about them as a person."

"What does mine tell you about me?" she asked quietly.

"That you're a hell of a mechanic, which I already knew. That you take care of what's yours. That just because something looks a little rough around the edges, doesn't mean it's not worth loving. That you value what you have. That you're practical. Should I go on?"

She shook her head silently.

Taking another risk, Casper lifted a hand and brushed the backs of his fingers against her cheek in a barely there caress. Her skin was soft and smooth. And even in the crappy lights of the parking lot, he could see her skin flush at his touch. She was so responsive, so honest with her unconscious reactions to him. It was heady to know he affected her so much, and not for the first time, Casper wanted to kick himself for not noticing sooner.

"Thank you for tonight. For making sure everything in my bird was top-notch. Safe. Perfect. For agreeing to come to Anchor Point. For being who you are."

"You're welcome."

Forcing himself to take a step back, Casper grabbed hold of the door frame with a white-knuckled grip. It was either that or wrap his arm around this woman and pull her against him and find out if her lips were just as soft as her cheek. "Go on. Have a seat. You can tell me everything she needs when we get to the bar."

She grinned and sat in the driver's seat. Casper closed the door and jogged around to the other side, looking around to check the area automatically. In the air, he felt fairly confident that he could see danger coming his way...or the instruments around him could. But evil could hide more easily on the ground. And while he felt safe on the naval base, that didn't mean it was completely danger free. He and his friends were trained to always be on the lookout for anything that seemed out of the ordinary. Thankfully, the parking lot at the hangar appeared safe enough at the moment.

He climbed into the passenger side of his car—which felt weird, but he'd never admit that to Laryn—and smiled as she gestured with her head to his seat belt impatiently. He buckled himself in and nodded at her.

She'd moved the seat up so she could more comfortably reach the pedals. Then she revved the engine and pulled out of his parking spot as if she were in one of the dirt races she'd attended so regularly as a child with her dad.

Casper laughed out loud and grabbed hold of the oh-shit handle above his head. He wasn't nervous, wasn't afraid. Laryn was full of surprises—and he couldn't wait to discover each and every little thing she hid under the stoic and serious face she showed the rest of the world.

CHAPTER EIGHT

By the time they reached Anchor Point, Laryn's cheeks hurt from smiling. Tate didn't seem discomfited in the least by her driving. She knew she had a lead foot and was a little reckless on the roads. It didn't help that the streets were fairly empty, since it was nearing one in the morning.

Tate's Taurus was in amazingly good shape for being as old as it was. Of course, it wasn't as ancient as her Civic, but she was still itching to get under the hood and take a look. The brakes felt as if they could use new pads, and there was a slight hitch when she pressed on the gas, making her think the lines needed to be flushed out.

She expertly parallel parked along the road before looking over at Tate. For a split second, she worried that she'd done what she usually did...turned a man off because she was more knowledgeable and had more skills behind the wheel than he did. But she should've known better. This was Tate. He had enough confidence in his own skills not to worry about someone else being better behind the wheel. If flying helicopters was an Olympic sport, he'd win gold every time. And probably have a shit-ton of endorsements as well.

"So? What's the verdict?" he asked.

"I'd give her a solid B," Laryn told him.

"Only a B?" he asked with a slight frown.

"That's better than average," she reminded him.

"But not an A," Tate returned. "Can you bring her up to snuff?"

In response, Laryn simply smirked and raised a brow at him.

"Of course you can," he said with a chuckle, answering his own question. "Come on, let's get inside and grab a drink before we're too late and they shut the place down."

Laryn nodded and got out of the car. That's when she happened to look down...and only then realized she was still in the coveralls she wore at work. Not exactly "going out" attire.

Doubts hit her hard. Behind the wheel or under an engine, she was confident and sure of herself. But in the real world? Not so much.

"Laryn?" Tate asked.

She hadn't realized he'd come around to her side of the vehicle, and he was now standing in front of her, looking at her with concern. She had no idea how long she'd been standing there, unmoving, but obviously it was long enough for him to wonder what the hell she was doing.

"I'm not dressed appropriately," she blurted.

"What? Sure you are."

Laryn let out an annoyed breath. "Tate, I'm wearing coveralls."

"So? I'm wearing my flight suit. As are the rest of the guys. No one is going to look twice at you."

That was the problem. Just once, she *wanted* to be the woman people stared at when she entered a room. Well...stared at for a reason other than wondering what the hell she was doing there because she looked completely out of place. That had happened to her more than once, and she wasn't looking forward to it happening again *here*, in front of Tate.

"Maybe I should just grab a taxi and go home," she hedged.

Once more, Tate stepped into her personal space. This time, the door behind her was shut. And he didn't simply crowd her; he put his hands on her shoulders and leaned in close.

When he'd caressed her face earlier on the base, it was all Laryn could do not to lean into his touch. For years, she'd dreamed of having Tate Davis look at her the way he had back there in the parking lot of the hangar. And now, here he was again...leaning into her, touching her. His thumbs caressed her collarbones gently, and even though she couldn't feel it through the material of the coveralls she was wearing, it still sent waves of electricity down to her toes.

"Are you naked under this?" he asked.

Laryn blinked in shock at his question. "What? No!"

"So take it off."

"Huh?"

"You aren't naked. Take it off if you're uncomfortable wearing it inside."

"But I'm wearing shorts and a tank top," she protested.

"And?" Tate asked with a small shrug. "Trust me, whatever you're wearing probably covers a hell of a lot more than what a lot of women will be wearing inside."

And that was a whole other problem. Laryn was curvy. She liked the coveralls because they hid a lot of the weight she'd managed to gain over the years. True, her shorts weren't exactly Daisy Dukes, but she still wasn't sure she was confident enough to wear them in public.

And the tank top was black, thank goodness, since it was more slimming than the white ones she sometimes wore at home, but again...it was a tank. And her boobs weren't exactly tiny.

As she silently went over her options, which weren't many, she stared at Tate. He was watching her patiently. It seemed as if he'd stand there for as long as it took for her to decide what she wanted to do. He wasn't glancing over at the door, as if he was annoyed at having to wait to join his friends. All his attention was on her...and all the while, his thumbs continued their gentle stroking.

Hoping she wasn't going to regret her decision, she said, "Okay."

"Okay?" he asked.

"Yeah. I'll take off the coveralls. But you need to step back."

He moved without hesitation, but his gaze didn't leave hers. Not until she reached for the zipper at her upper chest. As she lowered it, his eyes followed the movement. The moment was charged, and for the first time in her life, Laryn felt...sexy. The zipper went from her throat down to her crotch, and Tate watched as she inched it down as far as it could go.

Feeling nervous, as if she was undressing in front of a potential sexual partner for the first time, Laryn shrugged a shoulder and the material fell over her arm. She did the same on the other side, holding the material at her waist so it didn't fall to the ground.

Tate's gaze flew upward, and she saw him swallow as her tank top was exposed. Glancing down, she saw her girls were thankfully fully covered by the cotton material, but she could see quite a bit of cleavage from her vantage point.

Suddenly feeling more self-conscious than sexy, she wiggled her hips, wanting this over with. But typical of her often-clumsy self, she misjudged where the material was as she tried to get out of it. At home, she always just let the coveralls fall to the floor and she stepped out of them. But since she didn't want them to land on the dirty ground—they could definitely be worn a second time before she had to wash them—Laryn pulled her foot up before the material had cleared it.

She would've fallen onto her ass and completely embarrassed herself if Tate hadn't reached out and wrapped his hands around her waist to steady her.

The coveralls fell to the ground anyway, but Laryn couldn't seem to make herself care. Not when Tate's hands were on her and she was practically in his arms.

He stared into her eyes for a split second before his gaze dropped. Remembering the view of her cleavage she'd had a split second earlier, she knew he was getting an eyeful from *his* vantage point.

To her surprise and amazement, she felt his hard cock against her for a moment before he eased his hips back.

She, Laryn Hardy, had given Tate Davis an erection? She couldn't have been more shocked.

"Damn," he said, sounding awed. Then he cleared his throat and asked, "You good?"

Laryn nodded.

He took a step back but kept a hand on her waist. Then his gaze went from her face to her chest to her hips, her legs, and back up. Then he took a deep breath and leaned down to grab her coveralls, which were lying in a heap around her ankles.

"Step out," he ordered.

Putting her hand on the car behind her so she didn't repeat her near fall, Laryn obeyed.

He stood with her coveralls in his hand and reached for the door handle to the backseat. He threw the garment inside without a second thought, then turned back to her. He didn't say anything for long seconds as he took her in from head to toe again.

"Should I put it back on?" she asked after a moment, worried that he thought she didn't pass muster. That he'd be embarrassed to be seen with her. The cotton shorts and tank top weren't exactly going-out clothes either, but then again, she didn't really go out much at all, so what did she know?

"No!" he practically barked. Then he took another deep breath and said in a calmer tone, "No. You look fine. Great. Perfect. You might want to...um...pull up your top a bit though."

Looking down, Laryn saw that her bra was peeking out a bit beyond the material of the tank top. Feeling her cheeks flush, she pulled on the tank, making sure it completely covered her. She fussed with it a bit, smoothing it down and brushing her hands over her thighs nervously.

"Now I feel frumpy," Tate grumbled.

Laryn huffed out a breath. "As if," she said under her breath.

But he'd heard. And he grinned. "I mean, I could take my flight suit off, but unlike you, I'm not wearing anything under it."

"Nothing?" Laryn blurted, her imagination taking over as she envisioned him peeling off his garment, as she had hers.

"Well, I'm wearing some tighty-whities, but trust me when I say they aren't nearly as sexy as what you've got on."

Laryn rolled her eyes. "This isn't sexy."

"The hell it isn't," Tate said almost breathlessly.

They stared at each other for a long moment, the air feeling charged between them, before Tate nodded toward the bar.

"Come on. The guys'll be worried if we don't get inside. You look beautiful, Laryn. I never would've guessed my mechanic was hiding such an amazing body under those baggy coveralls."

Then he took her hand in his, the grip tight, as if he thought she might run or someone might try to steal her away from him, and headed for the bar.

Tate opened the door, and it took her a moment for her eyes to adjust to the brighter lights inside. It wasn't totally lit up, but still much brighter than the outside had been. And to Laryn's surprise, it was much busier than she might've expected for an hour before closing time on a weekday. She followed Tate without complaint as he wove through customers standing around drinking, toward a table in the back of the room.

Half expecting to overhear questions about why Tate had invited her, Laryn was pleasantly surprised to hear nothing but happy greetings as they made their way toward the other Night Stalkers.

"Casper!"

"'Bout time!"

"Holy shit, Laryn—is that you?"

She couldn't help but sigh at the disbelief in Pyro's voice. "It's me," she said dryly.

Edge abruptly stood and held the back of his chair as he gestured toward it. "Here, take my seat," he told her.

Laryn could feel the blush on her cheeks, but she smiled at him and said, "Thanks," before she sat.

She felt Tate at her back, and his fingers brushed against her bare shoulder for a split second, sending shivers all the way through her once more.

"Damn, girl. You are smokin'!" Buck said.

"Buck," Tate warned from above her.

"What? I'm just sayin'."

"You're embarrassing her. Chill," Tate admonished in a stern tone.

"Didn't mean to. Sorry, Laryn. But seriously—you're hot."

"Buck!" This time, his tone was almost angry.

Not wanting to be the cause of a fight between friends, and feeling warm and fuzzy inside from the compliment—had anyone called her hot before? She didn't think so—Laryn looked up at Tate and asked, "Will you get me a beer?"

"Anything in particular?"

"Whatever's on tap."

He stared at her for so long, she got a little self-conscious again. She felt better now that she was sitting and not feeling quite so on display, but she still squirmed a little uncomfortably in her seat.

"You don't want a mixed drink? Maybe a frozen margarita? Or a glass of wine?" Obi-Wan asked from across the table.

She glanced over at him. "I like all those things. And I don't mind the occasional shot, but tonight feels like a beer night.

Besides, I'm driving, and beer doesn't affect me as much as hard liquor."

"Marry me," Chaos said dramatically as he pushed out of his chair next to her and dropped to his knees.

"Get up, asshole," Tate said, smacking his friend on the back of the head.

Everyone chuckled as Chaos got back into his seat. Even Laryn laughed at his antics.

"I'll be right back." Tate had leaned over and said the four words right into her ear, making goose bumps rise on her arms once more as his warm breath wafted over the sensitive skin of her neck.

She wasn't sure what she'd expected, but talk at the table turned to the trials and more technical aspects of the flight and how the MH-60 had performed.

This was a conversation Laryn was comfortable with. So when Tate returned and put a beer in front of her, and dragged a chair over from a table nearby that had recently been vacated, she didn't even blink as she listened and occasionally joined in the shop talk.

But she wasn't so into the conversation that she didn't feel Tate's leg against her own. They were all pretty crowded around the table, and even though the pilots weren't gigantic, they weren't small men by any stretch.

At some point, Tate got up to get a refill of the pitcher of beer they were all sharing, and it took Laryn a few minutes to realize he didn't return right away. Turning, she saw him standing at the bar talking to one of the waitresses...who was wearing a barely there push-up sports bra and a pair of boy shorts that were pulled up into her ass crack, showing off her butt cheeks. She had long blonde hair and flat abs. She also wore a pair of heels that had to be hurting her feet after being on them all night, but she didn't seem fazed in the least.

"That's Barb," Chaos whispered close to her ear, when he saw where her gaze had gone. "She's wanted Casper since the moment she saw him. He's not interested. Not in the least. But he's also way more polite than the rest of us. Trust me, though, there's nothing there."

Laryn forced herself to turn away. "That's fine. It doesn't matter."

"Doesn't it?" he asked quietly, studying her as he leaned back to sit properly in his seat.

Feeling as if some of the shine had been taken off the evening, Laryn paid more attention to the talk around her and less to what Tate was doing.

When he returned to the table, Barb was at his heels with a tray of shot glasses in her hand.

"On the house!" she exclaimed dramatically, rudely leaning between Tate and Laryn, despite the fact they were practically shoulder to shoulder. She made a point of putting a shot glass in front of each of the men first—all while bending low and flashing her tits, which were barely encased in the flimsy sports bra—before plunking the last glass in front of Laryn.

Picking up the drink, Laryn smelled it and wrinkled her nose. The drink might've been on the house, but it was definitely cheap vodka, not the top-shelf variety she preferred.

Glancing at the glamorous waitress, Laryn saw she'd stepped to the other side of Tate...and was staring intently at the shot glass in his hand. She had a weird look in her eye that made Laryn uneasy. Remembering the lessons her dad had hammered into her about taking drinks from strangers—and about reading body language—she opened her mouth to tell Tate not to drink it, but she was too late. Even as she had the thought, he tipped the glass to his mouth and downed the shot in one swallow.

The satisfaction in Barb's eyes was enough to make Laryn abruptly put her own shot back on the table with a thunk.

"Oh, you can't hang? It's okay, sweetie, not everyone can. Unlike me. I can handle *anything* these pilots want to dish out."

She didn't wait for a response, simply winked at Tate, then gathered the now-empty glasses, leaving Laryn's still full one on the table before leaving as abruptly as she'd arrived.

"What the fuck was *that* about?" Buck asked.

"She cornered me at the bar. Wouldn't stop going on and on about how proud of us she was, how she'd heard we had a top-secret thing today and she wanted to gift us with free shots. I tried to turn her down, but she just got more insistent. Figured it was easier to just go with it."

Obi-Wan shook his head. "She's gross. And no, Laryn, in case you're wondering about that inuendo she lobbed at you before she left, none of us have tapped that. Disgusting. No way."

Laryn couldn't help but smile at that, but she was still worried about the gleam in the waitress's eye when she'd looked at Tate. "You feel okay?" she asked.

"Yeah, why?"

She was probably being paranoid. There was no way Barb would be so blatant as to drug Tate when he was with his friends, right? She was obviously upset that he'd arrived with Laryn, but that didn't mean she was stupid enough to put something in his shot. It wouldn't make sense. How would she take advantage of him when he was with someone?

The more she thought about it, the more Laryn convinced herself that she'd imagined the look she'd seen on the woman's face.

"On that note, since Casper didn't bring that refill he went to the bar to get, and because they're gonna do last call before too long, I think I'm gonna head home," Chaos said.

"Me too."

"Same."

And just like that, the group collectively decided they were done celebrating.

Laryn was all right with that. The small amount of alcohol she'd consumed was making her tired. It had been a long day full of stress and adrenaline rushes. She was thrilled to have gotten to know the pilots she worked for better, but she was more than ready to go home to her quiet apartment and crash.

"I'll take care of the tab," Buck offered as he stood.

"Already did," Edge said, satisfaction easy to hear in his tone.

"Fuck, man, it was my turn," Buck told him, frowning.

"Gotta be faster than that, boy," Edge said with a chuckle. "I paid it when I went to the head earlier."

"Sneaky son-of-a-bitch," Pyro grumbled.

It wasn't long before they were all heading for the door.

Laryn looked around for Barb but didn't see her anywhere, which she thought was odd, but she was relieved not to have to see the beautiful younger woman again.

Everyone went their separate ways in the parking lot, and Laryn walked with Tate toward his car on the street. His hand was on the small of her back once again, and it was almost scary how used to that she was getting already.

As they reached the car, Barb suddenly appeared out of nowhere, scaring the shit out of Laryn and making her jump. She was kind of surprised Tate hadn't been startled as well.

"You headed home?" she asked him, not looking at Laryn.

"Yeah."

"You don't look good. You okay?"

Laryn glanced at Tate, and she realized Barb was right. His eyes looked a little glazed and he was weaving slightly on his feet.

That fucking bitch! She *knew* it! Barb *had* slipped something into the shot she'd given Tate.

"I'm taking him home," Laryn said firmly, moving closer to his side and putting her arm around his waist. She was relieved when he wrapped his own around her shoulders.

"No. I will. I just got off work," Barb insisted, putting a hand on Tate's other arm.

Laryn didn't want to get into a tug of war with Tate between them, but there was no way in hell she was letting this bitch go *anywhere* with him. It wasn't common for women to drug men and assault them, but it wasn't unheard of either. She supposed Barb would have some story ready for when Tate woke up in her bed. The little schemer might even be pregnant, and of course she would claim it was Tate's. Which was stupid, because he would definitely insist on a paternity test.

Or maybe Barb *wasn't* pregnant...yet. And she was hoping to rape Tate and get knocked up...then she'd have him on the hook for child support, becoming entrenched in his life for at least the next eighteen years.

Not happening on Laryn's watch.

"Back off, bitch," she growled, leaning toward Barb in a threatening manner. "He came with me, he's leaving with me."

"But you're...*fat!*" Barb said almost incredulously.

"I'm curvy, not fat," Laryn corrected. "And Tate doesn't seem to mind my curves. I know what you did," she hissed with narrowed eyes. "Drugging his drink. That's fucking low. *Criminal*. And I'm going to make sure you pay. But first, I'm going to take him home and make sure whatever you gave Tate won't fucking kill him."

"What? Me? I did no such thing!" Barb protested.

But Laryn could see the fear in her eyes.

"Back. Off," she growled.

To her surprise, Barb took a step back.

In the short time it took for her to have that little conversation with Barb, Tate had sagged against her so much, she was practically holding him upright. If she didn't get him into his car, it was likely he'd fall to the ground right then and there. And she had a feeling the last thing he'd want was for her to call an ambulance. She wished his friends were still around. She knew they'd kick themselves for not waiting until they were all safely in their cars to head out, after they heard what happened.

If she truly felt Tate's life was in danger, Laryn wouldn't hesitate to call an ambulance. But she recognized a roofie victim when she saw one. Her dad had explained the dangers of the drug to her when she was a teenager, and years later, she'd seen a woman pass out in a bar after getting dosed. Thankfully, her friends had seen what happened and took her home before she could be taken advantage of. Tate would wake up with a headache and no recollection of anything after taking that shot. It was a good thing he had the next morning off.

Without another word to the fucking waitress, Laryn turned them toward the Taurus. She managed to get the passenger door open and deposit Tate inside. After she'd fastened his seat belt and shut the door, she looked back at where she'd last seen Barb, but the woman was nowhere to be seen.

Vowing to contact the bar the next day and report what Barb had done, she went around to the driver's side and shut the door. Still fuming, and pissed at herself for not speaking up *before* Tate had been drugged, she started the engine and headed for her apartment.

* * *

Getting Tate inside wasn't easy. Thankfully, she didn't need to call any of his friends to help. She still had plans to tell them so they wouldn't fall victim to Barb's shenanigans in the future—not that she'd be working there any longer, hopefully—but for now, all her attention was on Tate.

He stumbled up the stairs to her apartment with her at his side, holding onto him for dear life. She thought he was going to fall on his face when she had to let go of him for a moment to grab her keys out of her pocket and open the door, but thankfully he stayed upright.

The second she got him into her room—she didn't have the heart to put him on the lumpy sofa—he fell face down onto her mattress. She managed to get his boots and socks off, but now came the hard part.

She planned to get him settled, then go into the other room to get some sleep—in between getting up to check on him every couple of hours, to make sure he was breathing and hadn't thrown up or anything—but first she needed to get him on his back and farther up on the bed.

Unfortunately, it seemed as if his assistance was now done. She couldn't exactly be upset about that, since he'd at least remained semi-conscious enough for her to get him up to her place.

Crawling onto her bed, she kneeled next to Tate and tried to push him onto his back. He didn't budge.

"Damn," she muttered. "I had no idea you were this heavy." She was well aware he couldn't hear her and wouldn't respond, but talking to him made her feel better. "What now?" she asked, more to herself than to the unconscious pilot.

Leaning down, she put her lips by his ear. "Tate?" she said quietly.

Then, more loudly, "Tate!"

To her delight, he smacked his lips a little. Maybe there was still hope to get his help.

"Roll over!" she ordered.

To her astonishment, he did—except he rolled *toward* her, knocking her on her back. Before she knew what was happening, he'd snuggled against her, throwing an arm around her waist and burying his head between her boobs.

The tank top she was wearing wasn't much of a barrier, and her nipples immediately hardened as he nuzzled closer.

"Tate?" she whispered, wanting to stay right where she was for the rest of her life.

He grunted in response and tightened his hold.

Closing her eyes, Laryn considered her options. She could stay where she was and slip out from under him once he fell completely asleep. Or she could do whatever was necessary to get out of this bed right now.

"Hot," he mumbled, as he hitched a leg up over her thighs, further trapping her.

She was pretty sure he was telling her that his body temperature was hot, not that he thought *she* was hot...as in good-looking, sexy, beautiful. As much as she might want to think that, she wasn't delusional.

In the next second, Tate rolled away from her and reached for the zipper on the front of his flight suit.

This was her chance to scoot off the bed and make her escape...but Laryn was spellbound. She couldn't take her eyes off his fingers as they made short work of unzipping the suit. Then his motions were uncoordinated and clumsy, but somehow he still managed to get both shoulders out of the material and push it down to his hips in record time.

Tate's chest was a work of art. He was so muscular, and she was transfixed by the freckles that did indeed cover his entire body. His abs flexed as he struggled with the flight suit. He wasn't coordinated enough in his drugged state to push it completely over his hips, which was probably just as well, because what she could see of his underwear was enough to make Laryn's heart rate spike.

The man was huge...down there. She'd felt him against her earlier tonight, but seeing a glimpse of his cock in those tighty-whities he'd mentioned made her lick her lips even as her mouth suddenly went dry. He had those muscles along his hips that most women went gaga over, and Laryn realized she was no exception.

Before she could get her brain in gear, he rolled again, trapping her against the bed exactly as before with his arm and leg. He sighed in pleasure as he snuggled into her chest.

"Comfy," he mumbled.

"Shit," she whispered.

Then she stopped breathing altogether when his hand slipped under her tank top and slid its way up her body. The heat from his palm was scorching as he palmed her generous breast over her bra and made a contented noise in the back of his throat.

"Tate?" she said.

He didn't respond.

"Tate?" she tried again, louder, hoping she'd be able to get through to him as she had earlier.

But it seemed that he was finally well and truly out.

She lay there staring at her ceiling, fighting with her conscience. She should do whatever it took to get out from under him. This wasn't right. He had no idea what he was doing. Consent was important to her—and to him too, from everything he'd said—and if she stayed where she was, she was no better than Barb.

Deep down, she knew that wasn't true. She'd done what was necessary in order to keep Tate out of that bitch's clutches.

But lying next to the man she'd admired...and loved...for so long was torture. Especially with his lips so close to her nipples. His hand covering her breast. His cock pressed up against her thigh as he nestled into her. It was everything she'd ever dreamed about. She knew he wasn't aware of what he was doing. She could literally be anyone, and he'd probably be doing the exact same thing. But her heart didn't want to listen to what her head was saying.

They were lying on top of the covers. Not that she was cold, not in the least, and she couldn't get under them to pull up the comforter anyway. And the lights in the room were still on, as she'd planned on getting Tate settled before heading out to the couch, but Laryn had never been more comfortable.

She'd just stay here for a moment longer. Wait until Tate was well and truly out, then she'd somehow slip out from under his grip and leave him to sleep off the drug. The morning was going to suck. She was going to have to tell him everything that happened.

KEEPING LARYN

Her eyes closed, and Laryn sighed. Lying under Tate was more comfortable than she'd imagined. She loved that he was apparently a snuggler...at least when he was unconscious. She wanted to stay awake, to soak in the moment because she was pretty sure after he woke up and figured out where he was and what was going on, he was going to be pissed.

But the day, and night, was catching up with her. The stress she'd been under with the flight trials, with Altan Osman threatening her, and after spending so much time with Tate was too much to overcome.

She was warm, comfortable, and...safe.

It was enough to have her falling into a deep sleep in moments.

CHAPTER NINE

Casper woke up with a headache, feeling like he did when he'd overindulged. He was actually a little nauseous as well, which wasn't normal for him after a night of drinking. He tried to remember what he'd drunk, but he couldn't remember much of *anything*. He remembered going to Anchor Point with Laryn, then hanging out with the guys...and that was about it. The rest of the night was a blank.

Anxiety hit him hard. Not being able to remember was scary as shit, and he was a man for whom control was very important. Opening his eyes, he realized he didn't recognize the ceiling he was looking at. It was light outside, which meant it was morning. Or afternoon? Shit, even not knowing what time it was upped his anxiety.

Turning his head to get his bearings, Casper froze at the sight that greeted him.

He was in a bed he'd never seen before. In a room he didn't recognize at all.

And lying beside him, was Laryn.

Then something else occurred to him. He was naked. Well, okay, not completely, but his flight suit was unzipped, twisted around his waist, and he was basically in nothing but his underwear. Laryn was wearing a tank top and shorts he vaguely remembered her wearing the night before, but the top was twisted and one of her breasts was on full display. He couldn't see her actual flesh because of her bra, but it was enough to make his cock harden and his fingers twitch with the desire to touch her.

But the most unsettling feeling was that he had a suspicion he'd *already* touched her. He didn't remember doing it, but the memory of her tit in his palm was as clear as if he'd spent the night pleasuring the woman.

Horrified at what he might've done when he was intoxicated, Casper moved. He practically threw himself off the side of the bed and promptly fell on his ass, tripping over his flight suit, which fell to his ankles as soon as he stood.

He discovered he was also dizzy as hell, and standing had made a million hammers start up in his skull. He sat up carefully, trying to understand what the hell was happening, just as Laryn peered over the edge of the mattress. His not-so-coordinated exit from the bed had obviously woken her up.

But instead of chewing him a new asshole for whatever he'd done to her last night, she looked concerned. "Are you okay?" she asked.

Casper could only stare up at her in confusion.

"Right, of course you aren't okay. You woke up in a strange room, in a strange bed, with the last person you thought you'd ever wake up next to."

Her tone was no-nonsense and matter of fact, and it surprisingly went a long way toward making him feel better. She was blushing though, which made him wonder anew at what had happened last night.

"What—" Casper was surprised his voice was so scratchy. He cleared his throat and tried again. "What happened?"

She sighed. "I'll get into that in a second. First, let's get you up. I think you'll feel better after a shower. I don't have anything else you can put on, so you'll have to make do with your flight suit until you can get home and change, but you'll feel more like yourself after a shower. I'll get coffee going while you're doing that."

Casper wanted to protest, but his brain still felt foggy. And he was still on edge for some reason, which wasn't like him. He wanted to insist she tell him right this second what had happened, but instead, he blurted, "Are you okay? Did I hurt you?"

Laryn had gotten off the mattress and, thankfully, straightened her tank top so she was now sufficiently covered once more. But covering up her womanly parts did nothing to make Casper want her less. She was gorgeous. Skin flushed from just waking, curves in all the right places, and her hair was thoroughly disheveled...sex hair. The woman had *sex hair*, and he couldn't remember a damn thing that happened.

"Hurt me? No, of course not."

She sounded so affronted that he'd even asked, relief swept through Casper. But her reply confused him all the more. If they hadn't had sex...why was he in her bed? And why the hell couldn't he remember?

"Come on," Laryn said. She walked over to where he was still sprawled on the floor and held her hand out.

Without thought, Casper took it and let her help him up. He grabbed his flight suit with his free hand and pulled it up, so he was no longer exposing himself, and followed behind as she led the way out of the room and into the hallway. She hadn't let go of his hand, and for that he was grateful. It felt grounding.

In a world that seemed upside down, she was suddenly the only constant.

He trusted her. Not only with his life when he was in a chopper, because there was no doubt the woman was a magician with the machines, but with his well-being in general. He was off-kilter and more anxious than he could ever remember being, even right before missions. But with Laryn at his side, he was able to control the unfamiliar feelings coursing through his veins.

She led him into a nondescript bathroom that reminded him of the one in his own apartment. Formica countertops, shower/tub combo, cheap fixtures, and fluorescent lights.

Laryn pointed to the toilet and ordered, "Sit."

Casper sat.

She began to open drawers and the cabinet under the sink, mumbling under her breath, before saying triumphantly, "Ah ha! I knew I had one in here somewhere." She held up a toothbrush still in its container. "Got this the last time I went to the dentist and, like a bad patient, I didn't switch out my old one. Stay," she ordered.

Bemused, Casper watched as she stepped out of the bathroom, then returned with an armful of towels. "There's a washcloth and hand towel here, as well as one for after your shower. Take your time. You'll feel like a new man after you wash off the funk. I'll be in the kitchen with coffee. I've got some bagels and some frozen hashbrowns I can make. Don't have eggs though, sorry."

"It's okay," he said.

With that, she stepped to the door, about to close it behind her.

"Laryn!" he blurted, not wanting her out of his sight for some reason. She felt like the only familiar thing in the world at the moment.

"Yeah?"

He wasn't sure what he wanted to say. She couldn't exactly sit in here while he showered. Besides, he was a grown-ass man, a Night Stalker. He didn't need someone to hold his hand while he got ready for the day. Except whatever happened last night was messing with his head.

"Thanks," he eventually said a little lamely.

In response, Laryn stepped back into the small bathroom

and came over to him. Casper widened his legs, giving her room to get closer. She didn't hesitate, stepping into his personal space. Because he was sitting, she was taller than him. She put her hands on his shoulders and looked into his eyes.

"You're okay, Tate. I know you're confused, probably anxious, still tired, and maybe even a little nauseous. From what I've read, that's normal. And I'll tell you *everything* over breakfast. Promise."

Licking his lips, Casper nodded slightly. She'd nailed the feelings coursing through him. Acting on instinct, he wrapped his arms around her waist and lowered his head to her chest. Her hands came up and caressed his hair as he rested against her bosom. He could feel her heat through her shirt, hear her heart beating under his cheek.

Her scent soothed him. Vanilla. He remembered that from the night before last. How her lotion smelled like cookies.

Another memory flashed in his brain. Of him lying against her, his hand under her shirt, his lips pretty much where they were right now...against her tits. A feeling of comfort engulfed him. That safe feeling returned.

It was way too soon when Laryn shifted against him, and he reluctantly dropped his arms and lifted his head. Without a word, she smiled at him before turning and leaving the bathroom, closing the door behind her.

Taking a deep breath, Casper stood and carefully stepped out of his flight suit. Leaving it on the floor and wearing only his underwear, he stared at himself in the mirror and saw a man who appeared to be on the verge of an anxiety attack. It wasn't a good look, and it definitely wasn't him.

He turned on the cold water and splashed some onto his face. Surprisingly, that made him feel much better. The water was a shock to his system, but it also seemed to bring some clarity. Laryn was right, he needed to shower. Clear his head. Find out why he was so groggy and out of sorts.

As he brushed his teeth, he thought over what he remembered of the previous day. The flight trials, the feeling of triumph. The congratulations from his friends, Laryn standing in the background looking proud of her work...as well she should be. Of asking Laryn to celebrate with them at Anchor Point. He recalled her being uneasy about wearing her coveralls into the bar and watching her strip them off. As far as he was concerned, that was the sexiest strip tease he'd ever been witness to...and Laryn hadn't even been trying to seduce him. Yet, she'd done it all the same.

But everything after that, until he'd woken up this morning, was a blank. He didn't remember if they'd met up with his friends or what had gone on in the bar. Hell, he didn't remember how he'd gotten back to Laryn's apartment. He hoped like hell he hadn't driven. But as soon as he had the thought, he dismissed it. Laryn wouldn't let him drive if he was impaired. Though, he couldn't imagine drinking so much that he'd had such an extreme blackout. He liked the occasional beer and shot, but he wasn't the kind of man to drink to excess.

So what the *hell* happened?

Spitting out a mouthful of toothpaste and froth, he leaned down and picked up his wrinkled-beyond-belief flight suit and hung it on the towel rack next to the shower. He turned on the water, then used the toilet while he waited for it to heat.

He was forced to use Laryn's shampoo, as well as her shower gel—which he saw was called Sugar Cookie—and he smiled at the thought of smelling like her. Some men would be turned off by that, but not Casper. He was secure in his masculinity. And besides, who didn't like cookies? There were worse things he could smell like. *Had* smelled like.

By the time he stepped out of the shower, he felt a hundred percent better. More stable. But now he needed answers. Answers only Laryn could provide. He pulled his underwear back on and zipped up his flight suit—wishing he had a pair of comfy jeans and a T-shirt right about now—then hung up the towel he'd used and opened the bathroom door.

* * *

Laryn stood in her kitchen and sipped the cup of coffee she'd poured herself. She'd changed into a pair of jeans and a sweatshirt. Not because she was cold, but because she felt as if she needed to put on some armor. Last night had been...well, frankly it had been a dream come true. Sleeping in Tate's arms had satisfied a long-held dream she'd had since she'd started working with him, as well as fulfilling an innate desire to be needed.

And there was no denying that Tate had needed her last night. Every time she woke up and tried to scoot out from under him, he'd gotten extremely agitated. He only calmed when she continued to let him hold her. At one point, he'd rolled Laryn onto her side—effortless for him, even in his sleep—and then curled against her backside, spooning her, and nothing had felt more right.

But now in the light of morning, she was going to have to tell him that he'd been roofied. She'd have to explain everything she'd done, and hope like hell he wouldn't be upset with her for not calling one of his friends, or hell, even the cops.

In hindsight, she felt so stupid. It was likely the drugs wouldn't be in his system anymore, so there wouldn't be proof of her story. Even his friends hadn't seen him so out of it he could barely stand. Basically, it was her word against Barb's. For all anyone else knew, *she* was the one who'd drugged him.

They could've driven to her place because he'd insisted on staying with her until Altan was investigated. Then Laryn could have slipped the drug into a drink when they got back to her apartment. She had no proof at all that Barb had roofied him, other than her instincts and how disoriented he'd been after that shot.

She'd messed up. Big time. She was disappointed in herself. She hadn't been thinking clearly, had only wanted to get him away from Barb and back to her apartment, where she knew he'd be safe. But her actions meant that he wouldn't be able to prosecute, and Barb would get away with what she'd done.

She'd worked herself into a ball of anxiety by the time Tate sauntered into her living room. Other than being a bit wrinkled, he looked a thousand times better. More like the man and expert pilot she'd gotten to know over the years.

Which was a relief—and also a letdown. She kind of liked the vulnerable man he'd been with her last night and this morning.

After handing him a steaming cup of coffee, she blurted, "I'm sorry."

He froze with his cup halfway to his lips, then leaned against the counter opposite where she was standing in the kitchen and took a sip of the hot brew. "This is amazingly good. Much better than the crap they have at the hangar."

He wasn't wrong, but Laryn wasn't in the mood to beat around the bush. "Last night, Barb put something in your shot. I didn't see her do it, but she was watching you way too closely and seemed extremely satisfied after you drank it. You started acting out of it, and when we went to the car, Barb was there, offering to take you home since you were so 'drunk.' But you *weren't* drunk. I saw what you had last night, and it wasn't nearly enough to make you as incoherent as you were. I know the signs of someone being roofied, and my dad pounded into my head never to drink anything that I didn't see poured myself.

"I told Barb to fuck off, and then you passed out on the way to my apartment. I got you inside to the bed, and you were pretty much out of it. I didn't undress you. You did that yourself. I swear, I didn't touch you or do anything inappropriate. I wasn't going to sleep in the bed with you but in your dazed state, you kind of knocked me over. You didn't hurt me," she rushed to assure him, when he seemed appalled, "but I was basically trapped under you, and I was tired from the trials and the stress of worrying about them, and you and Pyro, and I just fell asleep. Nothing happened, Tate. I *swear*."

She was breathing hard by the time she was done. Relieved to get the bulk of the explanation over with. He was sure to have questions, but those would be easier to answer than trying to explain why he'd woken up practically naked in her bed.

Peering up at Tate, she noted he didn't seem agitated or upset, which was a relief. In fact, he was still leaning against the counter separating her kitchen and living room, drinking his coffee.

"And which part of all that are you apologizing for?" he asked calmly, when she was done word vomiting.

"Well…for not calling one of your friends for help. Not calling the cops. Not beating the shit out of Barb and making her admit to what she did," Laryn said with a miserable shrug.

Tate set the mug of coffee on the counter, then he pushed off and walked around it, stepping into her personal space. He put his hands on either side of her neck, his thumbs resting on her lower jaw, and tilted her head up even more, so she had no choice but to look him in the eyes.

"Do I look like the kind of man who normally needs taking care of?"

Laryn swallowed hard. She couldn't read him. Had no idea if he was pissed off at her or what he was getting at with his question. She shook her head as well as she could with Tate's hands holding her still.

"Right. Ever since my mom left when I was four, I've been pretty independent. My dad brought Nate and I up to think for ourselves. We had chores to do around the house when we were five. I was making my own lunches at seven. I had my first job at fourteen, so I could contribute to the household expenses. When I joined the Army, I was the first one up in the mornings and I always made it a point to help the privates who were struggling.

"When I woke up this morning, I panicked. I had no idea where I was and had no memory of what had happened. Then I turned my head and saw *you*...and I relaxed. Well, *after* I fell on my ass. When I had a second to think, I had no doubt that I was safe because you were there. Am I pissed about being drugged? Fuck yes! Am I upset about how you handled it? No. Not even a little."

"I should've called the police."

"Maybe. Maybe not. You made the decisions you did and I'm here. Safe. Thanks to you."

"I think she was going to do something horrible," Laryn whispered. "I've known women like her. My dad told me stories about some of the things that happened to the dirt track drivers. The good ones. The popular, good-looking ones. How women would drug them, take them home, rape them in the hopes of getting pregnant. Just to have some kind of sick leverage over them. If the guys wouldn't marry them, they'd still be able to get money, child support, for years. It happened more than once. I couldn't bear the thought of that bitch doing something like that to you."

Tate leaned in and put his forehead against hers. He closed his eyes, and Laryn felt him shudder against her. She placed her hands on his sides, feeling horrible that he was in this situation.

Then his eyes opened and he pulled back, but only a fraction of an inch. "Thank you," he said quietly. "For having my back. For not leaving me to wake up alone. For taking care of me."

"You'd have done it for me," she told him.

"Damn straight I would," he affirmed. "Did I do anything last night?"

Laryn frowned. "Anything?"

"Was I inappropriate toward you in any way? I don't

remember anything after you took off your coveralls and we headed into the bar."

Laryn swallowed hard and shook her head. But this was Tate. He had a way of being able to read her like a book.

"What did I do?" he asked with a frown.

"It wasn't a big deal," she insisted.

"Laryn. What. Did. I. Do?" he asked again, using his officer's voice that usually got the lower-ranking soldiers to jump and do his bidding.

"You were out of it. And pretty much unconscious. You just... cuddled up next to me and slept."

"Then why are you blushing?"

Shit. Fine. They were adults. And as he'd said, he didn't remember anything. "Okay. You touched me. My chest," she hurried to explain, as his frown deepened. "Your hand went under my shirt and you cupped me as we slept. But that's it! I swear!" she exclaimed.

"Fuck," he muttered. His hands were still holding her face. "Now *I* need to apologize."

"Tate, it's *fine*. It wasn't a big deal. It felt nice," she blurted.

It was a huge admission, one she regretted as soon as she said it. But she needed to be honest with him. He was learning some pretty heavy things this morning. And the last thing she wanted was to add any guilt he might feel about what happened. It wasn't his fault that some bitch had roofied him. It wasn't his fault he'd passed out. And it definitely wasn't his fault that he'd felt her up...or that she'd enjoyed it so much.

"I didn't read anything into it. I know it was a situational thing," she hurried to add, when he didn't immediately respond.

"I regret a lot of things in my life," he said quietly. "But not being able to remember how you felt next to me, under my hand, is now right up there with the biggest regrets ever."

Laryn stared at him in shock. Wait—*what*? Had she heard him say what she thought he'd said?

His thumbs caressed her jawline once more before he dropped his hands and stepped back. Laryn felt unsteady on her feet. What just happened here?

Beeping sounded from next to her, and it took a few seconds for Laryn to realize it was her air fryer, letting her know the tater tots she'd put in to cook were done. Before she could move, Tate was there, gently pushing her aside and opening the drawer. She watched as he deftly poured them out into the bowl she'd put next to the appliance, then reached out and depressed the button to toast the bagels she'd already put inside.

As far as breakfasts went, it wasn't the healthiest. All carbs and no protein, but she'd make up for that by eating a healthier lunch and dinner. Tate made himself at home in her kitchen, going so far as to refill her coffee mug and practically pushing her out of the small area toward her two-person table against the window that overlooked the grassy area behind her apartment complex.

And leaving her feeling a little shell-shocked that he was cooking for her—could toasting a bagel be counted as cooking?—once again.

When it was done, he slathered the bagels with cream cheese and opened her spice cabinet, smiling as he reached for a bottle. He sprinkled her "everything bagel" seasoning on them and brought their plates to the table, going back to get the bowl of tater tots. He also brought over silverware for each of them, along with paper towels, then sat across from her.

"Looks delicious," he declared, before taking a huge spoonful of tater tots from the bowl.

As they ate, he asked, "How did you know she drugged the shot?"

Laryn had thought they were done talking about what happened, but she should've known better. And she didn't blame him. If *she* had no memories, she'd want every single detail too. Besides, this was how Tate was with everything. He wasn't content with surface-level explanations. He wanted specifics. He never let her get away with skimming over what she'd done to tweak his beloved MH-60. He wanted every nitty-gritty detail, even if he didn't understand half of what she was saying.

"Instinct?" she said with a small shrug after she'd swallowed a bite of bagel. Why did it taste so much better this morning than when she made the exact same thing and ate it on the way to work? Maybe because *she* didn't have to make it? Because she was eating breakfast with Tate after sleeping with him?

No. No, no, no. She had to shut that line of thought down. Yes, she'd slept with him, but not in any meaningful way. He was un-frigging-conscious. Had been *drugged*. It wasn't of his own free will.

"More," he insisted.

Laryn rolled her eyes. Yep, this was the Tate she knew and—

Nope. She wasn't going to finish that thought. "She'd been eyeballing you right before that. Shoving her tits in your face didn't seem to be working, and I guess she must've gotten desperate. She came to the table with a tray full of shots, and she made a point of putting the first one in front of you. When you picked it up, she was just kind of...staring at you so intently, waiting for you to drink. Just made me wonder why. And after you drank it, the look of satisfaction on her face was clear as day. At least to me."

"Do you think the others were also roofied?" he asked.

Laryn shook her head. "No. They all seemed fine. Besides, Barb had eyes for you and only you."

"I've never fucked her," Tate said bluntly.

Laryn was more than used to the way the soldiers and sailors she worked with talked. She wasn't offended by swear words in the least. She shrugged at Tate's confession. "Not my business."

"It is," he insisted. "She hits on anything with a dick. And I'm long past the point where I want sex simply to get off."

"I think she was threatened by me, which is ridiculous, but whatever."

"Why?"

"Why what?" Laryn asked with a small frown.

"Why is that ridiculous?"

She chuckled. "Because. I'm *me*. And she's everything I'm not."

"Thank fuck!" Tate exclaimed. "Look at me, Laryn."

Her gaze automatically came up and met his own suddenly intense stare. "She's a bitch. And I think we can both agree, now that she's stooped to fucking *drugging men* to try to assault and possibly blackmail them into either being with her, or possibly giving her money by using an innocent baby, she's also manipulative, conniving, and a sexual predator. You are *nothing* like her, and that's a good thing. If I'd woken up in anyone else's bed other than yours, I would've freaked out. I said this before and I'll say it again, I'm safe with you. You've proven it time and time again by making sure my birds are as safe as you can make them. I've been pretty clueless for years, but not anymore. I told you—I see you, Laryn. And things are going to change from here on out."

"Change?" she whispered, terrified about what that meant.

"Did you really like it when I touched you last night?" he asked, instead of answering her question.

"Uh...what does that have to do with anything?" she hedged.

"It has everything to do with *everything*. Answer the question."

"You know you're annoying, right?" she countered.

"Yup." He leaned forward after pushing his now-empty plate to the side. His gaze bore into her own, and Laryn couldn't look away if her life depended on it. "When I slipped my hand under your shirt, did you get goose bumps like I've seen you get a few times when I've touched you before? Did your nipples get hard? Did you want more?"

Laryn swallowed hard. His questions were intrusive and crossed a line she wasn't sure she should cross with him. But here in her apartment, after the best night's sleep she'd had in a very long time, after doing everything in her power to keep this man out of that bitch's clutches the night before, her defenses were down.

She was tired of hiding her desire for Tate. And this felt like the perfect time to fish or cut bait. Wasn't that why she'd considered taking another job? As far away from Virginia, and Tate, as she could get?

Taking a deep breath, and feeling as if she'd just jumped out of a plane without a parachute, she said simply, "Yes."

Tate sat back, and instead of looking smug or conceited, he looked...excited. Pleased. Relieved.

"I said it already, but if there's one thing I regret about last night, it's not that I didn't shut Barb down immediately. It's not neglecting to tell her we didn't want shots. It's not getting fucking roofied—but for the record, that shit sucks. It's not fun to wake up and not remember a damn thing. To have a huge blank space in your head when you *know* it shouldn't be blank. No...I regret not remembering how it felt to sleep next to you. How you felt under my hands."

The damn goose bumps were back. She couldn't control them.

And she'd pushed up the sleeves of her sweatshirt before eating, which meant Tate saw them...and smiled. Reaching out, he ran a finger over her forearm in a barely there caress. "Will you go on a date with me?" he asked. "We can go out to eat, or there's an ax-throwing place that might be fun. I bet you'd kick ass at that. Or we can simply go for a walk along a beach. Whatever you want to do."

Laryn wanted to pinch herself. Tate Davis was asking her out? She wanted to squeal in excitement. Or pass out. One of the two. She did neither. Instead, she gave him a shy smile and said, "I'd like that."

They sat there smiling at each other for a beat before Tate stood. He picked up her empty plate and his and started for the sink. But he suddenly stopped and turned around. Then he leaned over her, and Laryn lifted her chin to meet his gaze, anxious to hear what he wanted to say.

To her shock and delight, he didn't speak—he kissed her. It was a chaste kiss, a mere brushing of his lips against hers, but it sent bolts of electricity down to her toes.

"Thank you for watching over me last night. For having my back. I'll never forget what you did for me." His voice was earnest and heartfelt, and the way it made her feel, all warm and fuzzy, was better than the electric energy his kiss made her feel.

Then he continued to the sink. He rinsed the plates as Laryn brought over the empty bowl. After the dishes were put away, she wasn't sure what to do next.

Tate took the decision out of her hands.

"I need to head home. I want to change, call the guys, the manager of Anchor Point, tell all of them what happened. I'm thinking I probably also need to connect with Nate. He probably knows something is up with me, as that's how things sometimes work between us since we're twins. I want to reassure him that I'm good, and let him know how perfectly the trials went and to give him a heads-up that we're being deployed next week. I also need to call Tex. You should come with me."

But Laryn shook her head immediately. "That's a no. I'm not going to sit around while you're making your personal phone calls. I'll go into work. I do have other things to do besides work on your helicopters, you know."

"Bullshit," Tate said with a grin. "You know my choppers are your first priority."

The annoying thing was that he was right. "Well, I do need

to make sure *your* MH-60 is properly secured for her trip across the ocean to the destroyer."

His smile died. "Stay on your toes. With Barb the bitch out there having been thwarted by you, and Osman...you need to stay alert for anything out of the ordinary."

"I will."

Tate stared at her for a long beat before turning and heading down the hallway toward her bedroom. Laryn noticed for the first time that his feet were bare. There was something so intimate about seeing him without the boots he always wore.

When he returned, she hadn't moved, and he looked more like the cocky Night Stalker that he was. But there was a look in his eyes now that hadn't been there before. They'd been through something intense together, even if he didn't remember it. He was smart enough to realize the ramifications of what would've happened if she'd let him go with Barb. If she'd let her insecurities when it came to the other woman get the best of her. Or if her dad hadn't educated her on the dangers of drugs being put into drinks to incapacitate the recipient. So many things could've gone a different way last night, and Laryn was thankful she was able to prevent Tate from falling victim to a predator.

Instead of walking past her toward the door, Tate came straight at her. Laryn stared up at him as he approached and didn't flinch as he got into her personal space. He wrapped one hand around the back of her neck and the other around her waist as he pulled her close. Laryn melted against him and swallowed hard. The feeling of his calloused fingers around the sensitive skin of her nape made those stupid goose bumps return with a vengeance.

She liked everything about this man. His work ethic, his confidence, and yes, even his cockiness. When he wanted something, he went for it with no holds barred. And the fact that apparently he wanted *her* was still something she was trying to wrap her mind around.

"I'd like to kiss you again," he said, his lips hovering close but not touching.

Laryn licked her lips in anticipation but couldn't seem to get her vocal cords to work.

"Laryn? I need consent. You can say no. I know this is fast. But what happened between us last night—you having my back with no expectation that I'd understand or wouldn't for some inexplicable reason blame you, or accuse *you* of drugging me—made me throw my plan to woo you slow and steady out the window."

"You were going to...*woo* me?" Laryn asked in surprise.

"Yeah. I finally got my head out of my ass and realized there was a woman I liked, respected, and desired right in front of me, and I'd been a stupid jerk and missed it for three years."

Laryn wanted to cry. But she also tempered her excitement. She didn't want to get ahead of herself.

"So...may I?" he asked again, nodding a little toward her lips.

"Yes. Please," Laryn said on a sigh.

His head immediately lowered, and the second his lips touched hers, Laryn knew she'd never be the same again.

This kiss was different than the chaste "thank you" kiss he'd given her earlier. It started out sweet and gentle, but quickly flared out of control.

The hold on the back of her neck tightened as he growled deep in his throat. He licked her bottom lip, and Laryn opened for him. His tongue swept inside her mouth and took control, as she supposed he did with everything in his life. But Laryn was more than content to let him take the lead. It was all she could do to stay upright. Their tongues swirled together as each learned what the other liked. And when Tate nipped her lip, her belly swirled and those pesky goose bumps returned.

"Damn, woman," he breathed as he moved his lips to a sensitive spot under her ear.

Laryn could feel how much he apparently enjoyed their kiss,

his erection pressing against her belly as he held her against him. He lifted his head but didn't pull away or remove his arms from around her.

"When?" he demanded.

"When what?" Laryn asked, secretly liked his Neanderthal grunts when he was feeling extreme emotions. He was so different than the vulnerable man she'd cradled to her bosom earlier in the bathroom. But she liked both sides of him.

"When are you letting me take you out?"

"Um...I'm not sure. I think we both have a lot to do to get ready for deployment."

"I'm not waiting until after we get back. Once onboard ship, we aren't going to have any privacy, and I'm not going to expose you to any rumors or innuendos from people who don't know us or who think we're doing something we shouldn't. You aren't in the Army, and it's not forbidden for us to date."

"I'm not saying no or disagreeing, I just don't know when we'll have time," she told him, thrilled behind belief that he seemed to be desperate to take her on a date.

"We'll make time. Play it by ear. I'm still not comfortable leaving you alone at night, not with Osman being out there. Last night was bad enough because I was so out of it, I couldn't have protected you if someone broke in. But I'll also understand, considering how things between us have changed, if you aren't comfortable having me stay the night...even out here on your couch like I did before. I can rotate one of the guys to stay here if that would make you more comfortable."

Her heart fluttered in her chest. The concern this man had for her...and they weren't even dating yet...it was unexpected and wasn't something she was used to. "My dad would've loved you," she blurted. Tate was just like him, protective and alpha to the core.

"I wish I could've met him. He raised one hell of a daughter.

We'll talk later. I'll let you know what Tex thinks about this Osman situation."

"And what the manager of Anchor Point says? I planned on calling today myself," Laryn told him. If anyone had asked her before right this second, she would've said having a conversation with someone you loved while plastered against him, feeling his erection against your belly, after just being kissed as if the world was ending, would be awkward. But it felt like the most natural thing ever. And surreal to boot.

"Of course." Then Tate leaned down and kissed her again. But it wasn't quite as intense as before. His fingers tightened on her nape for a split second before he let go of her and took a step back.

"Thank you again, Laryn," he said quietly. Then he strode toward her door with the confidence she'd gotten used to seeing in the hotshot pilot.

"Lock this behind me," he ordered.

Laryn rolled her eyes. "I'm not an idiot," she told him a little huffily.

"No, you're not. Later."

And with that, he was gone.

Laryn hurried to the door and locked the bolt and put the safety chain on. Then she turned her back to the door and wrapped her arms around her belly. A smile formed on her face as she licked her lips and still tasted Tate there.

Everything was happening so fast, but she couldn't say she was upset about it. She'd loved Tate Davis for what seemed like forever, and it was surreal that he'd been in her apartment, kissing her as if his life depended on it. She had no idea how this might change their relationship at work. She worried about that, but *something* had to change. She'd been in a rut and wasn't happy, hence asking around about other jobs.

She regretted that now, especially if Altan Osman's threats

turned out to be serious. But she'd cross that bridge if and when she came to it. She was nothing if not practical. Right now she needed to shower and get to work. She had a chopper to help get loaded and she'd be pissed if anything happened to her baby en route to the naval destroyer. Tate's—and Pyro's—lives depended on nothing happening to the helicopter in transit. She needed to be sure she did everything in her power to mitigate that possibility.

Laryn was still smiling as she walked into her bathroom and saw Tate had hung up the towel he'd used, and it was right beside hers on the rack. A shiver ran through her as a glimpse into a possible future with Tate flashed through her head. Things might not work out between them, she was well aware of that… but what if they did?

Taking a deep breath, she did her best to tamp down her excitement. For now, she'd play the future by ear. Whatever happened, happened. She'd try to enjoy the ride and not get bogged down in the details.

But thinking about that kiss, and how amazing it was, made that almost impossible. Sleeping next to him and kissing him had rocked her world. If they ever got to a point of being more intimate…she might self-combust.

Laryn stripped and stepped into the shower and tried to figure out how she was going to remove the ridiculous smile from her face before she got to work.

CHAPTER TEN

Casper's call with the manager of Anchor Point was frustrating. He'd told the man everything that Laryn had seen and done, but without proof, the manager was reluctant to simply fire Barb. She'd never had any complaints about her in the past, and she was apparently a hard worker. There were no security cameras pointing at the bar that would prove she'd drugged his shot, and he argued that he couldn't simply take Laryn's word for what happened over that of his employee.

It wasn't a surprise, but it was still frustrating.

His teammates' reactions were more satisfying.

They.

Were.

Pissed.

He had to reassure each of them that he was fine, that Laryn had done what she'd needed to do in order to make sure he was away from Barb the Bitch and safe.

"She's done," Pyro had told him in a fierce tone.

Casper didn't bother asking what that meant; he didn't need to. By the time Pyro was done with her, the woman would be gone from Anchor Point...and probably from the Norfolk area, as well.

Next up on his list of people to call was his twin.

Nate answered after only one ring. "You okay?"

Casper was right; Nate had known something was up. "Yeah." He gave his brother the quick and dirty details about what had happened. Including how he'd woken up and had absolutely no recollection of the incident and how disorientating that had been.

"But you're all right now?"

"Yeah. Thanks to Laryn."

"Are you sure she wasn't in on it? That she and this Barb bitch weren't working together?"

Anger rose hard and fast within Casper. "What the fuck, bro? No! She wasn't working with Barb! I can't believe you'd even say that. I've known Laryn for three years, and I have no doubt whatsoever that she has my back. She literally has my life in her hands because of the work she does on my helos. If she wanted to hurt me, she's had more than her fair share of chances to do just that."

"She could've been doing what she accused the waitress of doing. Trying to trap you."

"You're making me regret calling you, Nate. Laryn's too honest to do something so awful. If she was interested in me, she'd just come out and tell me."

"Would she?"

Something in his brother's tone had Casper pausing.

"All I'm saying is, I saw the two of you together on that naval ship, after you rescued Josie, Kevlar, and me."

"Yeah, you saw her sniping at me for crashing her helicopter," Casper retorted.

"Yes, but it was the way she looked at you. With relief. She was using anger as a shield."

The argument Casper had ready got stuck in his throat. "How do you know?"

"Because I've got eyes. Look, you guys have worked together for years. You're amazing. Good-looking, if I do say so myself..."

Casper snorted. Since he and Nate were twins, it was hilarious his brother even said that in the first place.

"And you're polite, appreciative, and kind. Why *wouldn't* she fall for you? And if you showed no inclination to return any feelings she might have for you, always giving her shit like she's one of the guys, why would she open herself up to possible rejection? Seems like one sure way to have you for herself is to get knocked up...just like she claimed that waitress was trying to do."

Casper was done listening to his best friend, his flesh and blood, denigrate the woman who'd been there for him again and again. Who'd gone out of her way to make sure he was safe. Who'd calmed the anxiety coursing through his blood when he'd woken up with no memories of what had happened to him the night before.

"She's not like that. I've never been a POW, but I imagine when you realized what had happened after you were captured, you were as stressed out as you've ever been," Casper said in a low, controlled tone. "You didn't know what the future held, you were probably confused, hurting, and even scared. And then you realized you weren't alone. That Josie was there in that cell next to yours. It gave you a focus. Something else to concentrate on. That's how I felt, Nate. Adrift, disorientated, anxious. And then I turned my head and saw Laryn, and I realized I was safe. She'd never let something happen to me when I'm up in the air in one of her babies, and she'd never let anything happen here on the ground. And since when did you get so damn chatty, anyway? I think I liked it better when you weren't talking," he finished, sounding like a three-year-old who'd just had his favorite toy taken away.

Instead of getting pissed at him for his honesty, Nate simply chuckled. Then asked, "When we were in Iraq after that chopper went down, remember how I told you that I didn't know where Josie was from, or anything about her except that she was mine?"

"Of course."

"When I'm with her, I feel the way you just described feeling when you woke up with Laryn. Safe. And I'm sorry. I was kind of playing devil's advocate there. Wanting to make sure about Laryn. My advice for you? Don't get lost in your head. If you like your mechanic, go with it. Don't second-guess yourself or your feelings. She could be the best thing that ever happened to you, like Josie is for me. Doesn't matter that it took three years for you to see what was right under your nose. Just that you finally did."

"Yeah," Casper agreed quietly.

"I want to meet her. I mean *really* meet her, not just in passing like we did on that ship. I expect you to make that happen, Tate."

"Not sure what's going on with us," he hedged, even though he knew what he *wanted* to happen between them. "Or when I'll get the time to go out to California. We're headed back to the Middle East in less than a week."

"Shit. Keep me in the loop if you can," Nate ordered.

"I will. Same goes for you."

"Yeah. Tate?"

"Still here."

"Glad you're all right. It sucked on my end when you went blank. I wasn't sure what was going on. I'd like to be able to thank Laryn one day."

"I'd like that too. Stay safe, bro."

"You too. Later."

"Later."

Casper hung up and took a deep breath. Nate's needling to try to make sure Laryn had his best intentions at heart was annoying, but he understood where his brother was coming from. That he was simply trying to protect his twin.

He thought back to that moment in the mountains between Iran and Iraq, when Nate had looked him in the eye and claimed that Josie was his, even though he'd just met her. If he recalled correctly, Josie wasn't even speaking at the time because of the trauma she'd been through, and yet his brother still knew without any doubt that she was the woman for him.

Casper wasn't there yet with Laryn, but he could admit that he'd never felt about another woman the way he did about her. He'd never felt as if he could completely let down his guard with anyone else he'd dated. She had his back, one hundred percent, she'd proven it time and time again on the job.

Others might argue that any good mechanic would do the same thing...make sure that nothing was wrong with the choppers they maintained. But Casper had experience that said differently. Laryn was also the first person to greet him when he got back from a mission, wanting to know if anything felt off about the chopper, how she performed, if there was anything he thought needed to be tweaked. But it felt personal...as if she cared more about checking on *him* than her precious helicopters.

And thinking back over the years, at the ribbing and teasing they always engaged in, he realized what his brother said was right on the mark. He always fell back on their tried-and-true way of communicating because it was easy and familiar. And because he wasn't sure how to let Laryn know how much he appreciated what her concern meant to him.

He was like a third-grader pulling the hair of the girl he liked. Or chasing her around the schoolyard. Or putting a frog in her lunch box. And that shit was going to stop. Now. Today. He'd taken the first step by asking her out, but there would be no more needling her from his end. She was a professional, a damn good mechanic, and she didn't need him interfering with her job.

Thinking about Laryn and how she did everything in her

power to keep him safe when he flew, had him wanting to return the favor. He wasn't sure if Altan Osman was really a threat, but his gut was screaming at him that something was wrong there. He also hated that Laryn had been so discontent, she'd contemplated finding another job.

It was time to call Tex.

John Keegan, known as Tex to just about everyone, was a former SEAL who'd lost part of his leg and been medically retired. Since then, he'd spent his time working for the government and independently, assisting in locating those who were kidnapped, taken captive, or who'd simply disappeared. He had a soft spot in his heart for special forces members and their families, and word was that he'd helped to find dozens of people, bringing them back home safe and sound.

But he did more than find lost people...he was a computer genius, which was how he was able to track down the missing in the first place. Casper heard he had a room in his basement filled with computer screens that blinked with trackers Tex had given some of his closest friends and their families, just to keep an eye on them. He was able to hack into traffic cameras, phone records, social media accounts, emails, government computers, and otherwise get into the most protected and closed-off records to obtain any kind of information necessary.

And Casper needed his expertise. He needed under-the-radar intel that he suspected only Tex could get. He'd never spoken to the man, but his contact info had been passed around the special forces community. He'd gotten his phone number from a Delta Force operative he'd once transported on a mission, who was now living out in Texas with his wife and kids. Oz had nothing but praise for Tex, and he'd reassured Casper that if he was ever in a position to need the man, not to hesitate to reach out.

Casper wasn't sure if he actually needed Tex's special skills or not. He had nothing but his gut to go on, telling him that Altan

Osman's threats were to be taken seriously. He needed facts. And apparently, Tex could get them.

He dialed the number he'd long since memorized, hoping against hope Tex hadn't retired...or changed his number.

It rang three times before a man with a slight southern twang answered who could be no one other than the infamous Tex. "Who is this?"

Casper wasn't offended by the brusque greeting. He was actually impressed he'd answered the phone in the first place. *He sure didn't answer if he didn't know who was calling these days.*

"Name's Tate Davis. Go by Casper. I'm an officer in the US Army. Night Stalker. I need intel on a possible threat to the woman I'm dating."

"I'll call you back."

The phone went dead in his ear.

Casper was a little taken aback, but he didn't hold the man's actions against him. Everyone said he was the best, and if now wasn't the best time to talk, he'd wait.

It wasn't a long wait. Twenty minutes later, Casper's cell rang just as he was about to leave his apartment. It was from an unknown number, but he had a feeling he knew who was on the other end of the line.

"Hello?"

"Hey, Casper. Tex here. Sorry about that earlier. I don't really take cold calls from anyone until I check them out."

"And I checked out?" he asked, wondering how much this guy could've found out about him in twenty minutes.

"Yup. Distinguished Service Cross, Silver Star, Distinguished Flying Cross, three Bronze Stars, and ten Air Medals—four with Valor Device. Thousands of daylight flight time hours and almost as many nighttime flying hours. You embody the 'Night Stalkers Don't Quit' motto. Thank you for all you do, have done, and will do for my Navy SEAL brethren and all special forces. Now, what can I help you with?"

Casper wasn't surprised very often, but he had to admit, Tex had taken him off guard. If he knew about the awards he'd been given by the military, he probably knew about each and every mission that had *earned* him the accolades—which was impressive, because they were all top secret. And the man had learned about them in minutes. Everything said about Tex was obviously true. He felt better about calling him for intel, even if it turned out to be nothing.

He gave him a rundown of Laryn's situation and explained how Altan Osman worked for the Turkish government and had threatened her over the phone. "I need to know if he's an actual threat, or just frustrated because he thought he had a shot at getting one of the best MH-60 mechanics in the world to work on their newly acquired choppers. We're headed out to the Middle East next week, which I think is the first time I'm actually relieved to be going to that part of the world...gets Laryn away from home and anyone Osman might send to try to convince her to change her mind about working for him."

"I've never heard of the man, which should be a slight relief for you, as I know most of the major bad guys in the world. But that doesn't mean he's not a threat. The organizations I follow have been recruiting more and more people to work for them. Lower-ranking people. It's impossible to keep up. The current objective for most of them is more sleeper operatives. People who are paid to watch and listen...and to pass on intel. Not saying that's how Osman got Laryn's number, but it's worth looking into."

Relief swept through Casper that Tex wasn't blowing this off. That he was going to use his skills to help look into the situation.

"But I have to warn you," he went on. "I'm in the middle of something. I can't put all my resources on this right now."

"I understand." And Casper did. He didn't expect a man as

in-demand as Tex apparently was to drop everything for a stranger.

"I'll do my best to get back to you before you're deployed. In the meantime, I probably don't need to tell you to keep a close eye on Laryn. I've seen too many loved ones disappear because they let down their guard."

"No, sir," Casper told him. "I've already told her she's going to have a roommate for the foreseeable future until we can see if there's a threat and mitigate it if there is."

"Good. Your fellow Night Stalkers stationed there in Norfolk are all good people. Don't know Pyro, Obi-Wan, Chaos, Edge, or Buck personally, but I've read good things about them. I'll be in touch. Keep your woman safe."

Once again, the phone went dead in Casper's ear. He probably should be worried that this Tex guy knew so much about him and his fellow pilots—he assumed that's what the name dropping he'd done there at the end was about—but he wasn't. So many special forces personnel, both retired and active duty, wouldn't trust the man if he wasn't on the level.

But it was hearing the words "your woman" that struck Casper hard. He hadn't even been on a date with Laryn, but deep down, she felt like his.

He chuckled under his breath. He was more like his twin than he'd thought. Nate had known from the start that Josie was his. And while it had taken Casper a bit longer, he was beginning to think he was exactly like Nate. When he fell, he fell hard.

Determination swam through his veins. He'd wasted so much time. Laryn had been right in front of him and he hadn't seen her. Well, that was done. She'd proven time and again that she had his best interests at heart, and last night just solidified that even more. It was past time for him to return the favor. Let her know that he and his friends had *her* back. This distasteful Altan Osman business was just the start. He hoped Tex found nothing.

That he'd call back and tell him the man was nothing but an admin who thought he had more power than he really did.

Feeling better now that someone would be looking into the threat against Laryn, Casper picked up his sunglasses from the kitchen table where he'd left them and headed toward the door. He needed to update his friends about his conversation with Tex and reassure them again that he really was all right. He probably needed to talk them off the ledge where Barb was concerned, as well. But he understood. If it had been Pyro or any of his fellow pilots who'd been roofied and almost taken advantage of, he'd be in the same headspace that they were right now. On the warpath. Ready to scorch the earth to avenge them.

But thanks to Laryn, he was okay. Tex had been contacted, and his chopper was good to go for their next mission. Oh, and he had a date to look forward to. Yeah, things were looking up for him, and he was feeling pretty damn optimistic about the future. Now he just had to figure out where and when to take Laryn on their first date. He wanted it to be memorable but not over the top. Something she'd enjoy and remember for the rest of their lives.

The smile on his face as he headed into the parking lot toward his Taurus was probably cheesy as hell and would make anyone who saw him wonder what the hell was going on in his head, but Casper didn't care. Even after last night, and the possible threat against Laryn, he felt pretty damn chipper. Nothing could dampen his excitement right now.

CHAPTER ELEVEN

Fuck, nothing was going right.

Casper's mouth drew down into a scowl, and he couldn't believe what he was hearing. Shit had gone sideways on a mission in northern Syria, and he and his fellow Night Stalkers were needed, stat. There were pockets of ISIS operatives in the area, and they were proving especially proficient at targeting the choppers other Night Stalkers were using, shuttling special forces troops in and out of drop zones. More air power was needed to get boots on the ground to take out the insurgents before they succeeded in actually shooting down one or more of the choppers.

And that meant instead of in a week, his team was being deployed in two days.

Casper's plan to take Laryn on a date was disappearing in a puff of smoke, which irritated him beyond belief. It wasn't as if he couldn't still take her somewhere, but it probably wouldn't be as epic as he'd hoped. The last thing he wanted was anything run-of-the-mill, but it seemed likely.

Because no way was he waiting. Now that he'd made the decision to take her out, he didn't want a deployment to stand in the way. He wanted to make sure the woman knew how important she was to him *before* they left. And things would be different for this deployment than they'd been in the past. No more would Laryn be on her own onboard the ship. He'd never given much thought to how she'd spent her time on the carriers, but now he had an innate desire to make sure she was sleeping all right, eating healthy meals, and taking care of herself in what could be a high-stress environment. It was a huge switch, but one that felt right.

Of course, she might not want him to be so up in her business. Time would tell, but a good gauge of how things might go in the future would be how their first date went. Was she the kind of woman who liked or hated public displays of affection? Would she let him hold her hand? Or let him pay without arguing?

One area where he had no doubts about their compatibility was physically. He couldn't remember their kisses without getting hard. And how soothing just being next to her in bed had been. Yes, he enjoyed sex as much as the next man, but after this morning, he appreciated simply being with someone he could trust more than he expected.

"Anyone have any questions?" the colonel asked.

Casper had a ton of them, but his friends beat him to the punch and asked everything that was swirling around in his head. They'd already learned about the current conflict that had caused the uptick in ISIS activity, and what the special forces teams were doing in the area. They went over the terrain, how the Taurus Mountains served as a kind of barrier between Syria and Turkey, extending all the way to Iraq, both helping and hindering the missions of the SEALs and Delta Force operatives on the ground.

ISIS was beginning to make this area a new stronghold, and they had many hideouts and knew the territory well. The mountains made the Night Stalkers necessary, as their specialty was flying over and through terrain that regular pilots would have second thoughts about tackling...especially in the dark.

The missions would be dangerous as hell, but Casper wasn't worried. He and his team could handle it.

The colonel told Pyro when he asked that, yes, Laryn and a small handpicked team of mechanics would be accompanying them. Especially since Casper's chopper was going into combat for the first time.

Casper hadn't thought there was a chance she *wouldn't* be coming, which was probably stupid of him. Just because he wanted her there, and just because she usually accompanied them, that didn't mean she always would. There *had* been times when she'd stayed behind. But since she'd been told previously that she'd be deployed on their next mission, he'd just assumed that would still be the case.

He was very glad that she'd be safe on the naval destroyer though. He hadn't thought much about her safety in the past, much to his embarrassment, but now that he was interested in her as more than simply his mechanic, his mind couldn't help but turn to her safety. The thought of her on the front lines made him want to puke. She had some military training from when she was in the Army, but nothing like what he and the other pilots saw when they were on missions.

Thank God that wasn't a concern. Especially since, in a massive coincidence, they were headed into Turkey—where Altan Osman was from.

The meeting broke up, and Casper was anxious to see Laryn. But he sighed, knowing he had more work to do first.

"You talk to Tex?" Edge asked, after the meeting with the colonel ended and as they walked down the hall toward the next conference room, to start studying maps of the area where they'd be flying. Yes, the instruments on their choppers were top of the line and they relied on them when they were flying, but nothing beat having a good mental picture of the major topographical obstacles beforehand.

"Yeah. He's going to look into Osman. But he's got some other things on his plate before he can get to it," Casper told his friend, the others listening in.

"Might not be a bad thing that we're headed out in two days instead of a week," Chaos mused.

"Yeah, if that asshole has plans to try to intimidate Laryn here on her home turf, he'll have to wait until we get back," Obi-Wan added.

"And by then, hopefully Tex will have gotten more intel on the man so we know if he's a threat or not," Buck said thoughtfully.

Casper was more than relieved that his friends were on the same page regarding Laryn's protection. They'd already agreed with him that the Turkish contractor was a concern, but after she'd stepped in to protect him from Bitchy Barb? They were now all-in on watching over Laryn.

"I'd like to see him try to fuck with her. He'll find out what having six Night Stalkers on his ass feels like," Pyro muttered.

The situation wasn't exactly humorous, but Casper found himself smiling anyway.

Chaos held open the door for everyone and they filed into the conference room.

Casper's smile faded as he took in the uncomfortable chairs he and his friends would be spending the next several hours in. They had a lot of work to do, and not a lot of time in which to do it. Sparing another thought for Laryn, he figured she'd be just as busy. Once she'd learned they were leaving in two days rather than a week, she'd probably started hustling to make sure her tools were ready for transport. Yes, there were tools onboard the destroyer, but he knew from experience that Laryn traveled with her own set of customized instruments.

She'd also have her own meetings to attend with those on her staff who'd be traveling with them. They'd be briefed on the situation and atmosphere the pilots would be flying into, but not the nitty-gritty details. Laryn had a top-secret clearance, but that didn't mean she was privy to everything that happened on the missions he and his fellow pilots participated in.

Sitting with a sigh, Casper and the others began to pull the appropriate maps out of the large folders that had been delivered to the conference room while they'd been meeting with the colonel. The day had already been long, and it would just get longer. But unlike on any other workday, he had something to look forward to when he was done here at the naval base. Laryn. Seeing her and talking to her. It made the long-ass day a little more bearable.

* * *

Looking at her watch, Laryn saw it was eight o'clock. The day had flown by. It began when she'd arrived to find the MH-60 had already been loaded for transport, and, in fact, was already gone from the hangar, because the timeline for deployment had been moved up by five days.

The amount of work she had to get done made her day much more stressful than she'd hoped. She'd had no time to think about Altan, other jobs, if the workers who were in charge of transporting the MH-60 had followed every protocol to make sure nothing happened to it in transit, or even Tate.

She had meetings with the soldiers and fellow mechanics who'd be traveling to the naval destroyer with her, and made sure their paperwork was in order. Things like their DD Form 93—Record of Emergency Data—family care plans, making sure their beneficiaries were all up to date, as well as their wills.

For some people, it was a depressing part of the job...making sure that if the worst happened while deployed, their loved ones would be taken care of. But for Laryn, it wasn't a big deal anymore. Mostly because she didn't have family herself, and *her* beneficiary had always been a beagle rescue group she'd volunteered with at her previous duty station back at Fort Bragg, which had been renamed Fort Liberty since she'd been there.

But now that she had a chance to breathe, to think, she realized she was starving. Lunch had been some chips and a candy bar from the vending machine. She was grubby and needed a shower in the worst way. Her coveralls were streaked with grease from taking time out to troubleshoot some engine issues on an MH-47 Chinook. A much bigger chopper than the Blackhawk Tate flew, it was used for longer missions and could carry a ton of cargo, including lifting extremely heavy loads...like the iconic story about the Night Stalkers stealing an abandoned Libyan attack helicopter in the late eighties during a sandstorm.

Laryn stood at the side of the hangar for a moment, closing her eyes as she tried to decide what to do. Wait to get home to make something to eat? Stop and grab fast food? Forget food altogether and head home and crash?

Her phone vibrated in her pocket. Pressing her lips together in irritation, hoping against hope it wasn't her boss or someone else needing her to take a "quick look" at something for them, she pulled it out and looked down at the screen.

Seeing Tate's name made her heart beat hard in her chest for reasons other than annoyance. He'd sent her a couple of texts during the day, simply to check in. He'd told her that he'd called his friend Tex, who'd work on gathering intel on Altan. He also checked to make sure she was all right with them leaving sooner rather than later—not that he could've done anything if she *wasn't* okay with that, but she appreciated him thinking about her.

"Hey," she said as she answered the phone.

"I'm going to be at the hangar in two minutes. You still there?" he asked.

He sounded irritated for some reason. At *her*? Because she

was still working? Laryn's back straightened. Well, tough shit if he was upset. She had a job to do, just as he did, and just because they'd shared something pretty intimate the night before...well, that morning...didn't mean he could start running her life.

"I was just leaving," she told him curtly.

"Perfect. If you wait for me, I'll take you home."

"I need my car," she protested.

"Why?"

"Because. I need to get back here early in the morning, since we're leaving the day after tomorrow. There's still a ton of stuff I have to do. My work around here hasn't stopped just because I'm being deployed."

"Right. I understand that. I'm in the same boat." His tone was softer now. Less abrupt. "I meant, why do you need your car if we're going to the same place and both coming back to work at the ass-crack of dawn in the morning to continue preparations to head out?"

Laryn's mind drew a blank. She'd completely forgotten that he'd insisted he'd be staying with her, just in case Altan tried any funny business. Which was hilarious, because normally she wouldn't be able to stop thinking about him being in her apartment, especially after sleeping next to him all night the previous evening. Well...this morning.

Her brain felt foggy. With lack of sleep, with hunger, and with everything she still needed to do swirling around in it.

"Hold on to your arguments...I'll be there in a second and we can discuss face-to-face."

The phone went dead in her ear, and at any other time, with any other person, she probably would've been extremely irritated he'd hung up on her. But she preferred to talk about him staying over in person. He needed to know that she could take care of herself. Had been for a long time now. She didn't need him to protect her as if she was some damsel in distress. Her dad had raised her to be confident and independent. She didn't want anyone swooping in on a white horse to save the day.

In fact, the way she was feeling right now—on edge, confused about where she and Tate stood with each other, hopeful yet skeptical that he'd somehow, after one night, decided he wanted to go out with her when he'd practically ignored her for years before—she *hoped* some bad guy dared to break into her apartment to try to "convince" her to take the job in Turkey. She'd bash his head in with the giant wrench she kept in the apartment for that exact purpose.

"You look fierce. What are you thinking?" Tate asked as he entered the hangar from the open side door.

"I don't need a man," Laryn blurted.

"Okay."

"And I don't need you to babysit me. Because I can take care of myself."

"I know."

In a much less defensive tone, she said, "I don't know what you want from me."

Tate walked into her personal space and simply pulled her into a bear hug...which felt amazing.

Laryn closed her eyes and sagged into him. She was at the end of her rope for the day, and as much as she wanted to be the tough woman her father had raised, who needed nothing and no one, the truth was...this man was her weakness. And she was so damn tired. And *hungry*.

"I didn't get a proper lunch today. I'm assuming you didn't either, because we're a lot alike. We've both been on the go, go, go today. So what do I want from you? Right now, I want to feed you. Then I want to take you home and tuck you into bed and stay nearby, so you can rest peacefully, knowing if anyone dares try to use nefarious means to force you to work for them, they'll have to get through me first. I know you're independent and you can take care of yourself. This isn't about that. It's just taken me too damn long to get my head out of my ass and see what was right in front of my face, and now that I have, I want to see if two people who are a lot alike can make a go of things."

Everything he said, she'd dreamed of him saying to her. Resisting the urge to blurt out, "Yes!" she lifted her head, and instead sighed, "I *am* hungry."

"Yeah, me too," he said with a grin. "It's not ideal, and not what I wanted, but how about we go on that date I promised you?"

"Now?"

"Sure. Why not? The guys and I usually go out the night before we're deployed, if we have enough advance notice. It's kind of our last hurrah...just in case. It's a little morbid, but we're nothing if not practical. We all know how short life can be."

Laryn smacked him on the shoulder. "Don't say that!" she exclaimed.

Tate shrugged. "It's true. We like to go out, not talk shop, and enjoy each other's company one last time before we deploy. You'll see, it's not morbid at all. It's more a celebration of friendship."

"I'll see?" she asked with a tilt of her head.

"Yeah, because you'll be joining us if we're able to go out tomorrow. It'll depend on how late we get out of here. But that leaves tonight for me to take you on a date, just the two of us. What do you say?"

Laryn suddenly felt a lot less tired. Then she frowned and looked down at herself. "I'm a mess."

"You are. And it's adorable."

She scrunched her nose. "No, it's not. I smell like oil and grease. And I look like I've been crawling around on the floor, which I kind of have."

"I do admit that I like the vanilla cookie smell better, but this is us," he said with a small shrug. "You in your coveralls. Me in my flight suit. Wrinkled. Dirty. But still standing. Besides, no one is going to look twice at us where I want to take you. We aren't exactly going to a five-star restaurant or anything. Not this late, after such a long day...although I *do* want to splurge and do that with you at some point. But we don't have the time before we head out to the Middle East."

"Where *are* we going? You don't even know what I like."

"Salmich's Burgers and Hoagies."

Laryn's mouth immediately started watering. "Seriously?"

"Yeah. Why? You been there?"

"I *love* that place!" she exclaimed happily. "The hoagies are huge and *so* good!"

Tate grinned. "Awesome. So you'll let me drive and take you out to eat, and then bring you back to your place and spend the night?"

"Sounds like you've got the evening all planned, stud," Laryn teased.

To her amazement, Tate blushed. "I didn't mean that the way it sounded," he rushed to assure her. "All I meant was, you'll let me stay? On the couch? Tex will work on getting me the info I requested about Osman, but he can't get to it immediately, and I don't want to take any chances with your safety."

Laryn studied him for a moment. Then she nodded. She was too tired to argue about him staying the night. Besides...she *would* feel safer with him there. She still wasn't convinced Altan would do anything, that he had the contacts to harass her from the other side of the world, but when she thought about how she'd felt after he'd threatened her over the phone, she decided it wasn't exactly a hardship to have the man she'd had a crush on for years stay the night.

"Good. Come on, let's get out of here before someone finds us and asks just 'one more question.'"

Laryn chuckled as he grabbed her hand and practically dragged her toward the door. "You get that too?" she asked.

"All the freaking time," he muttered.

It didn't take long for them to get to his Taurus, and he was pulling out almost before she had her seat belt buckled. The drive to Salmich's didn't take too long at this time of night. They easily found a parking space in the small lot next to the hole-in-the-wall restaurant. It wasn't too far from her apartment complex, and was, in fact, on the same street, albeit blocks to the east from where she was.

They easily got a table inside and Laryn didn't even bother picking up the menu, she knew exactly what she was going to get...what she got every time. She was a creature of habit, and when the food was as good as it was, why not?

"I take it you know what you want?" Tate said with a chuckle.

"Yeah."

He took a moment to look over the menu and by the time the waitress stopped by their table with water, they were both ready to order.

"I'd like the Chicken in the Grass hoagie with extra cheese, please. Oh, and a side of diablo fries."

"And for you?" the waitress asked, smiling at Tate.

"Jalapeños Popper Burger for me."

After the waitress left, Tate grinned at Laryn. "I was going to ask if you like spicy food, but since you ordered the diablo fries, that answers my question. Are those for us to share?"

Laryn pretended to think about it for a moment. "I guess," she sighed.

They talked about nothing in particular until their food came, which was surprisingly quick, but considering the time, they were probably anxious to serve the food and close up.

Laryn tucked into her sandwich as soon as it arrived and closed her eyes with ecstasy after the first bite.

"Good?" he asked.

When she opened her eyes, she saw he was staring at her with a look she couldn't interpret. "So good," she said on a moan.

Tate licked his lips as he stared at her mouth, and she realized how she sounded...and why he was staring at her. And just like that, arousal hit *hard*. She'd been practically orgasming over the hoagie. No wonder he was staring at her with heat in his eyes.

"I'm tempted to ask for a box for mine," he said in a low, tortured tone.

Surprising herself, Laryn asked, "You don't think you'll need the energy it gives you?" Nodding at the burger in front of him.

The spark of lust in his gaze made her feel confident and sexy at the same time, even in her coveralls and smears of grease. Somehow, this man made her feel as if she were the only woman in the world. And the fact that he so obviously wanted her was heady.

Without a word, he picked up his burger and took a large bite. They ate quickly, enjoying every bit of their dinners. The fries disappeared just as quickly, as they shared the plate between them. By the time she was finished eating, Laryn was stuffed... but that hadn't diminished the spark of attraction between her and Tate that literally felt like a live wire.

"You ready to go?" he asked quietly after he'd paid the bill.

Laryn nodded. She'd been confident enough to flirt when the table was between them and they were busy eating, but when he stood and stepped toward her, putting his hand on the small of her back to encourage her to head for the door, she felt awkward once again.

This was Tate. The Night Stalker. The man other women acted foolishly around, trying to catch his eye.

"Stop thinking so much," he ordered as they walked toward his car.

"I can't," Laryn said honestly.

Tate walked her around to the passenger-side door. He took a long look around the parking area before turning his attention to her. He backed her against the door until she had to tilt her chin to look at him.

"I'm thirty-four years old, and I've never been turned on simply by watching a woman eat like I was with you just now."

Well. Alrighty then. That was blunt.

"And I'm thirty-five, and I feel the same."

"The way I see it, this can go one of two ways. We can go back to your apartment, say good night, and you can go to your room and get a good night's sleep while I crash on your sofa."

"Or?" Laryn worked up the courage to ask.

"Or, we can go back to your apartment, and you can take me to your bed and have your wicked way with me. We probably won't get a lot of sleep because once I see you, all of you, I'm going to want to make up for lost time...my fault, not yours."

Oh, Laryn wanted that. So much. But..."Is this because we're being deployed? If this is a matter of you scratching an itch, I'm going to have to pass. I'm not the kind of woman who sleeps around. I've got a vibrator and I know how to use it, thank you very much."

"Damn," Tate said under his breath, moving a hand down to his crotch to adjust himself. It was somehow the hottest thing Laryn had ever seen. He was uncomfortable because of little ol' *her*.

"This is not a one-night stand. I wouldn't disrespect you like that. There's something between us, Laryn. Something that I should've seen way before now. I'm an idiot, I already told you that. I've finally opened my eyes, and I have a feeling *whenever* we do decide to take our relationship to the next level, it'll change both our lives for the better. But I can wait. Things on deployment are going to be intense, as always. We won't have any privacy or a chance to see where things might go between us. But I'm telling you right now, things are still going to be different this time around. No more going our separate ways all the time on the ship. I want to eat with you, check in and see how you're doing, talk about the helicopters, and hang out with you and my fellow pilots whenever possible. Is that okay?"

It sounded like heaven to Laryn. Deployments had always been a bit lonely for her. She didn't fit in with the sailors and soldiers onboard. Since she wasn't an officer or even in the military any longer, people were reluctant to say too much around her. They certainly weren't going to go out of their way to befriend her, since it was likely they'd never see her again. So having Tate say he wanted to spend more time with her onboard was actually something she was looking forward to. It should make the deployment less boring and more bearable.

"That's more than okay," she reassured him.

"Good. So? Door number one or two? No pressure. Seriously. Just as you're an expert with your vibrator, my hand does the job when needed."

The thought of him masturbating in her shower, or even on her couch when she went to bed, made Laryn's nipples harden under her coveralls.

"Two," she blurted.

His pupils dilated before her very eyes.

To his credit, he didn't ask if she was sure. Didn't try to talk her out of her decision. He seemed just as anxious as she was to open door number two and see if their physical attraction was as intense as it seemed.

Before she knew it, she was buckled into her seat and Tate was driving like a bat out of hell toward her apartment complex. Neither of them spoke, but Laryn took a chance and reached out and placed her hand on Tate's thigh.

He immediately covered her hand with his and gripped it tightly. Holding hands with this man was more exciting, more arousing, than anything she'd done with anyone else. It was overwhelming and almost scary. But in a good way. An I'm-at-the-top-of-a-roller-coaster-about-to-fly-down-that-first-hill scary.

Laryn had no qualms about his driving abilities. The man was a highly trained Night Stalker pilot...if the Army trusted him with multimillion-dollar aircraft, not to mention the lives of the

SEALs and Deltas he routinely transported in and out of some seriously nasty situations, she could trust him behind the wheel of his car. Even while sporting the hard-on that was tenting his flight suit.

Seeing it made Laryn squirm in her seat. She might be making a huge mistake, sleeping with Tate, but fuck it. She'd wanted him forever, and she wasn't going to pass up the chance to see if all the sleepless nights thinking about him were worth the buildup in her mind.

Tate let go of her hand after he parked, but only long enough to walk around his car to her side, then he reached for her once more. He didn't speak, the anticipation building around them both as he walked up the stairs, towing her behind him.

He stood at her side as she unlocked her door, then he spoke for the first time since the parking lot of the restaurant. "Wait here," he ordered gruffly.

Confused, Laryn did as he asked and watched as he quickly searched the kitchen and living area of her apartment. She heard him open the shower curtain in the bathroom and open and close the closet door in the hall. She assumed he went into the second bedroom that was more like a junk room, which she used to hold stuff she didn't know where else to put, and then her bedroom, before he materialized in front of her once more.

"All clear," he said matter-of-factly.

It dawned on her then that even fully aroused, and anticipating a sure thing, he'd taken the time to make sure her apartment was safe.

Had anyone put her safety above their sexual needs before? No. The answer was definitely no. In her experience, once men had sex on the brain, that's all they could think about. Anything else was secondary. But she should've known Tate would be different.

He stepped into her personal space and gently cradled her head in his hands. Laryn felt his erection against her once more.

But he didn't grab at her, didn't immediately start stripping off her coveralls.

"Still good with your decision?" he asked quietly.

"If I said no?" she asked, more curious about his answer than really wanting to change her mind.

"I'd step back, say good night, and see you in the morning," he said matter-of-factly.

Yup. This man was definitely different than anyone else she'd been with. He was honorable. Rough around the edges, yes. Cocky, definitely. But good down to his core for sure.

"I haven't changed my mind," she told him, reaching around him and running her fingers through the hair at his nape.

"Thank fuck," he breathed before wrapping one arm around her waist and picking her up.

Laryn smiled as he carried her down the hall, her legs tangling with his as he walked. She tried to pull her knees up to make things easier for him, but he hadn't lifted her high enough and the angle was wrong. Instead, he almost tripped over their legs as he entered her bedroom, and Laryn couldn't help but laugh.

He chuckled as he finally put her on her feet by the mattress.

"That's new," he said casually.

"What?" Laryn asked as she looked up at him.

"Laughing. I don't think I ever really saw sex as fun before. It was always something I took very seriously."

"And you aren't taking this seriously?" she asked, more surprised than upset by his words.

"Oh, this is as serious as it gets," he told her, making those pesky goose bumps break out on her arms once more. "But it's also fun. I get to unwrap you. See what you're hiding under that hideous mechanic's tent you wear all the time. And I get to see what turns you on. I get to figure out if you're ticklish, if your tits are sensitive, and if you can come with my mouth on your pussy or if you need a rougher touch."

Damn. She wasn't going to survive this.

He grinned once more. "And that look on your face only makes this *more* fun for me."

"Do I get to do the same? Figure out if you like your nipples sucked, how much control you're willing to give me when I go down on you? If you're the kind of man who pumps, bumps, and grunts, or if you've got more finesse?"

Tate threw back his head and laughed so hard, Laryn might've been offended if she couldn't feel the evidence of how her words affected him. He'd gotten even harder against her belly, if that was possible.

"Pump, bump, and grunt?" he asked, still smiling.

Laryn shrugged. "It's a thing."

"I'm sure it is. But I'd like to think I'm not that guy. And if you want control, you can have it. Do you?"

She was tempted to say yes, to test that he wasn't lying, but truthfully, she didn't want to be in charge. She had to be in control in every other aspect of her life. She didn't mind handing over the reins in bed to her partner. As long as he knew what to do with that control, and he didn't take things too far. She wasn't exactly submissive, but she wasn't a Dom either.

"No," she told him simply.

"Good. Because while I don't mind you sucking my cock—in fact, that is now one of my biggest fantasies—I'm not sure I can give up all control. I'm kind of type A when it comes to that sort of thing."

It was Laryn's turn to chuckle. "Yeah, figured that out, Mr. Night Stalker, always-in-control pilot."

He smirked. Then sobered. "If at any time you change your mind, everything stops. You decide you want to mess around, but no penetration, that's cool. I can always stop. Just say the word. I don't want you to regret anything we do here. This is going to change us. For the better, but different all the same. I'm looking forward to that. I want it. But if you aren't sure, if you want to slow things down because we're moving so fast, I'll understand."

Time for some serious honesty here. "I've wanted you for three years," she confessed quietly. "Part of the reason I was looking into leaving was because of you. Because it was so hard to work with you day in and day out, and know that I didn't have a chance in hell of being with you the way I wanted."

"Oh, Laryn," Tate whispered.

"I'm not telling you that to make you feel guilty. I get it, your life was way different than mine. I just want to reassure you that I'm not going to regret tonight. How could I, when it's everything I've ever wanted for so long? I admire you, Tate. Respect you. You're a good man, pilot, friend. And knowing you take consent so seriously...it's the icing on the cake for me."

"I'm sorry I was such an idiot and didn't recognize what was right there for so long. Thank you for waiting for me."

He was thanking her for waiting for him?

Damn, she loved this man.

In response, she went up on her tiptoes and kissed him with every ounce of emotion she'd held in for so long. It was too soon for the words, but she could show him how important he was to her. How impressed she was by him.

CHAPTER TWELVE

It was taking all the control Casper could muster not to rip the damn ugly coveralls off this woman and throw her onto the bed to have his way with her. Every word out of her mouth made him want her more.

The guilt that he'd missed her attraction all this time was there, but maybe it was for the best. A year or two ago, things between them might not have worked out. But now?

Her lips on his felt like coming home.

He banded his arms around her and held her tight as he took control of the kiss. Her upper arms were trapped against her sides because of the way he was holding her, but he felt her hands caressing his sides as he re-learned her mouth.

She gave as good as she got, she wasn't a passive participant, and it made Casper harder than he was already. He was two seconds away from coming, which would be a damn shame because the only place he wanted to orgasm was deep inside her body.

It was an unusual desire for him. In the past, he hadn't much cared about when or how he came, just that he did. But he wanted to be as connected as he could be to this woman when he exploded.

And thinking about coming inside her made him think about babies. Which should've freaked him out. He'd *never* thought about children...except how to make sure he didn't have them prematurely.

Tearing his lips from hers, he looked at the woman in his arms and blurted, "Do you want kids?"

She blinked in surprise at the question.

Casper rushed to explain his line of thinking. "I was envisioning what was ahead of us tonight...after going down on you and making sure you're wet enough to take me without pain—I'm bigger than a lot of men, not bragging, just stating a fact—and I got to thinking about how much I was looking forward to coming inside you. Of feeling you massage my cock from the inside, how amazing that would feel. Made me think about birth control and children."

Casper had a feeling he sounded like a lunatic. If this were a casual hookup, it would be a totally inappropriate topic to mention. But since he felt down to his bones that this was anything *but* casual, that Laryn could very well be the woman he married and lived the next sixty years of his life with, he needed to know they were on the same page when it came to kids.

She licked her lips, plump from his aggressive kisses, and nodded.

Relief almost made Casper's knees weak. "I'm a twin," he reminded her.

She smiled. "I know."

"All I'm saying is that it's likely twins run in my family. That gonna be a problem for you?"

"Um...are we talking hypothetically?"

"No."

"No?" she questioned, looking surprised again...and a little worried.

"Laryn, I like you. A lot. And if things go the way I'm hoping they do between us, we're going to be long-term. As we established earlier, we're both in our mid-thirties. We have some time, but not a lot because I'd rather not be changing diapers and running after toddlers when I'm sixty. I'm just trying to figure out if we're on the same wavelength when it comes to kids."

"Are you gonna help with these twins? I mean, are you going to be the kind of dad who thinks it's solely the woman's responsibility to get up in the middle of the night when they cry? Who's too busy flying his helicopters to remember he has a family? What about changing diapers, or being the bad guy every now and then and saying no, so I don't have to be the mean ol' mom all the time? What kind of father do you intend to be? The answers to those questions will help determine if I'm all right with twins."

Casper couldn't help but smirk. This was the strangest conversation he'd ever had with a woman he was on the cusp of taking to bed. But it also felt like one of the most important discussions of his life.

"My dad was awesome. He was very hands-on. Did everything with me and Nate. He went to every extracurricular activity we had and did whatever was necessary in order to give us what we needed to be happy and healthy. But the most important thing he gave us was his time. He was there for us. That's the kind of dad I want to be. Present in my kids' lives. I wouldn't give up midnight feedings or daddy days out for anything. So to answer your question, I'll be the kind of father figure my children need...as well as the kind of partner their mom needs."

His answer came from his heart, and he practically held his breath to see how Laryn would react.

To his surprise, she pushed on his chest—hard—and Casper immediately dropped his arms from around her and stepped back, giving her space. He panicked for a moment, thinking he'd screwed this up somehow. Maybe he was too mushy. Not alpha enough. And he was definitely rushing things.

He opened his mouth to try to reassure her, but he didn't get the chance before her hands came up to the zipper of her coveralls.

She smiled at him with more confidence than she'd had outside the bar—the last thing he remembered of that awful night—as she unzipped them, then wiggled her hips and let the coveralls fall to the floor. She stood in front of him in a pair of black bikini briefs and a black tank top.

It took every bit of willpower for Casper not to come in his pants right then and there.

Laryn was curvy, he'd known that from seeing her the other night. But her thighs were now on full display, and all he could think about was getting between them. Touching them to see if they were as soft as they looked. The thought of those thighs wrapped around his ears as he ate her out almost made him hyperventilate.

"I'm on the pill," she informed him.

It took a second for her words to sink in. "What?"

"The pill. I want kids, but maybe not right this second. Assuming the tests you guys went through last month came out all right, if you wanted...I mean..." She was blushing now, and Casper's fingers itched to touch her. To strip off the rest of her clothes and have her stand in front of him completely nude so he could drink his fill of her.

"If you want to come inside me...you can. I'm good too. Haven't been with anyone in years. No one could compare to *you*, if I'm being honest."

It was all Casper could do not to throw this woman on the bed and rip off her underwear and plunge deep inside her. But as he'd told her earlier, he wasn't a small man, and the last thing he'd ever do was hurt her. Instead, he stepped back into her personal space and reached for the hem of her tank top.

"May I?" he croaked.

She lifted her arms above her head as she stared him right in the eye and gave him a small, shy smile.

That was all the encouragement he needed. He ever so slowly inched the material higher and higher. The anticipation was killing him, but it was making this moment all the more carnal at the same time.

Her hair fluttered around her shoulders after he'd gotten the tank up and off. She stood in front of him with her chin lifted and her shoulders back. She wasn't wearing a bra, probably because the tank top had built-in support. Her tits were...glorious. Large, but perfectly proportioned for her curvy body. Her areolas and nipples were a pinkish-tan color, and as he looked his fill, her chest began to rise and fall faster and her nipples hardened, as if begging for his touch.

But he wasn't done unwrapping the best present he'd ever received.

His palms itching to map her entire body, Casper did his best to be patient. He hooked his thumbs under the elastic of her underwear and slowly pushed the material down her thighs. She stepped out of the garment and kicked them to the side.

This woman was all his hopes and dreams wrapped up in one gorgeous package. He could hardly believe she'd been hiding this perfection under the baggy coveralls she wore every day.

The dark hair between her legs was neatly trimmed and the little belly pooch she had was so womanly, so sexy, so different from his own chiseled body, Casper was in awe. He reached out, his thumb caressing a small tattoo just inside her bikini line. It was a wrench. Which was so...*Laryn*, that he couldn't help but smile.

"I got that after my dad passed away. It's silly, but I wanted to carry a part of him with me at all times."

"It's not silly at all. It's sexy. And sweet."

Casper went to his knees. More like he collapsed at her feet.

His legs didn't feel as if they could hold him up any longer. But the position put his mouth at eye level with her pussy. He leaned forward and kissed the small tattoo.

He heard Laryn take a small inhalation as he lightly placed his hands on her waist and looked up.

"Tell me you want this," he said.

"I do."

"Tell me *what* you want. In detail," he ordered, needing to hear from her lips that she wanted him as much as he wanted her.

If he thought she was going to be shy and demure, he was wrong.

She smirked down at him and shoved a hand into his hair, curling her fingers so her nails lightly scratched against his scalp. "I want you to eat me out while you're kneeling at my feet. Then I want you to get naked and let me give you head. Then fuck me and come inside me like you said you wanted to."

Casper was moving before he thought about it. His hands tightened on her waist as he leaned forward and pressed his lips to her pussy.

She gasped and her stance widened, giving him more room to work. But it wasn't enough. Casper grabbed one of her thighs and lifted it to his shoulder, completely opening her up to him.

He aggressively went after what he'd been dying for—the taste of her arousal. He found her clit and licked it roughly, loving the way she squirmed in his arms and the little squeaks that escaped her lips.

He ate her out as if she were his last meal and he was dying tomorrow. Neither of them had showered, but that was the last thing on his mind right about now. All he could think about was making her come. He wanted that. Needed it.

And even with his face between her legs, or maybe because of it, he could smell cookies. That vanilla scent would from this point on make him hard as a rock. Because it would remind him of this moment. Of her arousal mixed with her sweet scent.

"Tate!" she exclaimed as he wrapped his lips around her clit and sucked. She jerked in his arms and both hands were now in his hair, holding on for dear life. Casper's cock was leaking precome like a sieve, but he barely noticed. All his attention was on the woman in his arms, under his lips. He licked, sucked, nipped, and drank down every drop of arousal she gifted him.

And when he shifted and got one hand between her legs, the feel of how tight she was when he eased a finger inside her made him grunt in anticipation. She was going to squeeze the hell out of his dick. It would be all he could do not to come the second he got inside her.

She was dripping all over his finger as he continued to lick her clit and began to lightly finger fuck her at the same time. Her hips pumped in time with his hand, and Casper couldn't help but be awed at the sensuality of this woman. She might be working in a so-called man's world, wearing clothing that hid every inch of her womanly body, but she was sex on a fucking stick, and he was the lucky guy she'd elected to give herself to. He vowed right then and there to never take her for granted. To make sure he told her every damn day how sexy she was.

Wanting to stay right in this spot for hours, but also wanting desperately to get inside her, Casper removed his finger and grasped her by the waist again. Then he stood abruptly, making Laryn screech as she suddenly fell backward onto the mattress behind her.

Casper was now hunched over her, holding her hips in the air as he sealed his mouth to her clit and licked and sucked aggressively.

Laryn immediately began to shake in his arms. Her thighs squeezed around his head, her hands grabbed his shoulders, and her belly clenched as she neared the edge.

"I'm close!" she informed him unnecessarily.

The signs of her orgasm were easy to read, and Casper had a feeling she'd never be able to fake anything with him. Not if this was how her body reacted right before she came.

When she finally exploded, it was so damn beautiful, Casper was in awe that he was the one who'd done that for her and was getting to experience it.

He lifted his mouth and looked down as she quaked under him. Her pussy lips were swollen and he could see her arousal leaking from between her legs. Not able to help himself, he leaned in and licked it up before it could fall to the sheets under her ass.

"Delicious," he sighed as his thumbs caressed her hip bones.

"That's it. I'm dead. You killed me," Laryn gasped.

Then her head came up, and she pinned him with a look full of arousal. "Naked. Now," she ordered.

The sight of her on her bed, chest flushed with her orgasm, legs still spread, pussy glistening with his saliva and her arousal, nipples hard and hair mussed, made Casper eager to do any-damn-thing she asked of him. Treason? Murder? Get down on his hands and knees and bark like a dog? No problem.

Reluctantly, he let go of her and stood. He made quick work of his clothes, annoyed by the feel of them against his skin.

When he shoved his briefs down his legs, she gasped again.

"Holy shit, Tate. That's not going to fit."

Damn, she was good for his ego. "I told you I was bigger than a lot of men."

"That's like...alien size or something. Does it vibrate?"

Casper laughed, once again shocked that he was having fun in bed. He'd always enjoyed sex, but not like this. The banter he and Laryn had engaged in at work was carrying over to the bedroom, and he freaking loved it.

"No extra alien features. And I'll fit. I have a feeling you were made just for me. Scoot up."

She moved onto the bed so her head was up by the pillows,

and Casper joined her. He lay down next to her and put his finger under her chin, forcing her eyes away from his hard-as-nails cock and up to his face. "I'll fit," he reassured her again. "You're going to be so wet, even wetter than you are right now, and so desperate to be filled, you aren't even going to think about me *not* fitting."

"Tate," she whispered.

The feel of her skin against his own was thrilling. And addicting. Casper ran a hand down the center of her chest between her tits, over the adorable womanly pooch of her belly, to her pussy. He covered her with his palm and eased his middle finger between her soaking-wet lips. He played with her as he leaned over and kissed her.

The kiss this time was slow and easy, but no less passionate. Her hips lifted into his touch as they kissed and Casper felt ten feet tall. This woman was perfect. She probably didn't think so. Could probably list a dozen things she didn't like about herself. But she was perfect for him. Finding out she was deeply passionate was icing on the cake in addition to everything else he already knew and liked about her.

He lifted his lips from hers and moved down her body, kissing and nipping her neck, then her collarbone, before moving down to her tits. He'd been dying to get his mouth on her since he'd seen her in that tank top at Anchor Point. And now, here he was. Fulfilling his fantasies.

"I want to touch you," she mumbled as he took one of her nipples into his mouth.

"You are," he muttered, before sucking hard and deep.

She let out a small squeak, even while arching her back and pressing up into his touch. She apparently liked that small bite of pain, and Casper smiled around his mouthful of soft flesh. His finger between her leg hadn't stopped moving either. He continued to dip inside her body and stimulate every inch of her pussy.

"Tate," she whined. "I want to give you pleasure too."

That stopped him in his tracks. Casper lifted his head and looked her in the eyes. "You think this isn't pleasurable for me?"

"Not as much as my mouth on your cock."

She had a point, but Casper wasn't willing to give up control yet. Didn't want to stop licking and sucking her tits. "Later, Laryn. I want to do this for you. Please?"

Her head fell back onto the mattress. "Gosh, it's such a hardship. Fine, if you must keep pleasuring me, go for it. But I don't want to hear any complaints later that our sex life is one-sided."

Casper found himself laughing again. Yeah, this was definitely a new experience, one he was already addicted to. "So noted," he told her, before lowering his mouth once more.

The next several minutes went by with no conversation between them, just moans from Laryn and lots of lip smacking on Casper's part.

When she began to tremble beneath him once more, Casper moved. He sat up and got between her legs, pushing her thighs apart and scooting as far forward as he could. She wrapped her legs around him without prompting and looked down between them.

Casper held his cock, which was throbbing, and rubbed the mushroomed head up and down Laryn's soaking-wet slit. "You were right, all my tests came back clear. And I haven't been with anyone in over a year. Can I really take you bare? It's okay to say no, Laryn."

"Please, Tate. I want to feel you. All of you."

That was all he needed to hear. Casper ran his cock up and down her folds for a moment, then used his palm to further lubricate himself with her juices. Laryn's eyes were wide and she looked nervous, which wasn't okay. She should be feeling nothing but arousal, not worry. When he took her, he wanted nothing but pleasure for her.

But he also wasn't a saint. He needed to feel her around him, at least a little bit. Casper nudged just the tip of his cock inside her—and from the feel of that tight squeeze alone, the desire to shove himself all the way in was strong. But his control was legendary.

"Eyes on mine, Laryn," he ordered.

Her gaze immediately swung up to his face and pleasure swam through Casper's veins. There was no doubt who was in charge right now, and it was exciting. To be completely responsible for another person's pleasure was a big deal. He wouldn't let her down. Using one hand to desperately squeeze the base of his dick to keep from prematurely ejaculating, his other hand went unerringly to her clit, roughly stroking.

To his delight, her hips immediately pressed upward, making his cock slip inside her a bit more.

"That's it, Laryn, just feel. I got you. You coming around my tongue earlier was like heaven. But feeling you grip my cock will be a dream come true. Trust me, Laryn. Let go."

* * *

Laryn could hardly believe she was here. In her bed with Tate's cock partly inside her. She'd wanted this for so long. And it was so much better than she'd dreamed. The man knew what to do with his mouth, that was for sure. She'd come so hard earlier as he'd eaten her out, and she was on the verge of another orgasm already, this one even bigger than before, if that was possible.

"Tate," she whispered, feeling overwhelmed. When he'd asked if she wanted kids earlier, she'd actually been disappointed that she was on the pill—which was crazy. Things between them were moving at the speed of light. She knew she loved this man, but could he honestly have a complete change of heart when it came to *her* in such a short time?

She wasn't sure, but she'd never regret bringing him to her bed.

"That's it, Laryn. I got you. Let go."

For some reason, she was terrified to come again. The first time was kind of a surprise. She'd never really loved men going down on her, but she'd obviously been primed and ready. Now she was thinking too hard. She looked weird when she came. A former partner had told her that. And Tate's position would let him see all of her. There was no hiding from him.

She was looking into his eyes, as he'd requested, but suddenly it was too much. All of this. She'd loved this man forever and if she disappointed him, if she couldn't take all of him, if he was disgusted by her body's reaction to an orgasm, if he decided after this was over that he didn't really want to be with her...she'd be devastated.

Laryn squeezed her eyes shut and willed her orgasm to fade.

Tate stopped moving, and she could sense him hovering over her. His dick was still only partially inside her, and it felt as if she was being split in two with just that much. She was going to disappoint him, which was soul-crushing.

She opened her mouth to tell him she'd changed her mind. That she didn't want this—which was a huge lie, but at this point, she'd do anything to protect her heart from breaking into a million pieces. But then she felt his lips on her cheek. Then her eyes. Then he nuzzled that sensitive place right under her ear.

He was kissing her in what felt like the most loving way. She was overwhelmed. Confused.

"I know," he whispered against her, reading her mind. "It's overwhelming. Huge. Feels like we're on the cusp of something big and scary."

"Something's big and scary, all right," Laryn couldn't help but say.

He chuckled, and she felt it between her legs as much as she did against her chest, where he was touching her.

"Open your eyes, Laryn."

She didn't want to. Really didn't. But she was a damn adult. She'd gotten herself into this position, literally, and she needed to woman up. Besides, this was Tate. The man who she'd cuddled against her breast when he was feeling vulnerable and confused after waking up the morning after the bar. The man she'd spent the last three years doing everything in her power to keep safe while he was doing his job. And the person she'd gotten to know in the last thirty-six hours was even better than the guy she'd known already.

She opened her eyes.

His ice-blue gaze was right there, looking back. The concern she saw was soothing, but the desire was still there as well. And it was that desire in the face of her being a flake that made her relax a fraction.

"Giving up control is hard. But it's not so difficult when you give it to someone you know will do whatever he or she can to keep you safe. Protect you. Do what's right. That's how I feel when I fly with Pyro. I know he has my back. If the shit hits the fan, I don't have to wonder if he has what it takes to persevere. In the air, on the ground, or if we get captured by enemy forces.

"And that's how I feel about you. Yes, I've questioned the work you've done on my birds, but I think it was only because I wanted a reason to spar with you. To listen to the passion in your voice when you tell me what you've done and why it'll keep my ass in the air, as you've so eloquently put it.

"When I woke up here, in your bed, next to you, those feelings solidified. I had no control over anything, and yet you kept me safe. Did what was right. You had my back. *I've got you, Laryn.* Watching you come apart in my arms will be a gift I treasure. Earlier was just a taste."

"Literally," Laryn couldn't help but say.

He smiled. "Yeah. You're beautiful. A fucking goddess. Knowing you've got a tank and undies on under your coveralls is going to fuck with my head from here on out. I'm going to have to learn how to fly with a damn erection."

Laryn giggled.

"Damn, I felt that on my dick," Tate said, as he straightened his arms and lifted off her a bit. "Look at us," he demanded. "We're amazing together."

Laryn's gaze traveled down their bodies to where they were connected. There still seemed to be an awful lot of his cock that wasn't inside her, and her pussy lips were spread wide around him...and it *was* amazing. "You have freckles on your penis."

He laughed. "Penis? Woman, I'll have you know, that's a cock. Or dick. Or manly love monster. Not a *penis*."

Laryn laughed harder. She liked this. The comfort of their banter. The fun. Swallowing hard, she admitted, "I want this. You. More than I've ever wanted anything. I'm just nervous."

"I know. But like I said, I've got you, Laryn. I'd rather eject from my plane deep inside North Korean territory than hurt you. Trust me."

Taking a deep breath, she nodded.

"Now, look at me again. Please," he tacked on.

She did as he asked.

Shifting above her, one of his hands went back between her legs and began to strum her clit once more. It wasn't long before she felt the orgasm that had been simmering under the surface of her skin begin to rise.

"That's it. Fuck, you're so responsive. It's a dream come true. I love how your body reacts to me. The goose bumps you can't hide when I do or say something you like. The way your thighs shake. Your belly clenches. It's all erotic as hell, and it's all I can do not to come just seeing it. Knowing I've done this, *I've* made you feel this way, it's a huge turn-on."

That was enlightening. Laryn realized she'd taken her previous partner's words to heart when she shouldn't have.

"Come for me, Laryn. Show me how good this feels."

It took another fifteen seconds of his almost rough stroking of her clit before black spots danced in front of her eyes and Laryn felt herself flying over the edge.

In the midst of her orgasm, she felt Tate slide all the way inside her. And instead of being painful, it made her pleasure increase. She could feel every ridge, every vein in his cock as he claimed her once and for all.

And she did feel claimed. She was extremely full, but somehow she wanted more. Laryn shoved her hips up, wanting all this man could give her.

"Damn. You. Feel. So. Good," Tate stuttered, holding himself still inside her as she continued to shake and convulse around him. "Your pussy is gripping my cock so damn hard. I can feel your muscles rippling around me."

"Move," Laryn ordered when she could speak, coming down from her orgasm.

She didn't need to tell him twice.

He braced himself over her and his hips began to rock back and forth in a slow, methodical motion. It felt good, but it wasn't enough.

"More, Tate. Harder."

"I don't want to hurt you."

"I'll hurt *you* if you don't fuck me properly," Laryn growled.

The second the words were out of her mouth, he began to move with purpose. His thrusts were fast and aggressive, and she could feel him bottoming out inside her each time. Nothing had ever felt better, now that he was fully inside her. And she was so wet from her most recent orgasm, the noises his cock made as he fucked her were sexy as hell. Lubrication was important. She knew that better than most because of her profession.

"I'm not going to last long," he panted.

Looking down their bodies once more, Laryn couldn't help

but be in awe of how they looked together. His fat cock, her pussy stretched around him, the way his abs clenched with each thrust...it was the most arousing thing she'd ever seen in her life. And it was happening to *her*.

"Can I come inside you?" Tate asked, the desperation easy to hear in his voice.

"Yes!"

Almost as soon as the word left her lips, he pushed inside her once more and stayed there. He looked up, closed his eyes, and his hips twitched against hers as he filled her to the brim.

Laryn could almost feel his cock flexing inside her as he emptied himself. She couldn't help but smile with satisfaction. *She'd* done that. Turned this unflappable man inside out. It was an incredible feeling.

When he collapsed on top of her, she wasn't prepared and let out a small grunt. He didn't put all his weight on her, but it was enough for her to feel completely surrounded by him.

Tate propped himself up on his elbows and stared down at her for a long moment.

"What?" she asked, praying he wasn't going to say anything that would ruin the moment. He was still lodged deep inside her body, and Laryn had no desire for him to go anywhere.

"Thank you," he said quietly.

"I think that's my line," she told him.

"No. What you just gave me...it was beautiful. Your trust...I never knew how amazing it could feel to be given trust so completely the way you just did. So, thank you."

And she thought he was going to say something to ruin the moment.

"I wonder if I can arrange to get a private bunk room on the ship," he mused a moment later.

Yup. There it was. Guys were guys. Always thinking about sex.

"Because I'm thinking my nights of good sleep are over unless you're in my arms."

"Oh," Laryn said in surprise.

He grinned. "You thought I was gonna say because I wanted to be able to have sex with you when we're deployed, didn't you?"

"Well, yeah."

"What we just did...it's too private to risk doing on a ship where your neighbor is literally inches away on the other side of a thin metal wall. Besides, I'd never disrespect you that way."

"But sleeping with me won't do that? Have people gossiping about us?" Laryn asked, genuinely curious as to his response.

"Not like hearing the squeals and moans coming from your mouth when I make you come," Tate said with a grin.

Laryn couldn't even argue that point because she wasn't so far gone that she didn't remember the sounds that escaped her mouth when she flew over the edge and he'd pushed all the way inside her. Pleasure mixed with surprise, and maybe even a pinch of pain. It was delicious.

"Whatever," she said with a roll of her eyes.

Tate chuckled, then wiggled around so he was no longer lying on top of her, rolling her with him so she was on her side. His dick was still buried inside her, and the position felt...right. Almost natural.

"This okay?" he asked.

"Yeah."

"You want to get up and get cleaned up?" he asked.

"I should."

"But?"

"I don't want to move. You feel too good."

"Same."

Laryn sighed with contentment. The upcoming deployment would mean she and Tate would be extremely busy. They wouldn't have time to simply soak each other in like they were doing now. The Night Stalkers were experts at flying at night, and if *they* were up, *Laryn* was up. She was never able to sleep while Tate was on a mission. She had a feeling her anxiety would be even worse now.

"Laryn?"

"Yeah?"

"This is gonna work. It won't be easy, but I'm going to do everything in my power not to screw this up. Because I know when I've got something precious and important, and you are all that and more."

Laryn wasn't sure how to respond to that, but she couldn't say anything even if she wanted to because her throat was suddenly tight.

As if he knew how emotional his words had made her, he kissed her on the temple and said, "Sleep. We've both got a lot to do tomorrow."

Her eyes closed and she was asleep in seconds, secure in the arms of the man she'd only ever dreamed of having.

* * *

"Yes. Deployed. That's what I said. But you should be happy. Now you don't have to send anyone else to *convince* her she should work for you. You can do it yourself."

"Why?"

"Because she and the pilots are being deployed to your backyard. The Mediterranean. My friend who works for the colonel in charge of the Night Stalkers said they'll be flying missions on the border of Syria and your country. In the mountains."

"When?"

"Not sure of exact dates."

"Well, get them! I'm not paying you to give me half-ass information."

"I know they'll be onboard in a few days. You have someone

there who can get you the information you need? Because the Navy isn't deploying me."

"Yes, yes. I will talk to them. I *need* Ms. Hardy. My country needs her. We have the MH-60s, but we don't have anyone to outfit them like the US helicopters. We need her to make them just as good or better. Money is no object. Once she fully comprehends the riches we can give her, she'll change her mind. I just need a chance to talk to her in person."

"Not sure that'll work, but whatever. I've given you the info I have. It's up to you to do something with it. I expect my money by tomorrow night."

"You'll have it."

Altan Osman disconnected the phone and sat at his desk, staring at the white wall of his small office. He needed Laryn Hardy. Badly. By all accounts, she was the best of the best, and his superiors were anxious to get their newly bought MH-60s ready for combat. They also needed the intel that the US government was keeping to themselves as far as specialized equipment onboard.

He wasn't thrilled about hiring a woman, as they were clearly inferior to men, but they needed the information she had in her head. Once they had that, they could eliminate the mechanic so she couldn't cause an international incident, then continue their plans for increasing their military power.

He'd told his contact on the US base that she'd be compensated for her work, but that was a lie, of course. Once the helicopters were upgraded, she'd be eliminated. A woman knowing top-secret intel about his government's military and what the country was capable of simply wasn't acceptable. He'd use her to upgrade the choppers, and then she would disappear.

Laryn hadn't been on his radar until he'd learned she was possibly looking for a job. It was perfect timing. Altan had hired several mechanics in the recent past who'd each claimed they had the knowledge to outfit the choppers with the same firepower and technology used in the United States, but they were all unsuccessful...and so they had disappeared as if they'd never existed.

Now the Gendarmerie was getting impatient, and Altan's time was running out. He either produced someone who could do what they wanted, or *he'd* pay the price.

And then, miraculously, Altan had gotten wind of Laryn Hardy, who had the experience and skill to do exactly what he needed. Except she'd had the nerve to turn him down.

No one turned down Altan Osman.

He had moles in governments all over the world. Men he paid exceptionally well to leak intel about just about everything having to do with military maneuvers, personnel, and equipment.

And now, instead of paying someone else to bring Laryn Hardy across the world to *him*, she was doing him the favor of coming most of the way on her own. He just needed a way to get her off that US naval ship. Now that he knew which one she'd be on, he could activate his moles who were currently working onboard that very carrier and in the area where the Night Stalkers would be flying.

The latter part would be trickier, because he needed their exact flight plan in order to have an extradition team ready, but money was a good motivator. He'd get what he wanted—namely, Laryn Hardy—and his country would be one step closer to becoming a superior military force. Once they possessed some of the US's secrets, their nearest enemies wouldn't dare mess with them. He'd be hailed a hero to his country and could live the life of a millionaire.

Women, fancy clothes, houses, servants...and the respect he'd always yearned for.

Laryn Hardy may have decided not to leave her job in the United States, but too bad. The moment she'd come onto his radar, her fate was decided. She'd work for Altan and his country, or not work for anyone ever again. The choice would be hers. And he'd be sure she made the right decision. One way or another.

Straightening, Altan reached for his phone once again. He had people to contact and plans to make.

CHAPTER THIRTEEN

The second Casper woke up, he knew where he was, who he was with, and what had happened hours earlier. And his cock remembered too, because it was hard once again and obviously wanted a repeat.

After they'd napped for about an hour, he'd woken Laryn and urged her into the shower. She'd had a long day, as had he, and they both needed to get clean. It had taken all his control not to make love to Laryn again, especially when they were plastered together in her small shower and covered in slippery soap, but she was half asleep and obviously needed to get some rest.

But now it was morning. They were both clean, rested, naked, and Casper was more than ready to show Laryn that what they had last night wasn't a one-time fluke.

He inched the covers down until she was bare to him, and had to smile at the way one arm was flung over her head and she was slightly snoring. She was adorable in sleep.

Inching down her body, he rested between her legs and began to lightly suckle her. By the time she fully woke up, she was dripping wet from both his mouth and her arousal.

"Tate?" she mumbled.

"How sore are you?" he asked.

"Not *that* sore," she said immediately.

Satisfaction swam through Casper's veins. He climbed up her body, then rolled her over until she was on top and put his hands under his head. "Good. Now's your chance. You said you wanted to go down on me..."

Laryn rolled her eyes but settled herself over him all the same. "Why am I not surprised you want a blow job this morning?"

"If you don't want to..." he started, pretending to try to scoot out from under her.

"I didn't say that," she said quickly, reaching down to grip his cock.

Casper immediately fell onto his back once more and shuddered at the feel of her hand around him. She had callouses he could feel with every stroke. It was a working woman's hand, strong and sure. And that was sexy as hell in his eyes.

When she leaned down to take him into her mouth, he swore he saw stars. Her hand and mouth coordination was a bit clumsy, but that made her enthusiasm all the more exciting and authentic. She wanted him, and even though it was obvious she hadn't done this a lot, her desire for him was as much a turn-on as her touch.

She sucked and licked and learned his taste and shape as she pleasured him. Casper hadn't thought it would be too difficult to control himself, because he didn't think anything could be better than being inside her, but he'd been wrong. Seeing Laryn's lips spread around him as she glanced up with those big brown eyes was almost more erotic than being inside her. Almost.

Without thought, Casper reached down and pulled her off his cock. Then he urged her forward until she was straddling him.

"Lift up a little," he ordered. She might be on top, but he

was definitely in control. She did as he asked, and he began to flick her clit, wanting her to get off at least once before she took him.

It didn't take long. She seemed as primed as he was, and she was soaking wet. It seemed that sucking him off turned *her* on just as much as it did him. Which was good to know. Again, his Laryn was passionate as hell, and he couldn't be happier about that.

She began to undulate over him, and it was all Casper could do to keep his fingers on her sensitive bundle of nerves. Her body betrayed her pleasure, and she began to shake and tremble as she orgasmed.

"Now, Laryn. Take me now!" he ordered, reaching down and holding his cock up for her to sink down onto.

She did as he asked, and it wasn't long before he was once more buried inside her perfect body. It seemed to him that she took him easier this morning than she had the night before. He was fucking made for her, and he couldn't be more pleased about that.

With him buried all the way inside her, she could give him some of her weight, and she rocked her hips back and forth until her orgasm waned.

Then he took her hips in his hands and said, "Your turn to take me now, Laryn."

The excitement in her eyes made a spurt of precome leak from his dick deep inside her. Resting her hands on his chest, Laryn lifted her hips, exposing his now glistening cock, before sinking back down. She did that a few times before speeding up her movements.

She felt amazing, and watching her bob up and down on him was almost as erotic as the way her body swallowed his cock each time she bottomed out on top of him. Her generous tits bounced with her movements, and her belly and thighs clenched as her muscles worked to take him.

"Beautiful," he murmured, reaching up and palming one of her tits. He squeezed it and felt her inner muscles respond.

This was amazing, and he could've lain under her and watched her fuck him all morning. But, unfortunately, they both had things to do. Work wasn't going to wait for them, and the absolute last thing he wanted was to have their relationship interfere with either of their careers.

"Faster, Laryn. Fuck me hard and fast. Now. Do it!"

She did. Her tits bounced harder and she moaned each time she slammed down on him. She felt incredible—but it wasn't quite enough.

Casper put his hands on her waist and held her still above him. "Can you hold yourself there?" he asked.

Laryn licked her lips and nodded.

He began to fuck her from below, harder and faster than she'd been able to manage from her position. Her head fell back and she cried out, then she looked down between them and watched him take her. Casper couldn't help but follow her gaze. They were beautiful coming together. His hard cock, her soft body opening to him. There was a metaphor in there somewhere, but he was too aroused, too close to the edge to think of what it might be.

Then he was coming. Pulling her down on top of him once more, and filling her to overflowing with his come. Looking up into her dazed eyes, Casper vowed to always remember this moment.

"*Now* I'm sore," Laryn said with a small smile, her hooded eyes looking down at him.

Concerned, Casper immediately lifted her off him and scooted to the side. "Damn. No time for a bath for you, but go take a hot shower. I'll start on breakfast for us."

"I was kidding. Well, sort of," Laryn told him.

"I wasn't. And I'd offer to come assist in taking care of you, but we both know that won't get us to work any faster."

She grinned.

Casper swung his legs over the side of the bed, feeling better than he had in months. And not because he'd just had more sex in the last eight hours than he'd had in the last year. It was starting his day with Laryn by his side. He was as comfortable with her as he was with his fellow pilots, and that was saying a lot. He was excited about the change in their relationship and how that might carry over to the workplace. Some people might not want to work with their partners, but he had a feeling being intimate with her would only make them both better at what they did.

Leaning over the bed, grinning at how she immediately pulled the sheet up to cover herself, Casper gave her a fast kiss but didn't pull away.

"Today's gonna be busy. Hell, the next couple of weeks will be busy, but I'm going to hold last night and this morning in my head, and when I'm feeling overwhelmed or pissed off, I can take out the memories and calm myself. You do that for me, Laryn. Give me a safe place to go when I need one. When people piss me off."

"What about when *I* piss you off?" she asked with a cheeky grin.

"You don't."

She flat-out laughed. "Yes, I do. When I won't do what you say, when you say it. When I disagree with you. When I contradict you in front of your friends."

It was Casper's turn to grin. "Truth? I like that you aren't a pushover. I need more of that in my life."

"Well, you've got plenty of it with me, bub. Just because we're sleeping together doesn't mean I'm suddenly going to turn into a simpering miss. I'm still going to do what's best for that chopper you're flying, and not necessarily what *you* want or think is best."

"I'd expect nothing less. Just one more way you've got my back. Up. Shower. Hot water. Then food."

"Ugh. You, man. Me, woman," Laryn teased.

Casper kissed her once more, then turned to leave, knowing he was flashing his ass at her and not caring. He leaned over to grab his briefs and flight suit from the floor and turned to see Laryn's gaze was right where he wanted it...on him. He shook his ass at her, loving the laughter that rang out behind him as he walked out of the bedroom. This time, he had a change of clothes in his trunk, which he'd go grab before seeing what he could scrounge up for breakfast.

The thought that he couldn't wait to bring Laryn back to his place—where he had a full pantry stocked with all sorts of things he could make for her—flashed through his mind. But if she felt more comfortable with him being in her space, he had no problem with that either. He'd just have to go to the store and fill her pantry with more choices for when they got hungry.

Feeling like a different man this morning, Casper barely resisted the urge to whistle as he prepared to get on with the day.

* * *

As the day went by, it was a struggle to hold on to the carefree feeling he'd had that morning, but recalling the look in Laryn's eyes after she came, and after he emptied himself inside her, was enough to help keep him calm when the chaos of the upcoming deployment threatened to take over.

It felt as if they were being rushed, which they were. The Army and Navy were desperate to get them deployed because the terrain the SEALs and Deltas were being shuttled in and out of was brutal. They'd lost two choppers in the last two days. Thankfully, all the pilots had been able to eject, and they were extracted before being taken captive by the ISIS operatives in the area.

Casper's eyes felt gritty. He hadn't gotten nearly enough sleep, but he wasn't complaining. Thinking about Laryn and what they'd done together was enough to send a shot of adrenaline through his bloodstream. She was...unbelievable. More than he'd ever expected. She was his perfect match. He was sure of it.

Many people would scoff at that. Tell him he was thinking with his dick and not his brain. But other than his twin, he'd never felt so at ease with someone as he did her. He didn't feel as if he had to be someone he wasn't when he was with Laryn. She got him.

Knowing each other for years obviously helped with that feeling of comfort when they were together. And the fact that they'd spent much of their time together last night *laughing*? Exchanging good-natured barbs? He freaking *loved* that. A good chunk of his life was spent being deadly serious. Being able to tease was one of the ways he relieved the tension that built up within him while working, whether flying or prepping for a mission.

And being able to do that with Laryn while making love to her? He'd never felt more complete.

He'd be an idiot to let her slip through his fingers without at least trying to make things between them work. Life as the partner of a military man wasn't easy. But she knew that very well, since she'd been a soldier herself and now worked as a contractor for the Army.

A small smile formed on his lips. His Laryn was stubborn. And tenacious. And her actions made him realize she hadn't been lying when she told him that she'd liked him for years.

On top of the guilt, Casper now felt a little sad that he'd wasted so much time, but again, he felt certain the time for them to be together was right now. If he'd noticed the little spitfire any earlier, things might not have worked out. And he was determined that they *would* work out. Now that he'd gotten to know the Laryn hidden beneath the large coveralls and a defensive attitude, he wasn't going back to the pilot-mechanic relationship they'd had before. No way in hell.

"Casper! You listening?" Chaos barked.

"Of course," he responded automatically, forcing himself to push away thoughts of the woman who'd taken up so much of his brain space recently. They wouldn't have any kind of relationship if he was dead. He needed to pay attention. He was the highest-ranking officer in their unit, he needed to get his shit together.

By the time all his meetings were finished, and he and his team were cleared to leave, it was closing in on ten o'clock. They'd been immersed in maps and intel all day. Everyone decided that their usual going-out-before-deployment was regrettably unrealistic. It was too late, for one, and everyone was exhausted. They all needed to be back at the base at oh-three-hundred—a mere five hours—to head overseas.

All Casper knew was that *he* was headed for Laryn's apartment. He'd managed to text her once during the day to check in, and it had taken her an hour to respond, probably because she was just as busy as he was with everything she needed to do before they left.

No one said much as they left the conference room they'd been hunkered down in and headed down the empty, dimly lit hall.

As Casper and his team dispersed toward their vehicles in the parking lot, he was focused on finding which pocket he'd stashed his keys. His head was down, and for once he wasn't on high alert for danger. Which was why, when he finally grabbed his keys and looked up, he stumbled at the sight of someone leaning against his Taurus.

Not someone. Laryn.

"Hey," she said softly. She was wearing the coveralls he'd

gotten so used to seeing her in, but now, instead of overlooking the fact there was a very sexy and curvy woman underneath the practical and manly outfit, his mouth watered, thinking about the secrets that only he knew. How she probably wore only panties and a tank top under that outfit. How she liked her nipples sucked to the point of pain. How she trembled and shook right before she came. How tight and wet her pussy felt wrapped around his cock.

"Tate?" she asked, straightening and looking concerned.

"Sorry. Long day," he said, which wasn't a lie. He wasn't sure she'd appreciate knowing the thoughts running through his head every time he saw her now.

"Yeah. I went home and when I didn't hear from you, I called one of the guys I know on night duty, and he said that you and the others hadn't left yet. Instead of texting, I figured I'd come in person to see if you were too tired and wanted a ride."

Oh, he wanted a ride all right.

Shit. He had to stop thinking about sex when he was around her. Yes, she was sexy as hell, but she was so much more than that. Considerate, kind, thoughtful.

"Tate? Are you all right?"

He sighed and ran a hand through his hair. "Yeah. Can't seem to concentrate. My brain is stuffed full of everything we went over today. I'd love a ride. But I need to stop at my place to pack before we head to yours."

"Um, well...about that. I figured since you hadn't been home in a couple of days, and that it's likely if Altan *is* a threat—that's still a big if, by the way—he wouldn't know about you and me, or where you live. So I went ahead and packed what I need for deployment. It's in my trunk. If it's okay with you, if you want... wouldn't mind...maybe I can go back to your place tonight? You can pack, then we can see if we can get any sleep before we have to come back for our flight."

Good Lord, this woman. She was two steps ahead of him,

something he was grateful for. Casper took a giant step forward and took her face in his hands. He leaned down and kissed her the way he'd been thinking of doing between briefings all day.

To his gratification and satisfaction, she latched onto his wrists with a firm grip and gave as good as she got. Laryn was no shy teenager, she was a woman who knew what she wanted, and Casper was the lucky son-of-a-bitch she seemed to want.

Aware of the ticking of the clock, he pulled back but kept his hold on her.

"I take it that's okay with you?" she asked with a smile.

"That's more than all right with me," he reassured her. "I can't wait to see you in my bed. Your hair strewn on my pillow. Your vanilla cookie scent permeating my sheets. Please tell me you brought some of that shower soap or lotion with you."

She rolled her eyes at him. "I did."

"Thank fuck. You want to drive my car?"

"Okay. But are you sure?"

"Yeah. Why?"

"Because you're you. The hotshot pilot. The guy who wants to be in control at all times."

"You've already driven my car, Laryn. Besides, you're right. I'm beat. I can't think straight. And I trust you."

To his surprise—and horror—tears filled her eyes.

"What? What'd I say? Shit, Laryn, don't cry!"

"Sorry, sorry, sorry," she said, reaching up and dislodging his hands from her face as she frantically wiped under her eyes. "It's been a long day for me too. And I had visions of you coming to your senses and wondering what the hell you'd done last night and wanting to backpedal. Telling me that now wasn't a good time to date since we're being deployed. Or maybe that, since we work together, it wasn't a good idea at all."

"Fuck that. This is the best idea ever. And I *have* come to my senses...and opened my eyes to the beauty that's been in front of me for years. No backpedaling, Laryn. Unless you aren't sure about us."

"No!" she exclaimed, making Casper feel better. "I haven't changed my mind."

"Good. Thank you for thinking ahead and coming to get me. Assuming you're okay with leaving your car in the lot while we're gone?"

"Yeah."

"Good." Realizing his key ring was still dangling from his finger, he held out the keys to her. She took them with a small smile and headed toward her Civic, which she'd parked just a couple spots away. It took them seconds to grab the backpack and two duffel bags she'd brought and throw them into his trunk. The drive to his apartment didn't take long either, since, like Laryn, he'd chosen a small apartment complex not too far from the base. Because this was a military area, there were a lot of apartments available to accommodate the personnel who were constantly coming and going.

She expertly backed into a space, and Casper met her at the back of his car.

"You need the duffels?" he asked.

"No. Just the backpack. It's got my overnight things and clothes for the flight tomorrow."

Casper grabbed it and put it on a shoulder, then reached for her hand as if he'd done it every day for years. It felt natural.

After walking up to the third floor, he opened his apartment door and let Laryn enter first. He tried to see his place from her eyes, but had no idea what she'd think. He was a bachelor and his apartment reflected that. There weren't any homey touches, just his big television that he barely had time to watch, lots of clutter on the kitchen counter, shoes on the floor, books he'd half read strewn about the room. But it was clean. If there was one thing he'd learned from being in the Army, it was the importance of bleach in his life.

"So?" he asked.

She looked at him and shrugged. "It's an apartment. You hungry? I've already eaten, but I can find something to make for you real fast while you pack...if you want."

"Sounds perfect. I've got some leftover taco stuff from the other night. The lettuce might be brown, but the cheese, tomatoes, sour cream, and meat should still be fine. Besides, it needs to be eaten or thrown away since we're leaving."

"On it," she said, putting her backpack on the floor.

"And feel free to get rid of anything in the fridge that won't survive the couple weeks we're gone."

"Will do," she said, walking toward his galley kitchen. The apartment was set up much like hers. Galley kitchen, living area, hallway with the two bedrooms and one bathroom.

Casper watched Laryn make herself at home in his place and realized he didn't feel the slightest bit uncomfortable having her there. The few times he'd brought other women home, he'd been a little on edge, hoping they didn't read anything into being there. Feeling uncomfortable when they touched his stuff, inspected his kitchen.

But with Laryn, he *wanted* her to touch. To make herself comfortable. To rifle through his things.

Reaching down, he picked up her backpack before heading for his room. He took a moment to soak in the sight of her bag on his bed. It was pathetic, to be so happy about seeing her things in his personal space.

Closing his eyes, he wondered if this was what Nate had felt the first time he'd seen Josie. Of course, their situation was much different than his and Laryn's. His twin and Josie had been prisoners of war in a shithole of an Iranian prison. But that feeling of knowing deep in his gut that Laryn was meant to be his...was that what Nate felt, why he'd called Josie "his woman" so soon after meeting her?

It had taken Casper a lot longer, but now that he'd opened

himself up to the possibility of a relationship, he was all in. And it felt right.

Shaking his head, he spun around and headed for his walk-in closet. It was one of the reasons he'd chosen this specific apartment, because the closet in the main bedroom was huge. He had a lot of flight suits he kept impeccably ironed and carefully hung. He'd needed the space to store them all, plus his boots and other flight gear.

Now, as he looked around the closet, his brain was mentally rearranging the space to make room for Laryn's stuff.

Laughing at the way he was getting ahead of himself and realizing exactly how tired he was, Casper got to work packing his own duffel bags for deployment. The scent of spicy taco meat began to waft into his room as he worked, and once again he felt warmth spread through him. It had been a very long time since anyone had taken care of him the way Laryn was. It felt good. Really damn good. He would never take her for granted. And he vowed to return the favor tenfold. If anyone deserved to be taken care of, it was Laryn Hardy.

* * *

Laryn had taken a chance with packing her bags for deployment and driving to base to wait for Tate to get out of his meetings. But thankfully, that chance had worked out. She was in Tate's apartment, his kitchen, making him dinner before they'd crash for a few hours.

It made her mind spin to think of how she'd gotten here. And the thing was, she had no idea what she'd actually done to finally make the man of her dreams notice her. But she wasn't going to question it. She was going to enjoy their time together for as long as it lasted.

Because she still wasn't convinced this would be a long-term relationship, no matter how badly she wanted that. The sex was out of this world, and Tate was thoughtful and kind. But would that change once the threat he thought she might be under was mitigated? Once they returned from deployment and things got back to "normal," whatever that was?

She had no idea, so in the meantime, she was going to enjoy whatever stolen moments she had with Tate. And part of that enjoyment was taking care of him. Long ago, she used to cook for her father, and it satisfied a need deep inside her to nurture. He'd taught her everything he knew, looked after her, protected her, was her champion, and she'd done what she could to make sure he understood how much she loved him for it.

Now she'd do the same for Tate. He was exhausted, and he needed to be alert and ready for whatever mission he might be sent on as soon as they landed. She'd already made sure his chopper was in tip-top shape, and now she had a chance to make sure his body was ready as well. She could feed him, take away some of the everyday burdens he had, like going through his fridge to get rid of anything that might grow legs and try to walk off while he was gone.

She smiled at the thought as she grabbed the remainder of an open block of cheese and a few bell peppers that definitely wouldn't survive being in the fridge for a few weeks.

"What's that smile for?"

Laryn nearly jumped out of her skin at the sound of Tate's voice right behind her.

"Jeez! Don't do that! You scared the crap out of me! Why are you walking around like Mr. Silent, anyway?"

He chuckled. "I made plenty of noise. You were just too engrossed studying my vegetables to notice."

The words popped out before she could stop them. "I like inspecting your vegetables," and her gaze flicked down his body toward his crotch.

He laughed even harder and grabbed her around the waist, spinning her around. Before Laryn knew what was happening, he'd picked her up as if she weighed nothing and plunked her on top of the counter. He crowded closer, between her legs, and rested his hands on her hips. They were eye to eye now, and Laryn could see dark circles that weren't usually there, and the lines around his eyes were more prominent than they'd been that morning.

His hands started to roam, and as much as she craved him, as much as she wanted him, the clock was ticking and they both needed sleep.

She grabbed his hands and shook her head. She tried to look as stern as possible, all while knowing her heart rate had picked up and her panties were getting damp thinking about all the things he'd done to her already.

"Food," she said. "Then sleep. We don't have time for kitchen hanky-panky. Did you finish packing?"

"Yes, ma'am," he said with a small grin. "Duffels are by the door, ready to go."

"Good."

Neither moved as they stared at each other. Then Tate spoke. "I want you. But I'm dead on my feet."

"I know."

"I know you know, I'm just trying to tell you, badly, thank you for being you. For picking me up, for making dinner. For not letting me do things I want to do so badly, but wouldn't be smart. Like eating you out right here on my counter. Then turning you around and bending you over my couch and taking you from behind."

Laryn swallowed hard and couldn't stop herself from glancing toward his couch. It was way too high for her feet to be on the floor if she was draped over the back of it. And thinking about having no leverage, no control over their lovemaking while he took her from behind, was almost enough to rip off the T-shirt Tate had put on and say to hell with her plans for them both to get as much sleep as possible.

"Damn, I love that look in your eyes," Tate said. Then he leaned his forehead against hers. "Rain check. I want to make love to you on every surface of this apartment. The shower, here on the counter, the couch, the desk in my spare room, and my bed. Especially my bed. But we have all the time in the world for that. I'm looking forward to simply holding you as we sleep almost as much. Almost."

Laryn let out a huff of breath. "Yeah."

He still didn't move. His eyes were closed as his forehead stayed on hers.

"Tate? Did you fall asleep?" she whispered after a long moment.

"No. Yes. Maybe."

That made her smile again. "Food. You need to eat."

"Yeah," he sighed and reluctantly straightened. "Thank you, Laryn. Seriously."

"You're welcome. Scoot back so I can get down."

Instead of moving, he tightened his hold and lifted her from the counter to the floor.

"Want to give me some room here?" Laryn asked again, as he stayed plastered to her side.

"Nope."

She rolled her eyes but, deep down, she loved having him so near. She managed to dish up the taco salad she'd prepared for him and, by unspoken agreement, they both stood in his small kitchen while he ate leaning up against the counter. It didn't take long. He was either hungry or more than ready to go to bed. Probably a little of both.

"Go get ready for bed. I'll be there in a moment. I just want to wash the dishes and put them away," Laryn ordered.

"Leave them."

"No way. Not when we're leaving for who knows how long."

"Fine. But if you're not in my bed in five minutes, I'm coming to find you."

"Promise?"

To Laryn's surprise, the expression on his face wasn't teasing. He stared at her with a look so intense, it took her breath away. "I'll always come for you, Laryn. Now that I've seen what I've been missing, I'm planning on making up for lost time."

"Tate," she whispered.

"Five minutes," he repeated, then turned and headed for the front door. He double-checked the lock, then did the same to the locks on the windows.

She realized he probably did that every night. It was a little OCD, but she didn't mind. As a single woman, she did her part to follow as many safety protocols as possible herself.

Laryn's rush job on the dishes wouldn't impress anyone, but she was eager to see Tate's bedroom, his bed. She'd imagined it in her head for so long, she wondered if it would live up to her fantasies.

She noticed for the first time that her backpack wasn't on the floor where she'd left it, and she smiled as she headed down the hall. Peeking into the bathroom, she saw her bag there on the counter. Knowing her five minutes had more than passed, she rushed through getting ready for bed, changing into her shortie shorts and tank top she liked to sleep in. She wasn't sure how tonight would go, if Tate would keep his hands to himself or if *she* would. It seemed whenever they were near each other, especially in a bed, it was almost impossible to keep from touching.

Taking a deep breath, and trying not to feel ridiculous for the few extra seconds she took to smooth some of her cookie lotion on her legs and arms—and even her boobs—she made her way to the main bedroom. Tate had left a small lamp on to one side of the bed, and everything else was in shadow when she walked in.

The bed was a king, which she wasn't surprised about. It took up quite a bit of the floor space. There was a dresser, taller than it was wide, with a couple framed pictures on top. A large window with dark curtains, which had been pulled closed, an open door that led to what looked like a huge closet, and that was about it.

After the cursory look around, her gaze was drawn back to the bed, and the man on it. Tate had gotten under the covers and they were pulled up to his waist. His chest was bare, and she wondered if he was wearing any pants or underwear. His eyes were closed and it was obvious he was fast asleep.

Her heart turned in her chest. He was so exhausted, he couldn't even wait five minutes for her to come to bed. She had no doubt he'd probably had plans for her when she got there, despite their earlier talk. Even if she'd claimed they both needed sleep, she couldn't help but guess he wouldn't be able to hold back once they were in bed.

Honestly, she was a little disappointed, but no way in hell was she going to wake the man. The lives of who knew how many SEALs and Deltas relied on Tate being at the top of his game when he got behind the controls of his chopper. And that included being caught up on his sleep.

Stepping forward on silent feet, Laryn clicked off the light on his side of the bed. He didn't even stir. She walked around the bed and slowly, carefully climbed onto the mattress. She wanted to moan at how perfect it was. Not too hard or soft. It was literally exactly the kind of mattress she preferred.

She could've stayed on one side of the bed, it was literally big enough that they didn't have to touch when they slept. But she wasn't that strong.

Scooting closer, Laryn gently pressed herself against Tate, smiling when she realized he was wearing a pair of boxer shorts. It was funny, because so far she'd only known him as a briefs man. She figured they gave him more support when he was wearing his flight suit.

It felt extremely intimate to learn the underwear preferences of the man she'd crushed on forever, but also very satisfying. As she slowly lay her head on his chest, he stirred. Moving his arm so it was around her and holding her against him tightly.

"Sorry," he mumbled. "So tired."

"Shhhhhh. Sleep," she murmured.

He sighed deeply, then stilled.

Laryn smiled against his shoulder and closed her eyes. She'd never been a good sleeper. She jerked at every little noise, worried about people breaking in, thought about things she should've done during the day...wondered what Tate was doing. But at that moment, she had no thoughts in her head other than how comfortable she was and how safe she felt.

She was obviously just as tired as Tate, because she fell asleep in minutes, more content than she'd been in a very long time.

CHAPTER FOURTEEN

Casper woke up with his belly growling. Turning his head, he saw it was two-seventeen in the morning. Thirteen minutes before his alarm was set to go off. He'd managed to set it before he basically passed out.

The reason he woke up hungry was obvious.

Laryn.

And her cookie lotion.

He smiled and closed his eyes once more, enjoying the moment. He'd meant to stay awake until she came into his room. He couldn't wait to see her in his bed for the first time. He'd planned, despite his words to the contrary, to eat her to an orgasm, then hold her as she fell asleep against him.

His damn exhaustion had claimed him before he could put his plans into action. But he had to admit there was something so calming about holding Laryn as she slept. Even in sleep, she clung to him. It made him feel ten feet tall.

He dozed for the thirteen minutes until his alarm went off.

Laryn stirred in his arms and groaned when she realized it was time to get up.

"Hi," he said quietly after he'd shut off the annoying buzzer from his phone.

"Hi," she returned.

There was so much Casper wanted to say. To do. But they didn't have time. And things were still very new between them. So he simply kissed her forehead and said, "I'll be done in the bathroom in a few minutes. I'll make coffee to go while you shower, if that's okay."

"That's perfect. Thank you."

Reluctantly, Casper scooted out from under her and the covers and stood. Then he turned and placed his palms on the mattress and leaned down. "Best night's sleep ever," he whispered, before kissing her lightly on the lips.

He left before he did more than that, before he gave in to the urgent feeling deep inside him to claim this woman. There wasn't time, and he didn't want to rush their first time in his bed. It was a stupid thing to think because they'd already made love, but this was his space. His domain. And it felt different to be with her here. More real for him, somehow.

Which didn't make sense, considering things between them already felt as real as they could get.

Mentally shrugging, assuming it was a guy thing, he hurried to shower and do what he needed to do in the bathroom so he could turn it over to Laryn and get some much-needed coffee made for them both.

One thing was for sure, he felt different waking up with her by his side. The day didn't seem so mundane. So routine. Everything felt special with her there. The possibilities for the day seemed endless. It was a euphoric feeling. One he liked a hell of a lot.

* * *

That euphoria didn't last very long. Only until he and Laryn parted ways when they arrived at the base. She had to go make sure last-minute preparations for departure were done on her end. To check on the mechanics who were making the trip with her. And he had to meet his team and attend one last briefing about the situation they'd be flying into.

The plane ride across the world was frustrating. He and his friends were seated in one area of the plane, and Laryn and the men and women who worked for her in a different area. That was how it had always been in the past, but now the seating arrangements irritated Casper.

They landed and had to be shuttled to the destroyer, and Casper was able to finagle a seat next to her in the chopper. He pressed his thigh against hers but didn't dare do anything more that might make her uncomfortable around their teams.

It was the smile she aimed his way that warmed his heart though. While she was definitely in professional mode, as was he, it felt good anytime they shared an intimate look.

As soon as they landed on the deck of the destroyer, they went their separate ways once more. Him to check in with the other pilots onboard and to meet with the special forces teams about the situation on the ground, and her to check on the choppers, which had arrived before them.

Hours later, Casper was feeling jet lag and the little sleep he'd managed to get before leaving the States. He was also hangry, and he wanted to check in with Laryn and see how she was getting on.

"Where's the fire?" Pyro asked, as he and Casper strode down the corridor toward the mess hall.

"You aren't hungry?" Casper asked, instead of answering his question.

"Starving. But since I'm not holding my breath that what they've got cooking in the galley is anything worth busting my ass to get to, I can wait the extra thirty seconds it'll take to get to the mess hall and have it served up. Let me guess...Laryn?"

Casper shrugged, unwilling to pretend she wasn't important to him. That things hadn't changed between them. "Yeah. Just want to know how her day went and how the birds look."

"I'm sure they're fine. With Laryn in charge, how could they be anything but?"

His friend had a good point.

"This is serious, right? You aren't just fucking with her, literally or figuratively?" Pyro asked nonchalantly. "I mean, it would suck to lose her because you can't keep your dick in your pants."

Pyro wasn't denigrating Laryn, but it was still difficult to stay calm. "It's serious," he told him.

"Cool. I like her."

Casper gave him a sideways glance.

"Not like that," Pyro was quick to reassure him with a chuckle. "Jeez. Things got serious between you two pretty fast, huh?"

He nodded. "Let's just say I got my head out of my ass and opened my eyes to what was right in front of my face. I'm grateful no one else caught her eye while I was being a dumbass."

Pyro laughed and smacked his shoulder. "She's good for you, I think. The guys and I have always wondered why you two sniped at each other so much, and it makes sense now."

"What does?"

"You liked her. Even when you were teasing her. Maybe you thought you shouldn't go there, or that she was too good for you, or some other bullshit reason to stay away. So you told yourself that you weren't attracted to her. But you still couldn't resist getting under her skin anytime you had the chance."

"What are you, a psychologist now?" Casper grumbled, secretly thinking his friend was right.

"Naw. Just a guy who sees things."

"I wish you'd have seen this one coming so it didn't take me so long to let her know I wanted to take her out."

Pyro chuckled again.

They reached the mess hall, and Casper looked around eagerly when they entered. To his disappointment, he didn't see Laryn anywhere. He and Pyro went through the line and loaded their trays before sitting at a large table. It didn't take long for Buck, Obi-Wan, Chaos, and Edge to join them. Just when Casper had given up on seeing Laryn, she walked into the huge room.

He was on his feet before he even realized he'd moved.

She looked as tired as he felt.

"Hey," he said as he approached.

When she realized it was him, she smiled, and it transformed her face. How he'd never noticed how pretty his mechanic was, or acknowledged it at least, he had no clue.

"Hi," she returned.

"Everything all right?" he asked, accompanying her to the line for food.

Instead of answering, she raised a brow and asked, "You don't think I can carry my tray all by myself? Or are you getting seconds?"

Casper felt himself blushing, and he shrugged. "Just wanted to see you. Talk to you. It's been a while."

"Oh. And it hasn't been *that* long. Not really."

Casper made a point of looking at his watch, then said, "Six hours, fourteen minutes, and forty-three seconds."

She chuckled. "That long, huh?"

"Yup. You had a chance to check out your berth yet?"

She gave him an incredulous look.

"Right, sorry. You were elbow deep in the guts of my chopper, I'm guessing?"

"Yours and the others. I wanted to make sure your MH-60 made the trip all right—which she did—and the other two choppers were still up to par. You guys still heading out in the morning?" She started down the food line, grabbing a little of everything and piling her tray high.

"Yeah. For a reconnaissance flight. Get the lay of the land, so to speak. Then we'll head back here, debrief, get some sleep, and head out on our first mission tomorrow right after the sun goes down."

Laryn nodded.

Casper grabbed a water for her and gestured toward his team's table.

She sat down and smiled at everyone. "Hey."

"Hi."

"Yo."

"All settled in?"

She chuckled at that. "As settled as I'll get, I guess. You guys?"

Everyone agreed.

Laryn ate quickly, which Casper assumed was because, like him and his fellow pilots, she could get called away for an emergency at any time. Really, when they were onboard a ship, they were all on call 24/7.

Talk at the table turned to the choppers she maintained, and Laryn reassured everyone that things looked good for both the morning flight and the actual missions they'd be going on the next evening.

"You done for the night?" Casper asked. "With maintenance, I mean."

"Yeah. Unless I get paged."

"Shall we go find our berths?"

She gave him a side eye. "If that was code for hanky-panky, I'm thinking...no."

Everyone at the table laughed.

Laryn's cheeks were pink, but she met Casper's gaze without backing down.

"No funny business. This isn't the time or place. But I do want to make sure you've got everything you need and that we know where you are...just in case."

She tilted her head and stared at him without blinking for a long moment. Then she said, "You really were serious about things being different."

"Definitely," Casper told her with a firm nod.

"I'm good. I have everything I need," she said.

"Give it up," Chaos said. "When Casper gets something in his head, there's no convincing him otherwise. If the man wants to make sure you're settled in and don't have a bunk on the bottom level of the ship, where it stinks like fuel and is noisy as hell, you should let him."

"Wait—you can get me moved if I'm under the water line?" Laryn asked. "Why didn't you say so? Let's go!" She smiled to let everyone know she was joking.

But he figured there was probably an ounce of honesty in her words.

Buck reached over and grabbed her now-empty tray and stacked it on top of the other six trays in his hand. He carried them over to the bins, where he threw away their trash, then put the trays on the belt to go into the kitchen to be cleaned.

Casper's fingers itched to grab hold of Laryn's hand as they all stood to head out, but he refrained. Instead, he leaned close to her as they walked and said softly, "Long day, huh?"

She nodded as she looked up at him. "Yeah."

"Did all your equipment make it all right?"

"Uh-huh. How were your meetings?"

"Long. But informative. The mission will be tough, but nowhere near the most difficult we've had. It'll be fun to fly at night through the mountain passes."

Laryn rolled her eyes. "Fun. Yeah, right. You're a weirdo."

Casper merely smiled. "Takes one to know one."

She huffed out a breath of laughter. "That's mature."

Casper was having fun already. Maybe that was why he'd needled this woman so much in the past. One, because she never seemed to take offense to his teasing, and two, because he loved seeing her exasperated responses.

"What's your berth number?" Casper asked.

"Four A."

"We're twenty-six A and B. We've got three-man berths."

Laryn smiled at that. "I think I'm in a berth with twenty-three other women."

Casper frowned. "You should have more privacy than that."

"No, I shouldn't. First, I'm not an officer. Second, I'm only here temporarily. I would never want to take a room away from someone who lives onboard for months or years at a time. It's fine, Tate."

"Maybe you can sneak up to my berth and sleep in my rack with me."

She flat-out laughed at that. "You do remember how big these racks are, right?" she asked. "They're tiny. Barely enough for me to roll over and not touch the bed above me. You might have more room since you're a hotshot pilot, but I'm guessing not *that* much more."

She was right. Damn it.

"I still don't like it."

Laryn stopped and looked both ways in the corridor. The other pilots had peeled off to head to the floor where they were bunking down. Seeing no one, she stepped into Casper and put her hands on his chest and went up on her tiptoes. She kissed him hard and fast before stepping back.

Casper's hands shot out and gripped her hips, but he didn't haul her back into him like he wanted to. There was no telling when someone would come down the corridor. He didn't want any rumors to start about him and his mechanic. Not because he cared, but because he'd never do anything that might hurt her career or cause people to gossip about her.

"What was that for?" he asked.

"For everything. For letting me eat with you. I usually find an empty table or one without many people. For wanting me to have a private room, even if it's never going to happen. For wanting to be with me."

"When we have more time before a deployment, I'll see what I can do about getting you in a berth closer to me and the guys. And maybe we can plan time to eat in the mornings and at lunch, so you don't have to eat by yourself."

"I'd like that."

Casper wished he had his phone on him so he could take a snapshot of the shy smile Laryn was giving him. He wanted to be able to see it whenever he needed a pick-me-up. It was almost scary how fast this woman had gotten under his skin and into his heart.

"Come on, let's go find where I'm staying so I can make sure my stuff was delivered," Laryn said

Casper's fingers brushed the small of her back and he wished he could keep them there, but he dropped his hand and followed closely behind Laryn as she made her way down the corridors to her berth. When they arrived, he waited while she entered, and she reappeared thirty seconds later.

"All good?" he asked.

"All good. My stuff is there and my rack is on the bottom, which I prefer."

"I'm glad."

"Me too. So...what time for breakfast?"

Thinking about his schedule for tomorrow's morning flight, Casper said, "It's going to have to be early. Maybe meeting up tomorrow wasn't the best idea."

"It's okay. I need to get up and get to the helo hangar anyway, you know that. If you're up, I'm up."

"True. Okay, oh-five-hundred?"

"Perfect."

They stood there for a moment, simply staring at each other.

"I want to kiss you," Casper said softly.

"I want that too. But...probably not a good idea."

She was right, but that didn't mean Casper liked it. "If you need anything—I mean, *anything*—come up to my berth. You won't disturb me or anyone else. Okay?"

Laryn nodded. "It's dumb but...this is hard. I know it was only two nights, but I got used to having you around."

"Same," Casper said, amazed that he knew exactly how she was feeling.

"Sleep well. You need to be rested for tomorrow's reconnaissance flight, then the mission tomorrow night."

"I will. You too. Don't need my mechanic screwing up any easy shit, like not checking oil levels because she was up all night, dreaming of her hunky pilot."

Laryn burst out laughing and rolled her eyes as she shook her head. "Not conceited at all, are you?"

"Nope. Not at all."

They stood there for a beat before Casper forced his feet to move away from her. "See you at the mess hall in the morning."

"Yeah."

He turned and headed back the way he came, feeling a hole in his gut at walking away. Truthfully, he didn't like the feeling. It made him question what the hell he was getting himself into for a split second. Then he shook off the thought. Would he rather go back to being alone and not having stomach pangs and feelings of uneasiness...or deal with working with the woman he was sleeping with, who made him laugh and had his back at all times?

It was an easy decision.

Learning how to be romantic partners with someone he worked with was going to take some time, but Casper was ready for the challenge.

* * *

"Tomorrow night? Perfect. I've got people ready to intercept," Altan said, satisfaction heavy in his tone. "How're you going to get her into that chopper?"

He listened as the man on the other end of the line explained what he'd done.

"There's no guarantee it'll work, but I've got some ideas to make the situation even more urgent. To make it seem like they have to take off immediately or be grounded. Guarantee those hotshot pilots won't want that. And from what I've learned of the mechanic, she won't let them leave without knowing exactly what's wrong with her precious chopper."

"This needs to work," Altan threatened.

"And like I said, there's no guarantee. It's not exactly easy to get a fucking mechanic off this ship, especially to get her inserted into the middle of a top-secret mission. You should be thanking me, not threatening me," the man growled.

Altan did his best to rein in his temper. He needed to get his hands on Laryn Hardy, and he had no choice but to depend on others to make it happen. Yes, he could wait until she was back on US soil and get one of his contacts in the Norfolk area to break into her apartment and spirit her away, but then he'd need to get her *off* US soil, which was even more difficult than getting her off that destroyer.

No, if he could get his hands on her while she was in his territory, he'd have more support from his government. After all, entering the country without proper documentation or permission would mean he could brand her a spy. Keep her under lock and key, force her to use her expertise on their newly acquired MH-60s.

Her being on that chopper when it went into the mountains to retrieve the soldiers nosing around, looking for assholes hiding in the nooks and crannies, was paramount.

Altan didn't give a shit about ISIS. They were more annoying than anything else. The ragtag group of men and boys in the mountains would be dealt with later. And hell, if America wanted to come in and take care of them for his country, that was more than all right by him.

His only concern was Laryn. In order to increase their military strength and defend their territory, he needed the knowledge she had in her head. She'd share that with his people or die. He'd make sure of it.

"Let me know how it goes down," Altan ordered.

"I'll be in touch when I can. Not sure when that'll be, as my ass will probably get chewed out for this stunt I'm about to pull. The money you promised better be in my account by tomorrow morning."

"It will be. And don't fucking threaten me again," Altan said, before severing the connection.

He sat back in his chair and pressed his fingertips together under his chin. This had to work. It just had to. He needed that American bitch. It wasn't even natural that she was a mechanic. She should be home having babies and serving a man. But the fact that the best MH-60 technician in the world was a female would hopefully make her easier to break.

"Come to papa," he whispered, before reaching for the phone once more. He needed to make sure the men he had in place on the ground were ready. It was going to take quite a few people to move Laryn from the mountains to his facility. Hopefully during that time, she'd figure out that her best option was to do whatever she was told, as soon as she was told to do it.

If she was cowed and broken by the time she arrived at his doorstep, all the better.

Feeling hopeful, Altan dialed a number and waited impatiently for his contact on the other end to pick up.

CHAPTER FIFTEEN

Laryn watched carefully as the MH-60s Tate and his fellow Night Stalkers would be flying to pick up a group of Navy SEALs were moved to the top deck of the destroyer. She didn't know what the special forces troop was doing in the mountains, and she didn't want to know. All she cared about was making sure the helicopters were in proper working order and that nothing went wrong while Tate and his team were doing what they did best.

She'd seen videos of some of the things the Night Stalkers put their choppers through, and they made her heart lodge in her throat. The places they were able to go, the risks they took, it was terrifying. But watching those videos made her all the more determined to give them the proper tools to do their job. That's how she looked at what she did. She was a tool in their arsenal, nothing more, nothing less.

The area around her was a hub of activity, with mechanics and sailors moving here and there and calling out to each other. But all of Laryn's attention was on the three helicopters that had been used earlier for the reconnaissance flights and then stored back below decks until now. She wanted to make sure nothing happened to them as they were moved. This was nothing she hadn't seen or done hundreds of times before. But it was one of the most crucial last steps. The last thing she wanted was one of the rotor blades brushing against the side of the hold as a chopper was raised.

The flight that morning had been uneventful, at least according to Tate. He and the other Night Stalkers had gotten some good intel about the terrain they couldn't get from simply looking at maps and charts.

They'd all been pretty amped up at the late lunch they'd shared. Laryn loved that she was included in their group now. It might have been her imagination, but she also could've sworn that she was treated differently this deployment by the other sailors around her, as well. Night Stalkers had an impressive reputation, and it appeared that being in their inner circle made her more than a simple mechanic.

She should be irritated at the revelation, but she wasn't stupid. She knew how the world worked. Blue-collar workers weren't held in as high esteem as their white-collar colleagues. But when push came to shove, they were probably more valuable. There was a huge shortage of all kinds of blue-collar labor in the US. Positions no one wanted to do but were needed desperately. Linemen, plumbers, carpenters, welders, truck drivers, and so many more.

One of the sailors working in the area brushed against her, making Laryn jump. She was on edge; she always was when Tate was about to head off on a mission. She'd always managed to keep her feelings to herself, but she wasn't sure how she'd be able to keep from showing her concern this time.

It was different now. Much more personal. She'd gotten even closer to Tate, and the thought of anything happening to him made her want to puke. She had a feeling she was being extra abrupt and short with anyone who tried to talk to her, but that was the only way she could keep a handle on herself.

Making her way to the top deck for last-minute inspections,

Laryn purposely kept her distance from Tate and the others. She was also getting to know his team on a more personal level, and that made watching them climb into their seats and fire up the engines harder, as well. Knowing they were about to put themselves in danger, and thought doing so was *fun*, was extremely distressing. But they were professionals, as was she.

As if she could feel Tate's gaze upon her, she lifted her chin to look through the glass behind which he was sitting.

He gave her a small smile and a thumbs-up. With a shaky hand, she returned the gesture, praying harder than she ever had before that he'd return safe and sound.

The pilots started their engines and the rotor blades began to turn.

Then shit went sideways.

She could see Tate and Pyro having an intense conversation, complete with hand gestures. Then someone on the flight deck yelled her name and motioned for her to move closer to Tate's chopper.

Frowning in concern, Laryn jogged over to the side of the machine. The man took off his headset and jammed it onto her head. Surprised—as *that* had never happened before—she heard Tate's voice in her ears.

"Laryn? Are you there?"

"I'm here," she said into the mic in front of her mouth.

"There's a fucking light on. The FLIR. It's flickering. Why is it fucking flickering?"

Laryn was shocked. The Forward-Looking Infrared light should definitely not be flickering. It was working perfectly both before and after their flight that morning. And they could *not* go on this night mission without it. It allowed the pilots to essentially see in the dark.

"Incoming intel from boots on the ground. They're surrounded and need immediate extraction," another voice said through the headset.

"Damn it! Laryn, can you fix this or not?"

She could. And she would.

Turning to the man hovering next to her, she gestured for him to put his hands together to make a step for her. He looked confused but did as she ordered, and before she knew it, Laryn was inside the chopper. She hurried toward where Tate and Pyro were sitting and threw herself between them, reaching for the panel that protected most of the switches and wires that connected the multimillion-dollar electrical equipment used on the chopper.

She frantically searched for any kind of loose connection, praying it was a simple fix and the team could be on their way.

"My FLIR is out as well," Edge said through the headphones.

"Motherfucker," Pyro swore.

"I'm good," Buck added.

"Laryn?" Tate asked, amazingly sounding calmer than just a moment ago.

"There's a loose wire. I'm going to wrap it with some tape. That should fix it."

"Should?" a new voice asked through the headphones. "You have to go. *Right now*. If you don't get out there, those SEALs are as good as dead."

Laryn should've felt flustered or anxious. But her hands were steady as she reached into one of the pockets of her coveralls and pulled out a roll of electrical tape. She quickly wrapped the wire for the FLIR to another one to stabilize it. "Tate? Is it back?"

"Back," he said, relief and satisfaction in his tone.

Laryn hurried to put the panel on and backed out from between the two men. She turned to leave, but Tate's next words stopped her.

"It's off again. Shit—no, it's back. *Fuck*, what the hell is going on?"

"It's go or no-go time," the voice in her head said.

"Go!" Laryn impulsively yelled. She sat down in one of the seats in the back of the chopper and strapped herself in.

"Laryn, get out!" Tate ordered.

"You need me! If it goes out again, I can fix it," she told him, confidence in every word.

"No! You are not coming with us into a hot zone!"

"We have to go..." Buck urged.

"I'm grounded," Edge said.

"Fuck!" Tate swore again.

"Either take off now or you're grounded too," the voice said in her ear.

"Buck needs backup," Pyro said, looking over at Tate.

"*Fuck*," Tate growled one more time—then Laryn felt the chopper lurch as he began to rise in the air.

What the hell was she doing? Laryn wasn't sure, but there was no way Tate and Pyro could fly without the FLIR working properly. And if it went out again when they were in the air, they were in big trouble. She couldn't do a complete workup while the machine was in use, but if it was something as simple as a loose connection, or even a blown fuse, *that* she could easily deal with while on the move.

The man who'd been yelling at them to "go go go!" was giving coordinates through the headset and updating both teams of pilots—and her at the same time—on the condition of the SEALs on the ground.

It didn't sound good. They'd been ambushed and were running low on ammunition. It was going to be extremely dangerous to pick them up and not get shot down in the process. Laryn understood that, but strangely, because she was watching Pyro and Tate work together to fly the MH-60 she'd spent so much time on, and hearing them communicate with Buck and Obi-Wan on how to approach the area, she felt much calmer than if she'd still been on the ship, waiting and hoping everything went all right.

From what she understood, Tate and Pyro were going to provide cover for Buck and Obi-Wan. The other chopper would land and pick up the SEALs. They'd hopefully be in the air before anyone on the ground could get close...or could use an RPG to disable either chopper.

The plan was risky, but the firepower from the MH-60 would hopefully convince the operatives on the ground to back off, that they were outgunned.

There was no chance to talk to Tate without anyone and everyone on the headset hearing, but he did turn around and gave her a long, intense stare Laryn couldn't interpret. She thought she saw anger, but she also saw a hell of a lot of concern in his blue eyes.

She nodded at him, trying to tell him that she would remain right where she was. That she would stay out of the way and only get up if something happened to the chopper. But she wasn't sure she was successful in conveying everything she wanted to say with a simple look. She had a feeling Tate was going to have lots of words for her when they arrived back at the ship.

The back of the chopper was pitch black as they flew as fast as they could toward the coordinates where the SEALs would be waiting for extraction. Laryn couldn't see anything out the front of the chopper, and it wasn't as if there was a window she could roll down. Not that she'd be able to see anything anyway, as she doubted the mountains had many lights.

She trained her gaze on the instrument panel instead. She couldn't see all of the dash from where she was sitting, but she could see that damn FLIR indicator light. And when it started flickering again, she saw the moment it happened. She didn't need Pyro's tense "Casper" to bring her attention to it.

Laryn immediately unstrapped herself and went to her knees, inching forward once again to get to that damn panel. This time she was going to check the fuses. She hoped like hell one was simply loose.

"Hold on," Tate called out just before he banked left.

Laryn's hand flew out and landed on his thigh as she held herself up.

As soon as they turned left, the chopper went back to the right. They were weaving all over the sky. It was exciting, but also scary as hell, and Laryn had a momentary pang of regret. What the hell was she doing here again? Oh yeah, if she didn't make sure the night-vision technology worked, they were all doomed. As were the brave men on the ground.

Determination welled inside her, and Laryn focused on what she was doing. Leaning closer, she took out the small penlight she always carried. Being careful to cover most of the beam so it didn't blind the two pilots using their headsets with night-vision, she used it to examine the small fuses.

Bingo. There was one that was barely attached. Reaching forward, Laryn pushed it in, satisfaction settling in her gut as it sank home. Looking up, she saw the light that had been flickering was now once more shining steadily.

Slamming the panel door back on for the second time, she scooted backward toward the seat she'd vacated.

The sound of gunfire was extremely loud all around her, despite the headphones.

The entire chopper vibrated as Tate and Pyro fought the ISIS operatives on the ground.

Laryn was glad now that she couldn't see what was happening. This was freaking scary. And even though she was glad she was there to help fix the FLIR, she wished she could wiggle her nose and be back on the ship, safe and sound, even if she'd be worrying about the fate of her pilots. Especially Tate.

"Three o'clock!" Pyro exclaimed.

"I see 'em!" Tate said as he banked hard to the right.

The vibrations and noise from the missiles they were firing made Laryn hunker down next to the nearest seat. She hadn't been able to get back into hers with the way Tate was flying. It was all she could do to hold on and not go flying across the wide empty space behind the pilot's seats.

"Going in for extraction." Laryn heard Buck say.

"We've got your six," Pyro assured him.

Several tense moments went by as Tate and Pyro continued to fly around the area and shoot at what she could only assume were enemy forces on the ground.

"Problem," Obi-Wan said. "We've got two SEALs missing. They were injured and weren't able to make the pickup. They're almost a klick to the east."

"We've got 'em," Tate said immediately.

"We can't stay. Got two men bleeding out," Buck informed them.

"Go! We'll get 'em and be on your heels," Tate ordered, turning the chopper toward what Laryn assumed was the east.

She held her breath. This was almost done. All they had to do was pick up the last two injured men and they'd be headed back to the ship. She had a feeling this little jaunt wasn't exactly going to make waiting on the ship during future missions any easier. Having firsthand experience about what they went through, what they did, would make her stress levels soar even higher.

"You see anything?" Tate asked Pyro.

"Nothing. Wait, there's a few heat signatures to the north of the LZ."

"We'll make a pass, see what kind of firepower they have."

Laryn held her breath as the chopper flew in what she presumed was a circle.

"Nothing. They're not firing."

"I don't like this," Tate said. "But we have to get those men."

"When we land, I'll get out and provide cover," Pyro said.

Get out? Laryn didn't like the sound of that...but it made sense. If the SEALs were injured and there were men nearby, probably hostiles, *someone* would have to make sure they kept their distance as the SEALs made their way toward the chopper.

But what if they couldn't walk? How would they get there?

Worry ate at her gut, but she kept her mouth shut. She wasn't the expert here. Yes, she'd gone through basic training, but that wasn't going to help in this situation. The best thing she could do was stay out of the way, let Pyro and Tate do their thing. They were trained for this.

"Here we go," Tate said as the chopper began to descend. Fast.

Just when Laryn thought they were going to slam into the ground, Tate pulled up slightly and she barely felt a bump as they landed.

"Go!" Tate said.

Pyro took off his headset and flew past where Laryn was huddled on the floor of the chopper. He slid the large side door back and disappeared into the darkness.

What seemed like minutes went by, but it was probably only seconds before she heard Pyro yelling.

Tate obviously heard him too, because he swore, then he was out of his seat. He didn't take time to explain what he was doing. He didn't need to; it was more than obvious he was going to help his friend and fellow pilot.

Before he left, he paused, taking time he most certainly didn't have to reach into the holster strapped to his thigh. He pulled out the firearm he kept there and handed it to Laryn without a word.

There were so many things she wanted to say, but there was no time for any of them.

Before she could blink, Tate jumped out the open door and ran toward the sound of Pyro's voice.

Laryn took off her own headset and knelt by the edge of the open door, peering into the darkness, straining to see or hear anything as she gripped the pistol Tate had given her so tightly, she had no doubt her knuckles were turning white with the pressure. The rotor blades were still spinning above her head and she held her breath, hoping against hope to see Tate and Pyro returning with the injured SEALs any second now.

To her surprise, it wasn't either of the pilots *or* the special forces soldiers who appeared as if out of nowhere. It was three men. She might've thought they were also SEALs, based on their size—except they were literally dressed from head to toe in black, including masks pulled over their faces. Only their eyes were showing, and these men weren't injured in any way.

She heard shots ring out in the direction Tate and Pyro had gone, but the men didn't even pause. They came right at her, reaching up and grabbing her by the front of her coveralls and roughly pulling her out of the back of the helicopter before she could even think to use the gun Tate had given her. The weapon was wrenched out of her hand as Laryn opened her mouth to scream. Then a black-gloved hand clamped over her mouth, silencing any noise she might've made.

Laryn fought with every ounce of strength she had. She was in deep shit, and she knew it. Her only chance was to get away and hide in the darkness. Wait for Tate and Pyro to return. And they *would* return, she knew that without an ounce of doubt.

As one man struggled to control her, to keep her contained as she thrashed and squirmed and tried to bite the hand that covered her mouth, one of the other men leaped up into the MH-60.

Laryn had the horrified thought that he was going to lie in wait for the others to return, then assassinate them—but instead, the sound of automatic gunfire broke out from inside the bird.

She was confused for a split second, then realized what the guy was doing. He was shooting up her chopper! She could see sparks flying from the cockpit as bullets ripped through the metal.

"Noooooo!" she yelled, but it was muffled behind the hand covering her mouth. Tate and the others definitely weren't leaving. They weren't going to be able to use the MH-60 as a weapon against the people who had her in their grasp either.

No. That chopper wasn't going anywhere anytime soon. The number of bullets the asshole continued to spray into the cockpit guaranteed that.

She still expected the men to wait around to ambush the pilots, but to her surprise, the one holding her began to drag her away from the helicopter.

Fighting harder, not wanting to become a prisoner of war, Laryn did her best to try to get the man to loosen his grip. Just when she thought she might do it, that she might get away, the man who'd been serving as a lookout, his rifle at the ready, turned toward her.

The last thing she saw before she was knocked out was the butt of his rifle, coming at her face.

* * *

Edge paced the room the pilots had taken over for their use on the destroyer. On aircraft carriers, they had a ready room specifically for pilots. He didn't really care one way or another, as long as they had someplace to prepare for their missions and go over intel.

"Laryn wouldn't have messed that up," Chaos said. He was also pacing the room.

"I know," he said with a nod.

"I mean, a fucking loose connection? How does that even happen?"

Edge didn't bother to respond this time. He was as irritated and bothered as his copilot that they'd been taken off the mission at the last minute. Both pilots were now listening to the radio chatter as their team headed inland to pick up the SEALs.

His phone vibrated in his pocket, but Edge ignored it. All his attention was on the conversation they were listening in on.

But the second the phone stopped vibrating, it started up again. Edge didn't have anyone back home who would be so desperate to get a hold of him. No wife—his ex didn't count; she wouldn't contact him if she was literally dying, she hated him that much—no kids, no parents, no siblings. And his best friends were deployed to this destroyer with him.

He ignored the cell again, but when whoever was on the other end called a *third* time, Edge huffed out a breath of annoyance and reached for the damn thing. He had no idea who could be calling, as this was his emergency phone; it used satellites instead of cell towers, and he hadn't given the number to many people.

"What?" he barked into the phone.

"Is this Roman Aldrich?" a man asked. "Edge?"

"Who wants to know?"

"My name is Tex Keegan, and I'm trying to get a hold of Casper. Is he there?"

Edge blinked in surprise. He knew about Tex. Everyone did. He was also aware that Casper had contacted him about the guy in Turkey—Osman, he thought his name was. The man who had threatened Laryn. But he hadn't thought much about her situation since arriving on the destroyer, where he assumed she was safe.

"No. He's on a mission."

"Fuck."

"Why? What's wrong?" Edge asked, stopping in his tracks. He could see Chaos turning toward him with a questioning look on his face and immediately put the phone on speaker, so his friend could hear whatever it was Tex needed to tell them.

"Right, so...I suppose I should ask why you aren't on that mission with him, but at this point it doesn't matter. Altan Osman? The man he asked me to look into? That guy is bad news. And to answer Casper's question, yes, he's a threat to Laryn Hardy. A *huge* fucking threat. He has the power to get to her pretty much anywhere—including on your naval base. Where is she?"

Edge's blood ran cold. "She's onboard the MH-60 with Casper and Pyro." He explained what happened, how both his and Casper's choppers had malfunctions with their FLIR.

"That was no malfunction," Tex said. "The man has connections. It's how he learned Laryn might be available to hire. How he got her phone number without her giving it to him. He works for the highest levels of the Turkish government, and they're very determined to get their military up to the same standards as other, more powerful countries.

"I'm *positive* he's got people on his payroll who work on that destroyer. I'll look into money trails as soon as we hang up, but I'm guessing at this point, it's moot. What's done is done. Given what you've told me, I'm guessing Osman paid someone for intel about Laryn *and* your mission. That person probably sabotaged your choppers in a way that would necessitate Laryn jumping onboard and riding with them. Osman isn't stupid—he's crazy smart, actually. While there's no way he could guarantee she'd insist on going, or being ordered to go with the chopper, the bottom line is that's exactly what he wanted, and it's what he got. This is not good. Not good at all."

Edge had a feeling when Tex said something wasn't good, it *really* meant they were royally fucked.

"You need to tell Casper not to land under any circumstances. I have no doubt Osman has boots on the ground, that he's ready and willing to do whatever it takes to get his hands on Laryn. Casper needs to get their asses back to the ship, and she needs to be locked down. I mean it, Edge—no contact with *anyone* other than you and your team, because there's no telling who Osman has in his pocket."

"That's not going to be easy. Laryn isn't going to want to sit on her ass when her choppers need maintenance," Chaos said, speaking for the first time.

"Who's that?" Tex asked impatiently.

"Chaos," Edge said.

"Well, would Laryn prefer to be a guest of the Turkish military for the rest of her life, forced to break the oaths she's made to keep any and all intel about our military and the technology in our birds to herself?"

"No."

"Contact Casper. Let him know. I'll continue to try to unravel threads on my end and find out who he's paying for intel and to sabotage the choppers."

"You really think someone onboard is working for him? And that they disabled the FLIR on the slim chance that Laryn would go on the mission? That's a huge leap. If the control tower wasn't on their asses to get their asses moving, if the SEALs hadn't needed an extraction ASAP, no one would've ever allowed Laryn to stay in that chopper. Especially Casper."

"That's *exactly* what I think happened. And is that level of pressure to take off normal?"

Edge huffed out a harsh breath. Now that Tex brought it up, he realized it wasn't normal at all.

"Right. That's what I thought. I don't care what you're interrupting—get a hold of Casper and tell him the CliffsNotes version of what I just told you. He has to protect Laryn at all costs."

"Even at the cost of those SEALs' lives?" Edge asked.

Tex was silent a moment, then he whispered, "Fuck. Contact him. I'll be in touch. Keep me updated with what's happening."

The line went dead, and Edge put his phone back in his pocket as he looked at Chaos.

They shared a deeply concerned look between them, before Chaos turned and headed straight for the radio at the front of the room. Edge was right on his heels.

As they approached, they realized that while they'd been talking to Tex, the shit had hit the fan. Two injured SEALs had been separated from their team, and Casper and Pyro had volunteered to extricate those men. Buck and Obi-Wan were already on their way back to the ship with the other injured SEALs, so they could get immediate medical attention.

The entire mission, from the Night Stalkers' perspective, had gone to hell.

They were too late. Casper and Pyro weren't responding. They'd obviously already landed the chopper and were probably in the middle of attempting to extricate the SEALs. But the big question...what was Laryn doing?

With Tex's words ringing in his ears, Edge held his breath, hoping against hope that he'd hear one of his friends reply any second now with the good news that the SEALs had been rescued and they were on their way back to the ship.

"Casper, this is Chaos. Come in," his fellow pilot said, continually trying to get in touch with their friends.

Listening intently for any sign of Casper and Pyro's return to the chopper, Edge jerked violently when the sudden sound of gunfire echoed throughout the ready room.

Then the line went dead.

Edge's heart sank.

It seemed unlikely, and improbable that Osman would have managed to put people in place at the exact right spot to be able to snatch Laryn...but somehow, Edge knew that's exactly what had happened.

Osman had done the impossible. Edge had no doubt he'd managed to follow through with his plan, and Laryn was now in the hands of the Turkish government...or at least one particular man, who seemed determined to get any and all information out of her that he could possibly get.

Chaos continued trying to get a hold of Pyro or Casper through the radio, but the line was totally dead. They had no idea what was happening there in the mountains or if their fellow pilots, the SEALs, or Laryn were all right. All they could do was wait for intel. From Tex. Hopefully from Pyro and Casper. From someone. Anyone.

No, that wasn't all they could do. They could get to their chopper, hope like hell one of Laryn's fellow mechanics had been able to fix their FLIR, and get their asses in the air.

* * *

"I've got this one," Pyro said as he lifted the obviously critical SEAL over his shoulder in a fireman's carry.

Casper didn't bother responding, simply wrapped the second SEAL's arm over his shoulder and grabbed him around the waist.

The foursome began to hobble back toward the chopper. Unfortunately, he'd landed farther away than he would've liked from where the SEALs were holed up waiting for extraction.

When they heard something to their left, both the SEAL under his arm and Tate grabbed their pistols and shot in that direction.

Shit, shit, shit. Nothing about this mission was going right. From the fucking FLIR malfunctioning, to the asshole yelling in his ear to hurry up and take off, to Laryn being on the chopper, to them having to land and both him *and* Pyro having to get out of the chopper to extract the SEALs.

He was going to have some serious words with Laryn when they got back to the ship. Both about how the hell the FLIR could've gotten fucked up *and* her insisting on accompanying them on the mission. He could admit that without her there to fix the FLIR a second time, Buck and Obi-Wan would've been fucked. Without their night-vision, Casper wouldn't have been able to provide fire power from the air.

His thoughts were irrational, and he knew it. They were a result of the panic he'd felt at having her in this situation. Fear for her safety. He certainly didn't want to leave her while he went to help Pyro, but didn't feel as if he had a choice. He couldn't sit there and listen as one of his best friends was in danger and certainly couldn't leave those SEALs to die.

But he'd left *Laryn*. Alone. In the middle of enemy territory with only his sidearm for protection. None of this fucked-up situation was her fault.

He was practically dragging the almost-unconscious SEAL back toward the chopper when he heard a sound that made his blood run cold.

Automatic gunfire.

Laryn!

While they'd been busy extracting the SEALs, someone had obviously circled around to the helicopter.

Kicking himself for being so stupid, Casper wanted to drop the man in his arms and sprint toward their landing site. But he couldn't leave this man behind. He might have his own wife and family back home. Feeling torn, and more terrified than he ever remembered being before, Casper moved even faster in the direction of the chopper.

Just as he and Pyro arrived in the clearing with the SEALs, the sound of an engine starting up to the north echoed in the otherwise suddenly quiet night.

"Laryn!" Casper yelled, knowing it was stupid to bring so much attention to his location, but fuck it.

There was no response.

Casper placed the SEAL on the ground and without checking with Pyro, ran toward the helicopter, his weapon drawn, ready to kill anyone who dared touch his woman.

And yes, Laryn was *his*. He'd figured that out the second he'd had to take off with her sitting behind him in that chopper. The fear he'd felt in that moment had been so out of the ordinary, it could only be because it was no longer simply *his* life at stake. It was the life of the woman who'd somehow managed to burrow into his heart.

He understood Nate perfectly now. All too well. He'd known from the start that Josie was his. It had taken him longer, but now Casper had no doubt that Laryn was the woman he was meant to spend the rest of his life with. Have kids with. To laugh and argue with for as long as they both lived.

"Laryn!" he called out again, to no avail.

Without thought, he leaped into the back of the open chopper. It was a stupid thing to do. Whoever had been shooting earlier could've been waiting to ambush him.

But the chopper was empty...and shot to shit.

The silence fully registered then. The rotors were no longer spinning. And from the looks of the instrument panel in the beam of the pen light he held up, the MH-60 wasn't going anywhere anytime soon.

The chopper Laryn had worked so hard to get up to speed, to make safe to fly, to outfit with all the bells and whistles he and his fellow Night Stalkers needed to perform their dangerous missions...had been taken out in less than a minute by automatic gunfire.

"Son-of-a-*bitch*!" he seethed, turning. He didn't care about the chopper, it was just a hunk of metal.

Laryn was gone.

Whoever shot up the helicopter had made it impossible to follow the vehicle that left the area—the one that had surely taken Laryn.

Grabbing the backup radio clipped to his flight suit, Casper quickly called for assistance. He was all business while he spoke with the person on the other end, summing up the situation and letting him know the SEALs were in critical condition and needed immediate extraction. With a lump in his throat, he also informed the person on the other end of the line that one of his staff had been taken hostage. Laryn wasn't a US soldier anymore, but she was working for the government. Not only that, but she had knowledge they surely wouldn't want getting into the wrong hands.

Getting her back was a matter of national security. But for him? It was the difference between living the rest of his life as a broken and lonely man, or living the life he truly felt he was meant to live...with Laryn at his side.

CHAPTER SIXTEEN

The automatic gunfire that echoed through the mountains when someone destroyed their bird were the last shots Casper and Pyro heard. It was as if, now that the SEAL team was gone, and the last two men had been recovered, the operatives in the area had all bugged out.

Casper figured that was exactly what had happened. And it couldn't be a coincidence. Shit went sideways in missions all the time, but this one seemed to have more than its fair share of fuckups.

After calling for backup, he joined Pyro outside the chopper with the two SEALs and got to work trying to stabilize the men. He had questions, lots of them, but he wasn't sure what the men would be able to tell him.

The man Pyro had carried was still unconscious, with a head wound that was bleeding heavily. His friend immediately attempted to stop the flow, or at least slow it down. There was no telling if the man would pull through, but Casper knew from experience how hardheaded SEALs could be. They seemed to be able to defy the grim reaper himself on occasion.

He turned his attention to the man he'd dragged into the clearing. He was still conscious but seemed confused.

"Thought there was a chopper," he said.

"There was. It got shot up. It's unflyable," Casper told him.

The man snorted. "Thought you Night Stalkers could fly anything."

While Casper appreciated his attempt at humor, he wasn't ready to find anything about this situation funny. Not when Laryn had been taken.

"What's your name?" Casper asked him, as he did his best to staunch the flow of blood coming from his thigh. He started a tourniquet as he spoke.

"Mustang. That's Pid. He going to be all right? His wife, Monica, and his daughter need him to pull through."

"Pyro's got him. What about you? You got a family?" Casper wanted him to think about what he had to live for.

"A wife. Elodie. We're trying to get pregnant but it hasn't happened yet."

He nodded. "Well, hang in there. We've called in for backup. Almost seems as if the locals planned this," he said, moving on to what was rolling around in his head and needing his suspicions confirmed or debunked. "Was this mission out of the ordinary for you and your team?"

"No. Not in the least. Things were fine. Nothing unusual. We joined another SEAL team, and we'd obtained the intel we went in to get. Hadn't run into any hostiles, then they suddenly arrived as if out of nowhere. Waited until we were in this valley and opened fire. They surrounded us and pinned us down. But...I'd swear they weren't shooting to kill. They could've easily used an RPG and taken us all out. It was as if they were prolonging things for some reason."

Fuck. Casper looked over at Pyro, and he saw his teammate frowning as he worked on the other SEAL.

"Then they managed to separate Pid and me from the rest of

our group. One second we were together, working our way toward the extraction, and the next, they laid down gunfire to cut off the two of us, and we got pinned down behind a group of boulders. We heard the choppers but couldn't get to them. We told our guys to go, to get the hell out, and at first they refused. But they all have families too..." he sighed. "I ordered them to go, and they finally did, but not before making sure we wouldn't be left behind. Thank you for coming for us," Mustang told him.

"You're welcome. I hate to be the bearer of bad news...but I have a feeling your separation from the group was a setup."

"To what end?" Mustang asked.

"To get a hold of my mechanic."

Mustang looked surprised. "Explain."

So he did. He told Mustang about Laryn's expertise. How she'd worked on all the Night Stalker helicopters for the last three years. About his previous MH-60, how it was destroyed in Iraq, and how Laryn had worked day and night to get his new one up to snuff. About the countries that had been trying to recruit her—including someone representing the Turkish government. Then finally, how they'd just been deployed to the destroyer yesterday, and despite his chopper being in perfect working condition stateside, suddenly his FLIR had gone out right when he was scheduled to take off for this mission.

"It seems unlikely that someone would be able to arrange a kidnapping as elaborate as this. So many things could've gone differently that would've made it impossible."

"I understand," Casper said. "And I agree. But I've still got a bad feeling in my gut that says differently. That says this was all carefully planned, and we played right into the hands of the asshole who desperately wants Laryn's expertise for himself and his country. I've asked a man named Tex to look into the guy for me. Maybe you've heard of him?"

"Tex?" Mustang asked, his face registering his surprise. "Of course I've heard of him. I consider him a close friend, actually.

Let's just say he's been very hands-on with my team and when it came to keeping our women safe. If he's looking into this, he'll figure out what's going on sooner rather than later."

"I hope so," Casper said.

At that moment, a sound reached their ears, and Casper tensed as he turned and picked up the pistol he'd placed on the ground while tending to the injured SEAL.

It only took seconds for him to recognize the sound of rotor blades. Help was coming.

Relief made him almost dizzy. The assholes who'd shot up his chopper and taken Laryn didn't have that much of a head start. They'd be able to get Mustang and Pid medical help and see if they could locate the vehicle that had taken Laryn.

The advantage of this part of the country was that it was sparsely populated, there wouldn't be many trucks on the back roads...if they could even be called roads. He had no idea if it was Edge and Chaos coming in, or if Buck and Obi-Wan had dropped off the other SEALs and returned. Either way, they'd be up for combing the area for whoever had taken Laryn. They couldn't use their firepower on the vehicles for fear of hurting the woman he was desperate to find, but they could use the chopper at the very least as intimidation, and at best as a road block to make the vehicle stop.

A shoot-out hadn't exactly been on Casper's plans for the day, but he'd do whatever it took to get Laryn back safe and sound.

It hit him hard yet again, as he watched the MH-60 bank around, probably checking out the area for unfriendlies before it landed, that he'd failed to protect her. He'd talked a big game, asking to stay at her apartment just in case evil found its way to her door, claiming he'd keep her safe. And yet she'd been taken right out from under his nose.

He never should've left her alone in the chopper. He should've insisted she come with them to extract the SEALs.

It was a mistake he'd spend the rest of his life mentally berating himself for.

As he watched Edge land his MH-60, Casper's hands clenched into fists as determination filled him. He wasn't leaving the area until he had her back. They had too much to lose for him to give up. Night Stalkers Don't Quit. It was their motto. And he would never stop looking for Laryn.

As if Mustang could read his mind, the SEAL put his hand on Casper's arm. "You'll get her back. And if you need assistance, you've got my team. You didn't have to come for Pid and me, but you did. We won't forget it. We owe you."

"You don't owe me dick," Casper told him honestly. "You know as well as I do that we were just doing our jobs. But rest assured, if I need your help, I'll ask for it. I'm going to do whatever it takes, break whatever rules and laws I have to, in order to get her back. I didn't realize how much she means to me, only to lose her now."

Mustang nodded. "I understand that more than you know."

Talk became difficult as the dirt kicked up all around them from the rotor blades of Edge's chopper. Without a word, he hauled Mustang to his feet and put his arm around his waist. Pyro picked up the still-unconscious Pid—who was no longer bleeding—and they made their way toward the chopper.

Chaos immediately handed him a headset, and when it was settled over Casper's ears, he heard his friend ask, "Are we blowing it up or using a missile?"

It wasn't as if they were authorized to use the very expensive weapons onboard the helicopters in any old situation. It would be hard to use explosives to destroy yet another machine that Laryn had worked so hard to bring up to her demanding standards. It literally hurt his heart to destroy it, but they couldn't let the technology onboard get into the wrong hands.

His ass was going to be chewed for losing another helicopter so soon after the first, but it couldn't be helped.

"Missile," he said. "It's faster. We need to find a truck. It left the area not too long ago. It has to still be around here somewhere. Laryn's inside. They took her."

"Tex called. I'll update you later, but we figured she'd been taken. We looked around for any signs of life as we came in. Casper...there's nothing."

"How can that be?" he demanded, as Pyro closed the door and got Pid settled. "Your FLIR is working, right? It should pick up any heat sources, and people and a warm engine would definitely show up."

"I know, but I'm telling you, there's nothing out there."

Casper stared at his friend in disbelief. He'd been so sure all it would take was getting in the air and they'd find Laryn. But now Chaos was telling him that, somehow, she'd disappeared into thin air?

Whoever took her had to be hiding out in a large cave or something. It was the only possible reason for not spotting the vehicle. And her captors obviously knew the area like the back of their hand.

Like he'd told Mustang. They'd planned this kidnapping carefully.

Despair threatened to overwhelm Casper.

"We aren't giving up," Pyro said over the headset as he put his hand on Casper's shoulder. "But we need to get Pid and Mustang to the ship so they can get medical attention. I've stabilized Pid, but he needs a doctor."

His copilot was right, but that didn't mean everything within Casper wasn't rebelling. He couldn't leave Laryn. She was out there somewhere. Counting on him to ride in on a white horse and save her. He wanted to do that for her, just as she'd done that for him when he'd been at his most vulnerable.

But he could hear her in the back of his head, telling him to take care of the SEALs first. That she'd hold on until he could find her. That she'd be all right. That she was tougher than everyone thought, because her dad had taught her how to make the best of a bad situation.

Closing his eyes, Casper nodded.

He felt the chopper immediately lift off the ground. They banked around, and the sound of a missile being fired was loud in the small space, making the entire chopper vibrate. It felt different being in the back while the firepower was used, and Casper refused to watch the link he had with Laryn go up in smoke, literally. Blowing up the chopper that she'd put so much blood, sweat, and tears into...and time and love...felt awful.

Now that he knew Laryn better, he understood her love language was making sure he was as safe as possible while he was flying. She'd always done just that, the entire time she'd been working with him. She'd made sure everything on his chopper was in the best shape it could be...so he'd come back after every mission.

And he had.

But she hadn't. When push came to shove, he hadn't done his part in keeping her safe. It was a mistake he'd rectify or die trying. And it might come to that. It wasn't as if the Turkish government was going to admit one of their own had a hand in the elaborate scheme to kidnap one of the best and brightest minds the US military had working for them.

No, they were going to resist any attempts to get Laryn back.

Well, fuck them.

Casper concentrated on sending Laryn all the mental strength he could muster. He had to believe she was all right. That the crazy lengths Osman had gone to just to get his hands on her meant he wanted her healthy and uninjured as she was transported to wherever the Turkish military had stashed their newly acquired MH-6os. All he had to do was find where that was, get the government and his superiors to approve a mission to cross international boundaries, and get her back. Hopefully with as little bloodshed as possible.

Casper knew the challenge in front of him was daunting, but he wasn't a Night Stalker for nothing. He knew people, had some clout. And Laryn wasn't a normal mechanic. The knowledge she had about their choppers would surely mean her government would fight to get her back.

If they wouldn't, *he* would. And his fellow pilots would join him. Laryn would come home. No ifs, ands, or buts about it.

* * *

Laryn blinked, but it didn't do any good. The material placed over her head didn't let one speck of light in. She had no idea how long she'd been blinded, with her arms secured behind her back. Days?

She was more than sick of the damn hood. Of being treated as if she were a piece of baggage. She'd been hauled around and forced into one vehicle after another. Every time she tried to speak, she was told to shut up.

At first, she'd hoped to escape at the first chance she got, but she'd never had the slightest opportunity. The truck she'd been shoved into in the middle of the mountains had bounced and bumped over what had to be the worst road on the planet. After what she guessed was just fifteen or twenty minutes, it stopped for what seemed like hours. The air had been cooler, and she could only assume the truck had been driven into a cave or something to hide from anyone looking for her from the air. She could've sworn she heard a helicopter, but the sound was slight and far off, and any hopes she had of a fast rescue were dashed.

After that, she was moved into a different vehicle. Then another. And another. She estimated she'd been in at least thirty different vehicles at this point.

There was no way, even if Tate *had* been able to follow the truck she'd originally been taken in, he'd still be on her trail. Not with how many times she'd been moved from car to truck to car.

She had no idea where she was now, partly because of the hood over her head, but also because they'd been driving for so long.

She slept fitfully, unaware how much time had passed each time she woke. There were different voices around her each time she was shoved into another vehicle. Laryn wondered if the men tasked with making sure she didn't run, ensuring she ate stale bread every now and then, drank the water they poured down her throat because they didn't ever release her hands from their bindings, knew or cared who they were transporting, or why.

At first, she was afraid she'd be assaulted. She was the only woman with a group of men, and she'd stayed on high alert, determined to make it as difficult as possible for anyone to hurt her. But no one touched her except to get her from one car to another, or to assist her in eating and drinking. She didn't want to think about when she'd had to use the bathroom. It was humiliating, since they'd refused to untie her hands. They'd had to unzip her coveralls, pull her panties down, hold her arms so she didn't fall, then pull her underwear and clothes back up. All while she wore a hood.

With no idea how many people were looking at her, this was the first time in her life she hated the coveralls she wore on a daily basis. If she had on regular pants and a T-shirt, she at least wouldn't feel quite so exposed every time she had to pee.

Things felt different today, however. She could hear much more noise from outside the car. Even with the hood on, and lying on the floor of the vehicle—she thought it was a van of some sort, because the door slid shut, rather than slammed closed—the sound of horns blaring and other road noise was loud.

Being in a city was good, she hoped. It meant if and when she was able to escape, she'd hopefully be able to blend in and disappear. In the middle of the mountains, with nothing around, it would be impossible to hide from her kidnappers. But in a city? Laryn felt as if she had a fighting chance.

Throughout her ordeal, no one talked to her beyond telling her to keep her mouth shut. No one told her who had kidnapped her or why. But she had a pretty good idea.

Altan Osman.

No one else would go to the lengths he had in order to get her to work for him. Apparently, he didn't take rejection well. The good news for her was that he needed her healthy in order to do her job. The bad news? If he wasn't pleased with anything she did, he could easily kill her and get rid of her body and no one would know what had happened or where she'd gone. She'd be just another case of a person disappearing without a trace.

Laryn shuddered, forcing herself to take a deep breath. The hood smelled disgusting, and she immediately regretted her actions.

She simply had to figure out a way to stay alive long enough for Tate to find her. Stay alive and not give Altan Osman any of the top-secret information she was privy to. How the Night Stalkers operated. What technology the choppers contained. How the US military operated. She had a lot of information other countries would find extremely useful. The trick would be to make it seem as if she was scared shitless and giving up all the intel she had, while actually only giving away things that weren't top secret or particularly vital. How she'd do that, she had no idea. She was going to have to fly by the seat of her pants.

How long it would take for someone to come for her, Laryn wasn't sure. But she had no doubt that Tate would do everything in his power to do so himself. To be involved in whatever plan his higher-ups came up with. He wouldn't leave her rescue to the government. She knew that as well as she knew her name. But of course, that worried her too, because the last thing she wanted was for Tate to be in danger or get hurt.

The van slowed, and Laryn prayed she wasn't about to be shuttled to another damn vehicle. She was exhausted, sore from being restrained, and tired of being treated like a piece of lumber. When she came face-to-face with Altan, she'd make sure he knew how pissed off she was about this entire situation.

The noises from outside the van decreased as they drove slowly. Not for the first time, Laryn wished she could see. Any information she could get about her surroundings would be helpful when the time came to escape.

She heard two men talking, but didn't understand a word they were saying. Then they were creeping forward once more and, finally, the van stopped.

Holding her breath, praying she was at her final destination, Laryn jumped when the door next to her slid open. Her arm was grasped in a tight hold, making her cry out involuntarily in pain. Her upper arm had to be covered in bruises, because she'd been grabbed in the same place so many times while being dragged from one car to another.

Whoever had a hold on her didn't seem to care about her discomfort, but to her relief, he didn't just shove her into another car or trunk either. She walked next to him, trying to keep up with the long strides. The air around her changed from the dry, hot air she'd been in for the last who knew how many days, to the artificial coolness that could only come from an air conditioner.

But more than that, Laryn smelled the familiar scent of diesel fuel. Grease. And heard the clanking of metal against metal. They were sounds and smells she was intimately familiar with. They were comforting. The sounds and smells of a garage. It seemed they were the same no matter where in the world the garage was located. There could be cars or planes, choppers, or even lawn mowers inside, but it was still a garage.

The sounds of the garage became muted as a door opened then shut behind her. Only then did the man who'd been holding her let go of her arm. Then, to her immense relief, the cuffs holding her arms behind her back were cut free. The blood flowing freely into her hands made them tingle and hurt, even though the freedom of movement felt good at the same time.

Laryn immediately reached for the damn hood over her head without waiting to see if anyone gave her permission to remove it. She was almost desperate for some fresh air and to be able to *see* again.

The second the material passed over her head, she took a deep breath. Her eyes burned from the light, and she squinted, trying to take in her surroundings. Turning her head, she saw two men standing by the door she'd obviously just walked through. They weren't really looking at her, but staring into space above her head, instead.

Turning back around, she saw what she'd missed when she'd first taken the hood off.

A man was sitting behind a desk, leaning back, his hands behind his head as if he didn't have a care in the world. His dark hair and brown eyes were intense and calculating as he focused on her. His warm olive skin was weathered, as if he spent a lot of time in the sun, and he had well-groomed stubble on his face. Instead of making him look civilized, it added to his air of quiet menace. He had a lean, muscular build and hawk-like nose. And the stoic expression on his face, along with his thin lips pressed in a hard line, had Laryn suppressing a shiver.

This was a man who was used to getting what he wanted. Who had probably witnessed, and maybe even participated in, unspeakable acts.

If she had to guess, this was Osman. As they stared at each other, his expression transformed to a smug look of satisfaction, as if he'd just been gifted with his greatest desire. And he probably had. She'd been delivered to him on a silver platter—and his smugness made Laryn see red.

She held on to her temper by the skin of her teeth and instead of railing at this man for having her kidnapped, she merely said, "Altan Osman, I presume."

He smiled and nodded at her as he sat forward. "It's good to meet you in person. I hope your trip here wasn't too uncomfortable. Desperate times called for desperate measures. And since you refused to see reason, I was forced to take more drastic actions."

"By having me kidnapped?" she asked, keeping her voice even but unable to stop the question.

"Just so. I think you'll find that I'm a fair employer...as long as you do as you're told. I am reasonable. I know this is all a shock, but after a while, you'll see that it's a good thing. You'll have whatever your heart desires—money, food, clothes, husbands—in return for your knowledge and expertise in furthering the might and strength of our military."

Laryn swallowed hard. Husbands? No thank you. "I appreciate your offer, as I told you on the phone, but I have all the money, clothes, food, and men I want back home in the US."

Altan simply shrugged. "And now you'll have them here. Make no mistake, you'll be treated with respect and kindness in exchange for your skills. You resist, and your life can become... *difficult*, very quickly. But here's the thing—we will still get the information we want. So it's up to you if you want a comfortable bed to sleep in, good food to eat, and to be treated as a valued member of my team. Or if you want a room in the basement—fondly referred to by some as a dungeon—with no blanket, gruel for food, and to be treated like a prisoner.

"Now, I expect you'd like a shower and a good meal...but I suspect first you need some incentive. A reason to accept your new reality. I think a week downstairs would do you good. It'll show you *exactly* what will become your new normal if you don't wish to cooperate."

Laryn opened her mouth to protest, to scream at him to let her go, but before she could get a word out, the men who'd been standing by the door each took one of her arms in their big beefy hands and literally dragged her out the door.

She tried to struggle but it was useless. She managed to get her feet under her when they began walking across the large hangar, where she now saw the two barebones MH-60s were parked. They looked nothing like the machines she was used to working on for the US military. They seemed to be stripped down to their shells. Obviously when they'd been sold to Turkey, they didn't have any of the bells or whistles she'd gotten used to seeing on the Night Stalkers' choppers.

No one stopped what they were doing to watch her being dragged toward a metal door at the other end of the large space. It was as if she were invisible, as if the people working in the room were used to looking the other way when others were mistreated. It didn't bode well for her future.

One of the men opened the metal door and it slammed shut behind them with a loud, menacing *clang* that seemed like a death knell to Laryn. "Please," she whispered, hating that she was already reduced to begging. But the men acted as if they didn't hear her.

The air in the hallway was dank and stagnant. She could smell the metallic scent of rust, of mold and mildew, as if water had seeped into the walls over time.

They went down a flight of stairs and it got even darker and smellier the farther they went. Unwashed bodies, sweat, dirt, even dried blood. The scents all blended together, making her nauseous. The unmistakable smell of human waste made it even harder to breathe as Laryn was dragged past other cells, the men inside not even bothering to lift their heads as she went by. She wondered how long they'd been down here, what they'd done to get on Altan's bad side. But the fact that they seemed uninterested in anything going on around them didn't seem like a good sign.

She was brought to the last cell on the right and shoved inside. Laryn fell to her hands and knees but immediately sprang to her feet as the bars slammed shut. The two men left without a word, and she pressed her lips together in a desperate attempt to not call out, to not immediately agree to anything Altan wanted her to do.

When the men were gone, silence descended on the cells. An eerie silence that made the hair on the back of Laryn's neck stand up. Goose bumps rose on her arms, but not in the good way that often happened around Tate.

Despair threatened to overwhelm her...and she'd only been here a matter of minutes. She was tired, hungry, dirty, and scared shitless.

Backing away from the bars, Laryn stumbled and managed to catch herself by sitting down hard on the concrete "bed" against the wall. It was literally a block of concrete. No blankets. No pillows. Looking around, she saw there was only a hole in the floor for her to do her business.

Closing her eyes, she breathed in through her nose and out of her mouth, trying to stave off the panic attack that threatened. It took a hot minute, but eventually her heart rate slowed and she was able to think more clearly.

"This is a good thing," she whispered out loud, wanting to hear something other than the oppressive silence around her. She wasn't too worried about anyone else overhearing her talking to herself, because even if they did, it was likely they wouldn't care what she was rambling about...and couldn't even understand her anyway.

"It's a good thing," she repeated. "Being down here means giving Tate more time to find me. To come up with a plan to get me out of here. And if I'm down here, I'm not up there trying to figure out how *not* to give away the military secrets I've been entrusted with."

She was alive. She'd been given food and water. And although she was sore and her arms hurt, she hadn't been otherwise assaulted. Things could be a hell of a lot worse. She simply had to hang in there until help came. And it *would* come. She couldn't afford to think any other way. She'd do what she needed to do, for as long as it took, for someone to get her the hell out of here.

Laryn told herself that she needed to stay alert. She had no idea when rescue would come, and she had to be ready when it did. Night Stalkers Don't Quit. That was their motto. She'd worked with them long enough to know they took those words seriously. She might not be a hotshot pilot, but she'd worked alongside them long enough to absorb some of their pride in their unit, their traditions.

Then she thought about the Night Stalker Creed. She'd memorized a portion of it, because it seemed like such an honorable thing to swear to honor and obey.

I will never surrender. I will never leave a fallen comrade to fall into the hands of the enemy, and under no circumstances will I ever embarrass my country. Gallantly will I show the world and the elite forces I support that a Night Stalker is a specially selected and well trained soldier. I serve with the memory and pride of those who have gone before me, for they loved to fight, fought to win and would rather die than quit.

The words comforted Laryn. Made her able to relax when she curled up on the uncomfortably hard slab of concrete that would be her bed for the foreseeable future. She wouldn't embarrass her country by giving up their secrets.

She'd rather die than give up and quit.

Tate was coming for her, it was in that creed he'd vowed to live by.

Tears dripped down her cheeks as Laryn fell into an uneasy sleep. She dreamed about monsters with huge gaping mouths full of teeth coming for her, and Tate stepping between her and a monster, smiling as he turned to her and said, "I've got this."

That's what she was counting on.

CHAPTER SEVENTEEN

"It's been a fucking *week*!" Casper seethed, as he paced back and forth in a conference room aboard the destroyer.

The Navy SEALs who'd been extracted, including Mustang and Pid, were all going to be fine. They were flown to Germany, to the military hospital there, and then flew home shortly after. Casper learned that Mustang and his team were stationed in Hawaii, while the other team they'd extracted was from California.

He was glad for them, but frustrated beyond belief at the situation with Laryn. The colonel was also concerned, and he'd brought her abduction to the highest levels of the Navy and Army. But, as with most things in the government, decisions about next steps were slow in coming.

There'd even been an attempt at diplomatic talks, trying to get Laryn released peacefully, but the members of the Turkish government communicating with their own wouldn't even admit she was in the country. Could it be possible that Osman was acting independently? And his superiors didn't even know what he'd done?

In the end, it didn't matter who knew what—all avenues had been met with stonewalls. And Casper was done.

"Let my team and I go in," Casper pleaded with the captain in charge of the ship.

The room was full of more high-ranking officers than Casper had seen in one place in a long time, but he wasn't intimidated. Not in the least. He was more concerned about Laryn.

Pyro put a hand on his arm, and Casper took a deep breath. If he was going to help Laryn, he needed to get control of his emotions.

"Look, I understand Laryn Hardy isn't a member of the US military. But she was in the past. And she currently has knowledge about every top-secret modification the US has made to the helicopters we use on missions. That's why this Osman character was so desperate to get his hands on her in the first place. She's not some random mechanic. She's just as valuable to the Night Stalker missions as the pilots. Without her leading her team of mechanics and technicians, those helicopters might as well be ferrying tourists up and down the coast of Hawaii, checking out waterfalls."

The captain leaned back in his chair and looked deep in thought. Personally, Casper thought the admiral simply looked bored. Many people thought since the admiral outranked the captain, that he was in charge when he was onboard, but they'd be wrong. The admiral was in charge of the fleet of ships in the area, but the captain commanded the ship itself. So the fact that the admiral didn't look inclined to raise a finger to help Laryn didn't concern Casper overly much. It was the captain he had to convince.

"We know where she is," Pyro cut in.

"Right, because John Keegan has gotten involved," the captain said dryly.

"Yes. He's been watching the hangar where they've stored the

MH-60s they've bought. There's been a lot of activity there, trucks coming and going, but also personnel," Chaos said.

"Which doesn't mean she's there," the captain countered.

"True. But Altan Osman has also been there twenty-four seven. He hasn't left once, which is highly unusual," Buck pointed out.

"How the hell does Keegan know the whereabouts of a single person in the middle of a huge city? One in Turkey, at that?" the admiral asked.

"How does Tex know half the things he knows?" Obi-Wan countered. "He just does. And if he says that's where Laryn is being held, that's where she's being held."

"I'm not encouraging anything at this point, but let's say she *is* there. How do you propose to find her and get her out without blowing up the entire building, killing possibly hundreds of innocent civilians in the process?" the admiral asked. "Because I'm telling you right now, the president isn't going to want to do anything that would ramp up tensions in that part of the world... any higher than they already are."

This was Casper's chance. He leaned over the table and looked the captain in the eye. Not the admiral, but the man who had the power to approve any mission leaving from his ship.

"We take one chopper. Buck and Obi-Wan fly it in—at night, of course. The four of us—Pyro, Edge, Chaos, and myself—will be dropped off on the outskirts of the city, in the hills. From there, we'll then make our way to the hangar. From intel given to us by Tex, we know the east side of the building backs up to a neighborhood that's seen better days. That's our in. We enter, find Laryn, get to the roof, and Buck and Obi-Wan will drop in and pick us up," he finished.

There was, of course, a lot that could go wrong with the plan. But he had no doubt he and his team would figure things out on the fly if they had to. The main issue would be getting into the hangar without alerting anyone. Once inside, they'd do what they had to in order to liberate Laryn.

"You sound as if you have everything figured out," the admiral said, sounding skeptical.

Casper didn't respond, having no idea what kind of answer would appease his superior officer.

"What about the SEALs onboard this ship? They've got more experience than the four of you with this kind of extraction," the captain mused.

Casper's hopes soared. The man was listening to him. Not dismissing the plan out of hand. "True, but Laryn knows us. And we've had training, Sir. Maybe not as much as a SEAL or Delta, but enough to be able to succeed. Besides...this is personal."

"Personal?" the captain said, raising a brow.

This was the tricky part. If either officer knew the extent of his relationship with Laryn, they'd reject any plan he came up with that included his participation. "Yes, Sir. Laryn has been working with our team for years. Three, to be exact. She's the reason we've been so successful in our missions. It's been her attention to detail and work ethic that's kept the birds in such good working order."

"Besides the latest two choppers that were blown up, you mean," the captain said sarcastically, a smirk on his lips.

Casper refused to be baited, even though the man was being an asshole. "Neither of which was her fault. And she was able to get the last MH-60 ready in months. I don't know any other mechanic who could do that."

"True," the captain said with a nod. He drummed his fingers on the tabletop.

"You aren't seriously considering approving this insanity, are you?" the admiral asked.

"Actually, I am. If Tex Keegan says the woman is at that hangar, she very likely is. I've also worked with Casper and his team several times, and I believe him when he says they can handle the extraction. And I spoke with Mustang before he was shipped out with his team. He told me that if Casper and Pyro hadn't come to get him and Pid, they would've died out there. Even when it was obvious shit had gone sideways, they didn't abandon their duties. They stayed with Mustang and Pid and ensured they were extracted. Night Stalkers aren't going to turn their backs on a loyal member of their team. It's literally not in their DNA."

Then the captain turned and studied the men before him and said, "I don't want another chopper destroyed."

"Yes, Sir," everyone said at once.

"The thought of anyone being held against their will pisses me off. Especially not knowing what that young lady is going through, what her captors might be doing to make her more... receptive to helping them with their MH-6os."

Casper refused to even think about that right now. He'd already spent too much time wondering the same thing as he lay in his bunk each night. Warm and safe, his belly full, while Laryn suffered through who knew what. It was enough to give him nightmares.

"If you can gather any useful intel while you're there—what kinds of choppers they have, the technology they're using, things like that—it would be good."

"Of course."

"And you're to have your body cams on at all times. That's nonnegotiable."

Casper wasn't thrilled with that order, but it would make gathering data easier. All he had to do was take a moment or two to scan the place with the camera strapped to his chest and that would have to be enough, as far as intelligence gathering went. Others could analyze the footage when he returned. He nodded.

"You realize this is gonna be a disaster, right?" the admiral said to the captain.

Casper was sick of the man being such a downer. "With all due respect, you're wrong, Sir," he said.

"Did you happen to see the movie *The Ministry of Ungentlemanly Warfare?*" the captain asked.

Confused, Casper nodded. "Yes, Sir?"

"Good flick. Not a hundred percent historically accurate, but entertaining all the same. What I do *not* want to hear about is a similar number of bodies left in your wake as were taken in that film."

Casper's lips quirked upward. It wasn't exactly a smile—nothing about the situation made humor possible—but he couldn't deny there was a lot of bloodshed in that movie. And done so nonchalantly by the characters. They didn't break a sweat as they killed their way through the flick. "Affirmative. We *do* plan on making sure the man who planned this kidnapping is no longer a threat, however," he felt obliged to point out.

"I should hope so," the captain replied. "That's the reason I'm approving this mission. Yes, I'm concerned about Ms. Hardy, but I'd be demoted so fast my head would spin if I spent millions of dollars to send men who some would claim weren't qualified, into a country they shouldn't be entering, under the cover of darkness to rescue a mechanic."

Casper's hackles rose at hearing Laryn referred to with such detachment, but he didn't have time to comment—probably a good thing—before the man continued.

"But spending the money to take out an HVT who has connections and moles in our military? On our bases, on our ships, and on the ground? That is perfectly all right...and encouraged."

"Tex has passed on the intel he uncovered about Osman?" Edge asked.

"Yes. We know who he paid to force you to take off before the FLIR could be fixed, the sailor in Norfolk who tipped him off that you were coming to this part of the world in the first place, and the mechanic who temporarily disabled the FLIR in both choppers. And before you ask—no, you can't have two minutes with them in the brig. They've already been taken off the ship. They'll face judgement in a military court back home. But we can't leave a man with the kind of connections and power Osman has alive. *That* is officially your assignment. Get in, take him down, get out. If you find Hardy in the process, great."

That definitely rubbed Casper the wrong way, but he wasn't stupid enough to argue. He was ultimately getting what he wanted—permission to go find Laryn and bring her home.

"It's sixteen hundred right now. You'll leave at oh-two-hundred. That gives you three hours of darkness to get in, find your man...and woman...and get out. Understood?"

"Yes, Sir," all six pilots said at the same time.

The admiral didn't look happy, but he didn't contradict the captain's orders, thankfully.

Casper turned to leave the room, feeling more hopeful than he had in the last week.

"Casper..."

His friends filed past him as he turned to look back at the captain.

"Bring her home."

"I plan on it," he said with conviction, before following his friends into the corridor. They had some preparations to make, but nothing that would take eight hours. Time was going to tick by way too slowly for Casper's liking. This was their one shot to rescue Laryn, and he wasn't coming back to this ship without her. One way or another, her ordeal would end tonight.

* * *

Laryn was scared out of her mind, but she refused to give Altan the satisfaction of knowing how close she was to breaking. Every minute spent in that dungeon under the hangar was pure hell. Food was brought down once a day, and it was barely enough to sustain her. She was exhausted from lack of sustenance and sleep. There was no way to get a good night's rest on the concrete block that was her bed. No matter what she did, she couldn't get comfortable, which she supposed was the point.

Every day, Altan made an appearance in person to ask if she was ready to become his newest employee. Each time, she told him to fuck off.

Maybe not in those words; she wasn't an idiot. She knew Altan held all the power right now. He could make her life even more miserable than it was already, could simply decide to shoot her once and for all. The only thing she had going for her was the fact that he needed her. Needed her knowledge and expertise to outfit the precious MH-60 choppers he'd acquired.

It was only a matter of time before she agreed to work for him. Laryn couldn't continue with the way things were going for much longer. She needed more food, more water, more sleep. She'd been trying to delay as long as possible to give Tate time to figure out how to get her out of there.

Of course, he had no way of knowing where she actually was, but she had to believe he'd figure it out. He was smart. Really smart, and he knew people. Like that Tex guy. While she didn't think the military would send in an entire special forces team to get her, she hoped that maybe they'd consider her top-secret clearance worthy of putting together some sort of rescue plan. Or maybe they'd go the diplomatic route, which would be just as fine with her...but that kind of thing usually took time. Months. And while she could continue to stall for a while, she couldn't keep Altan at bay for that long.

At some point, she was going to have to agree to work on the choppers. But her plan was still to do everything in her power *not* to share any technology she knew was classified. She'd have to come up with something that sounded new and amazing, but in reality was tech most countries were already using. Like FLIR.

One of the main things she was concerned about in pretending to be broken and agreeing to Altan's demands was the whole "husbands" thing he mentioned in passing. She'd spent a good portion of her life being looked down upon because she worked with her hands, in a male-dominated profession. But she'd also been respected because of her skills. Laryn had a feeling that wouldn't be the case here. As soon as she'd given up all the knowledge she had, or pretended she had, she'd be expendable. And being under the thumb of one or more men as "husbands" wasn't something she would ever tolerate. Which meant the clock was ticking in more ways than one.

The pressure she was under was overwhelming. She wasn't sure she was as good an actress as it would take to fool Altan. The man was delusional, crazy, and cruel, but he wasn't stupid. He'd gotten where he was by being smart and having connections.

As if thinking of the man had conjured him up, Laryn heard footsteps coming her way. Shifting so she was sitting against the wall in as nonchalant a position as she could muster, she waited to see what new horror Altan was going to threaten her with today.

When he materialized in front of her cell, he was smiling, which she didn't think was a good sign.

"Good afternoon, Laryn. I trust you're well?"

What an ass. Of course she wasn't well. She simply stared at him.

"It's time," he told her. "Time to do what I brought you here to do. The question is, are you going to come with me of your own free will? Or are you going to make things difficult?"

Swallowing hard, Laryn said, "I'm ready."

He smirked. "Good, good. I knew you'd see things my way. This is Mert. He'll be your right-hand man. He'll be at your side from the moment you step out of your room, until you go to bed each night. Anything you need, he'll get for you. He'll also be taking notes and watching you carefully, because he'll eventually be your replacement."

In other words, he was her jailor. Great. Just freaking great. Then the last thing he said hit home. "My replacement?" she asked, proud that her voice only shook a little.

"Yes. When you have taught him everything you know, he will be in charge of the mechanics working on the helicopters."

"And where will I be?" Laryn couldn't help but ask.

"At home, of course. Women should always be in the home. Having babies and raising them. You can't possibly wish to continue working once you're pregnant. Mert has also expressed his interest in becoming your primary husband."

Fuck her. This was not getting any better. Laryn was tempted to tell Altan, *and* Mert, to go fuck themselves, but that wasn't going to get her out of this cell anytime soon. She had to be smart. Watch and wait for the right moment to get the hell out of there. Being alone on the streets was more appealing than being under this goon's thumb. The way he was leering at her already was enough to make Laryn's skin crawl. And she was looking pretty rough right now, after a week without a shower and very little food.

Mert was taller than her by quite a bit, and very muscular. In hand-to-hand combat, she'd definitely be at a disadvantage. He had dark hair, stubble on his chin, and he wore what looked like steel-toed boots, along with his military-issue pants and uniform shirt. He hadn't spoken a word, and she wondered if he even understood English. He had to, if he was going to be watching her so carefully and learning from her on the job.

"Come," Altan cajoled, holding out a hand. "Let's get you upstairs to your room. You can shower, have dinner, then start work."

"Now?" Laryn asked. She wasn't sure what time it was, but

Altan said "good afternoon." She hadn't expected to start working immediately, but she supposed she should've.

"Now," Altan said firmly. "We don't hold normal hours here. We work when work needs to be done, and a lot of work needs to be done to get our MH-60s operational. I'm sure you're aware of the tensions all around our country. We need to be able to protect ourselves in case the current situation blows up out of control."

She didn't like the usage of the pronoun "our" in that explanation. Not at all.

He motioned for Mert to open the cell door, and Laryn stood as he unlocked the thick bars. The man walked toward her and grabbed her arm, pulling her toward the exit.

Laryn's arm had just stopped being sore from all the manhandling when she'd been kidnapped. She wasn't ready to go back to being hauled around as if she were a recalcitrant child.

"I can walk," she said firmly, tugging on her arm, trying to loosen Mert's hold.

"Of course you can." It was Altan who responded. "Mert is just making sure you don't lose your footing. It's not exactly smooth down here."

He wasn't wrong, but when Mert's fingers brushed against her breast, Laryn's blood ran cold. Her watchdog was just as much a threat as Altan, but in a different way.

As they made their way past the other cells, Laryn couldn't help but glance inside them at the occupants. No one had made much noise in the week she'd been down here, and she could tell why...most of the men looked half dead. They didn't move as the threesome walked past. Didn't glance their way. Simply lay on the concrete beds, staring at the ceiling.

Laryn wondered how long they'd been down here, and what Altan was trying to force *them* to do.

She didn't have much time to think about that as they walked up a set of stairs, through one locked door, then another. She caught a glimpse of the large hangar as they went past a door with a window, before Mert paused at another flight of stairs.

"I will arrange for your dinner to be brought to your room. Ten minutes, Laryn. Then you have five to eat. I expect to see you down here to start work in twenty minutes, no later. Mert." He nodded at her jailor and went through the door into the hangar.

Mert pulled her up the stairs, and Laryn hated to admit that she was glad for his strength. The steps wiped her out, and she was dizzy by the time they arrived at the top. Mert pushed open the stairwell door and walked her along a quiet hall, stopping about halfway down at a door with the number four on its surface. He took out a key, unlocked it, and shoved her inside, slamming the door behind her.

It figured that the man had a key to her new room and she didn't. Laryn didn't see any kind of lock on her side of the door. Unable to help herself, she reached for the doorknob. It didn't budge.

Locked in. Perfect. Why was she not surprised?

She was uneasy that Mert could enter her room at any time, making her feel more vulnerable than if she was still locked in the cell under the hangar floor. Looking around, she saw she was in a room no bigger than a walk-in closet back home. It had a narrow cot that looked smaller than a twin-size bed and a table no bigger than a nightstand. At the back of the "room" was a metal toilet, a sink, and a shower head sticking out of the wall.

It was a step up from the cell she'd been in for the last week, but not a very big one. At least there was a blanket and pillow on the bed, even if the mattress on the cot was extremely thin. And a toilet. She was grateful to see that.

Conscious of time going by, and certain Mert would return in exactly ten minutes, as Altan had said, she took off her boots and peeled off the coveralls she'd been wearing for the last week. Her tank top and underwear soon followed. They were disgusting, but all Laryn's focus was on getting into the shower. There was a bar of soap lying on the side of the tiny sink, and she picked it up eagerly then turned on the water. It was little more than a trickle, but the water smelled clean enough.

Lathering the bar of soap, Laryn quickly scrubbed herself from head to toe. Then again. And again. She suds-ed up her hair, doing her best to wash it, even though the soap probably wouldn't be too effective. Anything was better than nothing.

A threadbare towel was folded and lying on the end of the cot. Aware that too much time had passed, Laryn tried to dry herself as quickly as she could. Her plan was to put her soiled tank top back on, since she literally had nothing else to wear, but first she'd wash her underwear and leave it out to dry when she was forced to go downstairs to the hangar.

She heard the key in the lock way before she was ready. Panicking, she did her best to wrap the tiny towel around herself.

Mert walked into the room, carrying a tray and a plastic bag. He stared at her with lust in his eyes, and adrenaline flowed through Laryn's bloodstream. He didn't force himself on her, didn't do anything more than stare inappropriately, but it still felt like a violation. Especially because she was sure he was thinking about later, when he didn't have a deadline, when he'd be free to take what Altan had so obviously already given to him —her.

Without a word, he put the tray on the table, as well as the bag. Then he turned toward the door. He walked out, locking the door behind him once more.

Breathing a sigh of relief, Laryn looked down at the bag he'd brought. Curiosity had her walking over to look inside—and pleasure hit for the first time in days.

Clothes. And they were clean.

Pulling them out, she saw it was a uniform, much as Mert had been wearing. There was no underwear, but she didn't even care. She dropped the towel and pulled the pants up her legs. They were too long and too big around the waist, but again... clean. There was no bra included in the bag, and Laryn refused to go without. So she reluctantly put her tank top back on. It almost physically hurt to wear the stinky garment, but she had no time to wash it before she was expected to get to work.

The shirt she was given, surprisingly, was too small. Whoever had estimated her size was an idiot, or they'd misjudged the size of her boobs. Maybe the shirt was meant for a man her height, which made sense, as he wouldn't have to worry about the extra room she needed at the bust. The buttons strained, but she was covered, that was all that mattered.

She put the clean socks on, they too were too big, but at the moment she didn't care, and quickly put her boots back on. She felt way too vulnerable without shoes on.

Her stomach growled at the smell coming from the tray, but Laryn quickly went to the sink and washed her panties with the bar of precious soap. She hung them from the shower pipe sticking out of the wall, then turned her attention to the food.

She had no idea what she was eating, just that it was the best meal she'd had in over a week. It was some sort of rice with sauce and mystery vegetables. She would've liked some protein, but beggars couldn't be choosers. She also gulped down the water that was included with the meal. She could almost feel her body soaking in the nutrients.

Suddenly, Laryn was so tired she could barely keep her eyes open. Being clean, having eaten, her body was ready to shut down, to replenish some of the sleep she'd missed while in the dungeon.

But that would have to wait. The key in the lock alerted her to Mert's return. His gaze went from her feet, up her legs, to her hand holding the waistband so the pants didn't fall down, up the straining material over her chest, and finally, to her eyes.

Her hair was still wet, hanging around her shoulders, dampening the material of the uniform top, and he smirked. He walked up to her and stood in her personal space, forcing Laryn to crane her neck to keep her eyes on him.

"Wives walk behind their husbands," he informed her, speaking for the first time. His English was impeccable, with almost no accent. If she'd met him in the States, she wouldn't have thought he was anything other than a man born and raised there, which for some reason made him all the more scary.

"I'm not your wife," she found the courage to say.

"Yes, you are. Altan gave you to me. That's how it works here. You do what he says, we *all* do what he says, and in return, he gives us what we need and want. What I want is a wife. And now I have one. Walk behind me. Three paces. No more, no less," he ordered, then turned toward the door.

Laryn was stunned. This couldn't be happening. But it was.

Mert got to the door and looked behind him. He saw she was still standing where he'd left her, so he turned and walked back.

Without warning, his hand flew out and he backhanded Laryn. Hard.

She fell onto the bed, hitting her hip on the metal frame and crying out in pain from both strikes.

"Wives walk three steps behind their husbands at all times," he repeated slowly, as if maybe she didn't hear him the first time. "If they don't obey, they are punished."

Laryn wanted to cry, but she wouldn't give this asshole the satisfaction. She slowly stood, her cheek throbbing. It was probably red, maybe even had the imprint of his hand. But she had a feeling no one would dare say a word about it.

He's coming, Laryn told herself silently as she fell in behind Mert as he left the room. *Tate's coming. You just have to hang on until then.*

But with every minute that passed, Laryn worried that she wasn't strong enough. That she wouldn't be able to do this. She was beginning to think that staying in the dungeon would've been preferable to whatever was in store for her up here.

Swallowing hard, she took a deep breath. Then another.

No. She *could* do this. Had no choice. She'd endure whatever she had to until help came.

Please let help be coming.

CHAPTER EIGHTEEN

Casper was as focused as he'd ever been before a mission. Buck and Obi-Wan were in the pilot and copilot seats of their MH-60. He, Pyro, Chaos, and Edge were decked out in all black clothing, bulletproof vests, and firepower that included grenades, flash bombs, pistols, and plenty of ammunition. Edge had first-aid supplies. Pyro was in charge of navigation; he had the best sense of direction out of all of them, both in the air and on the ground. Chaos was their eyes and ears for anyone coming up behind them...

And Casper had Tex in his ear.

When he'd called Tex to tell him that they'd gotten the okay to go in and get Laryn, the former SEAL had insisted on being involved. Casper had no problem agreeing. He needed all the help he could get. To find a way into the hangar, to find Laryn, and then to get the hell out of dodge.

Tex had maps, satellite feeds, and an almost supernatural ability to see through time and space to know what was going on. It almost felt as if he was physically there. And Casper was glad for the help.

"Things got busy tonight. More movement," Tex said in

Casper's ear as the MH-60 took off from the deck of the destroyer. This was it. They'd either return with Laryn in tow or die trying. And Casper had no plans on dying today. He had a life with Laryn to live. No way was he letting some asshole take that away from him before he'd had a chance to experience it.

"As I told you before," Tex said, "my suggestion is that you and your team approach the hangar from the east. Getting through the security around where the building is located won't be difficult, because there isn't any. They do have guards stationed at the main entry points of the hangar, but on the side where the neighborhood stands, there aren't any doors."

"So how are we getting in?" Casper asked.

"I said there aren't doors, but there are plenty of windows. You'll have to find one that's broken or open, or can be otherwise breached without making too much noise."

Casper nodded to himself as Buck and Obi-Wan flew over the dark waters of the Mediterranean toward the hills outside the city where Laryn had been taken. All things considered, the time between when she was taken and now was relatively short. But not short enough. Casper couldn't stop thinking about all the things that could've happened to her in a week's time. It made him feel sick inside.

He did his best to shut off those thoughts. His only objective was getting in, finding Laryn, and getting them the hell out. They could deal with the ramifications of whatever had happened to her when they were all safe. He supposed this was the moment when some men would decide they didn't want to deal with a woman who would almost certainly be dealing with some form of PTSD in the future. But not Casper. He'd never met a woman who was more his match than Laryn. Together, they'd figure out what she needed.

"You hear me?"

"Sorry, no," Casper admitted.

"Hey...everything I've learned about Laryn proves that she's tough," Tex said quietly.

Casper didn't love that the man had been looking into Laryn, but he supposed it was necessary...and he appreciated the assurance just then.

"I've known some amazing women over the years," Tex continued. "They all went through some shit, but with the support of their friends and their men, they're thriving today. I have no doubt Laryn will do the same."

Determination rose within Casper. Damn straight she would. She'd probably bitch at him for losing another chopper so soon after the last one. She'd complain about the workload she'd be under trying to retrofit another MH-60 and having to endure another test flight.

He took a deep breath and nodded. "Yeah," he said a little belatedly.

The rest of the flight was spent going over the layout of the hangar, at least from what Tex had been able to uncover. He wasn't sure of the number of employees who'd be at the warehouse at this time of night, but they were all hoping the number at two in the morning would be less than if they went in during the day or even closer to sunrise.

Before they knew it, Buck and Obi-Wan were hovering over the LZ and the Night Stalkers began to fast rope to the ground below.

When Casper was the only one left in the back, Buck turned around and said, "We'll be waiting for word to come in for extraction. Bring her home, Casper."

"I plan on it," he told his friend with a firm nod, before grabbing the rope and stepping out of the back of the chopper. It didn't take long for him to be on the ground next to his friends. No one said a word as they adjusted their small packs and began jogging toward the city. It was likely the chopper had been seen, but no one would know that it hadn't simply been off course.

That it had been dropping off four operatives intent on stealing back what was theirs.

Casper wasn't interested in what excuses the captain might give the Turkish government for their chopper being in their airspace. His only concern was Laryn.

The couple klicks to the city didn't take long, and soon the four men were weaving in and out of streets that had seen better days. Expensive homes and cars parked along the roadway had given way to the poorer section, which was their destination. The hangar that held the military's brand-new MH-60 choppers was in a run-down part of the city. Casper supposed that was done deliberately. To try to disguise exactly what was inside.

As they neared their objective, the four men slowed. The building loomed tall in front of them, in stark contrast to the two-story run-down apartment buildings and shacks that had been assembled nearby. Casper's heart was racing, adrenaline coursing through his bloodstream as he crouched under one of the many windows along the east side, just as Tex had suggested.

He could enable comms with the former SEAL with a simple press of a button on his radio, but Casper was done planning. He was ready for action. The first place they'd look for Laryn was the basement. Tex had let them know there was a huge room under the floor of the hangar. It could be storage, but Tex's intel said it was a dungeon of sorts. Full of cells reserved for men who'd been accused of treason or other high-level crimes. The thought of Laryn being down there made Casper want to puke, but it was the most logical place for Osman to stash her.

Tex had warned if she was down there, it wouldn't be easy to break her out. There were no windows on that level and the only way out was up one of two narrow staircases. It would be easy for them to be trapped down there, so they had to be very careful not to get caught.

The hangar where the choppers were located was much like any other. A large, open space with a few offices along the north and south walls. There was a catwalk around the entire area, likely so guards could keep watch over what was happening on the floor below.

Above that was an entire floor of rooms. Tex had guessed they housed the men who worked on the helicopters and airplanes stored in the building. If Laryn was in one of those rooms, Casper and his team would be hard-pressed to find her without raising alarm bells. It wasn't as if they could knock on every door and ask politely for an American woman.

It seemed getting into the country was the easy part of this mission. Casper wasn't above killing every single person who stood between him and Laryn, despite promising the captain that bloodshed would be kept to a minimum.

Taking out a snake camera—a tiny lens at the end of a flexible piece of metal, much like a snake tool used back home to clean clogs from toilets—Casper lifted it to the window nearest him and pointed it at the glass.

Watching the video being transmitted on the small screen on his wrist, Casper held his breath, not sure what they'd find.

To his surprise, the hangar was fairly busy. Lights shone in the middle of the cavernous space, making it easy to see what was going on. He spotted two MH-60 helicopters, with men walking around, under, and inside them. It was three-thirty in the morning, and it seemed as if the government wasn't wasting any time getting their new acquisitions battle ready.

"*Pbsst*."

Looking to his right, Casper saw Edge motioning him toward him.

"This window's open," Edge whispered.

What the hell?

"Open?" Chaos asked quietly.

"Yeah. I figured I might as well try to see if we could get in the easy way. I pushed up on the glass and the fucking thing opened," Edge said, clearly as surprised as the rest of them.

Casper shook his head in disbelief. So much for national security. But he supposed most people in this area knew better than to go into this building. Especially if the intel about working conditions Tex had passed along was any indication.

Lifting the camera once more, Casper stuck it into the open window, pleased at how much clearer the picture on the small screen became.

He took several precious minutes to look around carefully, racking his brain for a clue on how they were going to enter. While there weren't nearly as many people as Tex had estimated were working during the day, there were still way more than their four-man team had expected for the middle of the night. They'd been hoping to sneak in and stay in the shadows while they went to the staircase that led down to the cells beneath the hangar floor.

Then something caught his eye. He stopped the camera and panned back.

There!

One of the workers crouched under the nose of the chopper had long hair. It was pulled up into a bun, but now that he was focusing on the person, it was obviously a woman.

It was Laryn!

"She's there!" he exclaimed softly, with immense relief.

"Where?" Pyro asked.

"At the chopper on the right. Under the nose."

"How many guards are there?"

That was the weird thing. Casper didn't see anyone standing around with rifles or any other weapons, forcing anyone to work.

As he continued to watch, he was further confused by how... *normal* the scene looked. Laryn occasionally said something to a worker nearby, and that person would bring her some sort of tool. It literally looked like any other workday for her. Casper had seen her do the same things day after day while working on his own MH-60.

A moment of doubt assailed him. Was this not a kidnapping? Had he misunderstood the entire situation? Had Laryn *planned* this? She'd been the one to insist on staying inside the helicopter on the destroyer. She could've easily loosened the wires to the FLIR, then planned to jump in and save the day. She also could've passed along intel on where the extraction would be taking place.

But almost as soon as he had the thought, Casper dismissed it. Thanks to Tex, they'd found the men responsible for betraying their mission and sabotaging their choppers. And even if they hadn't, there was no way Laryn could've known they'd be landing. No possible way to know about the SEALs getting separated from their group. No way she'd betray her country. And *definitely* no way she would've put so many people in danger, just to take a new job.

No. She would've simply put in her resignation and flown to Turkey of her own accord.

Ashamed that he'd doubted Laryn for even one second, Casper continued to survey the hangar. He studied the workers around the helicopter. Many looked malnourished and skinny. They didn't meet anyone's eyes and there was no banter being exchanged back and forth between any of the workers. The hangar back home was a loud place when the mechanics were in there working. Lots of trash talk and joking around.

The men working here seemed as if they'd rather be anywhere else. And now that he was paying closer attention, there were a few men dressed in the same uniform shirt and pants as Laryn, who didn't seem to fit in with the other mechanics. They were muscular, tall, their gazes constantly sweeping the large room.

It wasn't obvious what they were looking for...unless they were there to make sure everyone was doing their jobs and no one tried to leave.

Frowning, feeling stupid, Casper realized for the first time that this wasn't a regular military operation. This was forced labor.

Osman was essentially a contractor for the government, and he apparently did whatever it took to keep his employers—the government—happy with his work. Including forcing men to work long hours for probably very little pay, and a few threats against their loved ones thrown in for good measure. The government might not even know one of their contractors had gone rogue and was kidnapping men and women to work for him.

Feeling better that perhaps the Turkish government wasn't falling back on Stalin-like practices from the Soviet era, Casper focused on Laryn.

She didn't smile, didn't try to make conversation with anyone—it was likely no one could understand her, or vice versa, anyway—and seemed to be working in one particular area under the nose of the chopper for a very long time.

Then it occurred to Casper what she was doing.

She was stalling.

Yes, there was a lot of sensitive tech equipment under the nose, but that stuff wasn't her area of expertise. She knew the basics, but she was better with engines and the more mechanical aspects of the bird.

One of the large men next to Laryn said something to her that Casper obviously couldn't hear, but he could see Laryn's reaction to the words. She tensed and shook her head. She looked exhausted, but she was standing her ground against the man.

Clearly ignoring whatever her reply had been, he grabbed her upper arm. Laryn struggled against him, to no avail, and he began dragging her out from under the chopper.

Casper had seen enough. They'd found Laryn, they wouldn't need to knock on every door on the upper level and wouldn't have to navigate the dungeon. They needed to move. *Now.*

"I'm going in," he told his team.

They didn't protest, didn't ask what the plan was. They'd worked together long enough, had to fly by the seat of their pants enough times, literally, that they'd figure out a plan as they went.

For a split-second, Casper thought about his brother. Nate would be appalled at the Night Stalkers' apparent lack of any kind of organized plan. As a Navy SEAL, he and his team probably had plans A, B, C, and even D before they set foot on any kind of transport.

But even the best plan could be fucked by one simple element that was out of their control. Casper and his fellow pilots' skills lie in making life-or-death decisions on the fly.

Because all the bright lights were currently pointed toward the MH-6os in the middle of the room, the beams didn't quite reach the walls of the cavernous space. Which meant the four men were able to silently infiltrate the building without anyone even noticing.

The lack of obvious weapons made Casper's hopes rise that they'd be able to grab Laryn and get the hell out of dodge without any—or much—resistance.

Looking around for her once he was inside, Casper had a moment of panic when he couldn't spot Laryn right away. Then a commotion on the other side of the hangar, near the stairs, caught his attention.

Laryn had managed to pull her arm out of the man's grip, and she'd fallen on her ass on the hard concrete floor. The man was standing above her, frowning.

"Get up!" he barked in a voice loud enough that it carried across the huge room.

"No! I'm not going anywhere with you!"

"You are. And this defiance will be punished. You'll learn to obey your husband one way or another. Now...Get. Up."

Husband? No fucking way!

Casper saw red. It was only Pyro's hand on his arm that kept him from rushing straight across the hangar floor to where Laryn sat on the floor. They'd been inching along the shadows on the outskirts of the room, trying to stay undetected for as long as possible. There was no telling the chaos that would explode once they were discovered.

But as Casper worked his way toward Laryn, needing to get to her as fast as possible, something strange was happening around them. They *were* being noticed...by the workers closest to them.

And no one was raising any kind of alarm.

Most of the men Casper had clocked as being guards of some sort were watching the scene between Laryn and the man who claimed to be her husband. They weren't paying any attention to the perimeter of the room, to anyone who might be hiding in the shadows.

With every second that passed, more employees spotted Casper and his team, but still no one said a word, solidifying his guess that no one was there voluntarily. They were forced labor, and not too keen on bringing any kind of attention to themselves.

Or maybe even hoping for their own opportunity to escape...

Making a split-second decision as he and his team approached one of the large hangar doors on the north side of the building, Casper grasped the handle of the door and yanked back, *hard*, praying it wasn't locked. Just like the damn window they'd used to gain entry.

It wasn't.

The door groaned and let out a horrible screeching noise, but it rolled back wide enough to allow several people to pass through side by side.

Then Casper aimed his pistol and shot a few rounds into the ground, just outside the door. The noise was startling in its loudness, especially with the hangar being so unnaturally silent.

He yelled, "Go!" as he pointed toward the now open door.

Several of the workers standing near him and his team looked confused, but he saw the exact moment understanding dawned.

All it took was one man making a break for the door to set off the others around him. Casper and his team were almost trampled as they rushed to get out of the way of the men racing for freedom.

He'd needed a distraction, and he'd gotten one.

The men he'd tagged as guards were now yelling, probably telling everyone to stop, to get back to work, but no one listened. They'd caught a whiff of freedom and were doing what they could to take it.

His attention now focused on finding his woman, Casper rushed forward, no longer concerned with staying in the shadows. No one paid attention to him and the others as they raced toward where they'd last seen Laryn.

But she wasn't there anymore.

Looking around frantically, Casper's heart fell into his throat when he didn't see her. Then he heard her scream. Turning, he saw a door.

Of course. The stairs. The man had dragged her into the stairwell, was probably taking her up to one of the rooms.

Pyro had obviously had the same thought, as he beat Casper to the door, pulling it open and holding it for the others as they ran through.

Laryn's voice was louder now, echoing around the stairwell.

"*No*. Stop! Let go of me, you asshole!"

It sounded as if they were at the top of the stairs above them. Then a loud smacking sound reached his ears, right before Laryn cried out in pain.

A sheen of red fell over Casper's eyes. The man would die for putting his hands on Laryn. He'd promised to keep casualties to a minimum, but he was looking forward to taking out this bastard.

A door clanged shut above them just as Casper started taking the stairs two at a time, desperate to reach her before the man got her inside one of the rooms on the floor above.

Not knowing if the man was armed, Casper quietly opened the door at the top in time to see Laryn literally being dragged down the hall by her hair.

She was kicking her feet and holding onto the man's wrist, trying to take the pressure off her scalp. She was also swearing like a sailor, using every curse word she'd learned over the years from working alongside her fellow blue-collar mechanics.

Casper rushed along the hall on silent feet, quickly closing the distance between himself and Laryn, endlessly relieved to have her in his sights, but hating the fear and pain he could hear under the angry words spewing from her mouth.

To his surprise, the noise in the hall wasn't making anyone open their doors to see what the commotion was all about. He had no idea why, but was glad they weren't going to have to deal with anyone deciding to join the fray.

The man holding Laryn glanced back when Casper was just feet away, maybe sensing his palpable anger, and his eyes widened in surprise. He moved his free hand to his waist, probably to pull a weapon, but Casper was already on him.

He tackled the man, knocking him backward and forcing him to let go of Laryn's hair. He heard her let out a squeak of pain, but all Casper's attention was on the man who'd dared to hurt the woman he loved.

The weapon he'd been reaching for was a knife, but he had no time to go for it again before Casper punched the man once, twice. Three times.

As Casper reached for his pistol, the man spoke, sounding outraged. "She's mine!" he claimed.

"She's not! She's a United States citizen who was taken against her will," he growled, pressing the barrel of his gun against the man's forehead.

He went still under Casper, smiling slightly, and said in perfect English, "She's my wife. She was given to me, and in *my* country, that trumps all other rights."

Casper was done talking. Fuck this. Fuck *him*.

He squeezed the trigger.

With his ears ringing from the shot, Casper was moving before the man even went limp under him. He stood and grabbed Laryn away from Pyro who'd gotten her clear when the fight started, and pulled her away from the very dead man behind her, holding her against his chest.

"I knew you'd come. I knew you'd come," Laryn chanted, as she held onto him for dear life.

She was trembling hard, and she felt skinnier than when he'd last held her. Hate for the situation she'd found herself in filled Casper. He regretted that Osman wasn't there for him to kill. The man would surely do whatever he could to get his hands back on Laryn, but that wasn't happening. Not as long as he had breath in his body.

"That's what happens when you bring a knife to a gun fight," Chaos said as he nudged the man's arm with his boot to make sure he was dead. "We going after Osman?"

Technically that was their one job. To find and take out Altan Osman. But with Laryn in his arms, obviously traumatized, the only thing Casper could think about was getting her the hell out of here. Making sure she was safe. He'd disregarded her safety one too many times already. No way was he doing it again. Even if it meant a reprimand on his record.

He shook his head. "We need to get her out of here."

Chaos nodded without hesitation.

Casper pushed a button on the radio in his ear.

"Tex?"

"Here."

"Got her. Call Buck. Tell him we're headed to the roof."

"Roger. Out."

Taking a quick second, he eased Laryn back and tried to assess her condition. She was bruised and looked shell-shocked, but none of her injuries looked life threatening. They needed to get to the roof and get the hell out of there. He had no way of knowing what was happening on the hangar floor, if the distraction of the workers making a break for it was keeping the other guards busy, but he wasn't going to wait around to find out.

"It's weird that no one has come out to see what's going on," Edge said from behind Casper, as he put his arm around Laryn, plastered her to his side and headed back down the hall.

"The rooms are locked from the outside," Laryn said in a shaky voice. "They couldn't come out if they wanted to."

No one said a word, but Casper felt sick inside yet again. He wanted to help the men, and possibly women, who were behind the locked doors, but his priorities were Laryn and his team. They couldn't wait around any longer than necessary. But he vowed to tell Tex everything he'd seen tonight, and perhaps the former SEAL could do something to help the people being forced to work here.

They reached the stairwell, and Edge pushed around Casper, opening the door and checking to make sure the coast was clear.

It was.

The men started up the last flight of stairs to the door that led to the roof. It was locked, but Chaos didn't hesitate to pull out his pistol and shoot the shit out of the mechanism. Metal fragments went flying, and Casper turned his back to the shrapnel to protect Laryn from getting hurt. She curled into his chest as his teammate made quick work of the lock.

And then they were standing on the roof. The air was clean, the night clear, and in any other situation, Casper might have taken the time to admire the view of the city from this vantage point.

They could still hear shouts below them, and Casper was relieved it seemed the escaping workers *were* still a distraction.

He could only hope their luck held and Buck and Obi-Wan would get there and get them the hell out of dodge before the shit *really* hit the fan.

They'd been lucky so far, and he prayed their luck held for just a little longer.

"Laryn? Look at me. Are you okay?"

She lifted her chin, and Casper wasn't happy at the dazed look in her beautiful brown eyes. She had dark circles under them, and she was still trembling. She looked overwhelmed, terrified, and unsure of herself.

But then she spoke. "I'm alive, and you're here. I'm perfect."

This woman. She slayed him. She'd been through obvious hell, yet she was still standing tall. Regardless, Casper intended to hear about every minute of what had happened to her since she'd been taken from him, so he could do everything in his power to lessen the impact of what she'd been through.

He took two seconds to appreciate the feel of Laryn in his arms. Bent but not broken, by any means. Something in his soul shifted at that moment. He'd been determined to find her and get her back, but hadn't been sure he'd be able to do either. And yet, here she was. It was a miracle. *She* was a miracle. His miracle. He vowed never to take her for granted ever again. He'd done that for too long as it was.

Just when Casper heard the most beautiful sound in the world, the whir of rotor blades, the stairwell door slammed open.

Moving on instinct, Casper shoved Laryn behind him and pulled out his pistol, his three friends doing the same. They moved closer to him and formed a wall between the stairwell and Laryn. They hadn't gotten this close to rescue to fail now.

A man stood in front of them, panting. His eyes were wide and crazy-looking. His dark hair was sticking up and his clothes were wrinkled. And, if Casper wasn't mistaken, his shirt was on inside out.

"No!" he exclaimed, ignoring the four guns pointed at him as he stalked forward.

"*Stop!*" Pyro exclaimed. "Right now!"

"It's Altan," Laryn said from behind them.

Casper wasn't surprised. That's who he assumed this must be. He was glad he was here—he'd be able to complete this mission after all.

The man was dead, he just didn't know it yet.

But first, Casper needed intel. He had about two minutes before Buck and Obi-Wan arrived. He'd do his best to get what he could from this man, what his country needed, before he ended any future threat to Laryn once and for all.

CHAPTER NINETEEN

Laryn stayed as close to Tate's back as she dared. She didn't want to be a hindrance to anything he needed to do, but she couldn't make herself break contact with him. He was her lifeline. Literally.

She'd thought that was it—Mert would get her back to her room and rape her. That was his plan; she'd had no doubt whatsoever.

She'd done her best to stall, to do basic maintenance on the MH-60, but she'd been exhausted and it was hard to concentrate when she was dead on her feet. When Mert had decided he'd waited long enough, grabbing her, it surprised the hell out of her, and her fight-or-flight response kicked in.

It was impossible to get away from him though. He was bigger, stronger, and wasn't weak from spending the last several days in a dungeon. The men around her were no help, as they were in the same boat she was...forced to work for Altan. It was easy to tell that no one was there willingly. They were most likely being blackmailed or threatened in order to keep working. Though, none of them had the expertise needed to outfit the choppers properly.

It was equally obvious that the workers were rotated in and out of the rooms on the floor she'd been taken to earlier that afternoon. Probably several men in each room, based on the number of workers on the floor at one time, versus the doors she saw in the hallway. All locked in, only brought out to toil in the hangar, while other workers took their places in the rooms. It was a miserable way to live, made clear in the lack of enthusiasm those around her had for their jobs.

It wasn't until Mert had gotten her close to the stairs that reality really set in. Tate wasn't coming, at least not yet, and her time was up. Mert was going to assault her, but Laryn wasn't willing to go down without a fight. She'd never stop resisting, stop fighting. Mert might claim her as his wife, but she'd never consent. Never be anything but a pain in his ass.

When he hit her, it hurt. A lot. More than when he'd hit her the first time. The pain shocked her enough that she'd sat on the floor, stunned for a moment, and that's when Mert made his move. He grabbed her again and pulled her up the stairs.

Laryn fought with all she had, but in the hallway, when he'd grabbed her hair and literally began dragging her behind him, all she could do was try to hold onto his wrist to lessen the pain.

Then one second she was being dragged toward her room, and the next, she was free, lying on the floor staring at the man she loved who'd appeared as if out of thin air.

Tate.

He was there.

He'd come for her.

Pyro had grabbed hold of her and pulled her away from Tate and Mert, but not before she saw Tate beating the crap out of the man who'd surely been going to sexually assault her. She didn't look away, not even when Tate put his gun against Mert's forehead and pulled the trigger. And then she was in Tate's arms. The relief she felt had been immense.

Things were kind of fuzzy after that, but she couldn't

concentrate on anything but the relief she felt being in Tate's arms.

They went up the stairs to the roof and the night air felt like a new beginning. Laryn felt as if she were floating. She had no fears anymore. Tate was there. He'd keep her safe.

She had no idea how much time went by when she was abruptly shifted behind Tate and all four men formed a human shield between her and Altan.

Seeing him actually snapped Laryn out of the semi-trance she'd been in since Mert's death. Now she felt anger building. Anger at the situation Altan had put her in. At his arrogance in thinking he could force not only her, but everyone else in that hangar to do his bidding. At thinking he could just give her away to Mert.

"It's Altan," she told Tate, but it was obvious he knew exactly who the desperate man was in front of them.

"Please! Stay!" he begged, glancing at the men, at the guns pointed at his head, at Laryn. "I need you!"

"You *need* to shut up," Tate countered.

"Everything I've worked for, all the contacts I've made, they'll be for naught if I don't get those MH-60s retrofitted. You're the best there is. You know all there is to know about those machines. *I need you!*"

Laryn opened her mouth to tell him to fuck off. That she didn't care if he was executed by his own government for not meeting whatever promises he'd made them. But Tate spoke before she could.

"Let's talk about those contacts," he said quietly. "How'd you get so many Americans to do your bidding?"

"Money," Altan blurted succinctly, as if it was obvious. As Laryn supposed it was.

"How'd you find them in the first place?" Pyro pressed.

"The dark web is a vast place, filled with people looking for money in exchange for information. Look...Laryn. I am sorry about how all this went down. But I promise things will be different now. You don't want a husband? Fine. Is it more money you want? I can do that. I just need you to stay. You don't understand—"

"Don't even look at her, asshole," Edge growled.

"What's the matter? You been operating without your leaders' knowledge or permission?" Chaos asked.

The look on Altan's face answered the question without him having to say a word.

"You have," Tate said darkly. "Do they know *anything* about your little operation here? How you're using intimidation and threats to get the men to work? Or how you *kidnapped* Laryn to get her on your little project?"

"They don't care as long as they get their precious choppers!" Altan yelled. "And the ends justify the means! When they get an MH-60 ready to go that can hold its own against any other military aircraft in the region, they'll give me everything I was promised. Money, land, respect!"

Laryn was disgusted.

"And it doesn't matter how many lives you ruin to get there," Tate retorted.

"The men here are being compensated. Food, a room to sleep, work."

"They're *locked* inside those rooms!" Edge exclaimed. "And I'm guessing the food is shit too. And should we even talk about the men in the dungeon?"

Altan looked shocked. "How do you know about that?"

"We know everything," Tate said.

Laryn glanced behind her at the glorious sound of an MH-60, now coming in hot.

"We know you kidnap innocent women to force them to do your bidding. That you have no problem standing by while she's assaulted. That you think nothing of ruining the lives of the men you've forced to work for you...all for what? Money? Perceived power? The fact that your government has no idea the lengths you'll go to for those things makes me feel a hell of a lot better," Tate bit out.

"If you leave, you'll regret it," Altan said with hate in his voice. The fake penitence was now gone. Laryn shivered at the venom she heard. Toward *her*. "You brought this on yourself! You should have accepted my first offer. If you leave now, this is going to become an international incident. I wouldn't be surprised if the US found itself in the middle of a huge scandal, maybe even a war with my country! You can't just cross our borders without suffering the consequences. One way or another, I'll get you back. Mark my words, I—"

Laryn jumped at the loud report from Tate's weapon.

Altan fell to the roof with a thud, just as the MH-60 hovered in the air at the edge of the roof.

"Ready to go?" Tate asked calmly, as if this was just another day of work for him. And she guessed in some ways, it was.

Pyro was already running toward the chopper, and the other two men waited nearby, their weapons at the ready, just in case anyone else decided to check out what was happening on the roof.

Laryn's gaze went to Altan, who was lying motionless, blood slowly pooling around him. She looked back at Tate. "Is he dead?"

"Yes. No way in hell was I leaving him alive to come after you again."

"You were going to kill him all along?" she asked.

"Of course. Officially, that's the reason we're here."

"What were all those questions about? Why didn't you guys shoot him as soon as he showed up on the roof?"

"Intel," Edge said, answering her question. "We didn't think we'd get much, but if there was anything he could tell us about how he'd found his moles in our military, we needed that info."

Laryn wrinkled her nose. "Did you get anything out of what he said?"

"Plenty. Come on, let's get the hell out of here, yeah?" Tate didn't sound irritated or anxious. He gestured toward the chopper. "Our ride's here."

Edge got on one side of her while Tate was glued to the other. Chaos was close on their heels as they hurried toward where Pyro and the chopper waited. Buck and Obi-Wan hadn't landed on the roof. One skid was resting on the very edge, and they were hovering in the air. She was impressed all over again at the skills of these pilots.

Pyro and Tate lifted her into the back of the chopper, and she quickly moved to the side. It was a matter of seconds before the other men had joined her and they were rising into the sky. Buck and Obi-Wan gunned it, and they shot away from the hangar.

The last thing Laryn saw was the dark shape of Altan Osman, lying dead in a pool of his own blood on the roof.

Tate placed a pair of headphones over her ears before putting a pair over his own.

"Should we expect any kind of retaliation?" Buck asked in a tense, serious tone.

"Negative. Osman was rogue. Working outside the government," Edge told his friend. "I mean, they knew what he was tasked with doing, and were probably giving him money to get those choppers retrofitted, but it seems pretty clear they have no idea he's been kidnapping, threatening, and blackmailing his workforce."

"Fuck. Seriously?" Obi-Wan asked.

"He said you guys being here is going to cause an international incident. That his government wasn't going to be pleased you'd come here without permission. Did I cause a war?" Laryn asked, terrified to hear the answer.

To her surprise, the men around her chuckled. She was taken

aback for a moment before Pyro explained. "He was talking out his ass, sweetheart. If anything, *he* would've been the one in deep shit. I'm not saying the Turkish government hasn't done some sketchy things, but everything Osman did to draw attention to them won't go over well."

Tate's arm went around her shoulders, and he pulled her against him. Laryn immediately melted into his side. The last ten minutes or so seemed like a blur. One second, she thought she was about to be assaulted, and now she was back in Tate's arms and hopefully on her way to safety.

Her entire body began to shake. "D-d-delayed reaction," she said, closing her eyes and doing her best to curb her body's response to the adrenaline dump. "I'm okay."

"I've got you. We've all got you," Tate reassured her.

With her eyes shut, Laryn let go of some of the control she'd been using to keep her body upright. Every part of her hurt. She was exhausted. Could sleep—on a nice soft bed, with a fluffy pillow—for days. But she had no doubt there would be debriefings she'd have to attend once they got to the ship. She'd need to explain what happened to her and what military secrets she might have exposed.

She'd do whatever was necessary, because deep down, she recognized that she'd brought some of what happened to her on herself, just as Altan had accused. If she'd simply stayed quiet and hadn't thought to escape her feelings for Tate by taking a new job... If she'd gotten out of the helicopter after fixing the FLIR the first time...

"No," Tate said sternly.

Looking up at him, she frowned. "No, what?"

"This wasn't your fault."

Her eyes widened. "How could you possibly know what I was thinking?"

"Because I know you. This was all Osman's doing. All of it. Paying off people in Virginia and on the ship to find out your movements. To orchestrate that kidnapping. He got what he deserved, and you shouldn't feel a second of regret."

"For Altan? I don't. Not at all. He was a dick," Laryn told him.

The men around her all chuckled.

"Right. So what are you feeling guilty about? And don't say nothing, I can tell you've got regret swirling behind those beautiful brown eyes of yours."

Laryn sighed. She looked around at the other five men in the helicopter. "You all put your lives, and maybe careers, on the line for me. I know better than most that it wasn't a matter of simply flying in to get me. There had to be a ton of red tape, and I'm still worried about relations between Turkey and the US going sour because of all this."

"No one's career is on the line. And we were never in any danger. Hell, most of the men in that hangar were just like you, Laryn. They weren't there of their own volition. The second they had a chance to get the hell out, they did. I think when the Turkish government hears what Osman was doing, and how he was going about it, there won't be any ramifications," Edge told her.

"Are you being honest with me? Or telling me what you think I want to hear?" she asked.

"I try not to lie," Edge said earnestly.

It wasn't exactly a straight answer, but Laryn realized it was the best she was going to get at the moment. She took a deep breath, then turned back to Tate. "How are those two SEALs doing? The ones you and Pyro had to go get?"

"Is she serious right now?" Pyro asked no one in particular.

Laryn glanced at him and said, "Yes, I'm serious. Why wouldn't I be?"

"Maybe because you were just rescued after being kidnapped and having who the hell knows what done to you for the week it took us to get to you, and you want to know how the Navy SEALs are doing?"

"Well, yeah."

"They're good," Obi-Wan said from his copilot seat. "Mustang and Pid are back in Hawaii, being spoiled by their friends and family."

"Thank God. And they're okay? They'll be able to continue doing...SEAL stuff?"

More chuckles sounded in her ears through the headphones. "Yeah, sweetheart, they'll be just fine."

She nodded. Then she glared at Tate. "You wrecked another chopper," she said sternly, falling back into the comfortable sniping they were so good at.

"Oh no, I did not. I landed perfectly."

"Did you or did you not have to destroy that MH-60 I slaved over? Spent hours upon hours getting flight ready?"

Humor made Tate's eyes sparkle.

"We couldn't let it fall into the wrong hands," Pyro said, defending his friend and fellow pilot.

"I about died when that asshole shot it up," Laryn admitted with a sigh. "I guess I have more long days and nights to look forward to, huh?"

Tate nuzzled the side of her head. "Guess so. But am I allowed to admit that I'm not entirely upset about this turn of events?"

"You *like* when I'm overworked and stressed out?" Laryn asked, feeling more and more like herself. This was what she needed. A bit of normalcy to overpower the horrible memories of the last week.

"No. I like when we're stateside. Without a chopper, it's not likely we'll be sent on any missions anytime soon," Tate said.

"Not to mention the Army probably isn't so keen to see us lose another chopper so soon after the last two," Pyro said with a chuckle.

"We're out of Turkey airspace," Buck informed them all through the headset.

Laryn sighed with relief. She hadn't realized how tense she'd been, but she was grateful for everyone's attempt at distracting her until they were well and truly out of danger.

As Buck and Obi-Wan flew them all back toward the destroyer, Tate said softly, "You did good, Laryn. I'm proud of you."

"You have no idea *what* I did. What I went through. Maybe I was in a three-room suite with food piled high on trays and everything I asked for at my disposal," Laryn countered.

Tate looked at her, his expression serious. "You've lost at least ten pounds from when I saw you last. You smell like soap, but it doesn't completely disguise the scent of mustiness and decay in your hair, which tells me you were probably in the dungeon under that hangar. And I can tell just by your body language that it's going to take a hot minute for you to get over what happened.

"I'm here for you, baby. I'm a good listener, and I want to know everything you survived from the second we left to pick up the SEALs, until we found you in the hallway with that asshole. And if you don't want to tell *me*, you'll talk to a psychologist. Because I plan on us having a long, happy life together, and in order to have that, you can't be constantly thinking about what happened back there."

He was scowling by the time he finished speaking, and Laryn couldn't help but grin up at him.

"Nothing is funny about this," Tate growled.

"I know," Laryn said, sobering. "You want to know what I was thinking the entire time?"

"That you wanted to kill those motherfuckers?" Chaos asked.

Laryn gave his teammate a quick smile before turning back to Tate. "Well, yes, but the thought that kept rolling around in my head was, 'Tate's coming.' I had no doubt you were doing everything in your power to get to me, and all I had to do was hold on until you got there. I stalled as much as possible, figuring the evil I knew was better than the evil I didn't. Yes, I was uncomfortable, and scared, and hungry. But I wasn't tortured. Wasn't beaten. I was just stashed in one of those cells in the dungeon under the hangar for most of my time there. It was dark, smelly, gross, and uncomfortable...but again, I knew you were coming for me. I just had to hold on for one more day, one more hour, one more minute."

"Laryn," Tate said, his voice quivering with emotion.

"There's no crying in the Night Stalkers," she admonished gently, as she hugged the man she'd loved for what seemed like forever.

"Wrong," Edge piped in.

Laryn wasn't even embarrassed that she was having this pretty intense conversation not only with Tate, but five of his best friends. She knew these men, had worked with them for years. Respected them. Loved them, each in their own way.

"We cry," Edge went on. "We're human just like everyone else. And there's no shame in crying. We've all done it. Sometimes it's the only way to get the emotions out so you can continue on with life."

He wasn't wrong. But his words also made Laryn wonder what exactly *he'd* cried about. There was a lot about these men she didn't know. And she was looking forward to getting to know them all better. A lot better. Because if she had her way, she'd be spending a lot more time with them, time outside of work, which was more than all right with her.

She felt Tate's hand on the side of her head, encouraging her to rest it against his shoulder, which she did gladly. She was exhausted and she felt grubby, but at that moment, in Tate's arms, safe, she didn't really care.

Laryn had no doubt that the next few hours, or days, weren't going to be fun, but after surviving what she had...she could deal with "no fun" without any issues. As she lay against Tate, she felt the sudden need to lose herself in her work. To put the past behind her. And thankfully, she'd have lots of work to occupy her time and mind in the foreseeable future.

She had a lot to look forward to...the most important of which was Tate. Every indication was that he was completely serious about a relationship with her. Something Laryn still had to pinch herself to believe.

She smiled. Content to put herself in this man's hands. He'd more than proven that he could, and would, stand between her and anyone or anything that might harm her. She couldn't ask for anything more.

CHAPTER TWENTY

Casper was done.

The last week had been full of nonstop debriefings. He'd gotten his ass chewed for taking a civilian on that flight to extricate the SEALs. He'd argued that Laryn wasn't exactly a civilian, but since he was still kicking his own ass for not kicking her out of his chopper and taking his chances with the FLIR, he didn't protest too much at the reprimand.

When they'd arrived back in Norfolk, the meetings didn't stop. He had to meet with the colonel, explain what had happened in detail.

And amazingly...he found himself face-to-face with none other than Tex. The man had actually come down from his home outside Pittsburgh to meet with him personally.

The legend was actually pretty chatty, which was a surprise. He'd actually been listening in while they were rescuing Laryn, and he'd had no problem speaking up when needed during the mission. It might've been annoying, but instead, looking back, it was somewhat amusing.

Tex had been positively gleeful at the intel Osman gave up.

He encouraged Casper to keep him talking, to not kill him too soon. And once Tex felt he had what he needed to start tracking down the other moles Osman had paid off, he simply said, "War my ass. Kill him."

Casper hadn't hesitated. He'd shot the asshole through the heart...and it had been so satisfying.

In the meeting on base, Tex had a lot to say about the information he'd dug up on Osman and how he'd found the men and occasional women who were feeding him intel. Those soldiers and sailors were now in the process of being charged with treason, including the sailors who'd been onboard the destroyer.

Mustang had called from Hawaii, wanting to check on Laryn, and he sent best wishes from himself and his team, and of course their families. He'd extended an open invitation to Casper's team to visit them if they ever found their way to Oahu.

The one thing Casper hadn't gotten enough of since returning home was Laryn. She'd been just as busy. She had her own share of debriefings to attend, as well as meetings with one of the psychologists on base who specialized in military personnel who'd been POWs. Technically, her situation couldn't be categorized as a prisoner of war, but she'd still been held against her will, tortured mentally by being dumped in that shithole of a cell, and tortured physically by that asshole keeping her hungry, thirsty, dirty, and sleep-deprived.

One morning, when she'd woken up after a nightmare around three o'clock, she'd finally opened up to Casper about everything she went through. She'd admitted that the worst had been the hood she was forced to wear for several days as she was transported through the mountains to the city. She'd cried, and Casper had felt helpless to do anything but hold her as she let out the emotions she tried so hard to keep bottled up.

They slept in the same bed each night, but they hadn't made love since returning to the States. The timing wasn't right, and with Laryn still recuperating from her ordeal, the last thing Casper wanted to do was add the pressure of sex. He'd been overwhelmed with relief when she told him that she hadn't been sexually assaulted. It didn't really make the other things she'd been through any better, but he was very thankful she didn't have to deal with that additional trauma on top of everything else.

Besides the timing being off, they were both dead on their feet by the time each evening rolled around. So they'd eat dinner together, then cuddle on the couch. Before long, one or both of them would end up nodding off.

It was more than time for them to get a break from work; from everything that had happened. Laryn was already retrofitting another MH-60 for him and Pyro, and he knew from experience that her exhaustion wasn't going away anytime soon. She prided herself on being able to get the chopper mission ready faster than any other mechanic team in the Army.

He'd cleared a day off for her with the colonel, and his plan was to take her home and keep her there for a full twenty-four hours. No meetings, no talk of MH-60s, nothing but enjoying each other's company and making sure she knew where they stood.

As far as Casper was concerned, they were two people well on their way to spending the rest of their lives together. To getting married and starting a family. He wanted that. With her. And he wanted to make sure they were on the same page. Yes, she'd had a crush on him; yes, she'd admitted that the reason she'd looked into taking another job in the first place was because she didn't think he'd ever see her as anything other than the mechanic who worked on his choppers. But that didn't mean she truly believed him when he said he wanted to be with her, and only her. It was past time to erase any lingering doubts she might have.

Casper strode across the hangar and couldn't help but smile

at the ass-chewing she was giving one of the junior enlisted soldiers who'd just joined her team.

"Around here, we don't watch the clock. We do *what* needs to be done, *when* it needs to be done. You want to know why?" She didn't wait for him to ask. "Because these birds aren't carrying spoiled tourists who want a glimpse of a fucking whale. They're holding the bravest and craziest and most talented pilots we've ever seen. They transport the SEALs and Deltas who keep our country free. Who are doing the most dangerous things you could ever imagine. So staying an extra ten minutes to finish whatever we're doing before heading home isn't a big deal. It's not a sacrifice on our parts. And if you think it is, you need to find a new place to work, and definitely a new job. You got a problem with that, private?"

"No, ma'am."

"Good. Look, I'm a hard boss. I admit it. I expect perfection from everyone who works with me. And loyalty to the men who fly these machines. Their lives depend on us tightening every screw and something as simple as making sure every fuse is properly installed. Understand?"

"Yes, ma'am," the young man said again.

"All right. Go home. Think about what I said. If you decide to stay, I can tell you that you'll never be prouder to have a part in making sure our brave special forces soldiers and our Night Stalkers make it home safe and sound after every mission. If you want to leave, find somewhere else to work, no hard feelings. Think about it and we'll talk tomorrow."

"Not tomorrow," Casper cut in, making himself known for the first time and straightening from where he'd been leaning against a box of parts waiting to be installed on the shell of the MH-60 in front of him. "The day after. Tomorrow, you have the day off." He glanced at the young man. "And I'm thinking if you make any decision other than to stay, you're an idiot, private."

"Yes, Sir," the kid said, before saluting Casper, then hurrying away from them as fast as he could without actually jogging.

"What? I don't have tomorrow off," Laryn said, her hands on her hips.

She'd filled out a little since they'd returned a week ago, mostly because Casper had been doing his best to keep her fed. Her hair was shiny once more, even though no one but him really saw it since, while at work, she kept it in the usual tidy bun at the nape of her neck. She smelled like her familiar sweet vanilla cookie self, which pleased them both beyond measure. Her showers were a little longer than they'd been previously, but Casper completely understood. Being clean wasn't anything she'd ever take for granted again.

As she stood in front of him, irritation making her practically vibrate, Casper couldn't help but be thankful she was in his life. That she was here in front of him. Healthy and back to her normal bossy, prickly self.

"You do," he countered. "I talked to the colonel and he agreed that after everything, we're both due some time off."

"We?" she asked, her tense demeanor relaxing a fraction.

"Yup. You okay with that?"

"Are you kidding? Yes! Wait...are we going to be spending our time off *together*?"

"Of course. I have plans that include, food, a bed, and us not leaving it for at least eight hours."

"Ooooh, you're such a dirty talker. I can't wait to sleep for eight hours straight."

Casper burst out laughing. This woman was going to keep him on his toes, and he'd love every second of it. Closing the distance between them, he pulled her into his embrace and kissed her. The kiss wasn't as deep or passionate as he wanted, but they *were* still at work.

"Tate, you can't do that here!" Laryn protested, but she didn't pull out of his arms.

"I can and will. I'm done pretending I'm not crazy about you while we're at work. It's not forbidden, since you aren't enlisted and don't technically work for me. And after everything that happened, I refuse to not show you every chance I get how important you are to me."

"Tate." This time her voice was softer, full of affection. "Did you really talk to the colonel? Do we really have all of tomorrow off?"

"Yes to both."

"Awesome."

"In fact, our time off starts now. You at a point where you can get away?"

"Yes. I just need to talk to Chuck and let him know what needs to be worked on next. And since I won't be here tomorrow, tell him to check the engine mount to make sure there aren't any cracks or weak spots, since we'll be installing the engine in the next week. Oh! And I want to discuss calibrating the Engine Control Unit. The last thing we need is the freaking engine failing in the middle of a test flight because it wasn't calibrated right—"

"Sergeant Wells!" Casper yelled across the hangar, toward a group of men standing around.

One looked up, then jogged over to where he and Laryn were standing.

"Yes, Sir?" he asked, saluting his superior officer.

"I'm taking Laryn home. She won't be here tomorrow. Don't fuck up my chopper, okay?"

Chuck smirked. "Of course not, Sir. It's about time she got a day off."

"Tate! I need to talk to him."

"No, you don't. You need to go home. Relax for half a second."

"I agree," Chuck said. "Don't worry, we won't do anything you wouldn't approve of."

"You better not," Laryn said, narrowing her eyes and glaring at the man.

The sergeant simply chuckled.

Casper put his hand on the small of Laryn's back and pushed her toward the large open bay doors. "If you need anything... don't call," he told the sergeant.

"Roger."

"Ignore him!" Laryn called over her shoulder. "If anything happens, let me know!"

Chuck merely waved, then turned back to the group of men he'd been talking to before being summoned.

"That was rude," she admonished.

He simply shrugged. "If I let you have your conversation, it would've lasted for at least an hour. I simply took the more expedient route."

"You're annoying," she groused, but Casper noticed she didn't contradict him.

"But you love me anyway," he told her with a smirk.

"Yeah, I do."

Her words sunk in as they stepped outside, and Casper stopped in his tracks. "What?"

"What, what?" Laryn asked, looking around in alarm.

Casper took her face in his hands and tilted her chin up, so she had no choice but to look him in the eyes. "What did you just say?"

"Um...I don't know?"

"You love me?" he asked, feeling uncertain and off-kilter for some reason.

She chuckled a little nervously, then shrugged. "Oh. Yeah."

"You love me." This time it wasn't a question.

"Tate, I've loved you for years. We've talked about this. It's why I was looking for another job. Because being around you and having you not even know I existed was becoming too painful."

Without a word, Casper took Laryn's hand in his own and strode faster toward his car.

"Tate! What's the rush?"

At the passenger side, Casper turned and pressed her against the metal. He leaned in and said, "The rush is that I want to get the woman I love, who loves me back, to my apartment. My bed. I want to make love to her and show her in a million different ways how sorry I am that I didn't see the best thing in my life was right in front of me for years. Make sure she knows that from here on out, she comes first in my life. Before my job, before my team, before any kids we might have. You're my everything, Laryn Hardy. I'll spend the rest of my life making the last three years up to you if you'll let me."

"Tate," Laryn whispered as tears filled her eyes.

"No crying," he admonished, not able to stomach seeing her tears, even if they were happy ones.

"Sorry," she said with a sniff.

Casper wiped the wetness from her cheeks. "I love you, Laryn. So much it should scare me. But instead, it just feels right."

"Same."

"Good. So you have any objections to me taking you home and making love to you in my bed? My domain. I am man, hear me roar. Me man, you woman."

She giggled. "No."

"Good. Because when I'm done with you, you're never going to want to *look* at another man."

"I don't want anyone else. Just you. It's always been you, Tate."

Her words echoing in his brain, Casper leaned down and kissed her hard. "My brother wants to come out and meet you. *Really* meet you, not just in passing on a ship like last time. He'll bring Josie. You have a problem with that?"

"Of course not. I want a chance to get to know both of them

too. I really liked Josie when we talked on the phone the other night."

A bone-deep rightness settled in Casper's belly. He realized it was happiness. Contentedness. A feeling of having found someone who fit him perfectly. He'd only felt this way with one other person in his entire life before...his twin.

He stared at her for a beat, before pulling her away from the door and opening it. "In," he ordered.

Laryn rolled her eyes at him. "No, I thought I'd ride on top."

"I'll let you ride on top," he said suggestively.

"That was so corny," she sighed, but she was smiling when she said it, so Casper wasn't worried she was turned off by his crassness.

He realized he was smiling like a loon as he ran around to the driver's side. He couldn't wait to get them home and finally make long, slow, sweet love to the woman he wanted to spend the rest of his life with.

* * *

Laryn woke up and turned over, grinning when she saw Tate lying next to her with one arm over his head, mouth open, snoring slightly. When they'd gotten home the evening before, he decided they should eat before they went to bed, that they'd need the energy and calories for what he had planned for that evening. They'd both had a glass of wine with dinner, and when she'd gone into the bedroom while he tidied the kitchen, she'd fallen asleep before he'd even arrived. The full belly, the exhaustion of the previous week, of still recovering from her ordeal, and the alcohol, it had all combined to make her essentially pass out.

But now she was awake, after a full night's rest...and remembering the sweet way Tate had said he loved her had Laryn more than ready to make up for lost time. Yes, they'd had sex...made love...before, but this time felt different. Special. More permanent.

She eased the covers back, smiling as she remembered doing this previously, in her own bed. In her apartment. But this time, the second she wrapped her hand around his cock, he woke up. It took him only a split second to figure out where he was and who he was with. Then Laryn found herself on her back with a very aroused Tate hovering over her.

"Morning," he said huskily.

Would she ever get used to waking up with this man at her side? She hoped not. She hoped it would feel as special as it did right this moment.

"Morning," she told him with a shy smile. She had no idea why she was feeling so bashful all of a sudden. They'd slept plastered against each other for the last week, and he'd had his mouth between her legs before, not to mention his cock.

"How do you feel?"

"Um...good. Why?"

"Rested? Are you hungry or thirsty?"

"Yes, no, and no."

"I don't care who calls, who knocks on the door, or if aliens land outside this apartment building, nothing is going to keep me from making love to you."

Laryn shifted under him with arousal. "Sounds good to me."

"I love you, Laryn. It sucks that we lost so much time because I had blinders on for three damn years. But I wised up, and I'm so excited for what the future holds for us both."

"Me too," she said, feeling the pesky goose bumps she got so often around this man spring up on her arms. "I should warn you that I'm not going to be the kind of woman who quits her job to stay home and raise the kids."

Her words made Tate smile even wider.

"What? Why are you smiling like that?"

"Just hearing you talk about having kids with me makes me feel ridiculously giddy."

Laryn rolled her eyes. "I'm not ready right this second," she added.

Tate nodded. "But someday. I can't wait to see our little red-haired terrors running around. We'll go camping, I'll build a tree fort in the backyard of the house I'll buy for you someday."

"Wait, why can't I buy a house for *you*?" Laryn argued.

"I don't give a shit who buys what for who. Just that we talk about it beforehand and it's what's best for our finances."

"Good answer," Laryn said with a grin. "And I want to teach our kids, no matter if they're boys or girls, everything my dad taught me about cars."

"Sounds good. And I'm going to want to spend as much time with Nate as possible. And any kids they have. I want the cousins to be as close as siblings."

"That sounds awesome. I always wished for someone to hang out with when I was growing up. I think that's why my dad and I were so close. Oh! And we need a beagle."

"The one you want to name Waffles," he said.

"You remember that?" Laryn asked.

"I remember everything." Tate was still smiling. "I'm happy," he said almost reverently. "I know some people would say our relationship has moved too fast. That you being kidnapped just accelerated things even more and we need to hit the pause button. But screw that. I know what I feel, and I love you. I've known you for years and vice versa. You know all the negative things about me and yet by some miracle, you're still here. With me. In my bed. My job isn't easy, I'm away a lot…hell, so are you. But we can make this work. I know it. I'm keeping you, Laryn. You're it for me."

Laryn had never heard more romantic words in her life. When Tate said he was keeping her, it felt so different than when Mert had declared her as his. She *wanted* to be Tate's.

Wanted him to keep her forever and ever. "I never thought this would be my life," she said softly, her voice full of emotion. "I tried to be content just being around you and not being *with* you. Things won't be easy, but I hope I've proven to you that I have your back, and you more than did the same for me. Hey, wait...whatever happened to Barb the Bitch from Anchor Point?"

"She's gone."

"She is? What happened?"

Tate smirked. "Let's just say, rumors spread about Barb's...er... eccentric sexual preferences. All lies of course, and nothing illegal, but embarrassing enough that people laughed every time they saw her at work. Sailors who went into the bar joked about her, loudly. Basically, they made every shift she was working extremely uncomfortable. She was the butt of everyone's joke and she finally quit. I heard she left the state."

"Oh. Good."

"Are we done talking about other women?"

"I don't know, are we?" Laryn teased. She freaking loved this. Banter had always been a part of her and Tate's relationship, but if asked, she never would've guessed it would end up being one of the things she loved best about him. Along with his loyalty, work ethic, morals, sense of humor...she could go on and on.

"We're done," Tate confirmed. "I'm going to be the best partner you've ever had."

"You already are," Laryn admitted.

Tate's head dropped, and Laryn met him halfway, more than ready to feel him inside her.

What followed was one of the most intimate moments she'd ever had with another human being. It wasn't just that they were naked and making love, it was the way Tate looked at her as he slowly slid in and out of her soaking-wet body. How he licked his lips sensually, the sounds he made as he watched himself take her.

The pride she saw in his eyes.

He was proud to be with her. *Her*. The tomboy with calluses on her palms and grease under her nails. The girl who'd been made fun of for not wanting to get her hair done instead of going to the track and spending hours in the heat and dust.

Tate made slow, sweet love to her, showing her with his actions that every word out of his mouth earlier had come from his heart. And after she begged him to speed up, to let her come, he reached between them and massaged her clit hard enough to make her immediately explode in pleasure.

Then and only then did he begin to fuck her. As far as Laryn was concerned, that was still making love. Tate never stopped staring at her with his heart in his eyes. Was still very careful not to hurt her in any way as he was taking his own pleasure. Knowing she could give this man, a man who in her eyes had everything—an amazing brother, a group of best friends who would literally go through hell to make sure he was safe, a great job, and the admiration of just about everyone he met—something no one else could...the kind of love he needed...was overwhelming.

He groaned as he came. He held himself still as deep inside her as he could get, then suddenly fell on top of her.

Laryn grunted, then giggled.

He mumbled an apology but didn't move off her, though at least he shifted his weight so he wasn't crushing her anymore.

"That was...I have no words."

"What? The great Night Stalker has no words?" Laryn teased as she ran her fingernails lightly up and down his sweaty back. She felt a little turned inside out herself, but also energized.

"You want words? I love you. Being inside you feels like nothing I've ever felt before. When your pussy flutters—"

"Okay, that's enough words," Laryn said, interrupting him. She had a feeling she was blushing a bright pink.

He chuckled, and she could feel his belly contract against hers.

Then Tate brought a hand up to her forehead and smoothed her hair back. "Thank you. For trusting me to come for you. For not giving up. For being strong. For enduring. For simply being you. You're my everything, Laryn Hardy. I can't imagine my life without you in it."

The feelings inside her were so big, she felt as if she would shatter into a million pieces. Thinking about what she'd endured sucked, but honestly, she'd go through it all again if it meant she ended up right here. In Tate's apartment, his bed, his arms.

"I love you," she whispered.

"I love you too," he returned. Then he pushed up, making sure to keep his hips locked against hers, his cock deep inside her body. "And you look amazing on my sheets."

Laryn rolled her eyes. "You know that's ridiculous, right?"

Tate shrugged. "Maybe, maybe not. But I can't deny that things feel more solid now that I've claimed you in my bed."

Laryn's pussy spasmed around his semi-hard cock.

He grinned. "You like that I'm a caveman," he crowed.

"Whatever," she said, trying and failing to keep the grin off her lips.

"Like I said, you're perfect for me. But I'm not as young as I used to be. How about we get up and get some breakfast, then you can have your way with me again?"

Laryn had never been super sexual, but suddenly she felt as if she couldn't get enough of her man. She nodded, feeling shy again.

Tate stared down at her for a beat, then said, "I'm going to keep bringing up the idea of kids. Don't feel pressured. I just want to make sure to touch base with you about it now and then. Make sure we're both on the same page. When we decide we're ready, you can go off the pill. We'll see what happens. Okay?"

Laryn couldn't keep the happy smile off her face. She liked

that Tate wasn't assuming she wanted to have babies immediately. She wasn't ready yet, wasn't sure when she would be. But she nodded. Then warned, "Even when we decide to have kids, that doesn't mean it'll happen right away."

Tate grinned. "I'm good at everything I do. I have no doubt my sperm is up to the job. And reminder...twins run in my family."

The thought of having babies with this man, twins at that, made Laryn's ovaries go into overdrive. All of a sudden, she was tempted to tell him she was ready now. But that was lust talking. The reality was that their lives would change drastically once they decided to have kids. "I'd love a set of twins," she said softly. "Boys just like you and Nate."

"Girls. So you can teach them to wield a wrench and they can get out and change our tires if need be."

Laryn giggled.

"And...for the record...I hope you'll someday make an honest man of me. I don't care if you change your last name to Davis, and I understand it might take some time for us to get to the point where we're ready to get married, but that's the end goal for me. I'm not just talking about knocking you up without making things official between us. Not that I care too much about that, but the benefits for you and our kids would be better if we were married."

Warmth spread throughout Laryn at hearing him declare his intentions. If it was up to her, she'd marry Tate today.

In response, she pressed on his shoulder and he dutifully rolled, keeping their hips locked together. It was an impressive move, but she shouldn't have been surprised the cocky pilot could do it without any effort whatsoever.

She sat up, bracing her hands on his chest as she looked down at him. "When you're ready, say the word. I'm yours."

"Damn, I love hearing that from your lips," he said with a satisfied smile.

"How about we forget breakfast," Laryn suggested as she began to undulate her hips, stimulating his cock.

Tate inhaled sharply and his hands tightened on her hips, moving her the way he wanted.

"Who's hungry anyway?" he asked, the last word ending on a groan when Laryn tightened her Kegel muscles around him. "Do that again," he ordered.

She did, and just like that, the mushy man who'd declared his love and talked about babies was gone. He lifted her slightly and began to thrust up inside her from below. "Stay. Just. Like. That," he grunted as he fucked her.

Laryn moaned and threw her head back as the man she loved stimulated nerve endings she didn't even know she had. The noises their bodies made as they came together were loud, and in any other case, with anyone else, would have probably embarrassed her. But with Tate, nothing felt uncomfortable. Besides, those noises were a direct result of the pleasure he was giving her, and that he was receiving in return. She couldn't be embarrassed by that.

By the time they both came again, Laryn's thighs were trembling and she felt like a wet noodle.

Tate pulled out, eased her onto her back, then scooted off the bed. "Stay. Doze. I'll get breakfast started. When you feel like it, come on out." He kissed her gently on the lips, then headed for his closet. While in there, he casually mentioned that he was going to make room for her stuff later that afternoon.

Laryn turned onto her side and smiled at the thought of her clothes mixed with Tate's.

He came out, still completely naked, and smirked at her.

"Put some clothes on, naked boy," she teased.

"Why? I like when my woman checks me out."

"I'm not checking you out," she lied.

He lifted one of his brows, giving her a "sure you aren't" look. Then he stood in the doorway of his closet for a long moment, not moving toward the bathroom or doing anything other than simply staring at her.

"What?" she asked, wondering what he was thinking.

"Just enjoying the sight of you in my bed. Even if we're together for another seventy years, I don't think I'll ever get tired of it." Finally, he headed for the door, leaving Laryn almost breathless behind him.

She closed her eyes and thanked her lucky stars that she was right where she was. That Altan hadn't gotten his way. That Tate and his friends had been able to find her. That, even though there was some mental stuff she was still dealing with because of what happened, not feeling safe wasn't one of her triggers. Because with Tate, she had no doubt whatsoever that she was as safe as she could get.

Turning onto her back, she stared at the ceiling. She was sore between her legs—Tate wasn't a small man, after all—and she was still tired, which was a feeling she knew wouldn't go anywhere anytime soon, with all the work she had in front of her getting another MH-60 up to snuff for Tate. But she was content.

Many people wouldn't understand. They'd think because she'd been kidnapped and mentally and physically tortured, that she'd be jumpy. On edge. But she wasn't. Off-kilter a little, sure, but knowing she was loved went a long way toward healing her heart and her head.

Her belly suddenly growled, reminding Laryn that it was past the time she usually ate. Smiling, eager to see what Tate was making them for breakfast, she made herself get out of bed. She grabbed one of Tate's ARMY T-shirts and pulled it over her head. Maybe after they ate, they could try out the shower... together. It would be a tight fit, it wasn't really meant for two. But that was all right with her.

Making a mental note that any house they ended up in

needed a ginormous shower they could share, Laryn headed out of the bedroom toward the bathroom.

Life was good. Even if it didn't always go the way you wanted, when you wanted it to, it was still what you made of it...how you dealt with the blows you were given and how you treated others. Her dad had taught her that. And while Laryn had questioned his advice many times in her life, she realized her old man had always known exactly what he was talking about.

EPILOGUE

This wasn't happening.

But of course it was.

Amanda huddled in the hot, wet Amazon jungle and let herself feel a moment of despair. She'd gone to Guyana full of anticipation. With a desire to help. A bone-deep satisfaction that she was making a difference in the world. And now, here she was. Kidnapped. Hungry. Scared out of her mind.

She'd gone to Guyana to work with orphans. To teach them. To maybe bring some joy into their lives. And she'd done that and more. Until a week ago, when armed men had burst into the school and ordered everyone into trucks with heavy canvas hiding them from view.

When one of the local volunteers had protested, he'd been shot point blank.

Amanda was the only adult taken, and she was now tasked with keeping twenty-three scared-out-of-their-minds boys and girls, ranging in ages from four to thirteen, calm. Which was almost impossible when she was feeling anything but calm herself.

She wasn't sure what the men wanted. The trucks they were

in had to stop once the road ended and they'd been traveling for a week since then through the jungle without saying much except for them to shut up and walk faster. They stopped when it got dark every evening, but that was their only respite. Everyone was on edge and the lack of any information about why they'd been kidnapped was almost scarier than trekking through the jungle.

Amanda had been warned about the dangers of living so close to the border of Venezuela, but she'd regrettably dismissed her friends' concerns. She wasn't going to be stepping foot into the neighboring country, after all. She would be in Guyana. Safe. Minding her own business.

Except now, here she was.

And the worst thing about the entire situation wasn't the constant rain. Wasn't the gnawing in her belly. Wasn't being responsible for twenty-three little lives. It was the knowledge that there was no one coming to their rescue.

The organization she was volunteering with wasn't sponsored by the government. It was a small, independently owned group comprised of men and women who were doing the best they could for the orphans in their country.

Amanda had seen a small news piece about them on social media and was instantly intrigued. She'd contacted them, having felt restless and unappreciated in her teaching job back in Virginia for some time, and before she knew it, had signed up for a six-month stint. She'd had to quit her job, but she didn't think it would be difficult to find another when she got home. She was well qualified and experienced enough to be hired in pretty much any school district with an opening. The question would be, did she want to stay in teaching? She wasn't sure. She'd been using her time in Guyana to figure that out, confident that she would.

Now, for the first time in her life, her natural optimism had slipped away. Whatever the kidnappers wanted, it couldn't be good. Of that she had no doubt. And being the only woman in a group of terrifying and ruthless men wasn't a comfortable place to be. She'd been surrounded by kids since they'd been taken, which was one of the only reasons she figured she'd been left alone up until now. But it was only a matter of time before one of her kidnappers decided he'd take what she didn't want to give.

And she saw no way out of the situation. Even if the opportunity for escape arose, she wouldn't leave the kids. They were even more vulnerable than she was. They had no parents. No one to fight for them. She was literally all they had. Besides, she didn't know the first thing about jungle survival. Oh, she had some basic knowledge, but she got lost back in her own town in Virginia even with her phone on and Siri telling her which way to go. Two minutes on her own in the jungle and she'd be hopelessly turned around.

Her only chance was being rescued, but she wasn't anybody special. Didn't know any generals in the Army. Didn't know any politicians. Didn't have any contacts who would fight on her behalf. There were only a handful of acquaintances at the last school where she'd worked who might even wonder why she never got a hold of them when she was supposed to return to the States. Her parents had died a few years ago, and she had no siblings or other relatives that she was close with.

She shivered, even though it wasn't cold. It was the opposite, actually. Tilting her head up to the sky, she let the ever-present rain mingle with the tears on her cheeks. She'd never thought much about dying, and now she couldn't think about anything but. Her body would never be found, it would just decompose in this rainforest and disappear into the ground. Ashes to ashes. Dust to dust.

"Mandy, I'm scared."

Taking a deep breath, Amanda tightened her arms around the little girl in her lap. Sharon was seven, and had been extra clingy lately. But who could blame her.

"Me too," she whispered. "But it's going to be all right. We just have to be strong."

She didn't actually think it *was* going to be all right, but there was no way she was going to add to Sharon's fears. To any of the children's fears. Taking a deep breath, Amanda dug deep for the optimism she was known for.

"Someone will come for us, right?" Michael asked from her right. He was twelve, and had made himself Amanda's protector.

"Of course," she told him, lying through her teeth. The truth was, no one was coming. They were on their own. But she'd rather die than admit that to any of the children. They were all they had, and they'd stick together throughout this ordeal. No matter what lie ahead of them.

* * *

"Who are these kids and why does the government care about them?" Edge asked. He didn't sound irritated, just curious.

Buck was just as curious. They were used to being sent into battlefields with Navy SEALs or Delta Force operatives. Shuttling them in and out of dangerous terrain and situations while they searched for HVTs or other terrorists the US wanted to take out.

But currently, they were in a meeting with their superior at the naval base, and he'd just informed them that two of them were being sent to South America on a rescue mission, while the rest were heading to Mexico to help with some of the extreme flooding that country had experienced as a result of the latest hurricane to blast the East Coast.

"And why only one team?" Chaos asked.

The colonel held up a hand to stave off further questions. "I know this is unusual."

It was more than unusual, it was…weird. Strange. Fucking confusing. Buck waited impatiently for some answers.

"The vice president has a vested interest in Guyana. As a young man, he did a stint in the Peace Corps. Working as a math teacher in a remote village in Guyana. Throughout his career, he's kept in contact with people still working in the area, and they reached out to him a few days ago about an alarming situation. Venezuelan soldiers kidnapped a group of school children and took them into the rainforest across the border."

"Why?" Buck blurted, exasperated with the slow explanation.

The colonel frowned and continued speaking. "We aren't sure. The general consensus is that it has something to do with forced labor or consignment into the military."

"But these are kids, right?" Casper asked.

"Yes. But even ten-year-olds can hold and shoot a rifle."

Buck was disgusted. Once upon a time, Venezuela had been the paradise of South America. But over the years, the dictatorial government had stripped rights and forced its citizens to live under strict authoritarian rule. If they were now kidnapping innocent children from neighboring countries, would an annexation be far away?

"These twenty-three kids are a symbol. If we can rescue them, we're telling Venezuela that we see what they're doing and if they continue, the US won't turn a blind eye," the colonel went on. "But we want to keep this on the down low for now. Rescue the kids. Make our point without making this a huge international incident. How the government reacts will dictate the president's next move. He's not willing to go to war over this, but he agrees with the vice president that something needs to be done."

"And we're that something," Obi-Wan stated.

"Yes. Because you're the best at nighttime operations. You can get in, get the kids, get out."

"What's the plan?" Casper asked.

"We'll go over that once it's decided who will be headed to the Amazon, and who will be going to Mexico. Oh, and one more thing. There's an American involved. A volunteer at the school. A teacher, Amanda Rush. Our intel says she wasn't supposed to be taken, but she refused to leave the kids. It goes without saying that it's vital to recover her, because she's the excuse we're using to cross into Venezuelan airspace."

That didn't sit well with Buck. He had very fond memories of some of his teachers growing up. He was the poor kid. The one who never fit in. Didn't have many friends. And his teachers treated him with kindness. Encouraged him. Made him believe he could do anything he wanted to do...including becoming a pilot. Their government using this Amanda person as an *excuse* left a bad taste in his mouth. Especially because, apparently, she'd put herself in danger to protect the kids under her care.

"I'll go," he said, before turning to Obi-Wan and raising a brow, belatedly realizing that the decision to go to South America wasn't his alone. His copilot had a say too. Thankfully, his friend nodded in agreement.

"Any objections?" the colonel asked the others. When there weren't, he said, "Briefing tomorrow morning at oh-six-hundred. Wheels up for both groups at thirteen hundred. The president and VP want this done quickly. Dismissed."

Buck had a ton of questions, but they'd hopefully be answered in the morning. For the moment, all he could think about was Amanda Rush. Where was she? What was happening to her and the kids? Was she all right? Was she even still alive?

That last question had him frowning. Anyone who volunteered their time to help kids in need was worth their weight in gold. And thinking about her being hurt or killed because she refused to leave the orphans under her care to the mercy of their kidnappers, disturbed Buck in a way he couldn't understand or describe.

He was ready for this mission. To find Amanda and the kids and bring them to safety. He couldn't save the world, as he'd once thought when he'd first joined the military, but maybe, just maybe, he could do his part in saving one little corner of it. Amanda Rush's corner.

* * *

I think by now, if you're read any of my books, you know Buck's rescue of Amanda and the kids isn't going to go according to plan...but how far off course could it go? Ha! Very off course! Find out more in *Keeping Amanda*!

Scan the QR code below for signed books, swag, T-shirts and more!

Also by Susan Stoker

Rescue Angels Series
Keeping Laryn (July 1, 2025)
Keeping Amanda (Nov 4, 2025)
Keeping Zita (Feb 10, 2026)
Keeping Penny (May 5, 2026)
Keeping Kara (July 7, 2026)
Keeping Jennifer (Nov 10, 2026)

SEAL of Protection: Alliance Series
Protecting Remi
Protecting Wren
Protecting Josie
Protecting Maggie
Protecting Addison
Protecting Kelli (Sept 2, 2025)
Protecting Bree (Jan 6, 2026)

Alpha Cove Series
The Soldier (Aug 12, 2025)
The Sailor (Mar 3, 2026)
The Pilot (Aug 4, 2026)
The Guardsman (Mar 9, 2027)

SEAL Team Hawaii Series
Finding Elodie
Finding Lexie
Finding Kenna
Finding Monica
Finding Carly
Finding Ashlyn
Finding Jodelle

ALSO BY SUSAN STOKER

Eagle Point Search & Rescue
Searching for Lilly
Searching for Elsie
Searching for Bristol
Searching for Caryn
Searching for Finley
Searching for Heather
Searching for Khloe

The Refuge Series
Deserving Alaska
Deserving Henley
Deserving Reese
Deserving Cora
Deserving Lara
Deserving Maisy
Deserving Ryleigh

Game of Chance Series
The Protector
The Royal
The Hero
The Lumberjack

SEAL of Protection: Legacy Series
Securing Caite
Securing Brenae (novella)
Securing Sidney
Securing Piper
Securing Zoey
Securing Avery
Securing Kalee
Securing Jane

ALSO BY SUSAN STOKER

Delta Force Heroes Series
Rescuing Rayne
Rescuing Aimee (novella)
Rescuing Emily
Rescuing Harley
Marrying Emily (novella)
Rescuing Kassie
Rescuing Bryn
Rescuing Casey
Rescuing Sadie (novella)
Rescuing Wendy
Rescuing Mary
Rescuing Macie (novella)
Rescuing Annie

SEAL of Protection Series
Protecting Caroline
Protecting Alabama
Protecting Fiona
Marrying Caroline (novella)
Protecting Summer
Protecting Cheyenne
Protecting Jessyka
Protecting Julie (novella)
Protecting Melody
Protecting the Future
Protecting Kiera (novella)
Protecting Alabama's Kids (novella)
Protecting Dakota
Protecting Tex

Delta Team Two Series
Shielding Gillian
Shielding Kinley

ALSO BY SUSAN STOKER

Shielding Aspen
Shielding Jayme (novella)
Shielding Riley
Shielding Devyn
Shielding Ember
Shielding Sierra

Badge of Honor: Texas Heroes Series

Justice for Mackenzie
Justice for Mickie
Justice for Corrie
Justice for Laine (novella)
Shelter for Elizabeth
Justice for Boone
Shelter for Adeline
Shelter for Sophie
Justice for Erin
Justice for Milena
Shelter for Blythe
Justice for Hope
Shelter for Quinn
Shelter for Koren
Shelter for Penelope

Ace Security Series

Claiming Grace
Claiming Alexis
Claiming Bailey
Claiming Felicity
Claiming Sarah

Mountain Mercenaries Series

Defending Allye
Defending Chloe

ALSO BY SUSAN STOKER

Defending Morgan
Defending Harlow
Defending Everly
Defending Zara
Defending Raven

Silverstone Series
Trusting Skylar
Trusting Taylor
Trusting Molly
Trusting Cassidy

Stand Alone
Falling for the Delta
The Guardian Mist
Nature's Rift
A Princess for Cale
A Moment in Time- A Collection of Short Stories
Another Moment in Time- A Collection of Short Stories
A Third Moment in Time- A Collection of Short Stories
Lambert's Lady

Special Operations Fan Fiction
http://www.AcesPress.com

Beyond Reality Series
Outback Hearts
Flaming Hearts
Frozen Hearts

Writing as Annie George:
Stepbrother Virgin (erotic novella)

ABOUT THE AUTHOR

New York Times, USA Today, #1 Amazon Bestseller, and #1 *Wall Street Journal* Bestselling Author, Susan Stoker has spent the last twenty-three years living in Missouri, California, Colorado, Indiana, Texas, and Tennessee and is currently living in the wilds of Maine. She's married to a retired Army man (and current firefighter/EMT) who now gets to follow *her* around the country.

She debuted her first series in 2014 and quickly followed that up with the SEAL of Protection Series, which solidified her love of writing and creating stories readers can get lost in.

If you enjoyed this book, or any book, please consider leaving a review. It's appreciated by authors more than you'll know.

www.stokeraces.com
www.AcesPress.com
susan@stokeraces.com

facebook.com/authorsusanstoker
x.com/Susan_Stoker
instagram.com/authorsusanstoker
goodreads.com/SusanStoker
bookbub.com/authors/susan-stoker
amazon.com/author/susanstoker

www.ingramcontent.com/pod-product-compliance
Lightning Source LLC
Chambersburg PA
CBHW011002010725
28987CB00023B/110